3/05

FIC M
Martinez, Michele, 1962-
Most wanted
New York : William Morrow,
c2005.

09
1

GAYLORD MG

4/09

MOST
WANTED

MOST WANTED

Michele Martinez

WILLIAM MORROW

An Imprint of HarperCollins*Publishers*

This book is a work of fiction. The characters, incidents, and dialogue are products of the author's imagination and are not to be construed as real. Any resemblance to actual persons, living or dead, is entirely coincidental.

HarperCollins books may be purchased for educational, business, or sales promotional use. For information please write: Special Markets Department, HarperCollins Publishers Inc., 10 East 53rd Street, New York, NY 10022.

FIRST EDITION

Designed by Jo Anne Metsch

Printed on acid-free paper

Library of Congress Cataloging-in-Publication Data

Martinez, Michele, 1962–
    Most wanted / Michele Martinez. — 1st ed.
        p. cm.
    ISBN 0-06-072398-X (acid-free paper)
    1. Public prosecutors—Fiction. 2. Puerto Rican women—Fiction. 3. New York (N.Y.)—
Fiction. 4. Women lawyers—Fiction. I. Title.

    PS3613.A78648M67 2005
    813'.6—dc22   2004044964

05 06 07 08 09 WBC/RRD 10 9 8 7 6 5 4 3 2 1

FOR MY FATHER

Acknowledgments

I am forever grateful to the three people who took this novel from a glimmer in my eye to a reality:

My husband, Jeffrey, who had endless faith in me and supported this project in more ways than I can recount;

My wonderful agent and good friend, Meg Ruley, who made it all happen; and

My amazing editor, Carolyn Marino, who believed in an unknown and guided me with the greatest skill and insight.

I am also indebted to the following: Kara Cesare, Peggy Gordijn, Jennifer Civiletto, Martha Hughes, Randy Dwenger, Triss Stein, Nicole Gruenstein, Annelise Robey, Donald Cleary, and Andrea Cirillo, for their advice and support; Amy Mundorff of the Office of the Chief Medical Examiner of New York City and Lynn Sullivan, M.D., for vetting the gory details; and my son, Jack, for his boundless enthusiasm for this book and killer title suggestions (*The Mystery Bad Guy* being my all-time favorite).

MOST
WANTED

1

———

Melanie Vargas would normally never have dreamed of pushing her baby stroller into the middle of a crime scene. Sure, she was a dedicated prosecutor who believed in locking up the bad guys, but she was also a fiercely protective mommy to her six-month-old daughter. Then again, these were not normal times. Things were out of control in Melanie's life, in a big way. Not to mention that little Maya had a will of her own. You could almost say that Maya engineered the whole thing. Something huge was happening outside their window, and Maya didn't want to miss it any more than Melanie did. That *chiquitita* had law enforcement in her blood.

They'd been home in their apartment at ten o'clock on a steamy Monday night. Maya was screaming her lungs out, face bright red, as Melanie walked her up and down, danced with her, jiggled her around. Anything and everything to get her to sleep, but nothing was working.

Then, in a split second of silence while Maya drew a breath, Melanie heard the sirens. Not just a few sirens either, but the separate and distinct shrieks of police cruisers, ambulances, and fire trucks. A *big* response. She'd been a prosecutor long enough to know the difference between those sounds and know what they meant. A ruckus like that in a tranquil, fancy neighborhood like this? Highly unusual—and *serious*. Someone else had worse problems than she did tonight.

It took an eternity for Maya to suck that breath all the way in. But it came back out in one loud, piercing wail.

"Maya, listen," Melanie begged, moving frantically toward the window, trying to put a soothing sway in her step. "Do you hear that? Sirens. Sirens, *oiga.*"

She turned Maya around to face the rectangle of window above the humming air conditioner, bouncing her up and down. For a blissful moment, the distraction worked. Maya quieted, her sodden brown eyes focusing on the hazy, shimmering air beyond the glass. Then a new bunch of police cruisers sped down Park Avenue. Their sirens blared, but you couldn't see them at all from this angle. Melanie craned her neck to catch a glimpse of the wide boulevard, over the tops of the low buildings on her side street. Too late. They were gone. Maya swung a pudgy fist toward the window and started to howl again. Frustrated, obviously.

"I know, I know, *nena.* The view is not what it should be." She pulled Maya close, resting her cheek on her daughter's silky raven hair, so like her own, trying to comfort her with caresses. No good. Maya struggled and fussed to get free.

"You're not ever going to sleep, are you?" Melanie said, looking into her daughter's face. "That's it, baby girl. We're going out."

She turned on her heel decisively and headed down the hall to Maya's room. Yanking the stroller from the closet with one hand, she settled Maya into it and buckled the safety strap. The bunny night-light on the dresser cast a warm glow on Maya's wet cheeks as Melanie pulled lace-trimmed ankle socks onto her tiny feet. The baby's sobs quickly faded to hiccups. No doubt about it, this little girl was happy to be going for a ride.

When they reached the lobby, though, Melanie's doorman had other ideas. Hector was Puerto Rican like her, and the slight lilt of a Spanish accent in his voice always reminded her of her father. The feeling was clearly mutual, since Hector fussed over Melanie like a protective *papi* who was convinced she couldn't take care of herself.

"Aw, no! Where you think you going? Something nasty happening out there. Sirens and everything."

"Hector, I'm a prosecutor. I can handle a few sirens." She stopped short of telling him that she *liked* the sirens. They were *interesting.* They drew her more than they scared her away.

"What about this little one? She don't want to go out!" Hector protested.

Maya leaned forward eagerly on her puffy, diapered bottom, grasping the toy bar strapped to the front of the stroller. She had completely stopped crying.

"Oh, yes, she does! *¡Claro!* You should have heard her screaming five minutes ago. I'm going to walk her till she falls asleep."

"By yourself at this hour?"

Melanie shrugged. Hector studied her face.

"When Mr. Hanson coming home, *hija*? He on business still? 'Cause I ain't seen him around lately."

Steve Hanson was Melanie's husband. And no, he hadn't been around much lately, because Melanie had thrown his cheating butt out. She just hadn't brought herself to tell Hector yet. Or anyone else for that matter. Telling people would make it real, and she didn't want it to be real. The last few weeks were a bad dream she kept hoping she would wake up from.

The telephone at the doorman's station began to buzz.

"Answer your phone, Hector. And don't worry about us. We'll be back in ten minutes with this little girl fast asleep. Promise."

As Melanie exited the air-conditioned lobby, the heat and the racket from the sirens blasted her in the face. She drew a sharp breath and tasted something acrid. August in New York City was always unbearable, but this was different. The haziness smelled like smoke. She hesitated, looking down at Maya. Far from seeming troubled, her daughter gave a huge yawn and snuggled down into the stroller. That settled it. Melanie pointed the stroller south on Madison Avenue and headed in the direction of the flashing lights.

A few blocks ahead, people clustered in front of blue police barricades, rubbernecking wildly. The smoke in the air stung Melanie's eyes, but the crowds told her there was something worth seeing. She stopped momentarily to check Maya. Hah! Fast asleep already, black lashes resting against silken cheeks, a peaceful smile on her shell-pink lips. Melanie stroked her daughter's face. Amazing what an angel this one could be when she was quiet. Melanie pulled the stroller hood lower to protect her and made a beeline for the police barricades.

Two blocks down, she finally got a clear line of sight across the street to the source of the commotion. The posh, town-house-lined side street was a tangle of police cars. Two large fire trucks with American flags dangling from their backs were parked at unnatural angles in front of an imposing brick-and-limestone town house on the south side of the block. Hose lines ran through its massive, carved front doors and through the elegant windows on the first floor, crushing the lovely flowers in their window boxes. Firemen in full regalia ran back and forth shouting as water gushed out the front door and down the grand, curving limestone steps. Melanie thought about leaving, but she was definitely at a safe enough distance for the baby. Besides, now that she saw which house it was, she couldn't possibly leave.

2

——

Melanie crossed the street, staring wide-eyed at the Bensons' burning house. They were acquaintances rather than friends, but she knew them. Everybody did. They were like celebrities in her universe. Jed Benson had been a famous prosecutor in her office years ago, then left and made a bundle in private practice. A serious bundle, like major *lechuga*. Melanie had met Jed and his wife, Nell, once or twice in passing, though never intimately, never for long. She wasn't in their league. They were the types who went out every night in black tie and jewels and got their pictures in the paper the next day standing beside the mayor. The types you'd think would be immune to tragedy like this.

The crowd was too thick for easy movement. Melanie maneuvered the stroller as best she could to a spot a few feet from the police barricade. The medical examiner's refrigerated van drove up. The crowd-control officers pulled aside the barricade to let the van pass. You didn't call the ME unless you had bodies. Somebody in that house was dead.

A ripple surged through the crowd. A woman fought her way up to the police barricade and grabbed the arm of a young cop with a dark crew cut.

"Officer, please, let me talk to the firemen!" the woman shouted over the din. "I know the house! Let me help!"

Between the backs of the people in the crowd, Melanie recognized Sophie Cho, her college roommate, still her friend. Sophie was an architect, and she had spent the last year working on a renovation of the Bensons' town house that made the society pages. Not only was her livelihood burning to the ground here, but she was personal friends with the family. Sophie looked deeply alarmed, face pale, eyes dark with worry. Melanie angled the stroller deeper into the crowd, not stopping until she reached Sophie and the cop at the barricade. The cop looked at Melanie, clearly trying to place her.

"Yeah? What can I do for you?" he asked.

"Melanie Vargas from the U.S. Attorney's Office," she said, reaching into the handbag dangling from the stroller handle and flashing her creds. "You testified for me on a drug seizure a few months ago."

"Sure, okay, now I remember," he said, instantly more polite. "Did you catch this case? You need to get in?"

"You work for Lieutenant Ramirez, right?" she asked, dodging his question. Case? They must suspect arson. Now she was really curious.

"Yeah. The lieutenant's over with the fire chief," the cop said.

"Can I speak with him, please?" Melanie asked.

Motioning to a nearby patrol officer to take over his post, the cop walked off to find Rommie. Sophie, who'd fallen into astonished silence at Melanie's approach, turned to her now with a terrified look.

"Was someone hurt? Are the Bensons okay?"

Melanie reached out and squeezed Sophie's arm as reassuringly as she could under the circumstances. But how reassuring could she be? Things looked grim for whoever was in that house.

"Soph, I don't know anything more than you do, but I'm going to ask the lieutenant who's in charge of the scene. And if you think you can do something to help, we'll let him know that."

"Yes. Please."

As they spoke, Romulado Ramirez strode toward them, the other cops and firemen giving way to let him pass. He was dressed sharply as always, but disheveled, his dark hair plastered to his forehead with sweat, his expensive blazer streaked with soot and dust. He sidestepped the barricade and came up to her.

"How you doing, kid?" He hugged Melanie and kissed both cheeks.

He was dripping sweat, so much he got her face wet, and he held her for an extra minute, like he needed comfort. He must know Jed Benson. It made sense—they were about the same age, and Rommie had worked with prosecutors in her office for a lot of years.

Rommie glanced at her baby stroller but, in his confusion, hardly seemed to notice it. "I don't get it, I didn't even call your boss yet. She got ESP? How'd she know to send you over here?"

Melanie's boss, Bernadette DeFelice, head of the Major Crimes Unit in the New York City U.S. Attorney's Office, had a close personal relationship with Rommie Ramirez. They knew each other very well indeed. He would surely talk to her, so Melanie needed to tread carefully to avoid getting caught in a lie.

She kept it as vague as she could. "I'm here to check out the scene, Rommie. What's going on?"

Rommie shifted on his feet nervously. "How much did Bernadette tell you? I didn't know she knew already that Jed Benson was murdered. She's gonna be real upset. And you know it's never good to upset Bernadette."

Sophie gasped. Shock hit Melanie like a slap in the face. Jed Benson, golden boy, star, *murdered?* She could hardly believe what she was hearing. A victim like him, a neighborhood like this? Impossible! At least, extremely rare. But if it was true, it was the kind of high-profile case that could make a career. And make a girl forget her problems. She wanted in. No, she *needed* in. It was fate, *destino,* that had called her here at just this moment. She was too junior to get assigned such a juicy case in the normal course of things, she knew that. But being at the scene of the crime gave her an edge. She could turn it to her advantage. This was her big opportunity, handed to her like a gift just when she needed it most. She would *not* let it slip away.

MELANIE LOOKED ROMMIE straight in the eye and mustered her most confident, professional tone. "I'm ready to work the case. The fire was an arson, right?"

"Set to destroy evidence of the murder, looks like." Rommie nodded.

"So Benson was already dead when the fire started. How was he killed?"

"Hard to tell, it's such a mess in there. I gotta talk to the ME."

Sophie grabbed the stroller handles as if to steady herself. Melanie glanced over at her, but Sophie immediately took a breath and straightened up.

"He was the only victim?" Melanie asked Rommie. "No family members?"

"His daughter was . . . her fingers were cut off. Amanda. She's fifteen. Maybe to get information—who knows." He looked away, his voice breaking as if he might cry. After a moment he pulled himself together and continued. "The housekeeper was beaten. They've both been taken to the hospital. Nell Benson wasn't home and still hasn't returned. We're trying to locate her."

"Any leads on the perpetrator?"

"Fled. Blue-and-whites patrolling the area, but we won't even have a physical description until the surviving victims can be interviewed."

"Okay," she said. "Let's go inside and examine the crime scene."

Rommie was taken aback. "You want to view the scene *now*? Melanie, this isn't show-and-tell for the prosecutors. Besides, what's your jurisdiction? Murder isn't normally a federal crime. The state DA's gonna go ballistic if I let you in."

"I could ask you the same question," she replied evenly. "Why is a narcotics lieutenant running this murder scene instead of somebody from Manhattan North Homicide? But I figure you work out the politics on your end. I'll handle them on mine. If we get to the scene first, we get first dibs. The state DA will have to live with that. There's always a way to federalize a murder charge. I just need to hit the books and I'll find ten cases to cite to the judge."

He shook his head uncertainly. "I don't know, Melanie."

She had to find the right words. She risked playing the card of Rommie's relationship with Bernadette DeFelice. "I understand. You want to make sure everything's done right, out of respect for Jed's memory. But remember, you have a special relationship with our office. If we get the case, we'll handle it with kid gloves. We'll consult you every step of the way. You won't get that kind of access from the DA."

"You think your boss is gonna *consult*? Dream on, kid," he said. But she read something different in his eyes. He was calculating the benefit of his direct pipeline to Bernadette. Melanie stood her ground, watching him, sensing that she'd scored.

Finally he said, "I'm not gonna stand around arguing all night. We got work to do. If the state's not here yet, that's their problem. You're faster, you get the prize. I'm warning you, though, it's gonna be ugly in there."

"I'm a big girl. I'll be fine."

That left only one logistical hurdle—what to do with Maya while she went inside. Sophie regularly baby-sat for Maya. Unhappily single and dying for a child of her own, she begged to, in fact. But Melanie couldn't tell if she was too upset tonight. That reminded her—she'd promised to let Rommie know that Sophie wanted to help the firemen.

"Rommie," Melanie said, "before we go in, I need to introduce you to my friend Sophie Cho. She's the architect who worked on redesigning the Bensons' house. She knows it inside out. She wants to help any way she can."

"Architect?" That got his attention.

"Yes," Sophie answered.

"Do you have the blueprints for this building?" he asked.

Sophie froze up. "They're on file with the Buildings Department," she responded stiffly. "Why?"

"I need them right away."

"I don't have them," Sophie said, shaking her head emphatically. "But I could go inside and—"

"No civilians inside. You don't keep a copy for yourself?" Rommie scrutinized her suspiciously, as if he didn't believe her. He started to say something else, but one of a group of fire officials standing nearby called his name, gesturing toward the town house.

"All clear," Rommie said to Melanie. "I gotta get in there. I'll follow up with you later about those blueprints, miss. Here, gimme your name and number." He pulled a small memo book from his breast pocket. Sophie gave him the information. He jotted it down and disappeared back in the direction of the town house, leaving Melanie to follow.

"What was that about? Why did he want the blueprints?" Sophie asked.

"They're probably trying to figure out where the fire started."

Melanie reached out and smoothed Sophie's hair, studying her friend's face. Sophie's eyes were dry, but Melanie knew her well enough to understand she could be upset and never show it. Sophie kept everything bottled up inside. A short, intense Korean girl from Flushing, struggling to get to the top of what was, in New York at least, a cutthroat profession. She took a lot of things hard, and Melanie couldn't quite tell how she was taking this.

"Are you okay, *chica*?" Melanie asked gently.

"Me? I'm fine. It's the Bensons we should worry about. You need to *do* something, Melanie. I'll feel so much better if I know you're on the case. Let me take Maya home for you so you can do your job."

"Are you sure?"

"Of course I'm sure."

"Well, if you're really up for it. I know how good you are with her." It was true. Melanie totally trusted Sophie with Maya.

"Okay, then it's settled. Don't worry, take as long as you need. If I get tired, I'll snooze on the couch."

"You're the best, Soph! Thank you so much."

Melanie gave Sophie her keys and some quick instructions. They hugged, and then Sophie grasped the stroller handles and headed off.

Melanie turned to the crew-cut cop, back at his post alongside the barricade.

"I'm going in with the lieutenant."

She must have sounded more confident than she felt, because he immediately pulled it aside for her. He had no way of knowing this was her first murder scene. She'd seen autopsy photos, all right, but no matter how graphic or disgusting, pictures were pictures. Hardly the same as real human flesh, slashed, ripped, burned, staring you in the face. She hoped she wouldn't gag or faint. It's all part of the job, she told herself, nodding at him as she drew a deep breath and marched toward the town house to view what was left of Jed Benson.

3

The firemen packed up their gear, faces weary in the glow of the flashing lights. Their job was done. The cops and prosecutors were in charge now. Melanie splashed through murky water, hurrying to the basement entrance where she'd seen Rommie Ramirez disappear a moment earlier.

The wooden door tucked under the curving limestone staircase opened into blackness. As she approached, a Crime Scene detective clad in protective jumpsuit and face mask emerged, shutting off a heavy-duty flashlight. He yanked off his mask and hard hat and wiped his arm across his weather-beaten face, leaving a trail of black.

"Butch Brennan, right?"

"Hey, Melanie. Haven't seen you since that grand jury. You the prosecutor on this case?"

"Yes, I'm with Lieutenant Ramirez. I need to view the evidence."

"Seriously? Jeez, no offense, I know it's your job and all. But what's in there is nothing for a woman to see."

"I appreciate the concern, Butch, but I can handle myself."

"Okay, if you say so. The lieutenant's toward the back with my team, where the body is. I gotta go talk to the fire chief, or I'd take you in myself. You better cover your nose and mouth. The smell is pretty bad for a kill this fresh."

Butch marched off, and Melanie stepped through the door into the darkness. The stench hit her instantly. A powerful combination of charred meat, burned hair, and blood. A human being slashed to bits, fried to a crisp. The smell stopped her dead in her tracks, throwing her right back to that night. The smell of blood, on that night she tried never to remember.

"PAPI?" *MELANIE CALLED, staring at the sliver of light shining out from under the closed door to her father's office. Something didn't feel right here.*

She was thirteen. It was night, mid-January in Brooklyn. They lived over her father's furniture store. She'd come downstairs to get away from her mother's screaming, to do her homework in peace and quiet. Her father was in his office in the back, avoiding her mother as usual. But all the lights were off in the showroom, and she'd just heard a strange noise. Like a grunt of pain.

As she reached for the door handle, a muffled thud sounded from behind the door.

"Papi?" she called again, her voice trembling. No answer.

She turned the knob and pushed the door open. Her father sat in his customary place behind the desk. But the overhead light was off. The desk lamp cast a yellowish glow on the desktop, leaving his face and the rest of the room in shadows. There was something odd about him, about his posture, his expression. And something smelled funny. Metallic, almost, yet gamy.

She moved a step farther into the room and squinted to see better. Her father's longish black hair flopped over his brow as it always did, but beneath it an angry cut slashed downward across his forehead. Dark blood oozed down the side of his face, disappearing into his hairline, then reappearing again on his chin. He stared back at her, eyes glazed with pain, not moving.

"What—" she began.

"¡Corre!" her father choked out. "Run! ¡Fuera de aquí!"

A STRING OF emergency lights flashed on, snapping Melanie back to the present. The basement was intact, though damaged by smoke and water. Cops' voices floated out from a room down the hall, so she headed for it. The odor got worse as she approached. She gagged, yanking the neckline of her white T-shirt up over her nose and mouth, just as Butch Brennan came up behind her.

"Got the lights on," he said.

"Right." Her voice was muffled by her shirt, so he didn't notice its unsteadiness.

"Here. I got a spare face mask," he said, pulling one from a pocket of his jumpsuit. She put it on as they entered the room.

The square, windowless space had obviously been a home office. The richly carved shelves lining three walls were filled with the charred remains of books. Inside, the room reeked of vomit more than anything else.

"Jesus, which one of you faggots lost his lunch?" Butch called to three crime-scene cops who stood in a loose knot around Jed Benson's blackened corpse.

The corpse sat, contorted yet upright, in a chair pulled into the middle of the room, in front of an imposing wooden desk covered with the sticky ash of burned papers. Melanie didn't understand how he, *it,* was staying vertical. Jed Benson's face was a death's-head, blackened skin singed off in places, the skull a bloody unrecognizable pulp with a gaping hole in the forehead, crowned by pathetic patches of burned hair. The jaw hung open, as if in midscream. She found herself staring into his mouth, numb and nauseous, fixating on his dental work. His teeth were capped. So not all of Jed Benson's glamour came naturally. What he'd been wearing when he was killed, you couldn't tell. Shreds of fabric hung off the shiny mass of his flesh, scorched and bubbling wherever it wasn't obscured by sticky, dark blood.

One of the cops threw a cautionary glance at Butch, then jerked his head toward Rommie Ramirez, hunched over, just finished retching in the corner of the room. Melanie felt like throwing up, too, but she fought the urge. She didn't want them to think she couldn't handle this.

"Oh." Butch raised an eyebrow. "Been a while since you did a murder scene, huh, Lieutenant?"

Rommie straightened up, his swarthy skin now green, sweat standing out on his brow, and wordlessly marched out of the room. Everyone stared after him in surprise.

"What the fuck!" Butch exclaimed. "I heard that guy was in a tailspin. Now I see what they're talking about."

Melanie knew the gossip. At one time Rommie had been on the way up, getting named to high-profile commissions, even being mentioned as a possibility for deputy chief. Now he ran a respectable but run-of-the-mill drug squad. A decent position, but a demotion. She'd never really heard the reason. She liked him well enough to be concerned, but it wasn't really any of her business.

"That was plain unprofessional, if you ask me," Butch said, turning to her. "Him leaving makes you the lead investigator in the room, Melanie. My money says you got more balls than him anyway. Let me run through how we usually handle stuff. You let me know if it suits you, or if there's anything else you need."

Crime Scene cops are technical experts. They provide a crucial service to the investigators running a case, but they expect to be given a certain amount of direction. In Rommie's absence, that direction would have to come from Melanie. The need to focus saved her. She mustered her courage, walked right up to the body. A real prosecutor was hardened like a cop. Blood and gore were part of the job description.

"Jesus," she said, looking at it.

"Yeah," Butch said. "What kind of animal does this to another person?"

"Whoever he is, we'll get him," she replied, her voice calm and resolute even as her legs trembled. "Introduce me to your troops, Butch, and let's get to work."

"Castro and Jefferson here work for me. Dr. Joel Kramer is from the ME. We start with the body and work our way outward. Make, like, a grid of the room, then go over the floor real careful for hairs, fibers, blood spatters, what have you. Make notes of what's located where in the grid, photograph everything. Sound good?"

"Makes sense. You're the supervisor?"

"Yes, ma'am," Butch said.

"Then you're the one I'll call to testify in court, so you should take the photos of the body. Castro and Jefferson can do the rest of the room and the house."

"Sure thing." Brennan knelt down and unzipped a duffel bag sitting on the floor, removing cameras and notebooks and handing them around. He doled out assignments to Castro and Jefferson, who went off to fulfill them.

"What can you tell from the body about how the murder happened?" Melanie asked Kramer.

"Quite a lot, actually," Kramer replied. "The Fire Department responded quickly. The fire was out in time to save most of the flesh, so there's plenty left to work with. I've done a preliminary examination. Here, I'll show you."

Kramer walked up to the chair, extracted a collapsible metal pointer from his pocket, and opened it. He waved it over Benson's corpse like a magic wand. "First of all, you see the way the body has contorted. That's what we call pugilistic positioning. A natural contraction of the muscles that occurs when the body is burned. The fact that we see it indicates that rigor mortis hadn't set in at the time of fire. That's important, because we also see clear evidence of a gunshot wound to the head. Given lack of rigor, we can assume that the shooting and the burning of the body occurred within a relatively narrow time frame."

"Can you tell which happened first?" Melanie asked.

"Not without completing the actual autopsy. Now, take a look right here," Kramer said, directing his pointer at the large hole in Benson's forehead. "A gunshot entry wound. We know it's entry based on beveling we observe to the skull and the remaining flesh. The beveling points inward, indicating the bullet going in. The entry wound matches up to an exit wound right here." He walked around and pointed to a hole in the back of Benson's head, at about the point where the skull met the neck. "Again, we know it's exit because of the direction of the beveling, which points outward, thus the bullet going out. And from the relative positions of the entry and exit wounds, we can conclude that the shooter stood above the victim and fired downward, at relatively close range. The handcuffs the victims is wearing also suggest he was shot while sitting right here in this chair."

"Handcuffs? So that's what's holding him upright," Melanie said, studying the plastic twist-tie handcuffs that slashed deep ligatures into Benson's wrists. Chunks of flesh appeared to be missing from his hands. What remained was gouged in a familiar-looking way. "His hands. Are those—teeth marks?" she asked, gulping.

"Yes, not human, though." Kramer replied. "Animal, probably dog bites. They're all over the legs, too, and look. There's a similar-looking deep puncture wound in the remaining flesh on the neck. See, right here," he said, pointing to a deep gash in the charred skin of the corpse's neck.

Melanie nursed her growing rage, using it to fight back a wave of nausea that threatened to overwhelm her.

"On the gunshot, Melanie, we bagged the spent round," Butch said. "Nine-millimeter."

"Wouldn't common sense say the dog attack came first?" Melanie asked. "The gunshot to the head, at close range, finished him off? Then the fire was set to destroy evidence?"

"Makes sense," Brennan agreed. Kramer nodded.

"Okay, so let's talk motive," she continued. "Why sic a dog on him?"

"So many bites," Brennan said. "It's almost like he was tortured."

"Just what I was thinking. Lieutenant Ramirez said Benson's daughter was maimed. Tell me about that."

"Perp cut off some of her fingers. Fucking savage," Butch said bitterly.

"Was she shot?" Melanie asked.

"No, thankfully. She's in serious but stable condition," Butch said.

"So Benson was tortured," Melanie said, thinking aloud. "His daughter was tortured. Why do that? A grudge, maybe? The perp hated Benson so bad that he tortured his daughter in front of him, then tortured him before killing him?"

"The viciousness of the attack supports that," Kramer said.

"Or maybe the perp wanted something," she continued. "Money, information—who knows? Benson wouldn't give it up."

"Would you hold out if somebody was doing that kind of shit to you?" Butch said.

"Maybe Benson didn't hold out in the end. When Castro finishes dusting for latents, he should look for evidence of robbery. Open safes, jewelry boxes, drawers that are normally kept locked—that sort of thing," she said.

"You really think the motive could have been robbery?" Butch asked.

"Sure. You see carnage like this sometimes in a typical home invasion, where the perps force their way into a house to steal something they know is there. Whether it's drugs or money or expensive jewelry. Then again, you wouldn't expect something like that to happen in a neighborhood like this."

"You wouldn't expect the animal who did this to be walking around such a nice neighborhood in the first place," Butch said, shaking his head in disbelief.

"Tell me about it. I live a few blocks from here," Melanie said, going cold at the thought. A few blocks from this carnage, her daughter was sleeping.

"But he *was* here," she said. "We know that. And we know something else, something even worse. He's still out there."

4

The seven blocks between the Bensons' town house and Melanie Vargas's apartment were long and desperate ones for Sophie Cho. She trudged, hunched over, clutching the stroller handles for comfort, trying to keep visions of the Bensons' faces at bay. She had the baby to think of. She was very conscientious with Maya. She forced herself to pay careful attention to the traffic lights.

Guilt and anxiety were familiar emotions to Sophie, like old friends, but she'd never experienced them with this paralyzing intensity. She was first generation, grappling with the restrictions of her old culture, fighting to adjust to the new. Life wasn't easy. But still, she'd always done her best. She could look herself in the eye as she put up her hair every morning. She'd never had this feeling before, like she'd done something wrong, like it had terrible consequences.

She paused at the corner of Melanie's block. The doorman, Hector, stood under the long green awning leading to the curb, fanning himself with his cap in the wet heat. She thought he noticed her, but then he turned away to watch two small dogs yap wildly at each other, their owners yanking on their leashes to pull them apart. Hector was a nice man, with a jolly laugh and a paunch, always offering to fix her up with his accountant son. Would he read her guilt in her eyes now? Would he turn away in disappointment, in disgust?

"Hey, Miss Cho! How'd you get the little one?" Hector called, spotting her with the stroller.

She managed a demure smile as she approached him, always the polite daughter, even under stress.

"Melanie had to work. She asked me to bring Maya home and babysit."

"So late? Too much working for a mommy. Not good."

Normally she would've sparred with him gently about the importance of women working, but tonight every word of normal conversation felt forced. She couldn't do it. She stood there numbly, unable to muster any chat, choking on the humid air. Beneath her shirt, rivulets of perspiration slid down her back. The silence lengthened.

"I have keys," she blurted suddenly, her tone uncharacteristically sharp. Hector looked at her curiously.

"Sure, honey, it's late. You must be tired. Go on up."

At Melanie's floor Sophie stepped off the elevator onto the small landing and worked the keys in the lock easily. She should—she'd chosen the door hardware herself. She struggled into the brightly lit foyer, heaving the stroller over the threshold with one hand while holding the door open with her shoulder. Once inside, she couldn't help smiling despite her unhappiness. Melanie had left all the lights on, something Sophie herself was much too compulsive to do. She felt a great surge of affection for her friend, this baby, this apartment she'd renovated and then spent happy hours hanging out in.

Melanie's apartment had been one of Sophie's first architecture jobs after going out on her own, a vote of confidence, an early bankroll that set her on her way. She looked around the foyer now, eyes smarting with unshed tears, remembering how happily the three of them had worked together, how proud they'd been of the results. With a little taste, you could make your money go far. Elegant but not showy, still nice and homey. Sophie looked up at the ceiling, praying that nothing would have to change, that Melanie would never need to know what she'd done, that she'd still be welcomed here with open arms. But she was fooling herself.

Things had changed already. Hadn't they, after what she'd seen tonight?

A sigh caught in her throat, threatening to become a sob. She dropped the keys on a small wooden table, next to a tall stack of unopened mail addressed to Steve, and picked up a silver-framed photograph of Melanie, Steve, and Maya. The picture had been taken about six months ago, shortly after Maya came home from the hospital. In it she had the red, scrunchy face of an infant, so unlike her yummy plumpness now. Sophie lifted the stroller hood and gazed down at that sweet face, crescents of dark lashes resting against fat cheeks. She could almost be a Korean baby with all that black hair. She could almost be Sophie's own.

This child, this and no other, not even her own many nieces and nephews, had awakened the baby hunger she'd only read about in magazines. Now, when it seemed less and less likely she'd ever have one of her own. She'd been raised in a schizoid way, an American girl at school, a proper Korean girl at home, expected to steer clear of any entanglement with boys until an appropriate marriage was arranged with some son of her parents' friends. When the time came, she was in architecture school, having succeeded beyond her own wildest dreams, but poised to shatter her parents'. The few young Korean men who would look at a girl with her résumé dutifully paraded through, took tea, and went on their way, immediately seeing her lack of interest in them, in bearing their sons, in working at their grocery stores and manicure salons. By now they'd found other, more suitable wives, and Sophie had aged well beyond marriageability. As for Anglo men . . . well, she'd never connected with them. Besides, they didn't chase her the way they did some Korean girls of her acquaintance. She was too round, her short stature suggesting not the petite exoticism she privately accused them of seeking but rather a tendency to fat in later life.

Maya shifted in her stroller and gurgled breathily, sending a rush of pure love through Sophie's heart. She wheeled the stroller carefully down the hall to the smaller of the two bedrooms, glowing with golden light from the night-light, and stood reverently in the center of the room, breathing deep. It smelled of baby—the powdery smell from the changing table, the faint whiff of ammonia from the Diaper Genie. A happy nursery for a special little girl, with white furniture and a parade of pink wallpaper bunny rabbits marching around the top of the room.

Maya looked so comfortable that Sophie decided to let her sleep in the stroller until Melanie got home, rather than risk waking her by transferring her to the crib. She picked up a fluffy pink blanket that was folded neatly over the back of a white glider rocker. But as she bent to tuck it around Maya, a great wave of despair washed over her. She sat down heavily in the rocker, clutching the soft fabric to her chest, stifling her sobs as best she could to preserve Maya's tranquil sleep. Her vision blurring, she saw not Maya but Jed Benson's handsome face. What must it look like now?

5

___

The morning sun bothering his eyes. He sitting in a diner across from where he follow that Chinese bitch with the baby to last night, smoking a cigarette and watching. Watching and waiting, long as it took. With the look he give the waitress when she refill his coffee cup, she ain't hassling him about no cigarette. She know he hurt people, he hurt her if she give him an excuse. She look in his eyes and see that. He love the second when they figure it out.

But it piss him off when they think he stupid. Muscle and no brains. Now, how you gonna think that, with how small he was? How somebody his size get to be the most fearsome killer in five boroughs? Brains, that's how. Brains and planning. But people never see the work he put in, never give him credit. They think he just show up and do the drama, shooting and cutting. Killing is a tough game, takes mad planning. You need to scope your marks. You got to know when they come and when they go. Who else live in the house. What kind of firepower they got. When they sleeping and when they awake listening, waiting on you. You need the careful work first—*then* you do the drama.

Okay, the drama the best part. The look on their face when they beg for mercy. The noises they make when he slice through their flesh with his knife. He saw shit nobody else ever saw, felt like God with life in his hand. Life and death. Death with a capital *D*. But that the payoff, and you only get paid after hard work. He do the hard work alone. He case and he plan. The only one he ever brang was the dog, No Joke. So when it came to the killing, even if four or five shorties be on the job with him, he do it himself. He do the work, so he deserve the payoff.

The coffee taste like shit. The diner next to a bus stop. The exhaust fumes coming in the front door hurt his head. The morning after, he always fucked up, though. Crashing from the high. He spend days getting ready for last night's job, sitting quiet, nerves mad twitching. Watching the mark walk around like he all that, like he different than anybody else. Fucking joke. The only difference is, he overconfident. He stupid as a pig to know what he know and not see it coming. Most marks got the sense to know you coming, but not him. The connect at Queens Auto fix up the van to look like it from a flower shop. He sit on that house three days running, and still this motherfucker ain't catch on. A nigga in a flower truck sitting on your house for three days, you better fucking notice. If you don't, you see what happen.

He slam his cup down and laugh. A woman at the next table look up, snap him back to reality. Fuck, he so busy patting himself on the back, he forget to case. The building on a side street, diagonal-like from where he sitting. He pick this diner so he can watch the door, see if he spot that Chinese bitch again. The architect.

He don't like sitting here in the open, but he don't wanna bring the van too close to last night's job. This diner just a few blocks north from that house. Not that he listen to shit about don't return to the scene of the crime. Show you what TV know about the street. He always go back. It never give him trouble. He check out the scene the next day, see what the police up to, watch them looking for him. Get right up in their face, they don't even pay no attention. But they stop him last night, him and No Joke, so today he being careful.

Okay, shit go bad last night. One motherfucker screw up the whole scenario. First he show up late. That mess with the plan right there. Then, when the time come to do the deed, he lose his nerve. With all the delay, they hear sirens. They got to break out real fast. So they don't tie shit up neat the way they should. They all split in different directions. He take No Joke and go pick up the van where he parked a few blocks down, drop his mask and gloves in a trash can. He walking down the street, just chilling. But then he notice his shoes all covered with kerosene. His hands, too—that shit went right through the gloves. The sirens was coming, and he got concerned. Not nervous, just a little concerned. The residue and shit, they use that for proof if they catch you. So he take off his shoes and throw 'em under a car. And his hands, the only thing he could do was piss on 'em. A police come up. There he was, barefoot, pissing on his hands, No Joke looking like one nasty motherfuck. So what the cop did? Give him a desk appearance ticket for indecency and send him on his way. Can you believe that? It just make you laugh.

Now he planning Phase Two. Every job cast a shadow. Maybe somebody see too much or know too much or get in your way. Part of being good at killing is being thorough. You got to clean up afterward, even if you tired and don't feel like it. It bother him that he didn't get a chance to do it last night. That motherfucker gonna pay for that, 'cause now he was sitting in this diner casing again when he rather be home, sleeping it off. But you got to do what you got to do, and there was more of 'em to take care of. A few of 'em, matter of fact. Going about their business right now, not knowing they had an appointment with him down the road. He stubbed out his cigarette and threw a dollar down on the table. Fucking bitch waitress deserve to get ditched, but why attract attention with something stupid? Eyes on the prize. Time to check out that building across the street.

6

———

Maya sat in her bouncy seat with her favorite stuffed bear tucked in beside her, watching Melanie try on and reject garment after garment. This happened sometimes when Melanie was really exhausted. She just couldn't figure out what to wear to work, and it was never a good sign for the rest of the day. At least Maya seemed happy. Normally she fussed in that seat, much preferring the freedom of lolling on her back on a blanket, kicking her pudgy legs.

"*Qué chica buena,* sitting so nice for Mommy," Melanie cooed.

Maya gave a drooly smile, her dark eyes shining like two little coals, and grabbed her bear with her plump hands. She managed to get its ear up to her mouth. Melanie couldn't help smiling despite her bleak mood.

"You're getting awful good at that, *nena,*" she said. "Teddy's ears are in big trouble." She knelt down and hid her face momentarily in her daughter's neck, drinking in her milky fragrance. If only she could stay here forever and forget everything—her husband, her job. Call in sick and snuggle under the covers with Maya. But how could she? The minutes were ticking away. With her marriage in trouble, she couldn't afford to screw up at work. She pulled on a skirt and blouse that vaguely matched and quickly applied some lipstick. She'd do her eyes in the taxi. She was late already, and she had to face Bernadette this morning about the Benson case. That, she suspected, was the real reason for her trouble getting dressed.

It wasn't only Melanie. Everybody in the office was afraid of Bernadette. She was one of those bosses who gloried in persecuting their unfortunate underlings. She was obviously an unhappy person, but knowing that didn't make her any easier to deal with. Melanie was pretty unhappy herself these days, but she still treated people decently. Bernadette, on the other hand—one minute she was sweet as candy, but the next she was blasting you till it hurt. You had to respect her, though, because she was good at her job. Every once in a while, Melanie would set herself the challenge of figuring Bernadette out, getting along with her, even winning her friendship. It worked for a while. Bernadette would reward her with praise or a juicy assignment, and Melanie would be thrilled. Bernadette was her mentor, her role model—for a day or a week. It never lasted. Bernadette turned on her, every time. If Melanie's work was less than perfect, she wasn't worthy. If it was perfect, she was a threat and needed to be put in her place. Either way Melanie lost.

Dressed at last. She was about to pick up Maya and head for the door when a glimmer on the dresser top caught her eye. Her wedding and engagement rings. *Damn it!* She'd been doing okay, but this knocked the wind out of her. Unable to stop herself, she walked over to the dresser and picked them up, feeling their weight, letting them sparkle on her palm. She'd forgotten she wasn't wearing them. It was three weeks now since she'd told Steve to get out, but last night was the first time she'd taken them off. In her heart she and Steve were still married. Not just in her heart. Legally, they were still married, and Steve was begging her not to do anything to change that.

It was sometime after 3:00 A.M. when she took the rings off. She'd come home and crawled into bed after the Benson crime scene, positively wrecked, and the visions started pouring into her head. Not what you'd think. Not Jed Benson's corpse, but her own personal horror show, the one that played constantly now. One scene in particular made her rip the rings off. That cocktail party at Steve's firm six months ago, right before Maya was born. She hadn't found out for sure until five months later, but that was when she first suspected something was going on. She remembered the sensation of being *so* pregnant, her feet swollen, feeling like a cow in her maternity formal. And how that slut in her low-cut dress sashayed up to him. The way she touched his arm and giggled. Melanie knew instantly there was something between them. Maybe not actual sex, maybe not then, but something in the air. She knew, and yet she couldn't believe it. *¡Puta!* Melanie always dressed like a lady, and he goes for somebody so . . . so trashy, so *hoochie*-looking, with her boobs popping out. *Slut.* She *still* couldn't believe it.

The baby-sitter, Elsie Stanton, called from the foyer as she let herself in. So far Melanie had told Elsie that Steve was away on business—which was true, it just wasn't the whole truth. The tan line on her ring finger stood out against her skin. She swallowed her tears and shoved the rings back on. Not today.

Yanking open the Velcro strap on the bouncy seat, Melanie lifted Maya out and held her close, drawing comfort from her daughter's little body. Maya felt fluffy—roly-poly and weightless at the same time. Melanie rested her cheek on Maya's dark head and immediately felt something cold. She held Maya away, looked down at herself, and laughed despite the awful knot in her stomach. Kids kept you grounded, all right. A large wet circle of drool spread across the shoulder of her blouse.

"Didn't like Mommy's outfit, *nena*? Just like your Aunt Linda. Fashion police." She put her nose against Maya's tiny button of a nose.

"Good morning, Elsie. This baby just got her mommy's blouse all wet," Melanie said, walking into the foyer. Maya smiled and lifted her arms to Elsie.

"I always say it's plain foolish to wear fine clothes around little children. Come to Elsie, baby. As if it's your fault you're teething!" Elsie said, taking Maya.

"I wasn't blaming her."

Melanie sighed, resigned to being misunderstood. Good communication was not the hallmark of her relationship with Elsie, but she'd decided to live with that. As usual, Elsie was twenty minutes late, and, as usual, Melanie bit her tongue and didn't say anything. A large Jamaican woman in her early sixties with five children of her own, Elsie had worked for Steve's Aunt Frances for seventeen years, helping to raise Steve's three cousins. So it was taken for granted that, when Steve's youngest cousin headed to college just as Melanie's maternity leave ran out, Elsie would come to work for them, to care for Maya. If Elsie didn't take direction, if she made no secret of her disdain for Melanie's beginner-level mothering skills, that was nothing compared with her decades-long relationship with Steve's family. Melanie trusted her. One of her greatest fears was that Elsie would quit the minute she found out about the separation, forcing Melanie to hire some stranger if she wanted to keep her job. Melanie couldn't bear the thought of leaving Maya with a stranger. Just look at how she loved Elsie! She went to her so easily, her face lighting up, snuggling into Elsie's big chest. Already late, Melanie beat back her jealousy and headed for the door.

SHE CAUGHT A cab in front of the diner. As they headed for the on-ramp to the FDR, she held a tiny compact in one hand and applied mascara with the other, rehearsing lines to use on Bernadette. She'd marched into that crime scene and taken charge. She already knew more about the investigation than anybody else in the office. She was ready, willing, and able to handle a big case. The speech would sound great—if she ever got the chance to open her mouth. Hell, if she didn't get fired first.

Bernadette's was the corner office, sitting at the intersection of two hallways housing the Major Crimes Unit. Melanie took a deep breath, studying her nameplate: BERNADETTE DeFELICE, CHIEF. She squared her shoulders and walked as calmly as she could manage into the anteroom. Bernadette's secretary, Shekeya Jenkins, played solitaire on the computer as she fielded phone calls, working the telephone buttons with a pencil held gingerly between inch-long, gem-studded nails. Shekeya was the only secretary who ever lasted more than a week with Bernadette, and she prided herself on the accomplishment. She had elaborate braids bleached orangey-red, a big heart tattooed on her arm that said KWAME, and a poisonous tongue. Shekeya didn't hesitate to give back to Bernadette as good as she got. She raised her eyebrows at Melanie dubiously.

"You want an audience with Her Majesty?"

"Uh-huh. She on the phone?"

"What else? You on your own, honey, because the way she acting, I'm not buzzing her. Don't say I didn't warn you."

As Melanie moved toward the door to the interior office, Bernadette screamed, "Who the fuck is on line three? Why is line three still blinking? *Shekeya?*"

"She can answer her own goddamn calls, see how she like that," Shekeya said, turning back to her card game, a bored look on her face.

Bernadette sat with her back to the door, facing her computer and a bank of telephones, but turned as she heard the clicking of Melanie's high heels.

"Oh. Hold on. You, I wanna talk to," she said, picking up the telephone and pointing at a guest chair. Melanie sat down and listened. Might as well learn something. Bernadette was stroking the guy on the other end of the line. He was a boss at DEA, and Bernadette was trying to get some business out of him.

"Larry, don't worry for a minute, we can jam the thing through Washington in no time. I'll put my best people on it. You'll get a nice seizure, we'll get a few bodies to prosecute. Everybody walks away happy."

She was smooth, no question, yet the cracks were showing. It wasn't her looks, exactly, because Bernadette was still beautiful. But she was in her mid-forties now and overcompensating, fighting too hard. Her shoulder-length hair, once a rich dark brown, was colored an unnatural red. She wore too much makeup. And her clothes . . . well, tight clothes suited some people—take Melanie's sister Linda, a Latina diva if ever there was one. But on Bernadette they looked cheesy, desperate. Bernadette had never married, had no kids. A career spent sleeping with cops wasn't likely to pan out into anything permanent, but no other type of guy seemed to do it for her.

Bernadette hung up and focused on Melanie. It was scary, because she did *not* look happy.

"How did you know Jed Benson was murdered?" Bernadette demanded. Melanie knew from that tone she would never deliver the speech she'd been planning.

"I was there last night, at the scene."

"Yes, I know that, miss. I had to hear it from Lieutenant Ramirez instead of your sneaky little mouth. How did you know to go there?"

Melanie had guessed Ramirez would tattle to Bernadette, but still it infuriated her.

"It was an accident. I mean, it was a coincidence," she sputtered as Bernadette fixed her with a cold stare. "I live right near there. I was out for a walk, and I happened to go by and see the fire trucks."

"You just happened to be out for a walk?"

"Yes."

"Why were you out walking at ten o'clock at night?"

"My baby couldn't sleep. I thought a stroll would help."

Bernadette leaned back in her chair, seeming to accept her answer, but then sat up suddenly, jabbing her finger at Melanie. "Lieutenant Ramirez claims you said I sent you!"

"I never said that! I was careful to avoid saying that, in fact. It looked like an important case, so I wanted to grab it for us, Bern, before the state got it. Be aggressive, take a page from your book. So I bluffed him. Pretended I was supposed to be there. If he thought I was just passing by with my baby stroller, he never would've given me the time of day."

"So you felt that justified going outside the chain of command? Doing this without consulting me?"

"I thought it was what you would want me to do."

"Hmmmph. Well. You put me in a difficult position, girlfriend. Two of my favorite management principles are in conflict here. Do you know what they are?"

"No." She hated the meekness in her voice. Bernadette could always do this to her, reduce her to a timid little mouse. And Melanie was *not* easily intimidated.

"Principle number one: punish insubordination. Principle number two: reward initiative. Do you see how your actions force me to choose between them?"

"Yes." She despised her own weakness. But what could she do, not answer Bernadette's rhetorical questions? That would read like rebellion.

"I can't have my people running around this city barging into crime scenes without my permission. *I* bring in the business around here. *I* make the assignments. *I* maintain the relationships with the bosses at NYPD and the federal agencies. Not you, not anyone else in this unit. Me. Is that understood?"

"Of course, one hundred percent, Bern. I wasn't trying—"

"But having said that, I do try to teach you people to be go-getters, and your instincts were right in this instance. We should have this case. Jed was one of ours, after all. His murder should be ours." Her voice cracked slightly, reminding Melanie that the victim wasn't just any corpse.

"Bernadette," Melanie interjected, "I was at the scene last night. I have knowledge nobody else—"

Bernadette held up her hand. "Quiet, please, I'm thinking!"

Seconds passed as Melanie sat in suspense, waiting for Bernadette's verdict. Her boss's lips twitched into a sly smile.

"Pop-quiz time, girlfriend. How are you planning to federalize this murder charge?"

Melanie hadn't had one second to hit the books since stumbling across the Benson crime scene last night, but she could fake it when she needed to.

"Well, it depends on how the facts unfold, but there are several possibilities. May I borrow your code book?"

Bernadette reached back to her credenza, where several fat paperback volumes stood upright between metal bookends. She yanked out one called *Federal Criminal Code and Rules* and handed it across the desk to Melanie. Melanie opened it, pretending she had a plan, doing her best to keep her face blank but feeling herself flush as Bernadette watched her. Bernadette must have been working on a RICO case recently, because she'd tabbed the racketeering statute. The book naturally fell open to it.

"Here's an option," Melanie said, straining for a perky, confident tone. "Section 1959. Murder in aid of racketeering."

"Okay, but you'd have to prove up a racketeering enterprise. Not easy. Keep going. See anything else?"

Melanie flipped pages, trying not to look nervous. "We could use Section 1958. Murder-for-hire. It's a federal crime as long as interstate telephone lines are used and there's evidence of payment. Or the drug-murder statute, if we can link the perpetrator to narcotics."

Bernadette raised her eyebrows, smiling broadly, enjoying watching Melanie scramble. "You're really reaching with those. Your first shot was your best one, even if you only picked it because I had the statute marked. Give me the book, hon," Bernadette said, chuckling.

Melanie handed it back to her, spirits soaring at the sudden warmth in Bernadette's voice. "The point is, Bern, we have options. Something'll stick, I'm positive."

"You think on your feet, and I like that. Look, I'm gonna be frank. Your gutsiness last night weighs in your favor, but it's not necessarily enough. Normally I wouldn't consider handing you a case of this magnitude. It's not a matter of talent. You're good in front of a jury. You have a good head for investigation. But you've never been in the spotlight before. You've only done basic bread-and-butter stuff. And what's more, you're not performing up to your abilities right now."

"What do you mean?" Cold anxiety flooded her chest again. An encounter with Bernadette was always a roller-coaster ride.

"Well, honestly, I question your commitment to the job. You have a new baby at home. That may be a big deal for you, but it's no excuse as far as I'm concerned. I'm very aware of when my people come in, when they leave, how many weekends they're putting in, that sort of thing. I don't see you here as much as I'd like to."

"My husband's been traveling recently, so a lot's fallen on me at home, but that can change. I can get extra baby-sitting if I need to. I'll put in whatever time is required, I promise."

"We're talking a *lot* of time. Like, bring-a-toothbrush-because-you'll-be-sleeping-here kind of time."

"Understood. I can do it, Bernadette. Just give me a chance."

Bernadette cupped her chin in her hand and gazed at Melanie. "Hmm. You're hot for this case, I'll say that for you. And the politics would certainly work out well."

"Politics?"

"Yeah. The front office wants Joe Williams on this case. Joe's close to the big boss. You know how the black prosecutors stick together. I'd have a spy in my midst. No way am I gonna let that happen. Politically, I think I can push you as an alternative, because you're a twofer."

"A twofer?"

"Yeah, you know, two for the price of one? Hispanic and female? A new mom to boot? We promote pregnant women, that sort of thing?"

"I'm not pregnant."

"But you were."

"And I'm only half Puerto Rican. I mean, I grew up in a Puerto Rican neighborhood and all, but my mother is Italian."

"Well, don't go around telling people that."

Melanie laughed in astonishment, then fell silent. She could barely muster words to respond. She hated taking advantage of her heritage at work, playing it up to get a case. She was a talented prosecutor. Bernadette should choose her because she deserved the assignment, not because of her last name or her dark hair and eyes. Playing ethnic politics like that made her uncomfortable. How many times had she sat in court and realized that, going by looks, she could be the defendant's sister or girlfriend? Not that the shared ethnicity made her sympathetic. Quite the opposite. She knew better than anybody how crime ravaged her neighborhood.

"I don't see what anybody's ethnic background has to do with deciding who's the best prosecutor for the case," she protested.

"Oh, you don't, Miss Priss? Spare me! All that stuff matters big-time these days. How else do you think I can spin your appointment, given how junior you are? It's our best shot."

Shekeya buzzed Bernadette with an important phone call, so Melanie had a minute to think. She couldn't believe it, but she was getting cold feet. This was starting to seem like a bad idea. Not only was she overwhelmed at home, but the Benson case was a minefield. Bernadette would be watching her like a hawk. If things got to be too much, she could take a spectacular fall.

Bernadette hung up and looked at her. Melanie hesitated, then said, "Joe Williams is a good friend of mine. I don't want to steal the case out from under—"

"I can't believe this! You come in here begging for the Benson case, you convince me you're the right person for the job, and suddenly you choke? Do you think Joe Williams would think twice about stealing this case from *you*? This isn't Mommy and Me class where everybody shares. This is every man for himself."

"I just—"

"Let me help you out here, Melanie. Your other choice is *not* rushing out the door at five on the dot to relieve the baby-sitter. You've been back from maternity leave for three months now, and I'll feel justified in piling the work on whether we're talking case of the century or endless bail duty. Do I make myself clear?"

"Perfectly," Melanie replied icily.

"Good. Secondly, if that's the stick, here's the carrot. You'll be working with the best agents in the city."

"Agents? What agents? I thought Lieutenant Ramirez was doing the case." It dawned on her how odd it was that Rommie had left the scene last night and hadn't returned. A queasy stomach couldn't account for that. Had he been taken off the case?

"Romulado was too close to the victim. He may not have the emotional distance to work the case."

"I see," Melanie replied, although she really didn't.

"Besides, he's going through a very bitter divorce right now."

"Oh. I didn't even know he was married."

"Yeah, for about five minutes, and now she wants big bucks. Problem is, he already pays every red cent to his wife and kids from his first marriage. Poor thing can't get a break, at work or in his personal life."

"Sounds complicated."

"Yes, well, I've convinced him to disqualify himself from the Benson case for the time being. On the understanding that I'll supervise it personally, of course."

"Of course." Melanie could only imagine the nightmarish level of scrutiny that would entail. This got worse every minute.

"So as I was saying, the people assigned to the case are top-notch. Randall Walker from the PD and Dan O'Reilly from the FBI. They were partnered up on that gang-homicide task force until O'Reilly got transferred to work terrorism. Randall's a burnout case now, but there was a time when he was hands down the best detective in the PD. He was the first black guy to make first grade, so you can imagine how good he was back then. O'Reilly's the real star now, though. Smart and brash and as cute as they come. We were very fortunate to get him. His supervisor was a friend of Jed Benson's, and he detailed O'Reilly to us to work this."

"Maybe I should take a few minutes to think this over, Bernadette."

"Sorry, Charlie! You already sold me. The Benson case is yours. And you'd better get started, because I want charges brought within a week."

"A week? How can I possibly bring charges in a week? Have there been arrests? Are there even any suspects?"

"Oh, yeah, I figured you knew since you were there last night. Romulado says it looks like a paid hit. His best guess is, it might've been contracted to retaliate against Benson for a big case he did years ago. He put away the founder of a major Puerto Rican drug gang for a triple homicide. By the way, Puerto Rican suspects, Puerto Rican prosecutor? See what I mean? They'll love you on the six o'clock news, hon. Anyway, Delvis Diaz was the kingpin's name. So start with the theory that the murder was payback for that case, and see what you come up with."

"But how do we know we'll be able to catch the killers by then?"

"Since when do you need the suspects locked up in order to bring charges? What is this, Crim Law 101? Present the testimony, get the indictment voted, and seal it until you catch the perpetrators. Now, report to your office and get to work, kiddo. I'd hate to see Joe Williams get the glory while you're stuck in night court doing bail hearings for the next six months. Understood?"

They stared at each other across the desk. This battle was over. Melanie's only option was treating it like a victory.

"Understood. I'm sorry if I seemed nervous for a minute. It won't happen again. I appreciate your confidence in me, and I won't let you down."

"That's more like it. I told O'Reilly to stop by right away and give you the details. Now, get moving." Bernadette turned back to her telephone and began dialing. Melanie was dismissed.

Melanie walked down the hall toward her office, feeling like she'd been hit by a truck. Brooding over her encounter with Bernadette, she wandered distractedly into her office but stopped short in the doorway. A guy was sitting behind her desk, talking on her telephone. He looked up, and their eyes met. Bernadette, the case, everything fell away. She completely forgot what she was thinking about.

7
—

She'd never met the guy sitting behind her desk, yet she felt the shock of recognition. As they looked at each other, he blushed and lost the thread of his conversation.

"I didn't catch that. Say again?" he said into the telephone, making a visible effort to break off eye contact with her.

He must be Dan O'Reilly, the agent Bernadette had told her about. Melanie walked in and leaned back against her filing cabinet, checking him out. He was big and handsome, with a masculine face and thick dark hair, and he looked strangely familiar to her. Maybe she'd seen him around, or maybe he just had that all-American jock look a lot of cops and agents have. But it was more like she'd been waiting to meet someone who looked like him. Even the sound of his voice—the deep, comforting timbre, the slight New York accent—seemed right on the money, like something she'd been expecting to hear for a while without quite realizing it. He kept sneaking glances at her as he talked. Finally he hung up.

"Melanie Vargas?" he asked.

"One and the same."

"I should have known it was you. You look like your name."

"Yeah? Someone told me once my name sounded like a stripper's." She blushed bright red the second that popped out of her mouth.

"No comment," he said, laughing gently. He had a boy-next-door quality, clean-cut, sweet. "I'm Dan O'Reilly."

"I figured. Bernadette told you she's assigning me to this case?"

"She said probably. She had to work out the details."

"It's done. You're looking at your prosecutor." She sat down across from him and reached for some folders he'd spread on her desk. "What do you have for me?"

"Not so fast," he said, grabbing at the folder she'd picked up. They had a tug-of-war over it, their eyes locked together. She lost her nerve for a second and let go.

"What, you don't let the prosecutor see your files?" she said breathlessly. Her voice sounded young and foolish to her own ears. Stop that, she scolded herself. Act like a professional.

"I like to train my prosecutors early. I handle my files, you handle yours," Dan said. "That way we don't end up accusing each other of losing stuff or giving the defense things we shouldn't. Keeps things friendly."

"Yeah, well, if those are your files, then that's my chair, pal. Out," she said, feeling a need to take charge of the situation.

"Okay, okay." He laughed. "I guess it remains to be seen who's training who."

"Damn straight."

They switched seats. He was still smiling as he opened the folder and picked out a couple of rap sheets printed on rough yellow computer paper. She watched his hands move. They were solid and strong. He wore no wedding band.

She nodded toward the rap sheets. "You have suspects already? Quick work. I'm impressed."

"Can't say for sure they're the right guys. Ramirez has this idea Benson was hit as payback for locking up Delvis Diaz almost ten years ago."

"Oh, right. Bernadette said Diaz founded some major gang?"

"Yeah, a unit of it anyway. Heard of the Gangsta Blades?"

"Sure. They're everywhere. Puerto Rican, mostly retail heroin, right?"

"Uh-huh."

"I'm Puerto Rican, you know. Half," she said, studying him.

"Really? I thought so from the name, but then you talk just like one of those anchors from the TV news."

"This is work. I speak the King's English. Besides, I'm second generation. I barely even speak Spanish at home."

"Yeah? Where's home?"

"Manhattan now, but I'm from Queens originally."

"Whereabouts? I'm from Queens, too."

"It's really the Brooklyn-Queens border. Technically, it's Bushwick." She blushed.

"Bushwick? You're kidding," he said, clearly surprised. "That's a tough neighborhood."

"Well, right near the border with Ridgewood." She was acting like her mother, she thought, annoyed with herself. Her mother hated Bushwick and used to say they were from Ridgewood when they really weren't. Bushwick *was* rough, though, which was the main reason Melanie had worked her butt off to get out.

"You know," Dan said, "Diaz founded a crew called the C-Trout Gangsta Blades. Named for the corner of Central and Troutman in Bushwick. So if Ramirez is right, the perps in this case are probably Bushwick boys."

"Yeah, well, my mother never used to let us walk down that way."

"I don't blame her. Central and Troutman's been a major drug supermarket for the past twenty years."

"I'm aware of that."

"You really from Bushwick? 'Cause you sure don't seem like it." He glanced up at the diplomas on her wall, then looked back at her, scrutinizing her closely, like he was trying to solve a puzzle.

"Trust me, it's there. You can take the girl out of the block, but you can't take the block out of the girl. What about you? Where in Queens?"

"Belle Harbor, out in the Rockaways," he replied, naming a solidly middle-class neighborhood of mostly cops and firemen.

"Oh." She nodded.

"Could've guessed, right? I haven't come that far in life. Put me in a groove and I stay in it."

He looked down at the papers in his hands, seeming suddenly shy. There was something endearing about him.

"Okay, well. Diaz was a big local kingpin. Benson locked him up for a triple homicide and heroin distribution about eight years back," Dan said.

"He still locked up?" she asked.

"Yup. Three consecutive life terms at Otisville. He'll die there."

"So we track down Diaz's known associates on the outside and, bingo, find the killer? That sounds too easy. Besides, if Diaz was in for eight years already, why go after Benson now?"

"Good point, Counselor. Revenge doesn't usually wait that long. Look, I'm not saying this is the answer. The hit could've been for some other reason entirely. But I have to admit, there is some support for the Diaz angle."

"Such as?"

"We got two eyewitnesses. Benson's teenage daughter, who's not well enough to talk yet, and a Filipino housekeeper, Rosario Sangrador. Me and my partner, Randall Walker, already interviewed Rosario. She's scared to death."

"From what I saw last night, I can't say I blame her."

"You were at the murder scene?"

"Yes."

"Now it's my turn to be impressed. I saw the autopsy photos this morning. That was some nasty shit. You got a strong stomach for a girl."

He grinned at her admiringly for a long second. His eyes were very blue. Melanie looked down at the desk, trying not to notice. What was it about this guy? Handsome, yes. But normally stuff like that didn't even register with her.

"So where's the housekeeper now?" she asked.

"What?" Dan was looking at her, still smiling.

"The housekeeper. Where is she now?"

"Stashed out of town so nobody gets to her. She tells quite a story. Typical gangland home-invasion MO. Four or five guys wearing ski masks. We recovered one of the masks from a Dumpster near the scene. It's at the lab getting examined for hairs and fibers. Anyway, one guy rings the doorbell. When she answers it, they all push in. They got a big dog with 'em, kind of unusual, right? She never sees their faces. But she hears 'em talking to each other and she gets some aliases. I gotta admit, the akas come up in the NADDIS database as known C-Trout Blades. That's what makes me think Ramirez could be right with this retaliation idea. Why else would these gangbangers target Benson? Anyway, it's a place to start. Here, I'll take you through it."

He opened a folder and plucked out two mug shots.

"By the way, the reason me and Randall got tapped for this case is, we did a wiretap on the C-Trout Blades a few years back. Took down about forty guys, learned a lot about the organization. They're a nasty crew."

He laid the two mug shots on the desk in front of her. She picked one up and examined it, feeling a tingle of déjà vu. The boy in the picture looked to be about thirteen or fourteen, but he had a pointy, feral face, small eyes, and a cold, sullen expression that chilled her.

"Who's this? He looks very familiar," she said.

"His street name is Slice, but we don't have a true name for him."

"You have a mug shot, so he has a criminal record. How could you not have his true name?"

"The mug shot's from a juvie arrest about ten years ago. Apparently he was arrested under the name Junior Diaz, but it turned out to be false."

"Diaz? Like the gang leader."

"Yup, interesting coincidence."

"Maybe it's not a coincidence. A family relationship to Delvis Diaz would fit with the retaliation theory, right? Like, say, Delvis's little brother whacking Benson to avenge the conviction or something," Melanie said. "But why do you say it's a false name?"

"It didn't check out. At the time of arrest, he gave a false Social, false address. Apparently they didn't figure it out until later."

"Hmmm," she murmured. She was performing the same calculation she always did, whenever she came across the right type of suspect. A Bushwick kid, Puerto Rican, rough, a gangbanger. Certain things matched. But no. This one was too young, and according to the physical description on the pedigree sheet, much too small. She didn't see how it could be the same guy, that one she'd been looking for for so long.

"You say Slice looks familiar to you, though? Did you run across him in a case of yours?" Dan asked.

"I don't know. I can't place him—it's just a feeling. What else do you have on him?"

"Nothing solid. He's very careful. Won't talk business over the telephone, won't deal with strangers except through trusted subordinates—that type of thing. But my informant from that old wire tells me about Slice from way back. Says he's the real deal. Maybe twenty bodies on him. Real psycho. Likes to torture his victims first by cutting pieces off 'em. That's where he gets the aka. Oh, and generally kills all witnesses. That's how he stays out of jail."

"Then maybe it's not the same guy. *Our* perp left witnesses. He didn't kill the housekeeper or Benson's daughter," she pointed out.

Dan was quiet for a moment, pondering that. Their thoughts must have been following the same path, because when he opened his mouth to speak, she knew what he was going to say.

"He didn't kill 'em. *Yet.*"

"Yet," she repeated.

"Don't worry. We got security on both of 'em. In fact, I'm gonna call right now to tell those guys don't even leave their posts to use the john."

"Yes. Do that. I'm pretty good, but even I can't make a case if the witnesses are dead."

AS THEY TALKED, Melanie filled pages of a yellow legal pad with notes on what they needed to do. And do fast. Identifying and apprehending Slice was the top priority. If he was the perpetrator, they could assume he would try to eliminate the housekeeper and Jed Benson's daughter. They needed to stop him before he did any more damage.

Dan pointed to the second mug shot, of a huge, hulking guy who wore his hair in dreadlocks wrapped in a bandanna. "Jason Olivera, street name Bigga, a known C-Trout Blade. We should go after him because he's gonna be easier to find than Slice. Bigga has a rap sheet a mile long, small-time stuff mostly, but nasty. Assault, weapons possession. He's been getting arrested his whole life, never done a stretch longer than six months, and he's left a trail of addresses. I'm gonna start beating the bushes for him, hit all the locations from that old drug wire, see what crawls out."

"Okay, order your files from the old drug wiretap," she said, jotting on the legal pad with a felt-tip marker. "I'll order the records from the original Delvis Diaz case, the one Jed Benson prosecuted years ago. Who knows, maybe those locations are still active. And what about the informant you mentioned? Would he have any leads on where we can find Bigga?"

"If I can find my informant, I'll find Bigga," he said. "But so far the son of a bitch isn't returning my beeps. I've been working terrorism, so I haven't kept up with my old drug snitches."

"What about posting a lookout with the police in other jurisdictions?"

"Already taken care of. I had my office teletype all known information about Slice and Bigga to every state law-enforcement agency as well as Immigration and Customs. If they come into contact with the law or try to leave the country, we'll hear about it. But that's a big if. It can take years for something like that to pan out. To find 'em fast, there's no substitute for good old-fashioned shoe leather."

"I want to speak to the housekeeper and Benson's wife right away," Melanie said, "and his daughter the minute she's able to."

"Write that down. Oh, and I'll contact the lab to get copies of any test results. They already called me this morning. Apparently the crime-scene guys lifted a latent fingerprint from a can of kerosene left behind in Benson's house. They can't identify the print. It doesn't belong to any of the Bensons, but it doesn't match up with any violators in the FBI database either. If one of the perps left it, he has no criminal record."

"Was the print checked against our people?" she asked.

"They don't do that unless you ask for it special. It's like you're saying somebody screwed up the crime scene, mishandled evidence."

"They need to run that check. I like to know before the grand jury if the crime scene was contaminated. I can't worry about hurting some-body's feelings." She made another note.

"Okay. That's your call."

"That's all I can think of right now," she said, shaking her hand to stop it from cramping.

"That's plenty for starters. Let me have that list so I can burn a couple copies, wouldja? I'm gonna get with Randall Walker and divide up the work."

She tore off the pages and handed them across the desk. As he stood up to go to the copy station, she stopped him.

"Uh, can I ask you something about Randall?"

"What about him?"

"This investigation is gonna be pretty fast-paced. He's definitely up for the job, right?"

He sat back down, brow furrowed. "What's that supposed to mean?"

"Um . . . well, Bernadette said Randall's kind of burned out."

"Burned out? That nasty bitch. She has to bad-mouth everybody."

"So it isn't true?"

He sighed in frustration. "Look, normally I would never dignify bull-shit like that with a response. But you seem like a nice person. I hate to see Bernadette poisoning your mind with lies before you even meet Randall Walker, who happens to be one of the finest detectives I've ever worked with."

"Okay, so he's on his game? You'll vouch for that?"

"Maybe he has a little too much on his plate now, personal-wise, but he's still a great detective."

So there *was* something to this. She looked Dan straight in the eye. "What's the problem? Drinking? Marriage troubles?"

"I don't like to talk about my partner's personal business."

"Just give me enough so I understand."

"Okay. But it stays in this room."

She nodded, feeling honored he would confide in her. "Cross my heart."

"Randall's son died of a drug overdose about five years ago. His only kid. Randall's okay, but his wife is a mess. Never got past it. She's got a lot of problems, mental and physical. Diabetes, asthma, major depression. It really brings him down."

"That's awful!"

"Yeah. But seriously, Randall more than pulls his weight."

"Okay." She stared into his eyes, trying to decide if he was telling her everything. He fidgeted under the intensity of her gaze.

"And if for some reason he can't pull his weight, I pull it for him."

"Okay. Now I get the picture."

He stood up again, shaking his head.

"What?" she asked.

"Nothing." He broke into a grin.

"What?"

"Nah, it's just . . . I gotta watch myself with you. It's not smart to go telling the prosecutor everything. Only causes trouble. But I can already see that you're gonna get stuff out of me whether I like it or not."

He was looking at her eagerly, in a way she found flattering and un-comfortable at the same time. Could it be that he liked her? Instinctively she scooped up Maya's photograph, which sat on her desk in a frame that said I LOVE MY MOMMY.

"She yours? Can I see?" he asked quietly, glancing at her wedding ring. She remembered that she almost hadn't worn it this morning. Good thing she had. She wouldn't want to give a wrong impression.

"Her name's Maya." She handed him the photograph.

He smiled. Everybody always smiled when they saw those cheeks.

"What a cutie! How old?"

"Six months."

"I always wanted kids. Always thought I'd have a passel of 'em. Guess life never works out how you expect," he said, eyes somber as he handed the picture back.

Melanie carefully set it in its place. Dan left to make the copies. When she was sure he was gone, she kissed her fingertip and brushed it lightly across Maya's picture. She felt strange. Sad and weirdly guilty at the same time. She realized that it was because she found Dan attractive, and finding him attractive brought home to her how damaged her marriage was.

Dan returned from the copy machine. As he gave her back her list, she looked up at his face and couldn't help wondering how someone like him ended up single. He must be around thirty and so good-looking—maybe he was just a ladies' man. Maybe the stuff about wanting kids was only talk. Somehow she didn't think so, though. His sadness at the mention of kids had seemed genuine, making her identify with him, making her want to hear the story behind his solitude. But she would never ask him about it. She'd keep things on a professional footing—that was obviously the right thing to do. She just had a funny feeling it might not be so easy.

8

The slick tiles of the Lincoln Tunnel flashed by at warp speed as Melanie raced toward New Jersey in a government car, heading for the hotel where the housekeeper who witnessed Jed Benson's murder was under protection. A few hours after leaving Melanie's office with the to-do list, Dan had called from the hotel and told her to get there fast.

"We got a big problem with Rosario Sangrador," he said, his voice urgent. "She doesn't want to stay holed up anymore while we look for the perps, but she can't go back to her apartment while they're on the loose. Not only is she refusing to testify, she's threatening to run."

"That can't happen. We need her testimony."

"You better get here ASAP and talk some sense into her. Or else I'm gonna cuff her to the doorknob, and she's not gonna like that."

Black clouds hung low in the sky as Melanie pulled into the hotel's vast parking lot. The modern tan brick building stood apart, rising like a squat mountain from the deserted wasteland of on- and off-ramps. A hot wind coming off the parkway tasted of asphalt and rain as she gathered up her briefcase and slammed the door. She'd come armed with a hastily typed subpoena with Rosario's name on it. She'd use it if she had to, but it was always better if witnesses testified of their own free will.

Melanie rapped firmly on the hotel-room door. An eye appeared at the peephole. Dan opened the door, stuck his head out, and checked both ways down the corridor before letting her in.

"You didn't tell anyone where you were going, did you?" he asked.

"Just Bernadette, so she could sign for the car."

He frowned. "You filled out a sheet? Those things go to the filing pool. When you get back, you better pull it and white out the destination."

"You think so? That sounds kind of paranoid to me."

He shrugged, then turned and led her down a cramped foyer into a small room with salmon pink carpeting, pink and green upholstery, and blond wood furniture. It smelled stale, a combination of old cigarette smoke and room deodorizer. A petite, middle-aged Filipino woman with short hair and steel-rimmed eyeglasses sat on the bed staring blankly at the television resting on the bureau. She turned, and Melanie's jaw dropped. *Abuelita.* The woman was the spitting image of her grandmother, who'd lived with her family when Melanie was young. But the left side of the housekeeper's face was darkly mottled, angry bruises punctuated by the black railroad tracks of a stitched gash. Something stiff in her posture suggested she was in pain.

Rosario Sangrador stared at Melanie morosely. In the hostile blankness of her gaze, Melanie read fear.

"Rosario, I want you to meet somebody," Dan said. "This is Miss Vargas. She's the prosecutor. She's gonna put Jed Benson's killers in jail."

Rosario glared at Melanie. "I not testify. No way. Send me home now," she said, ignoring Melanie's extended hand.

Melanie walked over and snapped off the television. She moved a small armchair from the desk to the foot of the bed and sat down facing Rosario. Dan pulled up another chair nearby.

"It's Mrs. Sangrador, right, ma'am?" Melanie kept her tone deferential, sympathetic.

"Yeah, that's me." Rosario deliberately looked away toward the window, though the blinds were drawn and there was nothing to see. Melanie shifted the chair to place herself directly in the housekeeper's line of sight.

"Look, Mrs. Sangrador, I can see how scared you are. Believe me, I understand what you're feeling."

Rosario made eye contact, her face full of fury, the fury of someone who's been attacked. "How you understand? These men, they gonna kill me! He tell me if I talk to you, he come back and hack me in little pieces."

"Who told you that?"

"The man who kill Mr. Jed!" Rosario dropped her head to her hands, shoulders heaving. "You not care about me! I testify and they kill me!" she choked out between sobs.

Melanie got up and fetched her a tissue and a glass of water. Rosario took them, sipping the water, dabbing at her eyes carefully to avoid the stitches that snaked down her cheek. After a few moments, she quieted and looked up.

"I have a plan to keep you safe," Melanie said gently. "We can get you away from here, far away, where this man can't reach you."

"You pay my ticket? Because I don't got too much money."

"Yes. Not only will we transport you, but we'll pay your living expenses until the trial."

Rosario looked at her suspiciously. "What I got to do to get that?"

Melanie met her eyes. "I'm not gonna lie to you, Mrs. Sangrador. You have to testify. Now in the grand jury. And later at trial."

"No. No way." Rosario shook her head emphatically.

"Look, it's a free country. If you tell us to leave you alone, we will. But then we can't pay for the hotel and twenty-four-hour guard. That kind of protection is only for people who testify. If that's your decision, my case might be weaker, but at night I go home in one piece. For you it's a death sentence."

Rosario gasped, eyes wide with shock, but Melanie was only telling her the truth. She'd be doing her a disservice if she didn't. They stared at each other, Rosario's mind obviously racing behind her glasses. In the silence Dan's pager went off with a piercing wail. He jumped up and excused himself, stepping out into the corridor to return the beep.

When he came back a few minutes later, Rosario drew a breath and said, "Okay. I testify. But you promise me, missus, you promise me, right? You promise me I be safe?"

"Yes!" Melanie leaned forward and clasped Rosario's two hands in her own. "You'll be guarded at all times. You'll be completely safe. You have my word."

MELANIE CALLED THE grand jury clerk's office from the hotel and booked the next available time slot, spelling Rosario's name carefully for the clerk. Rosario would testify the following afternoon at three. In the meantime she needed to be prepped.

"Okay, Mrs. Sangrador," Melanie said, pen poised over her yellow legal pad, "tell me what happened. Take me through it, step by step."

"Nine o'clock last night, man come to door. Mrs. Benson away, and Mr. Benson downstairs in office, so I answer."

"Did you get a good look at his face?" Melanie asked.

"Oh, yeah! I never forget him!"

Melanie looked over at Dan, who leaned down and pulled the folder with the mug shots from his battered canvas briefcase. Before he could open the folder, she stopped his hand with a touch.

"Single photos aren't allowed," she said. "Did you put it in an array?"

"This ain't amateur hour, sweetheart," he said, meeting her eyes. Too aware of his warm skin under her fingers, she pulled her hand away. He removed a sheet of paper from the folder and handed it to her. It was a color Xerox containing six numbered photographs, all of teenage boys with short dark hair, no facial hair, and thin features. The mug shot of Slice was in position number four.

"Not suggestive in the least," she said, nodding. "I approve. Proceed."

"Okay. Rosario," Dan intoned, reading from the boilerplate printed on the back of the array, "you're about to view an array of six photographs that may or may not contain a photo of the individual in question. Hairstyles, facial hair, and skin tones may vary with time and photo quality.

Examine each photograph carefully, and tell me if you recognize anybody. Take as much time as you need."

Melanie held her breath as Dan handed the array to Rosario. The mug
shot of Slice was so outdated. If Rosario didn't recognize him, it wouldn't
mean he was the wrong guy, but it could torpedo their case.

Rosario snatched the array from Dan's hands, glanced at it, and jabbed
her finger at photo number four. "That him! Except he much older now."

Melanie breathed out. "Okay. What happened when you answered the
door?"

"I talk to him through video monitor. He say he deliver flowers for
Mrs. Benson. I say, why so late? Then I see he have jacket with name of
flower company, so I buzz door. Let him in. So stupid!" Tears welled in
Rosario's eyes again and slowly spilled over, reminding Melanie powerfully of the past. *Abuelita crying when she left for the airport. Melanie crying. No,
Abuelita said,* mi hija, *don't you feel bad. This not your fault. Your* mami, *she
send me away.*

"Oh, Mrs. Sangrador, this wasn't your fault!" Melanie exclaimed.
"Don't blame yourself! Anyone else would have done the same thing!"
Don't blame yourself, she told Rosario, though of course she blamed
herself for all her own problems. "What next?" she asked aloud.

"He push door in and grab me. I feel gun on my cheek, I scream. Then,
boom, he hit me with gun. That how I get this." She pointed to the
stitched gash.

"Did he say anything to you when he came in?" Melanie asked.

"He say, 'You make problem, I kill you.' Then he kick my feet, and I
fall down. He tie my hands with twist tie, like from garbage bag. Very
sharp. Hurt me. Then he walk back to the door and open it. His friends
come. They all wear black ski mask, I can't see faces. Oh, my God! And
they have big dog!"

Rosario began breathing heavily, wringing her hands. Melanie patted
her reassuringly and looked deep into her eyes, trying to convey
strength. "It's okay. Keep going."

"Four or five guys maybe, and big black dog. Dog jump for me. His teeth, snap snap like this." With her hand, Rosario mimed jaws biting. "They laughing. Say he smell my blood already."

"Were they armed?" Melanie asked.

"Oh, yes. Guns. Big guns, all of them. Same like that one." She pointed to the Glock protruding from Dan's waistband.

"Sure?" Dan asked, removing it and displaying it for her.

"Yes."

"Nine-millimeter semiautomatic," Melanie said, making a note on her legal pad. "Matches the shell casing recovered from Benson's office. Did you notice, Mrs. Sangrador, were they wearing gloves?"

"Oh, yes, and it very hot night, so I know. They not want leave fingerprints, right?"

"Right. What next?" Melanie asked.

"Next they pull me up so leader ask me questions. Where Mr. Benson, he want to know."

"Did they ask for Benson by name?"

"Oh, yes. Seem like they know him. Sometime they say Jed, sometime Mighty Whitey."

"They called him . . . what? Mighty Whitey, you said?" Melanie asked, making a note.

"Yes. And they know house. The leader ask me, 'Is Jed down in office?' he say. But I so scared I can't talk. I pee my pants. He very mad, push me down again. Kick me, call me names." Tears leaked from Rosario's eyes, and Melanie squeezed her shoulder.

"You're doing great," Melanie said. "Keep going."

"Okay. Then I hear Amanda. She screaming. They talk about they gonna rape her. I lay on floor. Pants wet, very cold. I get so scared I go away in my mind. Think about my church. Pray to Jesus. I not remember for a while."

Melanie remained silent for a moment, letting Rosario collect herself, then asked gently, "What's the next thing you remember?"

"I realize it quiet. They all gone except big one."

"Tell me about the big one. What did he look like?"

"Very tall, very fat. Name Bigga. But he wear mask. I never see his face."

"Did you hear anyone else's name?"

"Yes. The first one who come to the door, they call Slice. Later I see why!" She heaved a sob, her shoulders trembling visibly.

"Why?" Melanie asked.

"The way he cut Amanda!" Rosario was shaking all over.

"That happened in the office? Down in the basement?" Melanie asked.

"I not see. When I get there, her fingers gone already!"

"How did you get down to the basement?"

"Slice call Bigga on walkie-talkie. Say get some Clorox because he want do trick like he do with Colombian that time."

"What trick?"

Rosario shook her head violently, covering her eyes with her hand as if she could stop herself from seeing.

"Okay, let's take it one step at a time. Bigga asked you to get Clorox?"

"Yes. He pull me up. I show him Clorox in laundry room. Then we going back downstairs, but new man come."

"Another man came? You mean another perpetra— another bad guy?" Melanie asked.

"Yes. We hear tapping sound. He banging on door with gun. Bigga open door and tell him, 'Why you late? Slice very mad. Watch your back.' Like that."

"Did the new guy say anything?"

"He say, 'Fuck that little prick. I tell him I handle the problem—now look what he's doing.'"

"Was he wearing a mask? Did you ever see his face?" Melanie asked.

"He putting it on while he walking in the door. So I see he have brown hair. Nice brown hair. Like him." Rosario pointed at Dan's thick, wavy, dark locks. "So he take us downstairs. He know the way. He push office door with his foot, I remember. He not wearing gloves like the others."

Melanie scribbled a note. "That's great, Rosario. Details like that really help us. What did you see when you got inside the office?"

Tears spilled over and began rolling down Rosario's cheeks again.

"Inside, I see Mr. Jed, tied up in chair. Oh, my God, covered with blood! Blood everywhere! Smell like market back home when they kill the chickens. Dog have blood on his mouth, too, so I know he bite Mr. Jed."

"Now, tell me: What did they do with the Clorox?"

The tears were coming faster now. "Mr. Jed, his eyes closed. So Slice slap him, like one-two-three. Wake him up, you know? He tell him, you watch this, then you talk. He take needle from his pocket. Big needle, like from the doctor. He fill it with Clorox, then he grab Amanda's arm and poke it in. He put his thumb on the needle like he gonna push. Then he say, 'Hey, Jed, you know what Clorox do in the veins? You talk, or I push.'"

"'You talk or I push?' What does that mean, Mrs. Sangrador? Why did Slice say that? Were they asking Jed Benson for information?"

"I don't know. I not hear that part." Rosario looked down at her hands, folded in her lap, and took a deep breath. "He poke the needle in. Then I see Amanda's arm. Her fingers." She spoke under her breath, almost talking to herself. "Oh, my God. Amanda's fingers gone! And so much blood."

"Then what?"

"Room spinning. I see spots."

"Did you see who shot Mr. Benson?"

"Maybe I pass out. At least I feel dizzy, I close my eyes. So I don't see, but I hear it. I hear shot."

"You heard a gunshot?"

"Yes. Yes, I'm sure."

"Did anybody say anything? Before or after the gunshot?"

"I remember they arguing. Arguing a lot. Then boom."

"What happened next?"

"I running down hall, out basement door. Smoke everywhere."

"Did you see anyone else? Amanda? Slice? Anybody? Did you see how they got out or where they went?"

"No, nothing. Next time I remember, nice policeman is helping me. That's all. That everything I remember."

Rosario looked at Melanie and sighed, shuddering. Melanie leaned forward and hugged her. She felt the brace around Rosario's midsection, under her clothes. The housekeeper winced.

"Ooh, sorry," Melanie said, pulling away.

"I got broken rib."

"Oh, my. You poor thing. But you're amazing! You were so brave. I'm proud of you."

"Okay, so tomorrow I tell grand jury. You gonna be there?"

"Of course. I'll be the one asking you the questions. Just like today."

"If you there, don't worry, I do okay. But now I wanna rest. Maybe take more pain pill, watch a little TV."

"Of course. And Agent O'Reilly will get you whatever you want from room service."

"I like fish. They have fish?"

"Rosario," Dan said, "if they don't, I'll go out and catch you one myself."

DAN WALKED MELANIE to the elevator, right across the hall from Rosario's room. She pressed the button. He leaned against the wall, looking down at her. He was taller than she'd realized, wearing jeans and an old polo shirt that emphasized his muscular arms and shoulders.

"You were unbelievable in there," he said. "Not just another pretty face. You really turned Rosario around."

"Never underestimate me, pal," she said. He smelled clean, like soap. What was she doing noticing stuff like that? She took a step backward.

"Rosario gives us good information. But this doesn't come across like a retaliatory hit to me. It doesn't add up," Dan said.

"I agree. It could be the perps knew Jed Benson. They had a beef, or they wanted something from him. Maybe Benson represented a Blade in private practice and got in the middle of something, totally separate from the Delvis Diaz case. I'll contact his law firm. He was at Reed, Reed and Watson."

"Never heard of them."

"Oh, they're one of the biggest. Very fancy. We should interview Benson's wife, too. She wasn't there when this happened, but she might know something. If it was a paid hit, maybe there's some obvious motive we're just not seeing yet."

"That reminds me," Dan said. "The wife is at Mount Sinai with the daughter. That was Randall who beeped me before. The daughter regained consciousness. We should go interview her right away."

"Fine. I'll go, but you can't leave *her*." Melanie gestured toward the door to Rosario's room.

"I know. Randall's trying to get a guy from the PD twenty-four hours. With the terror threat and all, the Bureau won't detail somebody just to baby-sit a homicide witness."

"It's critical to have her door covered at all times. She's in danger. Besides, I promised her."

"Yeah, I noticed you in there making lots of promises with my resources, missy." Dan's tone was light, even flirtatious. He moved a step closer, looking down at her, and she found his nearness disconcerting. The elevator was taking way too long. She jabbed the call button. Don't just stand there staring at him, say something, anything, she told herself.

"She's the spitting image of my grandmother. Rosario is, I mean," she blurted.

"Oh, so that's why you're so hot to protect her. Reminds you of good old Granny."

"No, I want to protect her because she's our witness. I barely even knew my grandmother."

"She died when you were little?" he asked idly, obviously in no hurry to go back into the hotel room.

"She lived in Puerto Rico. Well, she lived with us for a while here, but my mom sent her back to San Juan in disgrace. Claimed she was stealing the grocery money to play the ponies."

"That's Puerto Ricans for ya. Bunch of track rats," Dan said. "With us Irish it's the booze."

"Hey! Watch it, buster."

"Take it easy, princess, just joking. You can't take me too seriously. But hey, don't worry. I'll take good care of Rosario for you."

The elevator finally came, and she hurried on, but he leaned against the door to stop it from closing.

"So what else?" he asked, his tone conversational, like he planned to stand there all day.

"Nothing else. Let go of the door before you set off the alarm, and I'll see you when you can get to the hospital."

"What, we can't shoot the breeze for a minute? This is a very stressful job, you know. I'm more productive when I take breaks."

She laughed despite herself. It felt good. "Enough. Back to your post, soldier." She knocked his hand away, watching him smile at her until the elevator door slid closed. Wait a minute, was she flirting? Did that count as flirting? She shook her head hard to erase the image of Dan's face, but it stayed on her eyes like she'd been staring into the sun.

In the parking lot, the sky was greenish black, the air thick and sluggish. She wished it would just rain already. But the nagging unease in her stomach wasn't caused by the weather.

Sticking the key in the car door, she stopped and looked up at the ugly hotel looming over her. She counted up five flights and found what had to be Rosario's room. The hotel was virtually empty; Rosario's was the only room lit up on the entire fifth floor. Anybody standing out here would see that and get a pretty good idea of where to find her.

Melanie scanned the parking lot nervously. It seemed empty, but deep pockets of gloom and the shifting wind wouldn't let her get comfortable about that. She smelled smoke and looked around for its source. A cigarette butt lay on the ground a few cars over, still smoldering. Somebody must have passed this way in the last few minutes. But where were they now? She hadn't seen anybody coming into the lobby as she left. Heart pounding, she yanked the car door open, dove in, and smacked the lock down. But then she sat with her hands on the wheel, telling herself to calm down. So somebody dropped a cigarette butt, she thought as she turned the key in the ignition. So what? No reason to think it was Slice.

He probably didn't even smoke. Besides, Dan was guarding Rosario. Melanie trusted Dan completely. She'd better be right about that. Because she couldn't imagine what she'd do, how she'd feel, if somebody got to Rosario. If she failed Rosario. She couldn't even think about it. That couldn't happen.

9
—

Melanie shivered as she hurried down the hospital corridor looking for Amanda Benson's room. The grimy, brightly lit hallway was overly air-conditioned, but that wasn't the reason for her chill. She'd just had a vision of how Amanda Benson would look lying in her hospital bed, maimed, disfigured, horribly burned. Still reeling from seeing Jed Benson's corpse last night, she didn't know if she could handle seeing his daughter.

She knew she'd found the room when she saw the crew-cut cop reading a newspaper in a chair beside the door—the one who'd manned the barricade at the murder scene the night before.

He nodded at her as she approached. "Prosecutor, right? Go ahead."

Motionless, a thin, pale girl was propped up in the hospital bed in the middle of the room, her eyes half closed and vacant. One arm was bandaged past the elbow, the other stuck with an IV. She breathed softly through her open mouth, and Melanie saw the silver glint of a retainer. So young. A kid, just a kid. The room swam.

"¡Corre!" *Papi had managed to say. Run! But instead Melanie took several steps farther into the office. She watched with horror as a fat droplet of blood fell from his chin and splattered on an invoice sitting on the desktop, making a sharp, clicking sound. Why was he bleeding like that?*

"¿Papi, por qué estás sangrando? *Did you cut yourself?" she asked.*

She asked, but she already knew. She knew he was there, she could feel it. A *man, a large man, breathing heavily, crouching behind the door.*

"Who are you?" someone asked sharply, snapping Melanie back to the present.

In the corner beyond Amanda Benson's bed, a blond woman and a tall, silver-haired black man had been engaged in urgent conversation. They'd both looked up when Melanie entered, and it was the blond woman who'd questioned her.

"I'm looking for Detective Randall Walker," Melanie said.

"That's me," the man said. He was neatly dressed in slacks and a dress shirt, his face grim and world-weary.

"Melanie Vargas from the U.S. Attorney's Office."

"Right, okay, heard a lot about you from my partner. Can we step outside for a minute? Excuse me, ma'am."

Randall grabbed Melanie's elbow and propelled her out into the hallway before she could protest.

"Good thing you showed up," he said in a low voice when they were out of earshot of the door. "I need reinforcements. She's giving me an unbelievably hard time."

"Who? Amanda?"

"No, her mother. The widow. Not too happy about my visit."

"Oh. What's the problem? Amanda looks better than I expected. Bandages and an IV, but no burns."

"She didn't get burned."

"I saw. I'm so relieved. I thought she would look much worse. But how did she escape? Benson was incinerated, and they were in the same room."

"We don't know. She was found outside the house, unconscious, and we can't figure out how she got there. You interviewed the housekeeper, right? Does she know?"

"No, she draws a blank from hearing the gunshot to when she's outside."

"Well, if her mother would give me half a chance, I'd ask Amanda how she got out. I'd ask her a lot of other things, too."

"So Amanda can talk? She's not too out of it?"

"I spoke to the doc on my way in. She came to about an hour ago for the first time since they brought her in last night. She was in surgery for hours. Three fingers severed right below the knuckle. Fingers couldn't be saved. I guess the . . . uh . . . the pieces, they were left inside, burned in the fire." He looked away as he said this. It was a tough thing to say.

That animal, hurting an innocent young girl! Once again Melanie vowed she'd get Slice. How would Amanda ever sleep peacefully again, if he remained at large? She'd be looking over her shoulder for the rest of her life. Melanie knew too well what that was like.

"But the doctor said she could be interviewed?" Melanie asked.

"He said we could try and see if she responds, that it can't hurt her. She lost a lot of blood. She was in shock when they brought her in. They put her under and operated to stop the bleeding. She's coming out of it now, but she's sedated and on heavy painkillers. Still, she might be able to give basic information if her mother would let us talk to her. I explained to the mother that the doctor says it's okay, but she won't budge."

"Let me try."

"You might as well. I'm getting nowhere."

They stepped back inside. Randall introduced Melanie to Nell Benson.

"Mrs. Benson," Melanie said with true emotion, reaching for Nell's hands, "I'm so sorry to meet you again under these circumstances. We've met before, at charity events. I met your husband, too. He was a remarkable man. I am *so* sorry for your loss. I can only imagine what you've been through since last night. You must be completely devastated."

"Why, thank you, dear. That's very kind," Nell answered coolly, immediately withdrawing her hands. She gave no sign of recognizing Melanie from their prior encounters. "I'm glad *somebody* around here understands the severity of the situation."

Randall shot Melanie a sardonic glance, as if to say, *See what I've been dealing with?* and Melanie examined Nell Benson more closely. Bosomy and blond, she might have been a homecoming queen in her day, yet there was the unmistakable whiff of ballbreaker about her. Her demure black suit did nothing to camouflage the steel in her dark blue eyes. And beneath its ladylike cadence, her voice resonated with a nicotine huskiness.

"Maybe you and I should step outside, so we don't disturb Amanda, and talk this over," Melanie said to Nell. If this woman put up a fight, Melanie would need to get tough. She wasn't sure if Amanda knew what was going on around her, but she didn't want to risk alienating an eyewitness by strong-arming her mother.

"I don't need to talk it over. I don't want her interrogated while she's under the influence of sedatives."

"Just so you understand, Mrs. Benson, we have no intention of *interrogating* Amanda," Melanie said. "This poor girl is not a suspect. She's the victim of a terrible crime. And the animal who committed it, who murdered your husband, is still at large. We have reason to believe he'll go after the witnesses to his crime, including Amanda. We're doing everything in our power to catch him before that happens. We only want to talk to her so we can protect her better."

Nell maneuvered so that she was standing between Melanie and the bed. "Don't try to go around me," she said. "She's underage. I'm her mother. I'll decide what's in her best interests. How can I let her be questioned when she's in this condition?"

"Please, Mrs. Benson, at least let us try! Amanda may have information that could lead us to your husband's killers."

"No! I said no, I mean no! I won't allow it!"

"Mrs. Benson, either your daughter speaks with us voluntarily or I subpoena her to testify before the grand jury. Believe me, that won't be an easy experience for her. After what she's been through, I'd hate to do it, but I will if you force me to. That's how much I believe it's necessary to protect her."

Nell Benson studied Melanie's face. Melanie stared back, standing her ground, letting Nell see she meant business.

"Maybe we *should* talk privately outside," Nell conceded.

"Certainly."

When Melanie and Randall both moved toward the door, Nell said, "I meant just you, Miss Vargas."

"Detective Walker is part of this investigation, too."

"No problem," Randall said mildly. "I'll take a load off, rest my feet for a few minutes." He folded his tall frame into an orange plastic chair in the corner of the room.

"Don't you talk to her while I'm gone!" Nell tossed over her shoulder as they left.

MELANIE LED NELL Benson to a spartan waiting area she'd noticed on her way in. Eight orange plastic chairs stood along a wall facing a noisy elevator bank, next to two enormous snack and soda machines. The chairs were empty. Melanie motioned Nell to sit down.

"Can I get you a soda, Mrs. Benson?"

"That would be great. I haven't had anything to eat or drink all day."

"Come to think of it, neither have I." Melanie looked at her watch. She would've guessed it was still morning, but it was past four o'clock already. She didn't have much change, but luckily the machines took dollar bills. She got two Diet Cokes and two Drake's Coffee Cakes.

"Sorry, this is the best I could do," she said.

"No need to apologize," Nell said. "I love these things. Gives me an excuse to eat them."

Nell ripped open the cellophane with her teeth and broke a piece off one of the coffee cakes. Melanie sat down and watched her devour it, brushing away the crumbs that fell on her expensive suit. Chanel. She recognized it by the intertwined Cs on the buttons. Those things cost a mint. Qué lástima, because Melanie would have liked to own one herself. Eating at such a time seemed bizarre to her. She'd barely known Jed Benson, her daughter wasn't lying maimed in a hospital bed, yet she didn't feel hungry in the least. Then again, she should give the poor widow a break. It didn't necessarily mean anything. People reacted to grief in different ways.

"Mrs. Benson, I understand your reluctance to let us speak to your daughter. I'm a mother, too. Your first instinct is to protect your child. But there's a lot more to fear from this killer's remaining at large than from our talking to Amanda."

"Are you going to eat that?"

"No. Please." She handed Nell the second coffee cake, then popped open the Diet Coke and sipped at it. The bitterly cold liquid set a vein in her temple to pounding. "As I was saying—"

"I heard you the first time. Look, Miss Vargas, I'm going to be completely frank with you. What I'm about to say is highly personal." Nell glanced around to make sure they were alone, then leaned toward Melanie, lowering her voice. "My daughter is a very fragile girl, Miss Vargas. Please understand. I can't have her interviewed. Before I could let you speak to her, I'd need to consult her psychiatrist."

"What exactly is the problem?"

"Amanda is very troubled. Drugs, bulimia—you name it. I placed her in an inpatient program at Wellmead. You know, up in Connecticut. It's a lovely facility. Girls from some very prominent families go there. It's almost like a summer camp, really. But Jed went and signed her out! He was such an indulgent father. He refused to accept that her problems were serious. I just keep thinking, if only he hadn't done that! She'd still have her *fingers*, for Chrissakes!"

Nell started to cry, sniffling vigorously, intercepting her tears with her fingertips before they could smudge her mascara. Melanie found a tissue in her bag and handed it to Nell. Tears welled up in her own eyes as it hit her what Nell was going through. She knew what it was like when ugly, despicable violence invaded your home, sneaked up on you, changed your life forever. She'd experienced that as a child, and now here was Nell Benson experiencing it as a wife and mother. Her husband murdered, her daughter horribly maimed. God, what could be worse? Melanie had fantasized Steve's violent death more than once lately, but she knew she didn't mean it. If it really happened, how would she face it, how would she go on? And to think of her baby daughter harmed, some part of her precious, pudgy little body cut—she couldn't imagine such grief. She could hardly stand it when Maya had the slightest cold. She reached out and stroked Nell's shoulder, overwhelmed by sympathy. Almost instinctively Nell shrugged off Melanie's hand.

"I'm fine, really," Nell said. She struggled to regain her composure, clearing her throat and sitting up straighter.

Stung, Melanie pulled her hand away. This woman was one tough customer. She obviously did not like to be touched.

"Take your time," Melanie said, in a cooler tone.

"Okay. I'm better." Nell forced a smile.

Melanie was starting to lose patience. Every minute she wasted with Nell was another minute Slice was on the street.

"Thank you for telling me about Amanda, Mrs. Benson. I completely understand your concern, but I still have to talk to her. She's an eyewitness. There's simply no way around it. I promise you, I'll be very gentle."

"Don't you understand? My daughter may become suicidal after what she's seen. Do you want that on your conscience?"

"Why would it be on *my* conscience? I didn't kill your husband. I'm just trying to catch the man who did." The attempt to manipulate her was obvious and upsetting. Melanie had to remind herself that Nell had just lost her husband and might not be thinking rationally.

"At the very least, I insist on having her psychiatrist present."

"How long would that take?"

"I'm really not sure. He's at Wellmead. I'd have to call and inquire."

"It's four-thirty now. I can postpone interviewing Amanda until later tonight to give you time to get the psychiatrist here."

"I can't commit to that. I have no reason to think he's even available tonight."

Melanie sighed and took a sip of her soda, buying a minute to think. Amanda was so groggy anyway that interviewing her right now probably wouldn't be fruitful. Maybe it made sense to wait a few hours for Amanda's psychiatrist to show up in order to win Nell's cooperation. After all, the other alternative was forcing the girl into the grand jury. Even putting aside Melanie's own qualms, it would look strange to the grand jurors to compel Amanda's testimony. They'd wonder what was wrong, why Melanie couldn't get Amanda to talk voluntarily. Come to think of it, she was wondering that herself.

"I could agree to wait until the morning, Mrs. Benson, on the condition that we proceed then whether or not the doctor is present. Oh, by the way, where were you last night when your husband was murdered?" The question just popped out.

"I was in East Hampton, having dinner with some girlfriends. I can give you their names if you'd care to check."

Nell looked Melanie square in the eyes as she uttered this. Her gaze was so cool and casual that Melanie wondered if she'd been waiting for that question. She decided to call Nell's bluff. She took a small notebook from her handbag and withdrew the tiny gold pen tucked into its spine.

"If you wouldn't mind," Melanie said, handing them to Nell. But Nell looked untroubled as she carefully wrote down several names in a girlish script.

"I'm giving you their telephone numbers as well. Feel free to call. They'll be happy to answer any questions about me. These are my Hamptons chums. We've been summering together for years. We have dinner together every Monday night."

"Without your husbands?"

"Of course. The wives and children spend the summers out there. The men are generally in the city during the week, doing whatever it is they do." Nell's condescending glance underlined the social chasm between them.

"Of course," Melanie said. She took back her notebook and looked at the names. She'd call each one of them, but she felt certain the story would check out one way or the other. Her imagination was working overtime. Nell Benson was surely completely innocent in her husband's murder. And if she wasn't . . . well, she'd be smart enough to manufacture an airtight alibi.

Back in the room, under Nell's watchful eye, Melanie told Randall that the interview would have to wait until later. She studied Amanda

Benson's face as Randall folded the newspaper he'd been reading and stood up. The girl was pale as snow, her eyes tightly closed now. She lay so listless that she barely seemed to breathe. How much could she do for them in this condition anyway? Melanie felt desperately sad for her. She could predict how it would go for Amanda—the nightmares, the flashbacks, the debilitating fear following her everywhere for years to come. Guilt-stricken, Melanie chided herself for making such an issue with Nell Benson about interviewing Amanda. Shouldn't she, of all people, have a little more sensitivity?

A FEW MINUTES later, when they were alone in the elevator, Randall said, "I don't get it. Why are we backing off?"

"It would look pretty damn weird to throw the maimed daughter in the grand jury under subpoena, don't you think?" Melanie's tone was defensive. Despite her sympathy, she wasn't convinced she'd made the right choice for the investigation. "I'm giving Nell Benson a chance to cooperate voluntarily. She says Amanda has psychological problems. She wants her psychiatrist there when we interview her. She's got a point, when you consider what Amanda's been through."

"Say we do like she asks. You really think she'll cooperate once the shrink gets here?" Randall asked.

"You don't?" His dubious look answered the question. "You get a weird vibe from her, too, huh?"

"I know stonewalling when I see it," he said.

"You think she could possibly be involved in her husband's murder?"

"Is it possible? Normally I'd say hell yeah. I been on the job a long time. Find a body shot dead in a ditch, the first thing I do is check the spouse's gun. Nine times out of ten, it still reeks of powder. But here we got reliable third-party information that some serious players are involved. Even if the wife would normally be a suspect, I don't see Nell Benson associating with gangsta types, do you?"

"Not hardly," Melanie agreed.

"Then again, she hinks me up big-time."

"Yeah, me, too, but could that be because she comes off as a rich, snotty bitch? I don't want to be influenced by personal animosity."

Randall raised a skeptical eyebrow. He was one to trust his own gut.

"Okay, then," Melanie continued, "maybe Nell's genuinely trying to protect her daughter. I mean, come on. The girl just got her fingers cut off by a psycho killer and watched her father get tortured to death. Put yourself in the place of a parent seeing a child suffer like that."

"Hadn't thought of it that way," Randall said, a catch in his voice. "Maybe you're right."

The elevator reached the lobby. As the doors opened, she read in Randall's face a lot of years of watching a child suffer.

"How old are you, Randall?" she asked as they stepped off the elevator and headed for the exit.

"Me? Forty-seven. But that's cop years. Twice as long as regular-people years, so really I'm ninety-four." He chuckled at himself, then turned serious. "But why do you ask, dear?"

"I don't know. Something in your face just now. You look like you've seen a lot."

He smiled wearily. "That I have. Including plenty of things I'd rather forget."

She wouldn't ask him directly about his son's overdose death. She didn't feel right about that. He might be upset that Dan had told her.

"The job must take its toll," she said instead, as they emerged onto the street. "How long until you retire?"

"Soon, very soon. And then you won't be seeing me around here no more. I'm gonna take my pension and my savings, buy a little shack somewhere with a stream out back. Somewhere warm, good for my wife's health. I'll catch a fish for dinner every night, and she'll cook it up just right."

"Sounds nice. Too quiet for me, but nice."

"Aw, you should give quiet a try. Good for the soul. Anybody looking in *your* eyes can see you need it as much as me."

She didn't respond. She couldn't, so taken aback was she that he saw through her like that.

"Need a lift?" she asked after a silence. "I have an appointment at Benson's law firm in twenty minutes, but I could drop you somewhere on the way."

"No thanks. I'm parked around the corner."

"Okay. Catch up with you later, then."

"Yup. You take care, child."

Melanie got into her car, turned on the engine, and pulled out into the stream of traffic. Because their conversation had taken a personal turn, Randall hadn't questioned her further about her decision to back off on interviewing Amanda Benson. But, thinking about how little information she'd gotten from this visit, she questioned herself.

1 0

Prestigious New York City law firms, rather than bustling with commerce, tend to be hushed and reverent places. The attorneys who work in them neither remove their suit jackets nor raise their voices. And they prefer to think of their profession as sublime and intellectual, rather than the hard-nosed business it really is.

Melanie recalled this attitude the moment she stepped off the elevator into the tasteful thirty-second-floor reception area of Reed, Reed and Watson. She'd spent two years after her judicial clerkship toiling in the silent law library of just such a firm, researching the fine points of re-insurance law and the Uniform Commercial Code. Occasionally the partners she worked for took her to lunch at some elegant old establishment. They all shared an uncanny ability to make restrained, polite conversation while revealing nothing whatsoever about themselves or their opinions. She never knew whether they liked her or merely tolerated her, or whether she had the slightest chance of making partner if she stayed for the requisite eight or ten years. The arctic chill of the place sent her fleeing the second she landed a prosecutor job.

As she approached the prim receptionist seated behind an imposing cherrywood desk, she understood that Reed, Reed and Watson was exactly like her old law firm. Which meant that it was better defended against outsiders than an underground bunker. She could be certain of getting the runaround. Politely, of course.

"Yes? Have you an appointment, miss?" the receptionist asked in a plummy English accent. She was of indeterminate age, wearing a high-necked silk blouse fastened with a cameo and half-rim glasses she peered over disdainfully. Once upon a time, Melanie might have felt intimidated. But now she had the power of the federal government behind her.

She flashed her credentials. "Melanie Vargas, U.S. Attorney's Office. I have an appointment with Dolan Reed regarding the murder of Jed Benson."

The receptionist sniffed pointedly, apparently finding the use of the word "murder" to be distasteful.

"Very well, then, I'll announce you. Please have a seat."

She gestured toward a nearby grouping of sofas and armchairs, impeccably upholstered in quiet shades of beige. A large oil portrait of a man dressed in the style of a century earlier dominated the sitting area. Melanie walked over and studied it. According to the tiny brass plate affixed to the gilded frame, it depicted one George Dolan Reed, founder of the firm. Presumably an ancestor of the man she'd come to see, with the steely eyes and Roman nose of a robber baron. Melanie stood gazing at the painting with her back to the receptionist, trying to overhear what the woman was saying into her wireless headset. The plush carpeting absorbed most of the sound. Melanie made out her own name and Jed Benson's, but little else. A young woman in a pink suit strolling through the reception area stared at Melanie searchingly, then moved on.

"Ms. Vargas?" asked someone close behind her.

Melanie whirled around. The woman who'd spoken was perhaps in her fifties, with a handsome face and matronly figure, wearing a tweed suit and low-heeled pumps.

"Yes?"

"Mary Hale," the woman said in a composed voice, extending her hand. Melanie shook it and winced. The woman's hands were meaty and callused, with one helluva firm grip.

"I'm a bit confused, Ms. Hale. My appointment is with Dolan Reed."

"Mr. Reed is our managing partner. As you can imagine, he's extremely busy. He asked me to handle this matter, since I'm on the assignment committee. I assure you, I'm quite familiar with Jed Benson's cases."

She started off down the adjoining hallway, leaving Melanie no choice but to follow. Just as Melanie had anticipated, the runaround. Naturally Dolan Reed would decline to meet with her. Hierarchy was everything in these places. The most senior partners were worshipped like oracles and guarded like the crown jewels. If she wanted results here, she'd need to play hardball and start issuing subpoenas.

Mary Hale opened the door to a windowless conference room furnished with a long, gleaming table surrounded by red leather armchairs. At the near end of the table, precisely aligned with the edge, lay a thin manila folder. Mary nodded toward it.

"Please have a seat, Ms. Vargas. I ordered a computer run of Jed Benson's current matters for your review. The results are in that folder."

Melanie raised her eyebrows skeptically as she pulled out the heavy armchair and sat down. Judging from the thickness of the folder, what it contained wasn't worth the trip to midtown. She opened it and saw she was right. A single sheet of paper bore the titles of three cases. According to the headings at the top of the page, the computer had spit out client-identification numbers and the hours billed for each case as well, but those columns were blacked out with thick marker. The page was virtually useless.

Melanie looked up at Mary Hale, who regarded her with cold gray eyes.

"Ms. Hale, there's been some misunderstanding. I told Mr. Reed's assistant when I made the appointment that we need to conduct a thorough search of all Mr. Benson's files."

"There *has* been a misunderstanding, then. If I'd known that, I would have told you not to waste your time. There's nothing here, Ms. Vargas. Mr. Benson's work for the Reed firm had nothing to do with his death."

"That's a judgment my office has to make after a full investigation. This printout is not sufficient. I need to know the substance of the matters Jed Benson was working on."

"I'm sorry, but that's out of the question."

"Oh? Why is that?"

"Privilege."

"Privilege?"

"Yes. Reed, Reed and Watson takes the position that our files are privileged in their entirety."

Melanie stood up. She was the same height as Mary Hale and looked her square in the eye.

"Take any position you like, Ms. Hale, but the law is the law. We both know attorney-client privilege is only for direct communications with your clients, and work-product privilege doesn't apply in a criminal investigation. That should leave boxes and boxes of documents available for my review. So where are they?"

Two bright spots of color burned in Mary Hale's cheeks. She hesitated, choosing her words with care. "Mr. Benson had not been . . . productive in recent times," Mary said finally. "There's not much in his files, I'm afraid."

"I find that difficult to believe. Reed is one of the top firms in the city. It's known for being polite but ruthless in weeding out dead weight. If Jed Benson wasn't producing, he never would have lasted here."

"Ms. Vargas, I'm telling you we have nothing responsive to your request. Are you questioning my word?"

"Ms. Hale, this is a murder investigation. I can't rely on your *word*. I'll wait here while you get the boxes, or else you can bring them to the grand jury when I subpoena you. Whichever you prefer."

Mary Hale gave a shocked little grunt. Rather than backing off, Melanie took a small step toward her, increasing the pressure.

"As I said, this is our firm's policy," Mary said huffily. "I can't make an exception without consulting my partners. If you insist, I'd be prepared to take this matter up at the next partners' meeting, a week from Thursday. If my partners agree, we'd produce the documents in a conference room here. You could make copies. No need for a subpoena."

"I expected that would happen today. Jed Benson's killer is still at large. I can't wait until next Thursday."

"I'm afraid you'll have to. We couldn't possibly convene a meeting before then, given everybody's schedules."

Melanie realized Mary wasn't giving an inch, at least not today. Why was she even bothering? She was wasting her time. She had subpoena power. She didn't need voluntary compliance.

"Tell Mr. Reed to expect my subpoena. Directed to him personally," she said, taking a guilty pleasure in watching the woman's face fall. "No need to show me out. I remember the way."

She picked up the manila folder, shoved it in her handbag, and headed for the door.

MELANIE STEPPED ONTO the elevator, thinking that little had changed in the few years since she'd left her old law firm. Back then she'd been utterly unable to read these corporate-law types, and she still couldn't. Mary Hale looked like somebody who was deliberately hiding something, but Melanie couldn't be sure. These places bred close-mouthed, uncooperative attorneys. Maybe Mary never produced documents until she was forced to, as a matter of principle. She probably prided herself on it. Whatever her motive, though, the result was the same. Melanie came away with nothing but a useless piece of paper.

She looked at her watch and sighed, annoyed at the time she'd wasted. She'd predicted this outcome, so why hadn't she dispensed with the courtesy visit and sent a subpoena in the first place? Just because Reed, Reed and Watson was such a big name? Next time she'd remember not to be impressed. To top it off, she was on the local. She tapped her foot impatiently as the elevator doors opened on thirty-one and a young woman got on. Melanie recognized the woman by her pink suit as the one who'd checked her out in the reception area earlier. She must be an associate here.

In defiance of elevator etiquette, the young woman faced Melanie and made eye contact, looking her full in the face. She was in her twenties, quite attractive in a wholesome sort of way, with wide green eyes and long, light brown hair. She took a step closer, leaning toward Melanie purposefully.

"You're the prosecutor?" she asked, her voice low and conspiratorial.

"Yes. Why?" Melanie's heart began to pound. She knew this was important.

The elevator stopped on thirty. As the doors glided open, the young woman snapped around to face the front, her face blank and composed, as if she'd never spoken to Melanie.

A middle-aged man in a charcoal pin-striped suit got on.

"Well, hello, Sarah," he said pleasantly. "Still buried in that Securilex transaction?"

When the doors opened on twenty-nine a moment later, they both got off. The woman was obviously not willing to be seen speaking to Melanie. Why not? Sarah. Melanie pulled out the manila folder and made a note of the name, nodding to herself. How many young female attorneys named Sarah worked at Reed, Reed and Watson? Shouldn't be too difficult to track down. Maybe her trip hadn't been a waste of time after all.

11

The streets around her office were clogged with cars and buses by the time Melanie got back downtown. It was rush hour, still threatening rain, and everybody in the world seemed to be heading home except her. She sat in traffic waiting to turn into the lot to return the borrowed G-car, stomach tight with anxiety. Where had the day gone? She'd never even called Elsie to ask her to stay late.

Walking into her building, too frazzled to make conversation, she pretended not to see Shekeya Jenkins heading straight for her. But Shekeya spotted her and called out her name.

"Yo, Melanie! Look, I got 'em done at lunchtime!"

Melanie couldn't help smiling. "Okay, lemme see."

She held out her hand, and Shekeya placed hers on it, fingers splayed. On each fingernail a white dove decal flew over a multicolored rainbow, set against a pearly blue sky decorated with gemstone stars.

"Wow, Shekeya, they're amazing!"

"Girl, that woman is an artist. She take half my paycheck, but it's worth every penny." Shekeya laughed but then turned serious. "Listen, you a decent person, so I'ma do you a solid. Word of advice: Watch out for the boss today."

"More than usual?"

"She got it in for you today, girl, most definitely."

"Why?"

"Beats me, but she just headed to your office with a mad bug up her ass."

"Oh, great. Just what I need. Thanks, *chica*." She squeezed Shekeya's arm.

Melanie worried the whole way up in the elevator, and rightly so. The security guard buzzed the bulletproof door to let her onto the floor. It opened directly across from her office, revealing Bernadette standing with her arms folded across her chest waiting for Melanie. Two of Melanie's colleagues, Joe Williams and Susan Charlton, stood near the fax machine halfway down the hall. As Melanie entered, they glanced at her with a combination of sympathy and embarrassment. Everybody in the office seemed to know before she did that she was in for a tongue-lashing.

"Bernadette, what's up?" Melanie asked, a note of annoyance creeping into her voice. All her boss did was make things harder.

Bernadette jerked her head toward Melanie's door. Melanie walked in. Bernadette followed, closing the door with a slam. The histrionics were part of her standard repertoire, but they alarmed Melanie nonetheless. What could she possibly be in trouble for?

"What the hell did you think you were doing with Amanda Benson?" Bernadette demanded as they turned to face each other on the small strip of floor between the filing cabinets and the desk. The exhausting day after the sleepless night had taken a toll on Melanie. She walked over to her desk and sat down heavily in her chair.

"Well? Answer me." Bernadette said, planting herself firmly in front of Melanie's desk, glaring down at her.

"Randall Walker and I went to interview her. What's the problem?"

"What's the problem? Threatening a victim in her hospital bed is the problem! Please, *tell* me you didn't really say you'd throw that girl in the grand jury."

"Her mother wouldn't let us near her. You would've said the same thing."

"I would not! When the girl is suicidal and the mother as well connected as Nell Benson? Please! You think you're a hero? All you're doing is buying us an expensive lawsuit. Use your brain."

It had started already, exactly the type of pressure Melanie feared when she took on this assignment. She was accustomed to running her own cases without interference, and she liked it that way. Normally Bernadette wouldn't question her interview tactics. She was much too busy to micromanage like that. Come to think of it, normally Bernadette wouldn't even know who she was interviewing.

"Did Nell Benson call you or something?" she asked, curious as to how Bernadette had found out. "I just left the hospital a little while ago, and I thought we'd worked out a deal."

"You thought wrong. She called Lieutenant Ramirez and raised hell."

"I thought Lieutenant Ramirez was off the case. What's he doing butting in?" Just what she needed—Ramirez still trying to run the case, meddling through Bernadette.

"Watch your tone! Romulado is friends with the family, and he's very upset by your behavior. Your so-called interview had all the finesse of a sledgehammer. You need to back off, girlfriend! If you embarrass me, I'll reassign you for poor performance, and that'll follow you around for the rest of your career. Is that what you want? Because you know I don't make idle threats."

Why on earth had she done this to herself, and at a time when her marriage was in a shambles? Melanie wondered. Work was her refuge, her salvation, especially at moments of personal crisis. She needed to keep her career on track, or she would never be able to handle all her other problems. Even if she choked on it, she had to appease Bernadette.

"Look, Bernadette, I understand that Lieutenant Ramirez is concerned for the Bensons' welfare. I'm concerned, too. That maniac Slice is still out there. He has a reputation for killing witnesses. I agreed to wait for Amanda's psychiatrist, but if I wait too long, Amanda could end up dead. I have no intention of having a witness killed on my watch. If you have a better way to handle it, please, tell me."

"I better, or we're all in trouble," Bernadette said. "First off, you need to calm down. The girl has a twenty-four-hour guard posted at her door, so cut the hysterics about witness killing. She's perfectly safe. Second, you need to handle the family better. It's all PR. Make a big show of backing off, giving Amanda a chance to get some strength back, so on and so forth. Like you're doing them a huge favor. Then, in a day or two, try again. If Nell Benson still gives you a problem, *that's* when you threaten the subpoena."

"Whatever you say, Bernadette. As long as we both know that the delay was your decision. A day or two can be a long time in an investigation like this. I don't want to be accountable for the consequences."

Melanie's frankness read like insubordination to Bernadette. She flushed an apoplectic red. "You're obviously missing the point," Bernadette hissed. "These complaints about your performance are very awkward for me. I better not hear any others, or you won't like the consequences. So do like I said."

"Okay." The fight suddenly drained out of Melanie. Some battles couldn't be won, she realized—like any battle with Bernadette.

Satisfied, Bernadette turned on her heel and marched out of the room.

Melanie slumped on her desk, pillowing her head on folded arms. She wanted to cry, but she was afraid if she started, she might never stop. She closed her eyes, breathing rhythmically, trying to calm herself, but a loud rapping on the open door shattered her attempt at a Zen moment. She jerked her head up. Maurice Dawson, the custodian, stood in her doorway supporting a large handcart loaded with boxes.

"Yo, Melanie, I got a big delivery here for y'all. This ain't even half of it. I got, like, twenty boxes."

"What is it?"

"Don't know. Come over from 26 Federal."

FBI headquarters. It had to be the files from the old wiretap Dan and Randall had done on the C-Trout Blades. Just as well. Work was her best refuge, she reminded herself again.

"Okay, thanks, Maurice. Just put 'em down on the floor wherever you can find space."

"If I do that, you won't be able to get out the door."

"It doesn't matter. The way things are going, I'm not getting out of here tonight anyway."

Maurice laughed, but she hadn't been joking.

AFTER MAURICE FINISHED stacking the boxes and left, Melanie checked her watch. It was a quarter to six, almost time for Elsie to go home. Even if Melanie left that minute, she'd still be late. She picked up the telephone and dialed.

"Hanson residence," Elsie answered.

"Hey, Elsie, it's me."

"Now, why you calling me at this hour? Aren't you supposed to be in the subway? I don't like the sound of this."

"I'm really sorry, but I'm running late. I'm caught at work. There's nothing I can do about it. Steve's in L.A. until tomorrow, so I was hoping you could stay a little late."

"Well, I can't tonight. I need more notice than that. Who's gonna give my kids dinner?" Three of Elsie's kids still lived at home. The youngest was twenty-one.

"I feel terrible asking this, but could they possibly order a pizza?" she asked.

"They like *my* cooking."

"Please, Elsie. I'll make it up to you. And I'll pay you overtime."

"I should *think* so. But I still can't stay. I'm not used to this. If Mrs. Hanson ever had a social engagement, she told me at least a week in advance."

"This isn't a social engagement. I have to work. My boss is on my back. It's not my fault."

"What kind of treatment is this, now? Mrs. Hanson never treated me this way."

"Look, Elsie, I'm really sorry. It's not my choice, believe me. I'll call around. Steve's parents are away in Maine, but I'll try my sister and my mom. Maybe one of them is free tonight. We need to talk, though. I'm under a lot of pressure at work, and I'm going to need some extra help from you in the next few weeks."

"Humph," Elsie grunted, not committing to anything.

Melanie hung up, flushed with anxiety. She'd never discussed over-time with Elsie before. It hadn't come up, because Melanie had stu-diously avoided working late since coming back from maternity leave. She rushed home to be with Maya at bedtime. But her banker's hours were about to end. Before Maya had been born, Melanie routinely worked until eight or nine o'clock at night. When she had a trial or a brief due, she'd stay at the office until eleven, even later, sometimes all night. The job demanded it. Bernadette had obviously noticed she was slacking off, and now, with the Benson case, no way would she get away with it. Melanie sighed deeply, knowing that her baby-sitting problems were just beginning.

She longed to give up and go home to Maya. But that wouldn't be do-ing right by her job. Time to call her mother or her sister. She'd been avoiding them the past few days, not wanting to let on about Steve's mov-ing out. They already knew about the cheating, and she couldn't stand any more of their sympathy. It came with a tinge of smugness, of how-the-mighty-have-fallen. Like, she might have a fancy diploma, but she couldn't manage her own life. As if they could. She almost wished she'd never told them, but that awful night she found out, it was either talk to somebody or go *completamente loca*.

She deserved the prize for the worst way to find out your husband was cheating. It was almost a month ago now. Maya had been five months old and really sick for the first time—103.6, vomiting, her little body burning up. Steve was in L.A. on a deal, and Melanie was alone with the baby, worried, on the verge of taking her to the emergency room. She needed to hear Steve tell her it would be okay. She dialed his hotel and asked the operator to put her through to him. It was after midnight in L.A., but the phone rang and rang. He must still be working, she thought. So she tried the conference room in his firm's L.A. office, where he'd been camped out the past few days. A woman answered.

Melanie never found out who she was, but this girl had an agenda. Far from covering for anybody or sparing anyone's feelings, she *wanted* Melanie to know.

"Oh," she said, "you're Steve's wife. Steve and Samantha left *hours* ago. If you can't get them in his room, try hers." Then she carefully spelled Samantha's last name.

Melanie's body went cold and still, but her hands trembled violently as she dialed the hotel switchboard again and asked for Samantha Ellison's room. When *she* answered, Melanie asked for Steve in a quiet, controlled voice. *Esa puta* handed the phone over to him. He said he would call back in a minute from his own room. She sat like a stone, barely existing, until the phone rang a few minutes later.

At least he had the dignity not to lie or make excuses. He told her that it had happened once before, that it was just sex, that Samantha meant nothing to him, and that he would end it right away. He told her that he loved her and Maya more than anything else in the world and that he hated himself for behaving this way. He couldn't explain why he'd done it. Stress, maybe? Things tough at work, the new baby, Melanie busy and cranky and unavailable. Samantha had thrown herself at him; they were far from home. None of it was any excuse. He knew that. He told her he would never forgive himself, but that if she could find it in her heart to forgive him, he would be the best husband to her for the rest of his life. He told her he didn't know how he would go on if she left him.

She couldn't get her mind around it. He came home the next day and threw himself literally at her feet. She just watched, dry-eyed, unable to feel anything, while he cried. He went out and bought her an expensive diamond bracelet. She looked at it with disgust and told him to take it back to Tiffany's. After several days of utter misery, she realized she needed some time alone. She told him to go stay at his parents' for a while. He took some suits over there. Then he got sent back to L.A. That was nearly three weeks ago. Since then he'd been back in New York for just one weekend. She let him stay in the apartment so he could see Maya, but she made him sleep on the couch. She barely spoke to him. After he returned to L.A., she mostly screened his calls. She had at least five saved voice mails and, the last time she checked, seventeen unopened e-mails from him that she was thinking about deleting. She knew she couldn't go on shutting him out. They had a child and a mortgage together. She had to make a real decision. But she couldn't imagine the future. All she could do was grieve for what they'd lost. She couldn't stand the sight of him, and yet all she wanted was to be with him, like nothing had ever happened.

She could sit here and wallow forever, but she had things to do. She considered calling her mother, then rejected it out of hand. Her mother wanted her to work things out with Steve. She couldn't listen to that right now. Her mother was a little too clear-eyed for Melanie's taste sometimes. *Grow up, Melanie, men are like that. Who should know better than me? Just be grateful he's trying to make it up with you instead of walking out. If I were you, I'd take that bracelet and anything else I could get my hands on, and make him account for his every move from now on.* No, she couldn't listen to that poisonous cynicism. Besides, her mother was too busy for baby-sitting. She was smack in the middle of her second youth, with a cute condo in Forest Hills and a good job as a bookkeeper for a flourishing dermatology practice. She'd gone blond after a lifetime as a brunette. She had at least two boyfriends that Melanie knew of, and she was addicted to swing-dance classes. No, Melanie would call only in a dire emergency.

Reluctantly, she dialed her sister's cell phone.

"*¡Dígame!*" Linda was out of breath. Car horns blared in the background.

"Lin, it's me. I need a favor."

"*Sí, claro, los Manolos.*"

"Manolos? No, no, it's Melanie."

"Oh, Mel. I can barely hear you. I thought you were Teresa. She's going to a benefit tonight, and she wants my brand-new gold stilettos with the crystals. Can you believe it? I paid five hundred Washingtons for those suckers. What's up?"

"Listen, I have a problem. I'm in trouble at work, Steve's still in L.A., and my baby-sitter is about to quit if I make her stay late."

"Let me guess. You want me to baby-sit Maya?"

"Yes. Would you?"

"Gee, sweetie, I don't think that's such a great idea. I'd probably drop her or something. Besides, I'm going clubbing later with a guy who can get me a meeting with the programming people at Telemundo. You know, about developing my show."

Linda was a fashion and entertainment reporter for a local cable news channel. She was damn good at it, too. She walked the walk, lived the same lifestyle her subjects did, made the connections. Speaking of which, Linda never went out until the small hours, and Melanie knew it.

"What time are you meeting him?" Melanie asked.

"*A medianoche,* downtown."

"Midnight? I'll be home before then."

"But I need to get my hair blown out."

"Use my hot curlers."

"Hmm. I do like those things. They give me good volume. But did you try Mom?"

"She's so on my case these days, I couldn't stand the thought."

"I hear you on that, *chica.*"

"Besides, it can take her an hour to get in on the train. Please, Lin, just say yes—I'll owe you so big."

"You're not gonna make a habit of this, are you? Because you know I'm low on maternal instinct."

"This is the first time I ever asked!"

"You take my next two turns going with Mom to Costco and it's a deal."

"You never take her anyway."

"Is that a no?"

"Okay, okay, fine! Get over to my house, though. Elsie's waiting."

"Never saw a woman so afraid of her own help. You should fire her ass."

"Be nice to her, please! *Te amo,* sis."

"Yeah, you better." Linda laughed and hung up.

MELANIE ORDERED A turkey sandwich and two cups of coffee from the diner across the street, then knelt down and started reading the labels on the boxes. She had only a vague idea of what she was looking for—something, anything, that could lead her to an address on Slice or Bigga. She'd done a few wiretaps in her day and knew how the files should be organized. But this was a big investigation, bigger than any she'd ever worked on, with numerous telephones tapped. Figuring out which telephones might have some connection to Slice without spending weeks reading every document—that seemed beyond the capacity of her already overtaxed brain.

She jumped when her phone rang. It was the guard in the lobby calling to say the delivery guy was on the way up with her food. She buzzed herself out through the bulletproof door and waited by the elevator, stomach rumbling. This would be her first meal since that bowl of Cheerios early this morning. The Benson case was good for her diet anyway. She'd lost twenty-seven pounds since Maya was born, but when she looked in the mirror, all she saw was the ten still to go. And they weren't coming off without her starving herself, which she wasn't good at, or hitting the gym, which she didn't have time for.

The delivery guy got off the elevator and handed her a dripping-wet plastic bag; it must've started to rain. She paid him and went back inside. Several of her colleagues were hanging out near the fax machine, shooting the breeze. Brad Monahan, a tall, square-jawed prosecutor with perfect Ken-doll hair, snapped his arm back and sent a Nerf football sailing right for her head. She deflected it with her free hand; it hit the floor and bounced under a nearby desk.

"You're supposed to catch it, Vargas," he called good-humoredly.

"Her hands are full, you moron," said Susan Charlton, a short, athletic redhead, perched against the fax table, arms crossed over her chest. Susan was a former Olympic swimmer and the only openly gay woman in the office. The same cops who called her "Miss Alternative Lifestyle" behind her back begged her to work their cases because she was so fierce in the courtroom. Melanie, Susan, and Joe Williams—who stood with Brad and Susan—had all started in the office around the same time and gone through basic training together. Brad was junior to the three others, so ambitious and competitive that they teased him mercilessly about it, but he was cheerful and fun to have around.

"You're losing it big-time, Vargas," Brad said. "If you can't catch a god-dam football, how you gonna command a courtroom?"

"Brad's favorite game isn't Nerf football," Joe observed. "It's keeping track of who has the most macho points."

Smiling, Melanie bent down and picked up the football. What the hell, she could take a little break, hang out for a minute, like old times. One thing she'd missed out on since Maya was born was the late-night cama-raderie around the office. Melanie and her colleagues were too busy to chat during the workday. Their only chance to see each other—to seek advice and trade war stories—came after hours, when the courthouse was closed and the phones stopped ringing. By rushing out every day at five-thirty, she cut herself off from them. That was a price she paid for mother-hood, a price none of them could relate to. Melanie was the only woman in her unit with a child. Almost none of the male prosecutors had families either. The job was too intense. It was for young, ambitious, *single* people. People with outside commitments just couldn't handle the pressure. She tried not to think about that, about how the two things in her life that were any good—work and Maya—seemed to conflict with each other.

Melanie made as if to throw the football in Brad's face; he laughed and pretended to cower behind his hands. She walked over and handed it to him.

"From what I hear, *you're* winning the macho contest," Brad said envi-ously. "Kicking butt and taking names. Her suspect's got, like, twenty bodies on him!" he said to the others.

"Really?" Susan asked. "Jed Benson's killer did twenty murders?"

"That's what the informants say," Melanie replied.

"And I thought I was hot shit doing the Vlad the Impaler trial," Brad said. "He only killed four people. Although a machete through the stomach, that should count extra, right?"

"Forget Benson's killer. It's Witchie-Poo who scares me," Joe said. "We saw her ambush you earlier, Melanie."

"Careful," Brad said, glancing around nervously.

"Don't worry, I saw her leave for the day," Susan said.

"So what was that all about? You okay?" Joe asked.

"She's all over me about the Benson case," Melanie said.

"Better you than me," Joe said, his eyes kind behind thick glasses. He really was a decent guy. She was certain it rankled that she had gotten a plum assignment over him, but Joe would never hold it against her. The son of a prominent African-American city councilman, Joe came from a family that expected him to go into politics one day, but he lacked the cutthroat personality for it. He was intellectual, refined, laid back almost to the point of meekness. Joe's most famous moment in the courtroom was when he fainted dead away during a blistering attack from the nasty Judge Warner for being late to court. He and Melanie had often helped each other out—he sharing his expertise on legal precedent, she tutoring him on the nuts and bolts of investigation and trial strategy.

Brad checked his watch. "Any of you fine people care to join me at Burger and Brew? Work out my trial strategy over a pitcher?"

"Sounds good," Susan said. "I'm ready to pack it in for the night, and I'm starving."

"Sorry," Joe said. "I'm due at my folks'."

"Melanie?" Susan asked.

"Nope. Wish I could, but too much work."

"What happened to the Vargas we knew and loved? Never met a margarita she didn't like?" Brad said.

Melanie laughed. "You're confusing me with someone else. I was never that much fun."

"Well, no time like the present to start, right?"

"Hey, doofus, leave her alone," Susan said cheerily, punching Brad on the arm, "Maybe if you quit partying so much yourself, you'd get the big cases. Let's go."

"I'll walk out with you," Joe said.

The bulletproof door slammed shut behind them, leaving the office more silent and gloomy than before.

1 2

The sky outside was black, sheets of water falling sideways in the wind. The rain pounding her window provided the only sound as Melanie hunted through a nearby box for something to read while she ate. She pulled out a random wiretap affidavit and brought it over to her desk, where the soggy plastic bag of diner food gave off a pungent pickle smell. Unwrapping the foil-covered sandwich, she bit into it and chewed the dry, tasteless turkey. Yuck. She hated bland food, but she was trying hard to be good. She thought longingly of the leftover arroz con pollo sitting home in her refrigerator. Lucky thing it wasn't here, or she'd scarf it all in about ten seconds and feel fat for the rest of the night.

She flipped to the last page of the affidavit, searching for a date. Attested to nearly four years earlier by Special Agent Daniel K. O'Reilly of the Federal Bureau of Investigation, it said. Such a pretty name, Daniel. What did the *K* stand for? Something Irish? Kevin? Kieran? Maybe she'd ask him. No, she wouldn't. She had to be careful with Dan, and she knew it. She was at a desperate place in her life, and he was *too* attractive. And sweet. Man, was he sweet. No. Stop thinking about him. The last thing she needed was a new man in her life. She wanted to work things out with Steve, if only for Maya's sake. Whatever else Steve was, he was a good daddy. Yes, think of Maya. Think of Maya, think of work. Stay focused.

Besides, Dan was so hot he probably had a million women. He probably wouldn't even like her back.

The affidavit began with a background section that detailed the gruesome murder case against Delvis Diaz, the C-Trout Blades founder. She read it and finally understood the chronology. Eight years ago, when Jed Benson was still a prosecutor, he'd locked Diaz up for three murders. Three consecutive life terms for torturing, mutilating, and killing three teenage gang members who were caught stealing drugs from him. Diaz had been in jail ever since. Flush with victory, Jed Benson had left the office, gone into private practice, gotten rich, and expected to live happily ever after. Expected never to hear from Delvis Diaz again. End of story, or so everybody thought until last night.

Meanwhile, the C-Trout Blades, that many-tentacled monster, regrouped and came back stronger than ever under new leadership. They ran a massive heroin ring headquartered at the corner of Central and Troutman in the Bushwick section of Brooklyn, complete with guns, drive-by shootings, push-in robberies—all the fireworks of a modern-day drug conglomerate. Dan and Randall had gone after this new generation of C-Trout Blades and made lots of arrests, filling up enough boxes to crowd her tiny office. That case culminated four years ago, with wiretaps, search warrants, and raids that swept up nearly forty gang members. Even if Slice and Bigga weren't gang members eight years ago when Delvis Diaz was locked up, they might well have been a mere four years ago when Dan and Randall had made their arrests. If they were, somehow they managed to escape detection. But her hope was they'd left some trace buried in one of the boxes sitting on her floor tonight.

Melanie gathered up the empty coffee cups and the sandwich wrapper, stuffed them in the plastic bag, and pulled herself to her feet. She walked out into the hallway and threw the bag into the trash by the Xerox machine to get that awful pickle smell out of her office. The hallway was completely silent, the only square of light the one shining from her own door. She returned to her office and dropped down onto the floor, facing the boxes, her back to the open door.

If she learned more about the gang's structure, maybe she could find a shortcut to the right files. She leafed through boxes of background documents until she found a good overview of the gang. The C-Trout Blades' drug operation was huge. Suppliers, mostly Colombians and Dominicans, delivered hundreds of kilos of raw heroin to mills set up by the largely Puerto Rican Blades in empty apartments all over Bushwick. The Blades operated eight or ten mills at a time, changing locations constantly to elude the police. In these apartments, teams of women worked in shifts around the clock under the watchful eye of a manager, cutting the raw heroin with filler and scooping individual dosages into tiny glassine bags sealed with custom-designed stickers.

The Blades sold two well-known brands of heroin. "Poison" was decorated with a scary black-and-white skull sticker, the brand name written in bloodred letters across its forehead. "Uzi" sported a realistic-looking decal of an Uzi, the brand name written in black letters along the silver gun barrel. Junkies had brand preferences like anybody else, and dealers came from as far away as Virginia and Ohio to buy these famous brands for their customers back home.

When a batch was ready, the mill manager summoned trusted junkies to test it. Too weak and it wouldn't sell, too strong and the customers died like flies from ODs. If the batch passed muster, it was sent out to the Blades' spots to be sold. The Blades ran retail spots all over New York City, most famously on Central and Troutman in Bushwick, where street pitchers sold dime bags to hordes of individual junkies. They also ran wholesale spots where out-of-town dealers could buy bundles of a hundred glassines at a time to sell at a markup back home. The Blades' gross revenues from this enormous operation ran upwards of two hundred thousand dollars a day, 365 days a year. Where had all that money gone? Melanie wondered.

Dan and Randall had busted this huge operation wide open. They'd started with a single snitch, somebody they'd arrested one night with drugs and a gun. On the way to Central Booking, they'd told the guy he was looking at mandatory ten to life on the drugs alone, with a consecutive five years for the gun. His options were limited: either flip or rot in jail for the rest of his natural days. He flipped. They got him released on bail and back on the street in no time. The only difference was, now he was working for the feds.

With the snitch providing them key information, they'd applied for and gotten wiretaps on several telephones. The most important telephone was the one located at the most important heroin mill—an apartment on Evergreen Avenue in Bushwick rented in the name of Jasmine Cruz. Jasmine Cruz herself was a low-level figure, probably somebody's girlfriend. Other than lending her name to the apartment and the telephone, she didn't show up much in the documents. But Jasmine Cruz's telephone served as the party line for the whole Blades hierarchy. Upper-level managers used it all day and all night to give orders to the Blades' entire street organization. If Slice and Bigga were members of the C-Trout Blades four years ago, Melanie reckoned, they should have been intercepted talking on that phone.

Driven by that thought, she stood up and began searching through boxes for more on Jasmine Cruz's telephone. She found a box labeled JAS-MINE CRUZ PHONE—SEARCH PHOTOS AND EVIDENCE and yanked the cover off. The first few folders held photographs taken by the search team after they raided the apartment. She leafed through the piles of eight-by-ten glossies. They all showed different views of a large living room, empty except for folding tables placed end to end to form a crude assembly line. The apartment itself looked dingy and run-down, with peeling paint and naked lightbulbs hanging from the ceiling. In the photos, folding chairs sat askew or lay on the floor, telling the story. Their occupants had leaped up and tried to run when the feds kicked the door in. Close-ups showed piles of packing materials for heroin: tiny glassine bags, rolls of stickers, dispensers holding coveted "spoons"—the same long-handled white plastic McDonald's coffee spoons Melanie recognized from her childhood. McDonald's had discontinued their use years ago, but the black market for them remained strong; the spoons measured a perfect single dose and deposited it easily in a glassine. A table in the corner of the room held several digital scales and at least twenty kilo-size "bricks" of raw heroin, still wrapped in tape and waiting to be processed.

She pulled another folder, labeled SEIZED PHOTOS FROM JASMINE CRUZ APARTMENT, from the box. Different from the large, uniform glossies taken by the cops, these were snapshots of all different sizes and qualities, taken by the gang members themselves. Left lying around the apartment, they were seized as evidence during the raid. Melanie's hopes rose at this typical sloppiness. Drug dealers and killers loved to record their exploits. She couldn't count the number of times she'd shown a jury the defendant's own pictures—posed holding his favorite gun or sitting in front of a big pile of cash. Her heart beat faster as she riffled through the contents of the folder, shuffling snapshots like playing cards. This might be something.

Most were pictures of young men she didn't recognize, in baggy clothes, flashing gang hand signals and covered with home-drawn gang tattoos, some brandishing their guns. None of them was Slice, but she hadn't expected to find him. From what she'd heard, he would never be careless enough to let himself be photographed. She leafed through these pictures hurriedly, impatient for something better.

Then, about halfway through, she came across several Polaroids of tortured animals. A cat and a chicken at first, their bodies mangled, torn to shreds. Something about the violence in the pictures seemed significant, although she couldn't have said why.

The rabbit Polaroids were buried at the bottom of the folder, the very last pictures she found. In the first one, she couldn't identify the animal. The copious blood threw her off, bits and pieces of fur awash in crimson muck, unrecognizable. But there was no mistaking the next one. The severed head of a rabbit, one ear ripped away, lying in a bloody pool on the floor of Jasmine Cruz's apartment. The next Polaroid was even clearer—the rabbit's decimated corpse, limbs missing. And in the bottom-right corner of that one, she finally saw it, what she'd stayed late to find. The blood-specked muzzle and large paws of a black dog, toying with the rabbit's severed head. The same dog. It had to be. The same black dog that Rosario Sangrador had seen, that had mauled Jed Benson and ripped his throat open. That dog was in Jasmine Cruz's apartment. Somebody there had taught it how to kill, and had snapped these pictures as souvenirs of the lessons. She turned the stiff Polaroid over. On the back the phrase NO JOKE was scrawled shakily in black marker, the capital letters lopsided, childishly formed. She took it as a message of evil intent, and it sent a chill of fear straight through her.

Or was the chill real? Leaning forward, hair spilling over her shoulders, Melanie felt a small draft kiss the exposed back of her neck. She heard no sound, saw no change in the light. But the stirring of the air told her that somebody stood silently in her open doorway, watching her. She knew this exact feeling. Knew it indelibly. Frozen, paralyzed, something dangerous behind her. Her father did what he could to warn her. "¡Corre, Melanie! ¡Él tiene pístola!" *She tried to run, but the man was too fast. Legs kicked out from under her before she knew it, carpet rushing up to meet her face. The flash, the thunder of the report.* "¡Papi, noooo!"

Here and now, she knew somebody was behind her. Whoever it was, he might have been standing there for a long time, so absorbed had she been in examining the photographs. She knew that the best option was to face him of her own accord. Why proclaim her fear by pretending to ignore him? Slowly and deliberately, she gathered her courage and turned around to see who stood behind her.

1 3

—

"Jesus, Rommie, they should make you wear a bell around your neck!" Melanie exclaimed. "You gave me a heart attack! How long have you been standing there?"

"Sorry, kid. Didn't mean to scare you," Rommie said from the doorway. "I stopped by to see your boss, but she was gone. Figured I'd check in on you."

"Oh?" she asked. Rommie had never shown this much interest in her before. Was he meddling again?

"I hope I'm not bothering you or anything," he added hastily, hearing the wariness in her voice. "It's hard for me, being off the case. Jed was a good friend, and I'm close to the family."

"So why get off, then?"

He walked in and half sat, half leaned against her desk, folding his arms across his broad chest, nodding approvingly as he eyed the open boxes and papers strewn everywhere.

"Hey, looks like you're really earning your stripes here. Good, excellent. Why'd I get off the case? Your boss, *hija.* She says I have a conflict of interest. You know, because me and Jed were close. That's what she *says.* But really she's worried I'll screw up a high-profile case, and it'll be the last nail in the coffin of her hopes to make me a deputy chief. As if *that's* in the cards."

His dark eyes were downcast. Rommie looked like a soap-opera star, almost too handsome for a cop, with capped teeth that stood out blazing white against his coffee-colored skin, perpetually tan from the sunlamp, and a powerful physique that generated rumors of steroids. But he had a tentative way about him, as if he were afraid of being disliked.

"I'm sure she doesn't think that!" But Bernadette had hinted as much.

"She tries to push me, you know, but what's that saying about a silk purse and a sow's ear?"

"Don't get down on yourself, Rommie."

"Whatever. I do my best, but I don't have any delusions of grandeur. Anyway, I'm grateful to Bernadette for looking out for me. She's a tough cookie, your boss, but she's a softy underneath."

The personal confidences were beginning to make Melanie uncomfortable. Too much information, thank you very much. She didn't need to hear what Bernadette was like *underneath*. Their relationship was one of those classic mutual-exploitation things, except gender-reversed. Rommie was hot-looking, in a flashy, obvious sort of way, and Bernadette was powerful. Then again, these days Melanie was hardly in a position to judge.

"So you came by for an update on the investigation?" she asked, changing the subject.

"Yeah, you know. See what's going on, see if I could offer any advice. What's that you've got there?" He held out his hand.

"Animal-torture pictures from this old Blades case." She stood up and handed him the Polaroids she'd been looking at. "Now you understand why I jumped out of my skin when you snuck up on me?"

He leafed through them quickly and handed them back with a shrug. "So?"

"These were found at a heroin mill on Evergreen Avenue when Dan O'Reilly and Randall Walker took down that big Blades case four years ago. I think it's the same dog that attacked Jed Benson."

"We're looking for a person, not a dog."

"Ha-ha, very funny. I understand that, but it's a link, don't you see?"

"Look, Melanie, I agree you should look to the past to solve Jed's murder. But not four years ago, even further. Delvis Diaz, the kingpin, the big boss, *el capitán*. Jed put him away. Delvis wanted revenge, so he reached out and paid for a hit. Simple as that. You don't need to waste your time with this crapola." He dismissed all the wiretap boxes with a wave of his hand.

"I'm exploring all the angles, Rommie. Don't worry, I plan to fully investigate your theory about Diaz."

He looked at her with a hangdog expression. "I know. I'm no rocket scientist. You don't take me seriously."

"I never said that! I told you, I'm planning to look into it."

"You don't believe me. I can see it in your face. But, really, I was there, Melanie. I know. I was in the courtroom when the guilty verdict was read. I saw the look in Delvis Diaz's eyes. Hatred like that doesn't fade. He waited for a clear shot, and he struck."

"Okay, I hear you."

"This is not *cabeza*," he said, tapping his head. "It's *corazón*. I know it in my heart."

"All right already." She laughed.

"Okay, I'm acting foolish. But this is a very hard thing for me, Melanie. I knew Jed from way back, loved the guy like a brother. I wanna see the pricks who killed him fry. I don't want anything to get in the way of that."

"I understand. I wasn't making fun of you, Rommie. I promise, I'm taking your idea *very* seriously."

"Good, because I trust you, kid. You're green, but you're ambitious. I'm betting on you to crack this one."

She flushed with pleasure at his praise. At least *somebody* had confidence in her.

"Tell me exactly what steps you think I should take," she said.

"First off, read up on Diaz. See for yourself what a scumbag he was. Go through the old files. Look for similarities in the MOs of Jed's murder and Diaz's murder of the three kids. I'm confident you'll find them. Then go talk to Diaz himself. He's housed at Otisville. Take Randall Walker with you. He's an old-timer. He was around back then. He'll know how to handle Diaz."

"Like Diaz is just gonna confess to ordering Jed Benson hit?"

"Probably not. I grant you that. But ask Diaz what he thought of Jed. I guarantee, you'll get an earful. Then maybe we can get Jed some justice."

"Those sound like reasonable steps to take. I'll find a way to fit them in. I swear, you seem more broken up over Jed Benson's death than his widow—"

She stopped herself short. What a fuckup! She realized the second she said it. Nell Benson had Rommie's ear, had already complained about her once today. Nell had a pipeline to Rommie, who had a pipeline to Bernadette. Of all the cases she could've gone after, she had to pick one with insane politics.

"I'm sorry," she blurted hastily. "I didn't—"

"No, no, it's okay."

"I didn't mean to imply—"

"Relax. Look, I know Nell gave you a hard time today. That's part of why I'm here."

"It is?"

"Yeah, she sent me to apologize. Nell's a complicated woman, and she's completely blown away by what happened. She might have come on strong. But she meant well, really she did. She wanted me to let you know she felt bad about the way she acted."

"Huh. Okay," Melanie said skeptically.

"Seriously. She has a tough shell sometimes, but that's only because she's had a hard life."

"Nell?"

"I know, she comes across as the lady of the manor, doesn't she? But she had a miserable childhood. Abusive mother, alcoholic father, the whole nine yards. Then she married Jed and thought she found peace, and look what happens."

A proprietary quality in Rommie's voice when he spoke of Nell caught

Melanie's attention. She felt suddenly worried on Bernadette's behalf. Nell would be quite a catch for someone like Rommie. Great looks, all that money. Poor Bernadette. But no, Melanie was imagining things, wasn't she? Projecting her own problems onto everybody else? Her experience with Steve had her thinking everybody cheated. Then again, Rommie had a reputation, and he had a track record. Here he was involved with Bernadette while he was still in the middle of a divorce from his second wife.

"Bernadette told me to back off and give the family some space," she said.

"That would be nice," Rommie said. "I know Nell would appreciate it."

"Okay, so that's what I'll do."

"Amanda was a messed-up kid before all this even happened."

"So Nell said."

"Besides, you got plenty of other leads to follow. Do like I said, check out Delvis Diaz."

"Okay, okay, I'll start tonight. I'll go down to the file room and hunt through the old boxes."

"You do that. And interview Diaz, too. Meanwhile, I'll dig up some informants who can give him to you on a silver platter."

"What do you mean?"

"You know, guys from his organization willing to testify that he maintained contacts on the outside, that sort of thing."

"Gee, okay. Any help you can give, I would really appreciate."

He smiled, reaching out and patting her arm. "You're a good kid, you know? I can tell, you're gonna go places."

"Ha, right. I'm not going anyplace tonight but the file room."

What the hell, Melanie thought as she watched Rommie's departing back. He was really a decent guy. And maybe he was right about the Delvis Diaz revenge angle. She'd follow through on her promise. After she finished with all the boxes littering her floor, she would go to the file room and hunt through twenty or thirty more. The night was still young.

14

The ice-blue neon sign in the storefront window flashed on and off like a blinking eye. ENVIOS, LLAMADAS, BIPERES. Come in and wire your cash, call your connect back home without the feds listening, grab a new beeper for your important deals. On this gritty stretch of Corona Avenue, everybody needed the storefront's services. The place would normally be hopping at nine o'clock, but it was pouring out tonight.

Dan O'Reilly pulled up parallel to the plate-glass window and idled the engine, peering through the rain to check who was working. A stocky guy with a shaved head stood behind the cash register. Pepe, the owner. Good. He trusted Pepe enough to do the meet here. Dan drove north and west several blocks before he found an obscure enough parking space, then sprinted back toward the beeper store, holding the *Daily News* over his head in the downpour. He didn't own an umbrella. That kind of concession to the weather, like protecting himself from anything, seemed weak to him. He was the sort to beat his head bloody against a brick wall, then step back, assess the damage, and beat it harder. Take what life hands you, keep your mouth shut, keep going—that was how a man behaved. You got your reward in heaven.

He ran through the alleyway behind the store and slid, cursing, down the slippery cement steps to the basement. Dank and foul, it was lit by a single naked bulb dangling in the middle of the room. He ignored the scurrying noises in the dim corners and raced through it, head down. Unfortunately, walking in the front door was not an option. Three generations of cop showed in his face, in his height, in the way he moved, like he was carrying a gun even when he wasn't. In this neighborhood, people toted all that up in a single glance. If they spotted him going in the front, Pepe's business would be dead by morning. Pepe would be dead by morning, for that matter.

Dan crept up the stairs to the ground floor, stopping to search through his overloaded key ring in the semidarkness at the top. He hit the right key on the third try, emerged into a large back office that ran the length of the store. The office doubled as a storage room for electronics. Open cartons and gadgets in various states of disrepair crammed every inch of space. A metal desk shoved into a corner groaned under a slag heap of invoices and paperwork. He maneuvered through the debris to the door opposite, which led to the storefront.

Cracking the door open an inch, he spied Pepe sitting on a stool, his back to Dan, behind a glass counter that held cell phones and beepers. The naked lady tattooed on the back of Pepe's neck gyrated over thick rolls of fat as he watched a Spanish-language game show on a small TV and scarfed something from a foil container held under his chin. The food smelled good. Dan was starving, but not much he could do about it right now. Maybe they'd get this over with quick and he could grab something on his way out. He only had a couple of bucks in his pocket after paying for Rosario's room service back at the hotel, but around here you could eat decent for that.

Just because nobody stood at the counter waiting didn't mean the phone booths were empty. He hadn't watched for long enough to be sure. So he opened the door cautiously and pitched his voice in a whisper.

"Yo, Pep."

Pepe whirled, stumbling off the stool and reaching for his waistband as the food clattered to the floor.

"Jesus, man, you fuckin' scared me! I almost pull my piece out and heat you up!"

"Sorry."

"You be *damn* sorry if you dead, man. Fuck! Look at my fucking em-panada!" He pulled some paper towels from a drawer and began mop-ping at the mess on the floor, shaking his head. "Jesus fucking Christ, that's my whole dinner right there!"

"Hey, don't bust my balls. I fuckin' beep you to give you a heads-up, and you don't call me back! What the fuck kind of cooperation is that?"

Pepe knew better than to ignore that edge of violence in Dan's voice. Dan wasn't crazy like some of them, but he'd do what was necessary to maintain command of a situation. Pepe didn't need any trouble.

"Yo, chill out, man, we cool, we cool. I'm a little wired is all. We had a few stickups on the block. You here for the room?"

"Yeah, I need it for a coupla hours maybe."

"Sure, no problem. Who'm I waitin' on?"

"Puerto Rican guy, heavyset. Wears his hair in dreads tied up in a do-rag."

"Got it."

Dan closed the door, walked over, and sat down in the beat-up leather swivel chair behind the metal desk. He hunkered against the hard seat, hoarding his body heat, trying to warm up a little. His jeans and shirt were soaked through. He ran his hands through his wet hair to shake out the excess water. He'd chucked the sodden *News* in a Dumpster on the way in, so he had nothing to read while he waited. But he didn't mind. Obsessive thoughts had pursued him like hounds from hell all day long. He gave in to them now, relieved to surrender.

This woman he'd met, he just sat there and thought about her. What she looked like, her voice, things she'd said. How she smelled. That per-fume she wore smelled like spicy roses. When they were waiting for the elevator before, he caught himself about to lean over and sniff her hair. He laughed aloud in the empty room at the memory. Pathetic, what a fucking idiot he was. The second he met her, he went wow, just from how she looked. Those dark-haired Spanish girls were the most beauti-ful. They scared him, but they knocked him out. Then he read the diplo-mas hanging on her wall and listened to her talk, and he was a goner. Man, she was smart.

This never happened to him. Women chased him, but mostly, since Diane, he felt more comfortable alone. Hit the gym, walk the dog, work like a fucking maniac—that pretty much summed up his routine. Every once in a while, he got drunk and wound up in bed with some girl he met in a pub. He'd get so depressed afterward he couldn't even look her in the face. And if she tracked him down, if she called, he'd freeze her out before it ever went anywhere. He couldn't help it somehow. He was beginning to think he'd be alone forever, even though he imagined himself with a nice wife and a houseful of kids somewhere, Jersey maybe, or Rockland.

Then, out of left field, he meets her. He'd only known her for a day, and already he was thinking up excuses to spend extra time with her. Was she working late tonight? Could he swing by after this, maybe say he was checking if the wiretap boxes showed up okay? He knew it was crazy. She was married with a baby, for Chrissakes. Even if he hadn't been to church since the divorce, he was still a Catholic in his heart. He oughta act like one, try harder to resist. But he just didn't think he could. It wasn't only her looks or her smarts—there was something else to it that he wasn't strong enough to fight. Something in her eyes he recognized when they met, like the loneliness he saw in his own every time he looked in the mirror. That feeling like she needed him, was what had him hooked.

He sat there thinking about Melanie Vargas, not even trying to discipline himself, that's how bad it was already, that's how much it'd taken over. By the time he looked at his watch, he knew this asshole wasn't showing up. He sighed and dug a damp scrap of paper from his pocket, moving some folders out of the way to uncover the phone on the desk. He dialed the pager number written on the paper, then punched in the callback number of the beeper store, followed by his personal code and 911. Much to his surprise, in a few minutes the phone rang. He reached for the receiver.

"Yo, Bigga," he said, "where the fuck you at?"

1 5

—

They gonna see how he get down when he mad, and it ain't pretty. He ain't like the way shit was unfolding. Sitting in a fucking closet in a fucking hotel in Jersey. He trying to be real calm about it, but he starting to get pissed. He feel it building, that humming inside his blood. He take that energy and put it to use. He always feel that way before he do something.

First off, his concentration got interrupted. He hate that more than anything. That weaselly little motherfucker call him before with the location on the maid, all worried she be telling, when he right in the middle of scoping somebody else. As if he already ain't screwed things up enough by arguing last night and bringing police down. That motherfucker got to go. Yeah, sure, he worried the maid be telling, too, but one thing at a time. Everybody be telling on this job—that's why he got to kill them all. No reason to interrupt what you doing. No reason to break your stride. You get nervous, you jump the gun, you make mistakes. He shoulda just stayed where he at, took care of the other one first. That other Chinese bitch, the architect. Ain't never bodied no Chinese bitch before that he could remember. He did that girl *China*, but she Colombian, they just call her that because she got them scrunchy little eyes. No, he definitely ain't bodied no Chinese bitch before, and now it look like he doing two in one night. When it rains it pours. Ha, he make himself laugh.

The rain. That another thing got him real pissed off. Rain make him sad. And it bad for planning, too. All them scary movies fucked up when they show the killing happen on some night with a big storm. Ain't no serious killer like to work in the rain. Slows you down, just like it slow down anybody doing regular shit. How you gonna stand outside and scope when it pouring like that? He sitting for a while in between the Dumpsters out in the parking lot. Good spot, too. The place real deserted, he stick his head up and scope what going on with her window. But then it start to rain so hard he getting wet. Couldn't even light a cigarette. The drops blowing on him. So he find a door in the back unlocked before he was really ready to go inside. Rain force your hand. Not to mention he gonna have to drive back from fucking Jersey in it. He hated to drive in it.

So he go in the stairwell for a while, but that wasn't no good. Too open. Whole fucking place deserted, but they still got some cleaning ladies and shit. He find a closet on the same floor as the mark, and he sitting there for a long time in the dark, waiting. He know her door taken care of, but he still worried about the bitch making noise. If he can't see her window, he can't know if she sleeping. He gonna have to wait real late if he want to get the jump on her. It better that way in a place like this, so nobody hear. He ain't come this far by taking foolish chances.

He don't believe in no wristwatch. Tell time by his head, and he always right. He smart with shit like that—not just time, but like how far one thing be from another, which window you got to go in to get to which apartment. His brain built for this work. So he know he got maybe another hour to wait before she be asleep. The lock been handled, so it wasn't no problem for him, and his eyes be all adjusted to the dark. No guns this time. Too loud. He like his knife best anyway. He lifted up his pants and took it out of the holster on his leg. He like to feel it in his hand. Maybe it catching the light from the crack under the door, because even in the dark closet, it shine real nice.

ROSARIO WAS SURE she'd fallen asleep with the TV on, but she must be wrong. It was off now, as she awoke from a vivid, pill-induced dream, mouth dry, body heavy to the point of paralysis. She had no sense of how long she'd been sleeping. In her dream she was back home. The strong sunlight and the bright colors lingered on her eyes, radiating circles of blue light out into the pitch-dark hotel room.

Her eyes quickly adjusted to the blackness, but her mind was foggy and sluggish from the painkillers. She knew the shape looming over her bed was important, so she struggled to decipher its meaning. It slowly came back to her why she was here in this room. The horrors of the night before, the blood and the fire. Suddenly she understood what the shape was. She opened her mouth to scream at the exact instant his hand shot out, fast as a bullet, to grab her by the hair. She listened as if from far away to the guttural, bubbling sound that emerged, not from her mouth, but from her slit throat.

1 6

———

Melanie couldn't decide which part of her job she loved best—the courtroom or the investigating. She was crazy for the courtroom. Standing up there in front of the jury, all eyes on her, she felt like a movie star. But discovering a smoking gun in a hot investigation—that was a huge thrill, too. *Smoking gun*. What a great phrase. It made her think of finding a murder weapon in the bushes when everybody else had missed it. That's how she felt tonight, like she'd picked up a gun with smoke rising from the barrel, held it in her hand. Only the gun was a cassette tape.

She kept a tape recorder in her bottom drawer. They'd stopped issuing them to prosecutors when wiretaps went digital. Now you could listen to recorded calls on your computer speakers. She'd meant to turn her recorder in to Supply, but who had time for administrative details these days? Lucky she hadn't, or she would've had to wait until morning to hear the tape. The C-Trout Blades wiretap was old style; the calls were all stored on cassette. She was so giddy with discovery she couldn't have stood the delay.

The animal-torture photos led her to it. When she saw the pictures of the black dog training to kill at Jasmine Cruz's apartment, she knew Slice had been there. Not only been there but hung out there, maybe even lived there, treated the place like his own anyway. You don't teach your dog to kill in an environment you don't control. And if he spent a lot of time there, no matter how careful he was, Slice must've talked on that phone. She would read every transcript in every box, if that's what it took to find it.

The task turned out to be easier than it looked, precisely *because* Slice was so careful. The regular players openly used Jasmine Cruz's phone every day. The wiretap monitors quickly learned their voices and labeled the transcripts of their calls with their names. The call she was looking for, she quickly realized, would stand out because it wouldn't bear the name of a regular player. Slice would be called "UM"—unidentified male. It would be a slip up, a one-shot deal, made in an emergency or in anger. Once she figured that out, things moved quickly.

She recognized it the instant she found it. The monitor had marked it as non-pertinent because they weren't discussing drugs. Maybe it wasn't pertinent to their investigation back then, but it was sure as hell pertinent to hers. She read along on the transcript as she listened to the tape, sure in her gut the "UM" was Slice. Who else would have that voice—low and urgent and dangerous?

(Incoming from cell phone)

JULIO ONE-EYE: Yo.

UNIDENTIFIED MALE: Yo, son.

JULIO ONE-EYE: What up?

UM: Put Jasmine on.

JULIO ONE-EYE: She sleeping.

UM: I said put her on! Wake her up, then. Fucking
                                    bitch, sleep all day!

JULIO ONE-EYE: Yo, awright.

(Pause)

JASMINE: Yeah, baby, what up?

UM: You got something you want to tell me, bitch?

JASMINE: No. What you talking about?

UM: If you got something to tell me, you know I better hear it from you first. You know that, or you know what happen, right?

JASMINE: Come on, now, don't talk crazy like that. I don't know what you mean. I ain't do nothing.

UM: Yeah, that the problem, you ain't do nothing. You supposed to do something, but you ain't do nothing. See, you figured it out. You ain't as stupid as you look.

JASMINE: Oh.

UM: *Oh!* Stupid cunt! My dog smarter than you. You don't do your job, and I catch you fuckin' sleeping!

JASMINE: Last night was real busy at the club, baby, so I couldn't do it. But tonight I see him for sure, and I get what you need. Don't you worry.

UM: You think you got the only pussy in town? You ain't handling this right. Mighty Whitey gonna lose interest, and then I ain't got no back door to him. If that happen, you useless to me. Think about what that mean for your survival rate.

JASMINE: Don't worry, baby. He like me real good. I be his criminal girl, you know? Word, I get you the shit tonight.

UM: You better, or you wake up with me standing over your bed. And I ain't be there to fuck you.

JASMINE: Okay, baby.

UM: Do it.

JASMINE: Yeah, baby, I promise, okay?

(End of call)

Calm down, Melanie told herself. She shouldn't assume the "Mighty Whitey" they were talking about was Jed Benson. Just because Rosario Sangrador said Slice had referred to Jed Benson as "Mighty Whitey" at the town house last night didn't mean anything. He probably called all legit people that, anybody who wasn't street. Slice and Jasmine were discussing somebody else. Assuming otherwise was taking a huge leap. She'd made an important discovery just by tying Slice to this location. She should be satisfied with that, not jinx it by asking for the moon.

But what if Mighty Whitey *was* Jed Benson? What if—four years earlier—Jed Benson had had a relationship with a woman who had a relationship with Slice? What if Slice had used Jasmine Cruz to get to Jed Benson, or to get something from him? Then something had gone wrong, and Slice went after Jed? No, it couldn't be. Impossible. It was completely inconsistent with everything she knew about this victim. Unless, *unless*, she didn't know everything there was to know about this victim.

That reminded her. She'd never followed up on that strange incident in the elevator at Jed Benson's law firm. It seemed less significant in contrast to this exciting new discovery, but still, it would take only a second to cover that base. She hopped on the Internet and pulled up the directory for the Reed firm. The firm's Web site posted photographs. Bingo. Within seconds she'd identified the woman in the pink suit. One Sarah Elizabeth van der Vere, a recent graduate of Columbia Law School. Sarah was twenty-six, from Grosse Point, Michigan, and she specialized in securities and ERISA law. Melanie clicked "print," and Sarah's bio emerged from her printer. She exited the Reed Web site and went to a telephone-directory program. Sarah lived within walking distance of the Reed firm, off Second Avenue in the Sixties. Melanie jotted the address and phone number onto the printout of the bio, grabbed the dog photos, the transcript, and the cassette tape, and stuffed everything into her big black leather shoulder bag.

She turned off her light, lingered for a moment in the doorway to bid a fond good night to her darkened office, then headed for the elevator with a light step. With all these leads, she'd wrap up this case in no time.

WHEN SHE CHECKED her watch in the elevator, it was after ten o'clock. Her finger paused in midair, about to press the "Lobby" button. All she wanted was to go home and watch Maya sleep, put her hand on that little tummy, follow it up and down with each breath. But she'd made a promise to Rommie Ramirez. They were putting a lot of faith in her with this case. She sighed and pressed "B" for the basement instead.

Closed files were stored in a secured room in the basement of her building. The basement stayed lit twenty-four/seven, and Melanie was grateful for this as she walked down a deserted mustard yellow corridor and came to a metal door marked DEAD FILE STORAGE. Even brightly lit, the basement was creepy enough to justify a door with the word "Dead" on it. She swiped her card key through the magnetic lock. The door swung open onto a vast, windowless file room, dimly lit by emergency lights. She would have to hunt for the main switch.

As she stood on the threshold, the room seemed oppressively silent. She imagined getting locked in. Nobody knew she was here. She could be entombed for days until somebody else came looking for a file. The thought thoroughly spooked her. Holding the metal door ajar with her hip, she rifled through her bag anxiously and pulled out her cell phone. No reception. If she did get locked in, she couldn't even call for help.

She propped her shoulder bag in the doorway to keep the door from slamming shut. There, problem solved. She stepped into the room, located the main switch and flipped on the lights, illuminating the enormous space. The ceiling was low, the room lined from end to end with rows of metal shelves tightly jammed with boxes, creating an enclosed, cryptlike effect. She walked to the central aisle, her heels ringing on the hard concrete floor and echoing back at her like the sharp reports of a pistol. The room stayed cool because it was in the basement, but the ventilation was terrible. The stagnant air, redolent of ancient cardboard and mold, tickled her throat. Melanie walked deeper into the maze of shelves, scanning the dates labeled on each row until she found the Delvis Diaz files—far from the metal door where she'd left her handbag, almost at the opposite wall of the building.

The Diaz files consisted of at least thirty boxes, packed tightly on a lower shelf, running the full expanse of a row. She hauled down the first few and began opening them to see which looked important. A box of evidence about the three teenage gang members who were murdered seemed worthy of more careful study, so she opened it and started going through folders. One file held photocopies of news clippings about the trial. The stories referred to the victims as the "Flatlands Boys" because their dismembered bodies were discovered inside an old refrigerator that had been dumped in the Flatlands, a Brooklyn landfill.

Melanie studied the grainy photographs of the boys, wholesome and smiling in their school pictures. They were so young—two were fourteen and the third fifteen—but still, according to the news reports, they were old enough to guard a heroin stash for the Blades. Several kilos of heroin had gone missing from that stash, and Delvis Diaz was convicted of murdering the boys in retaliation. The boys had been shot execution style at the stash house, dismembered with a hacksaw in the basement, and then transported to the Flatlands in heavy-duty plastic trash bags.

Next Melanie plucked a folder containing autopsy reports from the box. She held it in her lap, opened it, and gasped aloud. Body parts stared her in the face, in a photo stapled to the top of the pile. The victim's name was Melvin Atuna. He was fourteen when he died, and she was looking at an eight-by-ten glossy of his dismembered limbs. Two arms, two legs, displayed like wares on the green plastic trash bag they'd been discovered in. The limbs looked so real, so normal, except they weren't attached to anything, and they had several odd-looking wounds. The arms thick and chunky, the legs bulbous. She looked back to the article with the school photos. Yes, Melvin had been a tubby kid. The arms were laid out on the plastic bag to showcase their numerous crude tattoos, belying the broad, childlike face grinning in the other picture. The right biceps bore a clumsily drawn black gun, the words THUG LIFE written beneath it. The left displayed another, more significant home-drawn tattoo—a greenish blue dagger being struck by a red lightning bolt as two green droplets flew from the blade. So young, but not so innocent. According to the news articles, the tattoo meant Melvin was a member of the C-Trout Blades, the two droplets signifying that he'd already, at his tender age, killed two people on their behalf.

She could feel several more photographs stapled beneath the top one, but she couldn't bear to look at them. Not here in this creepy basement room, her heart still fluttering with the shock of seeing the first. So she flipped ahead and began reading Melvin's autopsy report. Halfway through she found something that made her gasp again. The report revealed that his dismembered body had been covered with dog bites, just like Jed Benson's body. She forced herself to go back to the photograph. Jesus, yes. Those wounds on his limbs. They were exactly like the ones she'd seen on Benson's corpse. How did she miss that? The tooth marks were unmistakable.

Rommie had predicted she would find similarities between the MO of Jed Benson's murder and the murder of the three boys. He was right. But what did the similarities mean? When Slice and his crew killed Jed Benson, had Delvis Diaz ordered them to copy the methods of his own murder of the Flatlands boys years earlier? Why would he do that? What purpose could it serve other than pointing the finger right at him? Did the black dog that Slice used to attack Benson actually belong to Delvis Diaz? Could it be the same dog that had attacked Melvin Atuna nearly eight years before Jed Benson's murder? She didn't think so. The paws in the Polaroid from Jasmine Cruz's apartment, presumably taken about four years after Atuna was killed, looked like those of a puppy, a successor, an imitator of the earlier killer mascot. But she'd study that carefully when she finished here. She was glad she'd thought to put the animal-torture Polaroids in her bag. She should just take these autopsy reports and head home right now, finish reading them in the comfort of her own living room. A deserted basement late at night was no place to study the handiwork of a psychotic killer.

As she began gathering up the autopsy reports, Melanie froze. What was that? She was certain the sound of shuffling paper had masked an unnatural noise back near the metal door. She held her breath for a moment, listening for the noise again.

The overhead lights went off, leaving the room lit only by the dim emergency lights. Chest heaving with fright, Melanie prayed it was a fluke. *Por favor,* let it be so. The powerful overhead lights must be on a timer to save energy. She got to her feet, her knees trembling, to go switch them back on. But even as she stood up, the emergency lights went out, too, plunging the windowless room into complete blackness. She stood utterly still, straining her ears to hear, close to panic. She was certain you could only turn off the emergency lights by flipping a circuit breaker and shutting down power to this room. It could mean just one thing: Somebody was in here. To get her.

A loud slam echoed through the room in the pitch dark—the metal door crashing shut. Was somebody locking her in here . . . or coming in after her? Either possibility struck her senseless with fear. She began to feel her way carefully along the row, her breath coming in shallow gasps. He would surely hear her breathing in the darkness and zero in on her location. Her glance flew around haphazardly and came to rest on an exit sign glowing red at the end of the aisle. She headed for it, stumbling over one of the boxes sitting on the floor, crying out in surprise. Now she was certain she heard footsteps heading toward her. Panting, she ran for the exit sign, praying she wouldn't crash into anything.

It was an emergency exit. She didn't hesitate. She hurled her full weight against the handle, setting off an alarm as she stumbled out into a brightly lit stairwell, one flight down from street level. She took the slippery steps two at a time, breathing raggedly, terrified of tripping in her high heels and getting cornered by whoever stalked her. The stairs were confusing. As the staircase curled around on itself, she wasn't sure whether the metal door she came upon would take her outside or lead her nowhere, trap her. She heard something behind her. No time to decide. She crashed against the door, tumbling out into pouring rain. She was in the deserted loading dock behind her building, convinced the footsteps were gaining on her.

1 7

―――

Gasping for breath and rapidly getting soaked, Melanie dashed around the side of the building to the cavernous, echoing plaza beside the towering courthouse. The plaza was deserted of people except for a lone homeless man wearing a plastic bag, but cars whizzed by on the slick avenue. She rushed toward the street, bent on hailing a taxi and getting the hell out of here. But the sight of passing traffic calmed her enough that her curiosity kicked in. She managed to slow down and look over her shoulder. She wasn't being followed. She heaved an enormous sigh. But then she remembered her bag, left propping open the metal door. She couldn't pay for a taxi home.

She stood in the rain and agonized about whether to go back for it. She couldn't just leave it there. Not only did it contain evidence she'd spent all night searching for, but it had her wallet and keys. If the person who'd chased her took those, he could gain access to her apartment, where Maya was sleeping. But she couldn't go back either. Whoever had chased her might still be down there. No way was she risking running into him again. Who the hell was he? How could he possibly have gotten in? The building was so well secured these days. Federal marshals during the day and private security guards, all retired cops, at night. A guard was stationed at the main entrance. Several others executed regular patrols throughout the building. Yet somehow he'd managed to get in.

As she stood there dumbly, uncertain of what to do next, somebody behind her called her name. She turned. Dan O'Reilly was striding toward her, coming from the direction of her building.

"THANK GOD YOU'RE here!" Melanie cried out when she saw Dan.

"Why? What's the matter?" he said, rushing up to her. "Are you okay?" She told him about being in the basement, the lights going out, the intruder chasing her.

"Hey, hey, relax. It's okay. Probably just a custodian or something, thought the lights were left on by mistake and he shut 'em off. But come on, let's go back and get your bag before somebody walks off with it."

"No, Dan, I'm telling you, it wasn't a custodian. Somebody came after me. I'm scared!"

"Don't be scared. Here, look at this." He lifted up his polo shirt to show her the butt of a silver gun protruding from his jeans' waistband. Even in her distress, her eyes took in the smooth muscles of his stomach. She tried not to notice, but it was just there to see.

"Okay," she said.

"I'll be right there with you, and I'm armed. Okay?"

"Okay."

He pulled his shirt down, taking her arm protectively, gently, leading her back toward her building. She relaxed, being with him. She felt safe, although she suspected he was merely humoring her.

"What the heck were you doing down there by yourself anyway?" he asked.

"I was working," she said, making an effort to sound casual. "With you lounging around ordering room service with Rosario, somebody has to solve the case. Oh, hey, speaking of Rosario, who's—"

"A guy from the PD showed up a couple hours ago, so I went to take care of some other stuff. Then I figured I'd swing by here to make sure those wiretap files showed up okay. Did they?"

"Yeah, they did, and, man, were they great. You're not gonna believe what I found."

Before she could describe the evidence to Dan, though, they reached her building. The security guard, a sour ex-cop, refused to let her in without her ID.

"I left it in the basement—"

"I don't care if you left it on the moon," he snapped. "Rules are rules. You show ID or you can't come in."

"Let me explain. I was in the dead-file room, and somebody turned out the lights. Whoever it was started to come after me. I had to go out the emergency exit."

"That was you who opened the emergency door? You know you set off an alarm?"

"I was running from somebody! There's been a security breach. You should investigate!"

"Hey, hon, I been on duty since six o'clock, and I checked everybody going in or out. The only security breach tonight was *you* setting off the alarm. We got two guys down there right now trying to figure out what happened." Shaking his head, he removed a walkie-talkie clipped to his belt and depressed a button.

"Yo, Pete, it's Artie. You read me?" he barked into the handset.

The walkie-talkie crackled loudly. "Yeah, Artie? What's up, over?"

"I got a prosecutor standing right in front of me cops to the whole thing. She heard a noise, thought someone was chasing her," Artie said sarcastically. The guy on the other end howled with laughter, then said he was on his way back up. Melanie started to protest, but Dan cut her off with a sharp tap on her arm.

"I was thinking maybe she heard a custodian," Dan said to the guard. "Anybody down there cleaning tonight?"

The guard shrugged. "Cleaning crew does the offices after hours, but they got no reason to go down to dead files. Maybe it was a pipe banging spooked her or something."

Dan said, "She forgot her pocketbook, so I'm gonna take her back down there to get it, okay? I'll escort her, and I'll let you know if we find the . . . uh, intruder." Dan practically winked at the guard.

"Right, okay, as long as you'll take responsibility for her. Sign in," he told Melanie. "I'll verify your ID on the way out. And please, honey, do me a favor. Stay away from the emergency exits." Smiling smugly to himself, he went back to his newspaper.

They got onto the elevator, and Melanie jabbed the "B" button furiously.

"What a jerk!" she said once the doors closed, quivering with rage. "How could you take his side? You don't believe me?"

"I wasn't taking his side, I was bullshitting him. I hate guys like that. Do their twenty years cooping under a bridge somewhere, ignoring their radios, and once they retire, it's downhill from there. He couldn't find his own ass in the dark with two hands and a flashlight. So I made sure we both got in, to do our own investigation."

They reached the basement, and the elevator doors opened. Melanie hesitated and swallowed hard. But Dan was with her. It would be okay.

"This way," she said, stepping out and leading Dan back down the mustard yellow corridor toward the metal door.

"You came down here without an armed escort? Man, you got nerves of steel."

"Yeah, and you should've seen the autopsy photos I was looking at when the lights went out! Severed limbs and everything!"

She managed a weak laugh. With Dan at her side, the whole experience might have been an amusing caper, or so she tried to tell herself. But when they reached the metal door, her laughter froze on her lips. The door was closed, her black bag missing.

"My bag is gone!"

"Huh. Maybe the guards found it?"

"Wouldn't they have said something?"

Dan looked up and down the hallway. Ten feet away her bag lay on the floor beside some trash bins.

"There it is!" he said.

She ran over and grabbed it. Turning it upside down, she dumped the entire contents onto the floor, and began rifling through to see what was missing.

"Anything taken?" Dan asked, coming to stand over her as she opened her wallet.

"I had about thirty dollars cash," she said. "It's gone, but my credit cards are all here. Oh, look, the compartment with my checkbook is open! I always keep it snapped."

"Any checks missing?"

"No. But the checks have my home address on them. Do you think that's why he opened it? To see where I live?"

"It could have just come open when the guy tossed your wallet. With the money missing, this looks like a simple purse snatch to me."

"Wait a minute!" Melanie exclaimed, suddenly realizing what wasn't on the floor.

"What?" Dan asked.

She picked up the black bag and looked inside. It appeared completely empty. She stuck her hand in down to the bottom, feeling around to be sure. Nothing. The tape and the animal-torture Polaroids had been in there, and now they weren't. They weren't on the floor either. They were plain gone. She looked up at Dan, thunderstruck.

"I found some important evidence tonight in your wiretap boxes. It's gone. I can't believe it! Why would a thief care about that?"

"What evidence?"

"A wiretap tape and some photographs. From an apartment belonging to a Jasmine Cruz. Who is she?"

"She was the subscriber on our busiest phone. A stripper at a club in Times Square if I remember right, probably a top guy's girlfriend. We never intercepted her in a drug call, so we left her out there when we took the case down. Why?"

"I think she was *Slice's* girlfriend."

"What makes you say that?"

She described the pictures in detail, how they showed the black dog being trained to kill and how they led her to the transcript of the call between Slice and Jasmine.

"I remember that call," he said. "Pretty scary stuff, the way he talked.

We were looking to ID that guy when we took the case down. I played that tape for every cooperator in the case, and they all claimed not to recognize the voice. More than once I wondered if they were lying to me."

"I'm sure they were. They were all scared to death to rat on Slice."

"Yeah. Huh." He seemed troubled by something.

"But, Dan, it's missing! The tape and the transcript and those torture photos. Oh, and something else. Information about a young woman who worked at Jed Benson's law firm. I think she might know something. Stealing money I can understand, but why would a thief take evidence? Nobody would want that stuff unless they were involved with the case."

"Jesus, look at this," Dan said, his attention caught by something over her head. She stood up and twirled around, following his glance. A security camera, mounted to the low ceiling, pointed directly at the entrance to the file room. She hadn't noticed it before. Standing on tiptoe and stretching out his arm, Dan was tall enough to reach it. He pulled a piece of shiny gray duct tape off the lens and showed it to her.

"This tape looks new. Somebody taped the lens, probably just now while you were in there."

"Who would do that?" she asked, although she had a pretty good idea.

"Somebody who really didn't want his picture taken," Dan said gravely.

"But not a custodian, right?" A chill shot right down her spine.

"I doubt a custodian would think about taping a lens, even if he's dirty and planned to toss your purse. That's something a pro does when he's planning something big. You could have been hurt."

He looked at her intently, like he was afraid she would disappear before his eyes.

"Do you think it was Slice?" she asked, giving voice to her deepest fear.

"I have no way of knowing that for sure. But maybe."

"Probably, right? Who else could it be? Jasmine Cruz wanting to hear the sound of her own voice?" She giggled nervously, but her whole body was trembling. "How the hell could Slice have gotten in here? He looks like a total thug. Even if the guy at the front desk is asleep at the switch, he'd've noticed someone like Slice. And the rest of the building is sealed up pretty tight. No windows that open, all the external doors alarmed."

"I agree it's strange," Dan said.

"I mean, how would he even know where to look for me? He must've had inside help!"

"From who, a guard?" Dan asked skeptically. "That's a serious charge. A guard probably wouldn't do something like that. Lazy is one thing, but dirty is something else entirely."

"Then how, Dan? You explain it to me."

"I don't know. If we can grab whoever chased you, we'll ask him how he got in, okay? Who knows—maybe it *was* Slice, and maybe he's still around. I need to do a floor-to-floor search."

"I'm coming with you. I'm not staying here by myself," Melanie said.

"Of course not. You shouldn't have been down here alone in the first place. This is a serious case. We should be taking more precautions. You can wait in my car. I don't want you in the line of fire if I find this guy."

Under other circumstances she would have protested, but now she was too shaken up. When she went after the Benson case like a demon, she'd never imagined the killer might train his sights on *her*.

18

Melanie rushed into the kitchen and threw her arms around Maya, who sat in her high chair smiling like the Cheshire cat, green muck dripping down her chin.

"You're still up! Mommy missed you so much!" she cried, hugging her daughter close. Maya surveyed her domain as if not a thing was wrong in the world. But Slice was out there. Dan had done a floor-to-floor search back at the office and come up dead empty.

"Mel, not that that's much of an outfit, but you're about to ruin it," Linda warned. She'd been gingerly administering pureed peas from two feet away in a futile attempt to protect her own clothes. As if on cue, Maya spit a fine green spray.

"*Mi'ja,* I told you, this is Versace!" Linda's bracelets jangled as she deflected the neon green spatter away from her midriff-baring blouse, which showed off the ruby in her navel and the large butterfly tattoo spreading its wings across her lower back. She sported a diamond-encrusted choker bearing the legend BORICUA CHICA. Melanie envied her sister's glam Puerto Rican style. Sometimes she wished she could be more out there herself, but she just wasn't like that.

"I'm happy to see her, but why is she up? It's past eleven! And why are you feeding her this late?" Melanie asked.

"*Muy buenas tardes,* Linda," Linda said. "*Muchas gracias* for baby-sitting, Linda."

Melanie caught a whiff of something and leaned down, sticking her nose under the high-chair tray.

"*And* she's poopy!" she exclaimed indignantly, straightening back up.

"Ingrate! Remind me not to do you any more favors. Look what time it is! I'm gonna be late for my date with Alberto, and this is the thanks I get."

"Wait a minute, Alberto? You mean Chester the Molester?"

"Did I call him that? Oops."

"He's almost sixty!"

"I decided I like older men."

"Since when?"

"Since he promised to help me pitch my show idea. Listen to this: a makeover show! *Me* giving beauty and relationship advice. I'm calling it *Muy Linda*! Get it? It means 'very pretty' in Spanish."

"Yes, thank you, I speak Spanish."

"God, you are *nasty* tonight."

"You're right. I'm sorry, I should be more grateful. I *am* grateful. It's just . . . I'm under so much stress lately."

Linda held out her arms. "*Ven aquí, chica.*"

Melanie walked over and put her head down on Linda's shoulder, burying her face in her sister's perfumed dark hair. Linda patted Melanie's back.

"Poor baby! Hey, who would've thought it would be you leaning on me? Some role reversal, huh?" In the roles they'd played since childhood, Linda was the popular, glamorous, wild sister, and Melanie the smart, sensible, together one.

"Could you *try* to sound a little less pleased about my life being messed up?" Melanie disentangled herself from Linda's embrace.

"It's nice to feel needed, that's all. Hey, you really do look upset. Bad night?"

Melanie filled Linda in on the incident in the file room.

"Oh, my God!" Linda said. "You could have been killed."

"Tell me about it! The FBI agent I'm working with said the same thing."

They were both silent, thinking about that.

"So who's the guy?" Linda asked after a moment.

"The killer?"

"No, the FBI agent. Were you two working late together?"

"Linda!"

"Aha, you're blushing! I'm onto something, right? What an instinct!"

"Can't you be serious for once?"

"I *am* serious. What's more serious than you working late with a hot guy?"

"Who says he's hot?"

"He's not hot?"

Melanie rolled her eyes and walked over to the sink. She grabbed a piece of paper towel, wet it, and began swabbing Maya's face.

"Yuck, how did it get in your hair? You need a bath, *nena*." Melanie lifted Maya from her high chair and carried her to the changing table in her bedroom. Linda followed. Melanie undid the tabs on the diaper and scrutinized its contents.

"Why do you have to *look* at it?" Linda asked, making a face.

"It's good to see their poop. That's how you know they're digesting okay. I wasn't with her all day, so it makes me feel like I know what's going on." She wiped Maya's bottom and shoved everything into the Diaper Genie.

"When it comes to dirty diapers, ignorance is bliss if you ask me," Linda said.

Melanie carried Maya naked to the bathroom, Linda buzzing after her like a hungry bumblebee at a picnic. As Melanie poured Baby Magic under the running water, Linda closed the toilet-seat lid and sat down.

"So what about this guy? I always tell *you* everything."

"I could have been killed, and this is what you're concerned about." Shaking her head, Melanie tested the temperature of the water, then lowered Maya's squirming body carefully into the bath seat. She used a plastic cup to splash water over chubby, glistening limbs, eliciting gurgles of pleasure.

"He must be a loser, or you'd tell me. The real hotties never went for you anyway. You had the looks, but you refused to do yourself up. Like you were above it or something."

Melanie knew Linda was baiting her, but she couldn't help herself. A lifetime of competing with her flamboyant sister won out.

"He happens to be incredible."

"¡Mami! So go for it!"

"¿Eres loca? I'm a mother. I can't just go around having affairs!"

"Why not? Steve did."

That stopped Melanie cold. Each time she was reminded of it, it hurt like new.

"You know I'm right." Linda insisted, nodding her head. "Revenge is in order here. Show Steve he can't walk all over you."

"That's a sick attitude. No wonder none of your relationships last more than two weeks."

"Maybe my relationships don't last because I don't want them to. Marriage sucks. Mom and Papi were at each other's throats. Steve cheated on you right after Maya was born. I mean, how low can you get? Not that I didn't warn you. I saw through that guy from day one. Too smooth for his own good, I said. But you like that. Reminds you of Papi."

"Shut up."

"It's true. Didn't I tell you what a bad sign it was that Steve cheated on other girlfriends? You had this information when you married him, chica."

"Those were girls he dated casually. No vows involved."

"Vows, my ass. Once a sleazebag, always a sleazebag. But no, you were too into him to listen to any sense."

"Linda, this is getting me mad."

"Why are you sticking up for him? I don't get it."

"He's my husband and the father of my child!"

"So? He didn't respect that. Why should you?"

Melanie squeezed out the washcloth, not saying anything, her mouth setting into an angry line. She felt like an idiot leaping to Steve's defense, the way he'd betrayed her. But Linda's cynical attitude didn't sit well either. Maybe she just didn't want to believe that her marriage was over.

"Hey, it's your life," Linda said. "But give me one good reason for staying with this bozo."

"One good reason? Maya! If it was just me, I would've served him with divorce papers by now. But what would that mean for her?" Melanie gently lathered Maya's dark hair.

"So you're not in love with him anymore?" Linda asked.

"I never said that."

"You're not sure, are you? You're not sure whether you still love your husband."

"That's not true. I definitely do." She did. Otherwise it wouldn't hurt this bad. She took a deep breath and fought back tears as she rinsed Maya's hair. "He swept me off my feet, you know? It was like something out of a movie. He had everything. Gorgeous, smart, well traveled, from a prominent family. All these fancy white girls chasing him, and he picks *me,* a nobody from nowhere, a kid from the block."

"Why wouldn't he? You're a fancy white girl in a hot *boricua* body, *mami.* He gets an exotica trip in the bedroom and an Ivy Leaguer with an A-plus résumé to hostess his dinner parties, all in one package."

"That's not fair."

"No?" Linda eyed her skeptically.

"Well, maybe," Melanie conceded. "But it's not like he's the only one at fault. I mean, sometimes I think *I* picked *him* for the wrong reasons."

"Sex and money, *chica.* Ain't nothing wrong with that where I come from."

"Sex, I grant you. But money had nothing to do with it."

"Oh, come off it! The way he wined and dined you. Took you to Paris for that long weekend a month after you met."

"That wasn't about money, Lin. It was about romance. It was about *culture.* I mean, Steve didn't just take me to fancy restaurants. He knew what wine to order and what fork to use. And afterward he'd take me to the opera and translate the German for me. Culture means a lot to me, with where we're from."

"What does it matter when the guy doesn't treat you right? You'd be better off with a blue-collar schmo who really loved you."

"Steve *does* love me! He's trying to make it up to me. Maybe with time I can forgive him."

"Well, if you're telling me your heart still skips a beat when he walks into the room, I guess I can understand that."

"Of course it does." She paused. "Because I'm thinking about killing him."

Linda laughed. "Now, what about this FBI guy? Does *he* make your heart skip a beat?" Melanie thought about that one a second too long. "Wow, I'm starting to think you're falling for him, Mel."

"Will you shut *up* about him already? I already told you, I would never do anything about it. Just because Steve was an asshole, doesn't mean I should sink to his level. Plus, this guy would never mess around with a married woman. He's incredibly sweet and decent. And he has sad eyes, like he's been hurt before." Linda looked at her dubiously. "I'm telling you, he's not interested in me. I mean, you should see him, he is so hot. And I have child-bearing hips." Melanie lifted Maya from the bath and, wrapping her in a hooded towel, carried her back to the changing table in her bedroom. Linda followed.

"You're kidding me, right? Is your mirror broken or something? You're totally gorgeous. You were before Maya, and you're even better now. You're all voluptuous, and you have that glow."

"I have ten extra pounds on me."

"So? Baby got back! Men love that."

"And you said yourself I don't do myself up."

"You could dress a little sexier, is all I meant."

"I can't dress like a hooker when I might get called to court any minute. Besides, my clothes are nice—they're just professional. I always wear lipstick and *tacones,* see?" She pointed to her sexy high-heeled shoes.

"I do see! Mr. FBI hunk is gonna be down on his knees begging for it."

"*¡Dios mío,* the mouth on you, *chica*! Nothing is ever going to happen, okay, so never mention it again."

"Why not? Hey, maybe he could move in here and guard you. Just like in *Someone to Watch Over Me.*"

Melanie threw the wet towel at Linda's head.

BY THE TIME Linda left, Maya was falling asleep in Melanie's arms. Melanie carried her to her room, lowered the crib rail, and gently tucked her in. Little baby, so tiny and vulnerable. She said a silent prayer that Maya would always be safe. Then she went to her room, put on an old cotton nightgown, and stepped into the bathroom to brush her teeth. Her face in the harsh fluorescent light was drawn, dark circles under dark eyes. But the thought of sleeping made her nervous.

She stood in the middle of her bedroom floor and looked at her king-size bed with its many pillows and fluffy comforter, feeling the silence of the apartment all around her. Who, other than her baby daughter, would hear her if she screamed? She hated to admit that she was afraid to go to sleep, but what other explanation could there be, when she was so exhausted and the bed was so inviting? Maybe if she played the TV or slept with the lights on.

Instead she decided to walk around the apartment and double-check all the locks. Always best to take action. Her stomach fluttered with nerves as she made her circuit. She tried to tell herself it was just hunger. Speaking of which—that arroz con pollo would sure make her feel better. She got to the kitchen and turned on all the lights, then headed straight for the refrigerator. Diet be damned. She was sad, tired to the bone, and *scared.* She needed comfort, which unfortunately she only got from starchy Puerto Rican food. Why couldn't she come from a culture where comfort food was steamed broccoli or something?

The plastic container was way in the back, hiding behind the little jars of baby food. She maneuvered it out and stuck it in the microwave. Waiting for her food to heat, she saw the light blinking on the answering machine. Two messages. Of course Linda hadn't bothered to answer her phone.

She hit "play," tensing up as the sound of Steve's voice filled the room.

"Hey, it's me. Listen, I've been trying to reach you all day. I really need to talk to you, Melanie. Please stop screening my calls. Okay? *Please?* I'm about to catch the red-eye, and who knows if I'll be able to reach you from the air. Please pick up. I know you're there, Melanie. It's after ten. Where else would you be?"

Linda was right. Steve took her for granted. She'd been in the file room getting chased at ten o'clock, not sitting home like some submissive wifey, but he would never believe that, not even if she told him. It was time to show him a new side of her. Maybe revenge *was* in order here. Hell, maybe she should just dump the son of a bitch and be done with it.

She jabbed the "delete" button angrily before the message was finished, then instantly regretted it. What if his plane crashed and that was the last she ever heard from him? Now she wanted the message back. He was trying hard to fix things, and she was giving him no hope. She thought about how sweet he'd been when she was pregnant—massaging her feet, carrying the sonogram pictures around in his wallet. But—who knew?—he could have been messing with Samantha already. Asshole. Just because he said it only happened a couple of times. Why should she even believe him? She hoped the plane fucking crashed. She'd get the insurance money and never have to see his lying face again. That's what he deserved. But the thought of him dead brought her up short. Oh, God, she really just didn't know *what* she felt these days, except that she'd better get started figuring it all out.

The microwave beeped. She grabbed a fork and stood there eating the fragrant, steaming rice straight from the container as she listened to the next message. It was from Sophie Cho.

"Melanie, it's Sophie. Listen, I really need to talk to you about something. It's very important. Please call me as soon as you get this message."

Sounded urgent. Melanie put the container down. The clock on the wall read 12:10, but she was tempted to call despite the late hour. Maybe Sophie had some information about the Benson case? Sophie had requested an immediate callback, and she hadn't put a time limit on it.

Melanie dialed Sophie's number and stood listening to the unanswered rings. She counted ten, then hung up and tried again, to be certain she hadn't misdialed. Again nobody answered, not even a machine. Sophie must have turned off the ringer for some reason. Melanie fished through the utility drawer, pulling out her address book, and looked up Sophie's cell-phone number. She dialed it and got voice mail.

"Hey, Soph, it's Melanie. It's Tuesday night . . . well, Wednesday morning really, about a quarter after twelve. Got your message, tried to reach you, but now I guess I'm going to sleep. I'll try you in the morning. But . . . um, if it's really an emergency, you can call anytime. I'm home now, okay? Bye."

It worried her that she couldn't reach Sophie. She threw the rest of the arroz con pollo into the trash, then double-locked the service door off the kitchen. In the foyer she double-bolted the front door and put the chain on. Turning out lights behind her, she went to her room and snuggled beneath the covers, leaning over to snap off her bedside lamp.

The second the lights went out, she knew she wouldn't sleep that night. She lay there, eyes wide open, staring at the ceiling. You never get true dark in a New York City bedroom without blackout shades, which she didn't have. Dim bluish gray light filtered through the drawn blinds, allowing her to see just well enough to set her nerves on edge. Familiar pieces of furniture seemed to loom at her like attackers. Every creak from the old walls echoed in her ears like footsteps.

The sudden shrieking of the phone on her bedside table startled her. Heart racing, hands shaking, she grabbed for the receiver and nearly dropped it.

"He-hello?" she said, breathing rapidly.

Dead silence on the other end.

"Hello? Hello? Who's there?" she asked, a tremor in her voice. She could hear someone breathing, then a click, and the line went dead.

Now she was really scared. She sat up and looked at her digital clock. Jesus, it was almost one o'clock in the morning. Who would call her and hang up at this hour? The caller ID was lit up in the dark room; it read "Private Number." It couldn't have been Steve. Or Sophie. They would never hang up like that. Slice? Light-headed with fear, she sat paralyzed on the edge of her bed for a long time, afraid to breathe, watching the red numbers change on the clock. She couldn't even bring herself to get up and turn on the light. She knew this feeling too well. Years of it. Insomnia, terror. After her father was gone, when she was still living in that same apartment with her mother and sister. Not like Bushwick had gotten any safer. Every night, lying awake in the top bunk listening to Linda breathe, thinking about the office downstairs, the place where it happened. Wondering when that animal would come back.

IT WAS NEARLY one-thirty when Melanie gave in and dialed Dan O'Reilly's pager number from the phone on her bedside table. She couldn't handle the anxiety any longer. He called back immediately.

"You're still awake," she said, relieved. She got under the covers, pressing the receiver to her ear in the darkness. It felt good to lie down.

"Melanie?"

"Yes."

"I almost didn't return the beep. I didn't recognize the number. We need a beeper code, you know." His voice was low and husky. She wondered if he'd been sleeping or if that was just how he always sounded late at night.

"Beeper code? Isn't that for drug dealers?" she asked.

"Nah, it's for anybody who uses pagers a lot. That way you can beep me to any number and I'll know it's you. This is your home phone, right?"

"Yes."

"You're not sleeping? Because your lights are out."

"I'm in bed, but I couldn't sleep. How do you know my lights are out?"

"Really? You're lying in bed right now, while we're talking?"

"Yeah."

"Oh."

"But I couldn't sleep. Listen, I beeped you because I'm scared."

"Where's your husband?"

"Mmm, traveling."

A flirtatious note crept into her voice despite her best intentions. Lying in the dark, overwrought, terrified, she was too weak to fight it. Talking to him made her feel so much better. She curled and uncurled her toes under the blanket.

"He left you all alone?" Dan said. "A very foolish man."

Her heart raced, in an exciting way this time. She should hang up. But what the heck, they were just talking, right? What harm could it do?

"Yeah, well, anyway, I'm by myself. I got scared of Slice coming after me. I figured I'd call so you could tell me I shouldn't worry."

"You shouldn't worry."

"Why shouldn't I worry? I have good reason to, don't I?"

"Because I'm sitting right out here in front of your house, watching the door."

"Seriously?"

"Yeah, seriously. I dropped you off before and never left. Think I'm gonna take a chance on you ending up looking like Jed Benson?"

"You're really in front of my building?"

"Yes, ma'am, and the service entrance is visible from here, too. So nobody can get in without me seeing."

"You've been sitting there all this time? You're crazy!" It moved her deeply, that he would spend his own time watching out for her like that.

"What's the big deal? Sitting up all night in my car is what I do for a living. Besides, after what happened tonight, this is probably the best spot to catch the bad guy."

She laughed breathlessly. "Oh, thanks a lot! You'll give me nightmares."

"I don't wanna give you nightmares. Only sweet dreams. Hey, think you'll dream about me?" His voice as he asked the question was endearingly nervous, as if he feared he'd gone too far. He *had* gone too far, and it surprised her. Could he really be interested in her like that? Wow. But if he was, she really shouldn't lead him on.

"Dream about you? We only met this morning," she said.

"Huh, that's right! We only met this morning. It's funny, I feel like I've known you for a long time. Do you feel that, too?"

"Well, it's been a long day. So in a way, it has been a long time." She yawned, exhaustion catching up to her. "Listen, I should get to sleep."

"Don't hang up. We can just talk until you fall asleep."

"What, and leave my phone off the hook? I can't do that." What if Steve called and couldn't get through? Hah, it would serve him right! But really, how would she explain it? Didn't she have enough problems?

"You really know how to shut a guy down, you know that?" Dan said. But she could hear a smile in his voice.

"Good night, Agent O'Reilly," she said, unable to resist smiling herself.

"Wait, don't go," he said. "What's your favorite number?"

"Um, I don't know. Seven? Why?"

"Lucky seven. I like that, too. So that's our code. If you feel scared, you beep me, put a seven in, and I'll rush up there and rescue you, okay?"

"Okay. So are you really gonna sit there all night?"

"I was planning to."

"Didn't we agree we would go to Otisville first thing, so we'd have time to interview Delvis Diaz before Rosario's grand-jury testimony?"

"Yeah, so? I was gonna pick you up at your office at eight. But I'll just pick you up here instead."

"But then you won't get any sleep. You won't even have a chance to shower."

"You're a very high-maintenance girl. Expect a guy to sit up protecting you all night and still find time to shower and shave and show up looking fresh as a daisy."

She giggled. "I have high standards. We'll have to see if you measure up."

"Okay, then. I guess once it's light, I better head home for some grooming."

"Seriously, you should go home. I'm fine, really. I feel better now that we talked." Now, why did she say that? She didn't want him to leave. She felt so much safer knowing he was out there. But she had to put a stop to this. Every second they talked was drawing them closer, and she felt it.

"I feel better, too," he was saying. "It's good. Talking to you, I mean."

"So you'll go home?"

"I'll hang out till I'm sure it's safe. Then I'll go clean up and pick you up at your office at eight. Me and Randall, okay?"

"Okay." They were both silent for a moment. She didn't want to hang up any more than he did, but she'd make herself do it. "Hey," she said.

"What?"

"Thank you. Really."

"Don't mention it. Sweet dreams."

She hung up, smiling again. But then the smile faded as she wondered what the hell she was getting herself into with him.

19

___

"Hello? Hello? Who's there?" Melanie had said.

Sophie Cho opened her mouth to answer, but no words came. Before she even realized it, her finger moved to the button and clicked off the phone. She couldn't do it. She'd decided she would, but when the moment came, she just couldn't.

She sat on the glossy hardwood floor and looked around her completely empty apartment. Her furniture was gone, taken away by the moving truck that afternoon. The problem seemed too big, so she'd pretty much made up her mind to run away from it. It was the only solution she could think of. Eventually it would come out, what she'd done, but she was a minor enough player in this drama that she had to think the police wouldn't bother pursuing her. So long as she went far enough away and left no forwarding address.

The possibility of anyone other than the police coming after her never entered her mind.

But even as she put her escape plan into action, she wavered. She was not an adventurous person. The thought of leaving behind everything she knew and starting over in some new, foreign place held not the slightest whiff of romance for her. It seemed horrible, in fact, like being sentenced to exile. When she really thought about it, was staying here and facing prison really any worse?

Such thoughts made her consider the possibility of confessing to Melanie. Surely Melanie, who knew her so well, could argue for leniency on her behalf. After all, who could have imagined such severe consequences flowing from one small, unorthodox bit of architecture? Sophie herself had never imagined it, let alone intended it. All she had tried to do was please a client. And yes, admittedly, she had filed false documents at his behest. Which was wrong. And certainly a breach of professional ethics. But anyone who knew Jed Benson would understand. Because he wasn't just any client—he was a particularly persuasive and persistent one.

It was her inability to say no to Jed that had caused this terrible problem. She hugged her knees to her chest and rocked back and forth, berating herself silently in her mind. Why had she agreed? Why, why, why had she been so weak? Was it that he'd turned her head? Such a handsome and powerful man, paying attention to her? This was very unusual in her experience. But no. She was realistic enough about her own modest charms to understand immediately that Jed was merely adding another inducement to the package, along with the monetary compensation and the promise of future referrals. So why, then?

In the end she had to come back to her upbringing. She was raised to place politeness above all other qualities. To say no to a patron, one older than she was and male, would have been unthinkable. So she'd said yes.

And now it was done, and the consequences were what they were. She could bemoan and agonize as much as she liked, but she had a choice to make. Run—or stay and face her punishment. She hid her face in her knees. She would sit here all night, if necessary. But by the time the sun came up, she must make her decision.

2 0

—

In the light of day, the desperation of the night before seemed alien to Melanie. Her fear had vanished, and with it the strange intimacy she'd felt as she lay in her darkened bedroom talking to Dan O'Reilly on the telephone.

Steve had something to do with that. He had woken her up, banging on the front door just as the sun was rising.

"Melanie!" he called. "The chain's on! Let me in!"

She jumped out of bed and hurried to the foyer in nightgown and bare feet. Tiptoeing up to the door, she peered through the peephole. Better make extra sure it was really Steve. After last night she couldn't be too careful.

The face was distorted by the lens, but definitely his. Not that that meant she should open the door. Steve was dangerous in his own way.

"Mel, I can hear you breathing. I know you're there."

She opened the door a crack, leaving the chain on. Steve was one of those rugged, sporty-looking blonds who tanned. Like Robert Redford in his glory days, Steve always looked as if he'd just climbed off the back of a horse or been squinting into the prairie sun. Okay, so he really caught those rays on the tennis court. But, hell, that turned her on, too.

"What are you doing here at this hour?" She made her voice as cold as she could manage. She knew she was vulnerable.

"Didn't you get my message? I took the red-eye. My plane just got in."

"So? Go to your parents'. You don't live here anymore."

His face fell. She noticed suddenly how exhausted he looked, unshaven, pale beneath his tan, his fine blue dress shirt creased from sleeping on the plane. She unfastened the chain and opened the door a little wider.

"Are you okay?"

"Please, Mel?" He sounded hoarse, even choked up. "Can't I come in? Can't I come in for just a minute and see you and Maya? I miss you guys so much!"

Didn't she miss him, too? And long for things to be how they were before?

"Okay," she said, opening the door, telling herself she'd probably regret this.

He rushed in, grabbed her, and held on like his life depended on it, and for the first time in a long while, she didn't push him away. He buried his face in her neck. She reached up to hold his head, to comfort him. His hair was shaggy, flowing over his collar. She used to remind him when he needed a haircut, but she'd stopped doing that after she found out about Samantha. It wasn't like him not to take care of himself. It meant he was suffering. She felt his pain as if it was her own. Wait a minute, it *was* her own! He was the one who hurt *her*! What was she doing comforting *him*?

"Steve—"

"No, please," he said, touching his fingertip to her lips. "Please, don't say anything. Let's pretend for a minute that this never happened. I miss you so much, Mel. I just need to hold you for a minute like normal, okay? Please?"

He looked into her eyes. Then he started to kiss her, slowly and deeply, until they were both breathing hard and his hands were wandering around under her nightgown. Before she knew it, they were doing it standing up against the wall in the entry foyer.

Okay, they always had amazing sex. Especially the make-up sex— *increíble*. Out-of-control crazy. She remembered a time on their honeymoon, on an overnight train in France, after a terrible argument. They'd practically wrecked their sleeper compartment, knocking an open bottle of red wine onto the carpet, breaking the folding bunk. He could always get her with sex. That and his sweet talk. But now, even with her behind bumping against the wall, her legs up around his waist as she cried out with pleasure, she couldn't forget all that was wrong between them. He *was* gorgeous. He *was* incredible in bed. He *did* push her emotional buttons. Trouble was, she couldn't forget he'd shared all that with another woman.

"Steve?" she gasped, her nails digging into the expensive fabric of his shirt. "This . . . is . . . *not* . . . a . . . good . . . idea."

"Ohhh, baby, you are so hot!"

Okay, maybe this was not the moment for serious discussion. She'd use him for sex, talk later. A girl has needs, after all.

When they were finished, he carried her into the bedroom and dumped her onto the bed, then collapsed beside her.

"God, I'm an idiot!" he cried. "What a tragedy."

She sat up on one elbow and studied him. Was it possible he shared her anguish? That he felt the same sadness she did, having sex, with their estrangement weighing them down? Maybe this guy was really ready to work on things.

"Why do you say that?" she asked thoughtfully.

"Because." He leaned over and kissed her lightly on the lips. "You are the hottest thing on this planet. That face, that body. Wild in the sack. What was I thinking, when I had this at home?"

It took a moment for his words to sink in. So if she had a bad hair day or gained a few pounds, he'd be out there looking for someone better?

"Steve, you're not an idiot." She paused. "You're an asshole."

She marched into the bathroom, slammed the door, and locked it.

"Melanie," he called a minute later from the other side of the door, "I'm sorry! It came out wrong, okay? I'm exhausted. I've been up for thirty-six hours straight. All I meant was, I'm crazy about you and I can't believe how I screwed up. Melanie?"

She turned the shower on full blast to drown out his words and stood under the scalding spray. She'd been so happy with him, and he had to go fuck it up just when they should've been closest because of the new baby, just when she needed him most. She knew she wouldn't stay with him if it wasn't the right thing. Where children were involved, she believed in forgiveness. But not if he kept acting the way he just did, like he truly didn't get it. And yet, what would happen if they couldn't put it back together? All her white-dress dreams would be over. She always promised herself that, no matter what, she'd never get divorced. She'd give Maya a better childhood than she'd had.

By the time she came out of the bathroom, Steve had crawled under the covers and fallen dead asleep. She looked at his handsome face and felt her heart break all over again. How many times had she watched him sleep, secure and happy in the knowledge that he belonged to her? Now he felt like a stranger.

She got dressed quickly. If she didn't leave right away, she'd go totally *loca*. Work was the answer. Work was always the answer. She'd go check out that new lead. Steve could stay with Maya until Elsie showed up.

She was heading out of the room when it struck her. Today was the day. She'd declare independence, then figure things out from there. She had to tug hard to get them off. She left the wedding and engagement bands on the bedside table, right where he couldn't miss them.

MELANIE WALKED THROUGH dappled light on a leafy block in the East Sixties, checking the numbers on the beautifully maintained brownstones. She found Sarah van der Vere's building and studied the names written beside the intercom. Sarah lived on the second floor, but Melanie didn't want to announce herself if she could possibly avoid it. Peering through a pane of etched glass set into the wooden door, she saw a mom in shorts and running shoes in the foyer loading her baby into a jogger-stroller. The mom turned and opened the front door. Melanie held it for her so she could maneuver the stroller through.

"Thanks," the mom said, looking at Melanie questioningly.

"I'm a friend of Sarah's," Melanie explained. "Two, right?"

"Yup, parlor level."

Whoever had taken the evidence from her bag last night knew that, too. She hoped they wouldn't decide to pay Sarah a visit, because the security here was nonexistent. With her black pantsuit, heels, and briefcase, Melanie looked plenty respectable, but still . . . The mom had let her in without checking at all. Life without a doorman. The place was beautiful, though, the foyer cool, elaborately wallpapered. In Manhattan real estate, you made trade-offs.

She walked up the stairs and pressed the buzzer outside Sarah's door. No answer. She buzzed again, holding the button down longer.

"Who is it?" a voice answered warily after a couple of minutes.

"Melanie Vargas from the U.S. Attorney's Office, Sarah. We met in the elevator at your firm yesterday. I'm here to talk to you about Jed Benson's murder."

Complete silence. A moment passed, then another.

"Sarah?" she called, more insistently this time.

"You have the wrong apartment. Go away."

"I know I'm in the right place. If you don't open the door, I'll have to come interview you at work."

Melanie held her breath, listening. A moment later she heard the sound of the chain being removed. Sarah van der Vere opened the door and stepped aside, frowning. Still in her bathrobe, wet hair streaming over her shoulders, she looked young, yet firmly in possession of herself.

Melanie walked past her into a large, loftlike space. The internal walls had been removed from what had once been a one-bedroom floor-through. Light streamed in through tall windows at either end of the apartment, reflecting off lovely hardwood floors. In the front part of the space, two love seats were arranged before a charming old mantel. Opposite, a sleek kitchen opened to the room, divided off by a marble breakfast bar and two high stools. At the far end, a queen-size bed stood against one wall, its rumpled sheets telling of a fitful sleep.

Melanie gestured toward the seating area. "Let's talk," she said.

"What do you want?" Sarah asked irritably, not moving from her spot near the door.

"You spoke to me on the elevator yesterday. I know you know something about Jed Benson's murder."

"I have no idea what you're talking about." Sarah's face was bright red, her breathing fast. Was she angry or scared?

"Are you afraid to talk to me, Sarah?" Melanie asked, searching her face.

"Afraid? No! I just don't know why you're here accusing me, that's all. Jed was my supervisor. I don't know anything about his death. Why should I?"

She was clearly lying. And the way she said Jed Benson's name had an interesting ring to it. An intimate ring. Melanie took a shot in the dark.

"Sarah, somebody wanted Jed Benson dead. Given your close personal relationship with him, you could be next. You need to talk to me."

"What do *you* know about me and Jed?" Sarah scoffed.

"We know a lot," Melanie bluffed.

Sarah stood there for a second in silence. Then, slowly, her chin began to quiver, her face crumpled, and she started to sob. There was a stagy, overdone quality to the display, and Melanie made no move to comfort her. Besides, it was too galling, given Melanie's own current circumstances. Sarah might be young, but she was old enough to know it was wrong to sleep with your married boss. And if the big secret was an affair with Jed Benson, it wasn't much of a lead. No reason to think such an affair would have caused Benson's murder.

Sarah got up and bolted for a door off the kitchen, leaving it ajar. Melanie heard the sounds of water being turned on and Sarah sobbing melodramatically.

"Go away! Just go away!" Sarah cried, and slammed the bathroom door.

Melanie sighed and checked her watch. She was due downtown in half an hour to meet Dan and Randall for the trip to Otisville. She needed to wrap this up and get on her way, and she hadn't gotten a single useful piece of information yet. But something told her not to quit. The karma here was weird.

She moved farther into the room, looking around. A side table next to the bed held a telephone-and-answering-machine combo with a caller ID display. Glancing at the bathroom door first, Melanie leaned over and began scrolling back through the caller ID, reviewing Sarah's telephone calls. All the calls in the past day or so had come from the same cellphone number. It had called her twelve times last night alone between 9:58 P.M. and 1:40 A.M. Someone had something pretty urgent to discuss with Sarah van der Vere. Melanie snatched her notebook from her briefcase and copied down the number.

"You okay in there, Sarah?" she called through the closed door.

"I *said* go away!" Sarah yelled between sobbing breaths.

Melanie crossed to a tall dresser standing against the wall opposite the bed and examined the things strewn across its top. A wallet, some jewelry, and a large, old-fashioned clock radio. She quickly went through the wallet. Nothing interesting, just cash and credit cards. The clock radio was odd. Clunky, cumbersome. She looked closer. The knobs were phony. She lifted it up and studied it. Huh.

"Sarah," she called, trying to keep the excitement out of her voice, "when are you planning to come out of there?"

"I'm not coming out until you leave!"

Melanie knew a thing or two about hidden cameras. Generally they broadcast to receivers equipped with video recorders. Judging from the vintage of this one, it probably had limited range, meaning that the receiver must be hidden in this room somewhere. The closet next to the dresser, perhaps? Caught up in the rush of discovery, anxious about getting caught snooping, Melanie didn't have a moment to waste. She hurried to the closet, turned the knob slowly to avoid telltale creaking, and eased the door open. Unbelievable, there it was. A video recorder, in plain view on the floor of Sarah's closet. Melanie knelt down and pushed "eject." A videocassette popped out. She held it in her hand, staring at it, heart pounding. You never could tell about people. The camera in the clock radio pointed directly at Sarah's bed. Maybe it was just her own private porno, but maybe she was blackmailing Jed Benson with tapes of their trysts. Difficult to imagine how that would result in *him* winding up dead as opposed to her, but still, this had to be important.

Sarah turned off the water in the bathroom. Swiftly, Melanie closed the closet and shoved the videotape into her briefcase. She headed for the front door.

"Look, Sarah," she called loudly, "I'll leave now. But I'm warning you, this isn't over." No response.

"Once you know you're needed for questioning, you can be charged with contempt if you leave town."

Nothing. This girl was beginning to annoy her.

"I'll pull the door closed behind me, Sarah. You'll be hearing from me."

2 1

——

By the time she got to her office, Dan and Randall were parked out front waiting for her. Randall unfolded himself from the front passenger seat and flipped it forward.

"Not only can't I fit back there, but it scares me," he said with a wry smile. "And that's after nearly twenty years on the job."

Melanie contemplated the cramped, cluttered backseat, littered with clothing, newspapers, and empty coffee cups. "Wow."

"Yeah. We've had reports of animal sightings," Randall said.

"You're killing me, botha youse," Dan groaned from the driver's seat. He came around to where they stood and gathered up an armload of clothing and garbage, dumping it wholesale into the trunk. He was freshly shaved, wearing neatly pressed khakis and a clean polo shirt. She wondered if he'd ironed the pants himself this morning to please her. He came back around, smiling.

"Okay now? Him I'm not surprised, he's a pussy-ass wimp. But you," Dan said to Melanie, looking right into her eyes, sending a jolt through her body, "I thought you had nerves of steel. Chased by a stone-cold killer in the file room last night, and you performed better than this."

"I'm very squeamish about dirt."

"Why doesn't that surprise me? Didn't I say you were high maintenance?"

Randall looked back and forth between the two of them. "Something going on here I should know about?"

Melanie climbed into the backseat, thinking she'd better put a stop to this thing. People were beginning to notice. It wasn't good for either of them.

"Hey, Randall, you weren't kidding. There's definitely animal hair back here." She brushed yellowish hairs off her black pants.

"My dog, Guinness," Dan said as he got back into the car.

"Sometimes I think O'Reilly likes that mutt better'n he likes people," Randall said. "The Irish are strange that way. Us black folks don't go in for consorting with no animals."

"Randall, you perv, you better not be implying anything about my dog."

"Not your dog, son, it's you I wonder about."

"I know character when I see it. Guinness is a purebred golden retriever. They may not be the smartest dogs, but they're honorable and true. Which is more than you can say for most people. You like dogs?" he asked, catching Melanie's eyes in the rearview mirror.

"Yeah, sure."

"Maybe you'll meet him sometime."

"Maybe." Her tone was unfriendly. He looked away sharply. It killed her to hurt him, but it was for his own good. Ring or no ring, she was still married, hardly a candidate for a new relationship. She wondered how this could have gone so far in one day.

"Uh, can you watch the road, please?" Randall said as Dan pulled out, nearly sideswiping another car. An awkward silence settled over them, lengthening as they headed for the West Side Highway.

"So," Melanie said, intent upon breaking it, "Dan, did you tell Randall what I found last night when I went through your old files? The phone call between Jasmine Cruz and the UM?"

Dan was silent, as if the road required his full attention.

"Yeah, O'Reilly here told me about the whole incident. We were talking about it just now on the way to pick you up, back when he knew how to speak." Randall's glance was half concerned, half teasing.

"Make up your mind. A minute ago I was talking too much and not driving right," Dan said.

"Okay, there he goes. Glad to have you back, son. My personal view, Melanie: I can't believe that was Slice who took the stuff out of your bag. I'm familiar with the security in your building, and I don't think it would've been possible for him to get in. At least not without some inside connection."

"That's what I said. He must've had an inside connection! We should follow up on that, maybe get the sign-in sheet from the security desk."

"No, no. I'm not saying Slice had an inside connection, but that it wasn't Slice in the basement last night. I don't go in for conspiracy theories. Usually the commonsense explanation is the right one."

"Who put the tape on the security camera, then?" she demanded. "Who stole the evidence from my bag?"

"Some low-life building employee doing a bit of thieving on the side."

"He takes a cassette tape, a transcript, animal-torture Polaroids, and thirty bucks? But leaves credit cards and checks? To me the money is a cover. It's the evidence he was after," she said.

"Why would a building employee want your evidence?" Randall asked.

"He wouldn't. That's why I'm saying it was Slice, or somebody close to him."

"Nah, I don't see it. I'm sticking with Ramirez's theory that this was a retaliatory hit, plain and simple. If we want answers, we should do exactly what we're doing right now—go interview Delvis Diaz. Diaz is the only known link between Jed Benson and the Blades, so that's the most promising angle, far as I'm concerned."

Melanie looked at Dan in the rearview mirror. "Is that your position, too?" she demanded, eyes flashing.

"I agree with you the tape is worth following up on. I'm trying to get a lead on Jasmine Cruz's whereabouts. If nothing else, she might know where Slice is. And Benson's phone records should be in today. If there was some kind of relationship between Benson and Jasmine Cruz, it should show up on his phone."

"I guess that's fair," she said grudgingly.

"Okay, so that's that. Anything else?" Dan asked.

"Yes, actually. I took an interesting detour on the way to work this morning."

She told them about the videocassette she'd taken from Sarah van der Vere's apartment.

"Gotta love a prosecutor who doesn't trouble herself about a search warrant," Dan said to Randall.

"Oh, Jesus, you're right!" Melanie exclaimed. "What was I thinking? I was so involved in playing cops and robbers I got completely carried away."

"Been there, done that," Dan said, laughing.

"Never did care for the Fourth Amendment much myself," Randall said.

"What should I do? Should I take it back?" she asked, truly upset at herself. To do something so careless—it wasn't like her.

"And what?" Dan asked. "Knock on her door and say, 'Here's the tape I pinched from your house—we're all done with it'? You'd burn our entire investigation."

"But it won't be admissible in court without a warrant!" she protested. "And any leads we derive from it are fruit of the poisonous tree, inadmissible also. Although only against Sarah van der Vere. And only if she ends up being a defendant."

"There, you see?" Dan said. "Not a problem. Sarah might be a porn star, but I'd bet good money she's not Benson's killer. So I vote we watch the tape."

"Sign me up for that duty!" Randall joked. "My wife don't let me watch blue movies at home."

RANDALL HAD CALLED ahead, so the staff at Otisville was expecting them. A heavyset young woman from the Liaison Office, with a bleached blond buzz cut, met them at the X-ray machine. Her name tag read LEONA BURKETT, but she didn't bother to introduce herself.

"Check your cell phones and your weapons," Leona ordered, snapping her chewing gum. She gave them receipts for what they checked and peel-off name tags to stick on their clothes, then led them through a bewildering series of grimy corridors and elevators, metal doors clanging shut behind them. The ill-fitting polyester pants of her uniform emphasized her wide rear end as she sashayed ahead, the keys on her belt jangling.

"Wait here," she barked, unlocking a gray metal door and motioning them into a small interview room. "Prisoner'll be up soon." She turned the key from the outside when she left, locking them in.

Claustrophobic and windowless except for a tiny pane of bulletproof glass set face high in the door, the room contained little beyond a battered steel desk holding a red telephone and three dilapidated swivel chairs. It was air-conditioned to an arctic chill and lit by a flickering fluorescent light.

"Not enough chairs," Melanie noted.

"That's okay, you sit." With elaborate courtesy, Randall pulled over a chair. "I owe you one for taking the backseat on the ride up."

"Don't count on me being so cooperative going back," she joked.

Randall's snappy rejoinder was cut short by the sound of another key in the lock.

The door opened, and two burly, pasty-faced guards entered, with Delvis Diaz between them. Diaz was shackled hand and foot, but he walked with attitude. Everything from the set of his square jaw to his narrowed eyes to his erect posture said *Fuck you* to anyone who cared to listen. Short, stocky, and powerfully built, he still wore his lank black hair in the style of gangbangers of a decade earlier, long and gathered into a ponytail on top, shaved underneath. Clad in a standard-issue bright orange prison jumpsuit, he sported around his thick neck the milky green plastic rosary beads allowed inmates, designed to snap apart if you tried to garrote your bunkmate.

One of the guards unlocked Diaz's cuffs, placed a hand on his shoulder, and pushed him down into a chair, fastening his right handcuff to the chair's metal arm.

"Looks like it's your lucky day, Delvis," the other guard said wolfishly, looking Melanie up and down.

"Watch your tone, pal," Dan warned.

The guard shrugged, as if to say *What's your problem?* but said nothing.

"Pick up that phone when you're done. It rings through to us," the other guard said. They left, locking the door behind them.

"The vermin that work in these places," Dan muttered, shaking his head.

Diaz looked at his visitors belligerently. "Who the fuck are you?"

In answer, Dan and Randall flashed their badges. Melanie sat down across the narrow desk from Diaz and extracted her credentials from her briefcase, passing them to him. He took them with his free left hand, glanced at them dismissively, and shoved them back at her.

"Say what you got to say, because you interferin' with my exercise period," he said irritably.

"We thought maybe you might want to help yourself out." Melanie said evenly, leaning forward in her chair slightly to make better eye contact.

"Yeah, like what? Giving up those assholes gettin' blow jobs from the inmates in the women's unit?" His gesture toward the door implicated the guards who had just left. "You don't need me for that. Everybody in this place knows."

"We came to talk to you about the murder of the man who prosecuted you, Jed Benson." Melanie looked him in the eye. He stared back, defiant yet calm, sizing her up and tipping back slightly in his chair. "I take it from your expression you're not surprised to hear that Mr. Benson was killed?"

"What goes around comes around." He smiled nastily.

Melanie exchanged glances with Dan and Randall. This guy obviously hated Benson with a passion. Perhaps she should take Rommie Ramirez's retaliation theory more seriously. At least she should treat Diaz as a viable suspect. She reached into her briefcase and took out a form and a pen, sliding both across the desk.

"These are your rights. If you're unable to read, Agent O'Reilly can read them to you. Initial after each paragraph to show you understand, and sign at the bottom."

"I can read. And I know my rights."

Diaz made no move to take the form and instead began rocking his chair back and forth slightly. With his long experience of the legal system, he surely knew that she needed his signature waiving his rights. Without it, any confession he made could be thrown out in court. But Diaz continued to rock his chair as if bored to distraction, saying nothing. Melanie decided to get more aggressive.

"I'm not gonna lie to you, Delvis. You're a suspect in Jed Benson's murder. Some people think you ordered the hit." He laughed derisively. She waited calmly for him to stop laughing, then continued in the same tone. "We're working the case, and I promise you we're gonna find the killer. And I don't mean just the shooter, but everybody who was involved, including the guy who gave the order. We took time from our busy schedules to come up here and listen to your side of the story. You should view it as an opportunity."

"Knock yourself out," he said, laughing again, rocking the chair more exuberantly. "Pin it on me. I don't give a fuck. I'm already doing three lifes."

"Times have changed, Delvis. Back when you were convicted of killing the Flatlands Boys, the federal death penalty was almost never applied. But it is now. It would be pretty easy to convince a jury to impose it on someone who got three lifes and still kept killing."

The chair stopped rocking, its front legs touching down. He sat up straight and looked at Melanie uneasily.

"Now that I've got your attention, what do you have to tell us?"

"I didn't do it."

"Let's start again. I wasn't expecting a full confession up front. Obviously you didn't do it with your own hands, since you've been locked up for over eight years. We understand that. We're looking for the guys on the outside, the ones who pulled the trigger. You could help yourself by giving them up and telling us where to find them."

"I told you, I'm innocent. I don't have no outside accomplices, because I didn't do the crime. Think about it. It's mad late in the game! I hated Benson, sure, and I'm glad he's dead. The prick fuckin' set me up. But if I was gonna hit him, why do it now? I'd of done it years ago!"

Dan and Melanie looked at each other. Diaz had just confirmed an idea they'd kicked around before. Retaliation usually comes when the shock of conviction is still raw. Not years later, when most inmates have re-signed themselves to doing their time. That was the biggest problem with the retaliation theory. Apparently, though, Randall felt differently. He wasn't buying a word Diaz said.

"I suppose you're gonna tell us you didn't kill the Flatlands Boys ei-ther," Randall taunted, cracking his knuckles. Melanie threw him a warning look. Antagonizing Diaz at this point in the interview seemed counterproductive to her.

"Matter of fact, that's right. I knew 'em, they worked for me, but I didn't never body 'em."

"Pffft!" Randall snorted. "Every piece a' garbage killer I ever met says he's innocent. If we listened to you scumbags, we'd empty out all the jails."

Diaz glared at Randall angrily but remained silent. Randall clearly would have kept going, but Melanie held up her hand for silence, not wanting to provoke Diaz further.

"It's natural Detective Walker would be a bit skeptical," she said, "since a jury convicted you of killing the Flatlands Boys. But we're very interested in hearing what you have to say about that trial. Like I said, we're here to listen to your side of the story."

"Maybe I'm 'a bit skeptical,' too," Diaz said. "I been telling y'all about this trial for years, ain't nobody listen. It was a fucking frame-up. If you want to hear that, fine, I'll talk. Otherwise I'm gonna go exercise."

His air of bitterness and resignation seemed authentic to Melanie. Whether or not what he said was actually true, she was starting to think that at least he himself believed it.

"I can't speak for anybody else," she said, glancing pointedly at Randall, hoping he would get the message and keep his mouth shut, "but I assure you I want to hear what you have to say."

Diaz looked Melanie in the eye searchingly, clearly weighing whether she could be trusted. She looked back steadily, patiently, trying to convey by the openness of her gaze that she would give him a fair hearing. Still he said nothing.

"What did you mean when you said it was a frame-up?" she prompted.

"Aw, come on!" Randall exclaimed.

"Randall!"

"Fucking waste of time. I thought we were here to get some work done!"

"He don't want me saying nothing!" Diaz practically spit. "He prob'ly know my conviction is bullshit. It's a fucking conspiracy, is what it is! You know who the main witness was at my trial? You don't even know, do you?"

"Who?" Her intuition told her something big was coming.

"You heard of this kid Junior Diaz? He go by Slice? Likes to sic a dog on people and then cut 'em up? You ever heard of him?"

"Yes." A chill ran down Melanie's spine.

"It was him. You go look at the trial transcripts, you'll see. He killed the Flatlands Boys, not me. He killed 'em, and then he testified that I did it. The real killer is the one who put me away."

THE NEWS THAT Slice had testified at Delvis Diaz's trial shocked Melanie completely. It meant Slice had been Jed Benson's star witness, had cooperated with the prosecution. That flew in the face of everything she knew about Slice. And not only about Slice, but about Jed Benson himself. Relying on the testimony of a vicious killer like Slice was a dangerous enterprise for an ethical prosecutor. And though the thought that Jed Benson could have conspired with Slice to frame Delvis Diaz seemed impossible to Melanie, nevertheless warning bells went off in her head. She didn't know enough about her victim. Jed Benson himself warranted closer scrutiny.

"Lemme explain a couple things, ma'am," Delvis Diaz was saying. "First off, who I am, who I was on the street. I was a drug dealer, a king-pin, real high level and shit. I sold drugs. Dope, mostly, and a little co-caine here and there. I had a real nice organization, back in the day. Killin' wasn't my thing, okay? Ask anybody. Step to me and I'll fuck you up. I won't have a choice. I'll have to, to stay strong in the streets. But I was a businessman, and violence is bad for business. Never believed in it."

"Every other scumbag like you says the same thing," Randall inter-jected with exaggerated disgust. "Admit to the drugs but not the mur-ders. Sometimes a jury is stupid enough to believe it. But they got it right with you."

"Randall, please!" Melanie snapped, wanting to hear more. "Let him talk."

"I can't believe you fallin' for this horseshit." Randall shook his head. "Fine, I'll just keep my mouth shut! Pretend I'm not here." Dan regarded Randall with bewilderment, then glanced at Melanie, raising his eye-brows questioningly. Melanie held her hand up again, struggling to pick up the thread of Diaz's words.

"Okay," she said, "so you were a drug dealer, not a killer, fine. But how do we get from there to a reputable prosecutor conspiring with a cold-blooded killer to set you up? I'm prepared to take this seriously, but you better have a damn good explanation and proof to back it up."

"Why does anybody do anything? Greed. Money. That's all. I saw it comin', too, but I was too fuckin' stupid, too soft, to do what needed to be done. See, Slice was with me from a shorty. He ain't got no daddy, and his moms was a crack ho who just kinda faded out. He attach himself to me when he was ten years old, call himself Junior Diaz after me. He wasn't born in no hospital, ain't got no government name anyway. So I took him in, raised him up, kept him from starvin', made him a player in my organization. But after all I did for him, look what I get." He glanced down at his cuffed hand, shaking his head, genuinely upset. "The boy'd been a big problem for a long time. Stealin' from me, beatin' on people when he shouldn't, cuttin' 'em up. I knew I shoulda bodied him—it was the only way. But I couldn't do it. So he set me up, got me out of the picture, so's he could be the kingpin himself."

"Okay, I understand Slice's angle. He wants to push you out and take over your turf. But what about Jed Benson? Surely you're not suggesting that he knowingly collaborated with Slice—"

Randall smashed his fist against the metal door. They all jumped. "Enough! I can't believe we're all standing here listening to this crap!"

Diaz went white, his eyes narrowing to tiny slits. "You don't wanna hear what I have to say? Fine, call the guards! I'm done!" he yelled.

"What? No, please!" Melanie pleaded.

"Think I ain't never heard of the right to remain silent? I'm not saying another word to this asshole. You want to talk to me again, come back without him. And bring my lawyer."

Melanie was powerless to try to change his mind. Once a prisoner invoked his rights, it was illegal to question him further. Diaz knew that. Randall had pushed Diaz to the breaking point, derailing the interview with his blatant hostility. To some extent Melanie sympathized. If you listened to the inmates, the prisons were overflowing with innocent people, every one of them with a hard-luck story. An old cop like Randall had very limited patience for that sort of talk. Most of the time, she didn't subscribe to it either. But there were too many unanswered questions in this case—about Slice, about Jed Benson, about the relationship between them. There was a real chance Delvis Diaz could shed light on those questions. Now Randall had blown it, and Melanie was angry and surprised. It wasn't what she expected from him. It wasn't good police work.

MELANIE WAS DULY irritated during the long march back through grim corridors to the lockers where they'd left their things. Only the presence of their bleached-blond escort checked her tongue. She wouldn't criticize Randall in front of the snippish Ms. Leona Burkett, but she'd let him have it the second they got to the car.

"By the way," Leona said as they retrieved their cell phones and beepers, "next time please have the basic courtesy to turn off your communications devices before you stow them. They've been making an unholy racket in there and giving me a headache like you wouldn't believe."

As if on cue, Dan's pager and Randall's cell phone began to shriek simultaneously, and Melanie's phone vibrated vigorously in her hand, startling her. They looked at each other for a split second before answering, their faces all registering the same terrible conviction: It had to be bad news.

22

The hotel off the interstate looked less threatening today in the blazing-hot sunlight than it had yesterday in the gloom. Now it just seemed antiseptic, institutional—an impersonal place to die. Standing in the parking lot, Melanie let her gaze travel upward once again to that fifth-floor window. She remembered what she'd been thinking looking up from this exact spot yesterday, that anyone could find Rosario. She knew how vulnerable Rosario was, and how afraid. Yet she'd driven away and left it to others to protect her, consigning her to die in this soulless outpost, far from home. The only way to redeem herself in her own eyes was to find Rosario's killer and bring him to justice.

Randall had bounded ahead, but Dan noticed her lagging and turned to wait for her. His face was troubled and grave, framed against the backdrop of flashing lights from the emergency vehicles in front of the hospital entrance.

He stretched his hands toward her in supplication. "Please, Melanie . . ."

"I blame myself more than I blame you."

He took several steps, closing the gap between them, clasping her shoulders and looking down into her face. "That's plain wrong! Look, it was somebody's fault. But it wasn't mine, and it sure as hell wasn't yours. There'll be an inquiry. We'll find out what happened."

"We know what happened. She wasn't properly protected. Whose fault

is that? Yours and mine, Dan. We knew she was at risk. We knew that animal was out there. We promised her she'd be safe, and then we left her
here."

"Yes, we left her here. We had to. What were we supposed to do, run
the investigation from a fucking motel in Jersey? We had work to do, for
Chrissakes!"

"We should have moved her!" she said.

"This guy is good. He would've found her anywhere. You know that."

"*How* did he find her, Dan? How many hotels are there in spitting distance of the city? A hundred? Two hundred? More? What are the odds
he'd find her in this one?"

"Come on, don't get crazy now. There's no evidence for what you're
saying."

She tried to shrug off his hands, but he held her fast. "Let me go. I
want to see her."

"Is that really a good idea?"

"It's not your choice. Let go, I said." She pulled free and brushed past
him, through the dingy lobby and into the elevator. He raced to catch up.

"I'm just trying to help you," he said, following her into the elevator.

"You want to help me, get more personnel on this investigation. The
three of us can't go on working this alone. Not if we want to keep our
witnesses alive, we can't."

"You think I haven't tried to get more men?" Dan said. "The Bureau
doesn't give a shit about straight homicides in this climate! If there's no
terrorists involved, it's not their problem."

"When it was just Jed Benson, fine, I understood that. But Slice struck
again. He hasn't stopped, and he's not going to."

"Believe me, I'm on *your* side. If it were up to me, we'd have ten more
guys right this minute. But the Benson case ain't the only thing going on
in this town."

"So we don't fit the mission statement this month? Do I need to write
some PR memo, spin it better, so somebody pays attention?" Her voice
dripped with disgust at herself, at her own performance, at him and his

agency. She was remembering Rosario, the mask of fear on her face when they first met, her brave smile once Melanie had convinced her she would be safe. Rosario, who trusted her. And paid the ultimate price for it. They needed to see, to understand what their inattention had done.

Dan sighed. "Okay, look. I'll make some phone calls as soon as we get upstairs, but I'm not optimistic. I hate to be crass about it, but the times we live in, two victims aren't enough to get anybody's attention. I'm just being honest with you."

Would he make a serious effort to get more personnel, as he promised, or was he merely humoring her? Was she the only one who took this investigation seriously? If necessary, she'd take matters into her own hands. She had no power to assign investigators, but Bernadette could intercede. Bernadette had pull. Yes, she'd speak to Bernadette, ask her to call the FBI and start making demands. They had to listen now, after this, after an innocent woman died on their watch.

THE FIFTH-FLOOR CORRIDOR was crowded with local cops and hotel employees straining to see into the open door of Rosario's room. A stretcher had been pulled across the doorway to block the curious from entering. As Melanie approached, the crew-cut cop from Rommie Ramirez's squad stepped up to it from inside and whisked it out of the way so she could pass, his eyes hollow. Dan followed, glancing at the cop curiously, his gaze prompting Melanie to wonder herself what Ramirez's underling was doing here. But as she walked down the narrow entry foyer and looked into the room, any natural thoughts fled her mind.

She absorbed it all in a glance that hit like a punch in the stomach. Rosario's severed head stared at her from a spot on the dresser right next to the television, its glazed, empty eyes wide open with surprise. Dried, blackish blood was everywhere—in cascades down the dresser, spattering the walls, in great stains on the pink carpet. The bed looked like tornado wreckage—a riot of bloody covers and pillows, a stiffening arm protruding from beneath a blanket. By the time Melanie snapped her eyelids shut a split second later, multiple images of Rosario's violent death were permanently imprinted on her brain. She would carry them to her own grave.

"Oh, Jesus!" Dan exclaimed. He was one step behind her, his words spoken practically into her ear, but they echoed as if from a great distance. Her legs felt leaden, rooted to the floor, while her head felt hot and prickly. The next thing she knew, she was sitting in the same chair she'd sat in yesterday, her head between her knees, breathing into a paper bag somebody had handed her.

"Better?" Dan asked, his hand on her shoulder.

"I think so. Did I faint?"

"Out cold. Lucky I caught you before you hit the floor. Easy does it. Come up nice and slow."

She lifted her head slowly, taking deep breaths. "I'm seeing stars, but I think it's okay." She sat up straight now, focusing on him kneeling in front of her chair so she wouldn't have to look at the room. "Yeah, I'm okay."

Holding on to the arms of the chair, she pushed herself to her feet unsteadily.

"C'mon, I'll take you back to the car," Dan said, standing up.

"You think I'm stopping after what I just saw? No way! I'm catching this scumbag. I want to talk to the Crime Scene team."

Dan knew better at this point than to try to stop her. Melanie motioned to Randall, who'd been conferring with a detective by the far window. Randall left him and came over to where she stood with Dan.

"Who's that? Is he in charge?" Melanie asked him.

"One of the Jersey guys. They haven't actually touched anything yet. Rosario was discovered by a cleaning lady who called the local cops. They responded a couple hours ago, but when they learned that Rosario was here under our protection, they had the good sense to call us before they did anything else."

"Some protection," Melanie said bitterly.

Randall ignored her remark. "Right after the locals arrived, the officer who was detailed to watch the door came back. I just debriefed him before you folks walked in."

"The guy with the crew cut?" She looked around the room but didn't see him. He must have left while she was blacked out in the chair.

"Yeah. He's devastated. More than that, he's scared, worried about his job."

"He fucking better be," Melanie said. She didn't usually swear like that, but it gave her some relief.

"Don't prejudge, Melanie," Randall said. "It really wasn't his fault. O'Reilly and I have been going around like beggars with our hands out to find people to work this case. Ramirez loaned me this kid. He was watching Amanda Benson yesterday, but she hired private protection, so he freed up."

"Smart idea, private protection," Melanie said sarcastically.

"Look, with funding cuts and all, Ramirez is terribly understaffed," Randall said. "He's only doing this out of respect for Jed Benson's memory. His squad had an emergency last night. They get a tip about a major cocaine shipment in a disabled tractor-trailer on the BQE, and when they go in to investigate, they wind up in a shoot-out. I'm not shittin' you—heard it over the radio myself. So this kid gets called away to assist. He's told a replacement is on the way, so he leaves. Turns out dispatch screwed up. Nobody got that call. The kid worked all night on the bust and came back here to relieve that other guy, only to find the place swarming with Jersey cops because of this mess."

"I feel for him. Poor thing."

Randall's jaw tightened. "Strikes me you're looking to point fingers. I don't really hold with that. People try their best, but shit happens."

"Our witness is dead—no, a lovely, decent, scared *human being* is dead, and the best you can do is say 'shit happens'? That's pathetic, Randall. You've been on this job too long."

"Hey, enough, don't get personal," Dan said firmly. "That's not productive. I know you're upset, but we got work to do."

Randall glared at her. "That's right, Melanie. You're wasting time and energy on this blame game. Meanwhile, our friend with the knife is thinking about where to strike next." He turned to Dan. "They haven't canvassed the hotel staff yet. I'm gonna start with that."

"Okay. I'll call over to the squad and see if we can get some more personnel," Dan said.

"What, like roadblocks and helicopter support?" Randall asked.

"Nah. Useless. From the looks of the blood, she was killed hours ago."

"I agree. Why chase a quarry that's long gone?"

"I'm talking about anticipating his next move."

Melanie looked back and forth between them. It was obvious what Slice's next move would be. "You mean Amanda Benson," she said.

"Yes," Dan said.

Randall nodded soberly. "You better make those calls fast. For all we know, Slice left here and headed straight for that hospital."

Randall walked away just as Butch Brennan and his crime-scene team arrived in force.

"Whoa, looks like you guys got a serious psycho on your hands," Butch said, dumping a load of equipment in the corner of the room and walking over to the dresser. "Look at this. My first severed head in five years. A real clean cut, too. Guy can chop, I'll say that for him. Hey, Castro, we need a few nice pictures of this one."

"You got it, boss. Pictures of the head. What else?"

"Any cuts on the body that show the size of the blade. ME'll compare 'em to cuts on Benson's body, and the murder weapon, if we get lucky enough to find it."

The crime-scene team took control efficiently, herding the rest of the New Jersey police out of the room and confining Dan and Melanie to the tiny entry hall so the team members could work without interference. While they waited, Dan and Melanie started working their cell phones, looking for reinforcements. Melanie tried without luck to reach Bernadette, who was out of the office until midafternoon. Dan left several messages for guys who he said owed him favors. Bottom line, they both came up empty-handed for the moment. After a while Randall returned, shaking his head.

"Of course nobody saw or heard a thing," he said. "Nothing that could help with time of death. No physical description either. Only thing is a pile of cigarette butts in a closet down the hall."

"That's something, anyway," Melanie said. "Let's have Butch's guys collect them for DNA sampling."

"Will do." He nodded gravely.

"Listen, Randall, I owe you an apology."

"I owe you one, too. I can see how upset you are. First time you lose a witness?"

"Yes, and I'm gonna make damn sure it's the last."

"Nothing worse than that. Except maybe losing a partner. I been through that, too. Look, honey, let me pass along something it took me a lotta hard years to learn. Play for your own team. Maybe that sounds cynical, but useful things often are. There's us and there's them. Pointing fingers at *us* only helps *them*. And this is one guy you don't want to help." His glance took in the whole blood-spattered room.

She wasn't sure she agreed with Randall's message, but before she could open her mouth to reply, Butch Brennan came over to give them a report.

"Whaddaya got, Butch?" Dan asked.

"Off the bat, different MO from the last time."

"How's that?" Melanie asked.

"Well, as far as I can tell, this is a straight knife job. No dog attack, no gunshot, no setting the remains on fire. As far as I can *tell*."

"What's that supposed to mean?" Melanie asked.

"Not everything's here to examine."

She felt light-headed again, but she managed to keep her voice steady. "What's missing?"

"Quite a bit. One of the arms. Both legs. The torso's here. It was under the blankets. But it's been cut open and, like, scooped out. You wanna know exactly what's missing from inside, you need to ask the ME."

"Why would he do that?" Dan asked.

A vision of the stolen animal-torture photographs flashed into Melanie's mind with such clarity that she gasped. They all looked at her.

"For his dog," she said with absolute conviction, remembering the bloodied paws and muzzle in the bottom corner of the Polaroid. "Slice took the parts for his dog."

"I bet you're right," Dan said. "That sick fuck."

"We've got to stop him. And we'd better get to Amanda Benson right away."

23

The cavernous main floor of Saks was jam-packed and noisy at lunch hour. Nell Benson strolled past the cosmetics displays, stopping occasionally to spray perfume across her wrist as she looked in every direction. Her senses were sharp, but they weren't doing her much good in this chaotic place. Vast flower displays and mirrored partitions impeded her view. Sound floated upward, became muddy, and disappeared into the vine-covered ceiling as into the dome of a cathedral. Still, she was relatively confident she wasn't being followed.

She took the lumbering wooden elevator to the fourth floor. Here everything was bright and open. She was certain now she was alone. Even so, she walked around, fingering a garment now and then, looking over her shoulder discreetly. Best to be careful. A saleslady, noting her expensive bag and the diamonds weighing down her hand, stepped forward and asked if she needed help.

"Just looking," Nell said. After a moment she headed for the ladies' room.

The waiting area smelled bad, so she raised her perfumed wrist to her nose. A young mother sat on the upholstered bench by the pay telephone, nursing her baby. Nell looked at her, frowned, and disappeared into a stall for a while. When she came back, the mother was still there.

Nell walked casually over to the makeup mirror and opened her bag, taking her time choosing a lipstick shade. She watched in the mirror as the mother closed her blouse, tucked her baby back into the stroller, and left.

When the waiting area was empty, Nell went over to the pay phone. She dug around in the bottom of her bag, the blinking green light of her cell phone providing just enough illumination to help her find a quarter. The plastic receiver was greasy in her hand as she dropped the quarter into the slot. God knew what you could catch from these things, but at least they still took change. She'd had a moment of fear about that in the elevator. When she got the dial tone, she punched in the number.

"Hello?" Rommie answered.

"It's Nell."

"Well, hello. What's this number you're calling from? I don't recognize it."

"It's a pay phone."

"A pay phone?" He sighed. "You watch too many spy movies."

"I'm just being careful. People could draw conclusions from our friendship."

"What's wrong with us being friends? I was friends with Jed, I'm friends with you. Big deal. Besides, I'm seeing Bernadette. Everybody knows that."

"Still, in a situation like this, with the will getting probated and all, appearances matter."

"So I take it that's why you haven't returned my calls?"

"Don't be so touchy. I called you yesterday. About that prosecutor, remember? The one who's harassing Amanda? And I'm calling you now."

"I called *you* three times last night to see how you were doing. It's one o'clock in the afternoon, and this is the first you get back to me? I've been worried about you."

"Come on, now," she coaxed, a honeyed note in her husky voice. "Be nice, Rom. I don't want to fight with you. If I haven't called sooner, it's only because I was at the hospital with Amanda. Do you have any idea how difficult this is for me, watching what she's going through? Can you even imagine?"

He was quiet momentarily. "No, I can't. But you know I've done everything in my power—"

"Of course. I know that, and I'm grateful, I really am. But tell me again, what are you doing to protect her now, right this minute?"

"You hired Bill Flanagan like I told you, right?"

"Oh, yes. He showed up this morning. To say I wasn't impressed is the understatement of the year. He reeks of gin! Reminds me of my father. There's nothing I hate more than a broken-down old wino."

"The guy hits the bottle, I'll grant you that. But he's one tough son of a bitch. Nobody gets past him."

"I'm taking your word on him."

"You won't be sorry."

"But is one person even enough? I mean, Amanda saw the whole thing. She could testify. That animal is going to come after her, I know it."

"Is she awake? Has she said anything?"

"She seemed better a little while ago when I left."

"That's good. That's a relief."

"But I want her left alone. And I'm afraid that prosecutor is going to come back today."

"I wouldn't count on it. They're busy doing other stuff."

"Well, if she does, I don't see how I can keep her away from Amanda."

"Like I said, nobody gets past Wild Bill." He paused. "Look, don't worry. You're worrying too much."

"You really think so?"

"Yes. Amanda will be fine. I'll come over there and guard her myself if I have to. And as for Melanie Vargas, look, if you really feel Amanda's not well enough to talk, she'll have to accept that."

"I don't know. She doesn't strike me as the type to just roll over."

"Don't worry. I have it under control."

She sighed. "I guess I should go back to the hospital to keep an eye on things."

"That's not necessary. Flanagan is there."

"Where else do I have to go? I took care of all the funeral arrangements yesterday."

"Where are you now?"

"At Saks."

"You went all the way to Saks just to use a pay phone? Man, you *are* under stress!"

"I wasn't about to use one on the street. Besides, I always feel better here. It's a very calming atmosphere."

"That's so *you,* Nell. No problem in life a little shopping can't cure." He laughed.

"I suppose, since I'm here, I could find Amanda something to wear to the funeral."

"Really? She's well enough to go?"

"We'll see. I'm hoping anyway. I can only imagine how much she'll resent me if I don't find a way to get her there. Years of therapy."

"Kids."

"Tell me about it."

"Okay, so do your shopping, and then I'll come over and we'll have an early dinner, order in room service or something. You shouldn't be alone right now. What's the name of that place you're staying?"

2 4

———

With all the ground they had to cover, their best bet was to split up. Randall would go to the hospital and check on Amanda Benson. Dan would head to Brooklyn to hunt down informants who might know Slice's whereabouts. And Melanie would return to her office. Her nominal assignment was to collect the records they'd subpoenaed and scour them for leads on Slice, but she had her own agenda, one she didn't reveal to Dan and Randall.

The security breaches on the Benson case troubled Melanie greatly. First the intruder in the basement stealing her evidence, then Slice getting to Rosario. How had he managed it? How did he even know where to look? She had to worry there was a leak somewhere, maybe in her office, maybe among the cops or agents. Maybe a sloppy, careless leak—or maybe an intentional one. Dan and Randall pooh-poohed her concerns. Fine, let them. She'd investigate and get to the bottom of this without them if she had to. She'd reached out and grabbed this case for herself, and she'd see it through to completion no matter where it led or what it took.

But acting completely alone, she recognized, was not an ideal strategy. Ferreting out wrongdoing or negligence in her own office or in the FBI was bound to kick up resistance. She needed backing from someone with juice. Her boss was the obvious choice.

With that thought in mind, she buzzed herself through the bulletproof door and hurried straight to Bernadette's office, not even stopping to put away her briefcase. Shekeya was sitting at her desk, eating a Big Mac and fries, reading a dog-eared copy of *People.*

"She back yet?" Melanie demanded, out of breath, "I need to see her right away."

Shekeya dipped a french fry carefully into some ketchup and chewed it slowly.

"Nope. Went to Washington. She got a meeting at Main Justice."

"I know, but wasn't she supposed to be in by now?"

"She don't inform me of her every move."

"Well, you booked her flight, didn't you? Can you check it for me, please?"

"Your panties in a twist, girl. Can't you see I'm eating?"

"Shekeya, it's important."

"So's my lunch."

Melanie folded her arms in exasperation, glaring at Shekeya.

"Don't give me that look. The boss ain't gonna come back any faster because you standing there with your face all ugly. When I'm done with my burger, I'll check it for you. Now, get your hiney back to your office." Shekeya shooed Melanie with a ketchup-besmirched hand.

Melanie sighed dramatically, but she had no choice. She turned and walked out into the hall. She knew Shekeya well enough to be confident she'd get the correct information in Shekeya's own good time.

AN HOUR LATER she was sitting at her desk scanning Jed Benson's telephone records and thinking about how to get her hands on the sign-in sheet from the security desk downstairs when Bernadette rapped loudly on her open office door.

"Shekeya said you were looking for me, hon," Bernadette said.

"Oh, Bern, I'm so glad you're back," Melanie said, hopes brightening. She really needed Bernadette's help; it was a relief that her boss sounded so *nice* for a change.

Bernadette walked in and sat down across from Melanie in the guest chair. She leaned forward, her features arranged in a look of motherly concern. "I heard your witness was killed. Are you holding up okay?"

"No, I'm not. I really need to talk to you."

"Oh, hon, I'm sorry I wasn't around earlier. I'm sure you could have used a shoulder to cry on."

"It's not that, Bern. I'm worried about the case. We had two major security breaches in the past twenty-four hours, and I'm beginning to think we have a leak somewhere. I really need some advice on how to handle it."

"A leak? What are you talking about? I'm sure your witness blew it herself by telling some idiot neighbor where she was or something."

"No, Bern, Rosario was completely terrified. She wouldn't have given up her location to her own mother."

"People are stupider than you'd think. Do me a favor, check the phone records from her hotel room—*then* come back and tell me I'm wrong. I'll bet you ten bucks there's some call on there to some cousin in Queens who blabbed to the whole planet."

"I really doubt it. Besides, Rosario's murder wasn't the only security breach. Somebody chased me in the basement last night, stole evidence from my purse—"

Bernadette laughed. "Yeah, I heard about that one. The security company complained, you know. I commend your nerve in going down to Dead Files so late at night. But next time be a little more careful with the emergency door, or we're gonna have to start paying them overtime for investigating false alarms."

"I didn't just hear a noise and freak out, Bern. Somebody was down there. Valuable evidence is missing."

"Melanie," Bernadette said sharply, "the perpetrator removed cash from your wallet, right?"

"Yes, but—"

"So don't give me partial information, miss, it's misleading. The cash is key. Some janitor obviously stole your money, and in the process he took your evidence by mistake. He probably dropped it in a Dumpster last night on his way to score a few dime bags with your cash."

"That's it? You're just explaining everything away without even investigating?"

Bernadette sighed. "Look, I understand you're upset. It's very traumatic when a witness gets killed. There's a natural tendency to see it as bigger than it is, as the result of some wild conspiracy. But that's just nerves talking. You want my advice? Calm down, do your work, and stop running off at the mouth with crazy theories."

Melanie stared at Bernadette in dismay. She couldn't believe that her boss wasn't all over these security breaches, that she wasn't helping her. Then it dawned on her that Bernadette had a huge conflict of interest here. Rommie Ramirez's squad had taken responsibility for protecting Rosario last night. The crew-cut cop had left his post to respond to a drug call. Did Bernadette already know that? Did she fear that an inquiry might negatively affect her boyfriend, further damage his already troubled career? Would Bernadette allow personal feelings to influence her professional judgment like that? She was obviously head over heels for Rommie. But covering up something so significant would put *her* whole career at risk. Melanie respected Bernadette too much to believe that such a thing was possible. Yet she couldn't deny that Bernadette was acting bizarrely nonchalant.

"Rest assured," Bernadette continued, "nobody blames you for what happened to your witness. When you're faced with a killer as smart and ruthless as this one, you're gonna experience setbacks."

"Rosario wasn't a setback, she was a person!" Melanie said. "There's a leak somewhere, and for all I know, her door was purposely left unattended. I think we need an inquiry."

Bernadette's eyes narrowed. "When you say something like that, I have a hard time deciding whether you're stupid or just reckless. You want an inquiry, you say? Those things never go the way people expect, you know, Melanie. If I were you, I'd make damn sure my own house was in order before asking for one."

"What's that supposed to mean?"

"You want to know how the killer tracked Rosario down and whether there was a leak? Have you examined your own conduct? Were you careless with information? Isn't it possible it was really *your* fault somehow, and not anybody else's?"

Melanie fell silent, thinking about the address she'd put on the G-car authorization and never found time to erase, about her call to the grand-jury clerk, about her other actions in the past twenty-four hours that might have divulged Rosario's location. What if it had been her fault? God, how could she ever live with that guilt? Her stomach sank. It must've shown in her face.

"Uh-huh, I thought so," Bernadette said with a knowing smirk. "Well, I guess that's why I'm here. To teach you greenhorns to look before you leap."

"I tried to be so careful—"

"Of course you did. And if you let something slip, I'm *sure* it was an accident, hon. That's my point, you see? Don't start pointing fingers, because nobody's perfect." Bernadette stood up and moved toward the door. "Speaking of not being perfect," she said, with a nod toward Melanie's desk, laden with piles of unopened subpoena responses, "this desk is a mess. Clean it up before something else falls through the cracks, would you?"

"Okay."

"And another thing. Romulado tells me Amanda Benson still is not well. So just stay away from there, okay? Focus on something else for a while. After all, you have plenty of other work to do."

After Bernadette left, Melanie went over her actions in her head. She was certain she'd never divulged Rosario's whereabouts to anyone outside her office. If someone from the office cribbed the address and leaked it, that person was complicit in murder. But she couldn't be expected to anticipate someone else's treason, could she? No, she was entitled to trust her own people. Only once she got comfortable with that did she begin to see that Bernadette had manipulated her. Bernadette had turned the tables, made her question her own conduct, distracted her. And left her empty-handed. No help on investigating the security breach, no additional staffing. She was determined to solve these murders, but she needed resources and proper support. She was starting to have a bad feeling about this.

MELANIE'S PHONE RANG some minutes later.

"Hey, what's up?" Dan said. "I thought it was about time to check in." His voice cheered her up so much that it scared her.

"You always check in with the prosecutor every few hours?" she asked breathlessly.

"With you I do. You miss me?"

Playing this game with him was dangerous. She'd end up in way over her head with this guy if she wasn't careful. She looked down at her bare ring finger, longing for the security of her wedding band. When she wore it, she knew where she stood in the world. She knew where the boundaries were.

"Any developments?" she asked Dan.

"Yeah, actually. I just got a lead on Jasmine Cruz from this scumbag informant of mine," he said.

"Well, that's good news, because I was just examining Jed Benson's telephone records, and she's all over them."

"No kidding!"

"Yeah. I'm starting to think she's it. You know, the missing link between Slice and Jed Benson."

"What's in the phone records?"

"Numerous calls in the last year from Jed Benson's cell phone to two phones subscribed in the name Jasmine Cruz. One landline, one cell phone, so he was calling her at home *and* on her cell. I'm talking like several calls per week, usually late at night. Long ones, too."

"Wow! All from his cell, you said, not from his home phone?"

"Yes, that's right. He didn't call her from his house."

"You know what that means?"

"Unfortunately, I do. He was hiding it from his wife, the jerk." She was thinking of her own innocent-looking home-telephone bills—they hadn't breathed a hint of Steve's cheating. "I have a feeling Benson got around. Sarah van der Vere practically admitted they had an affair. And these phone records suggest the same thing about Jasmine."

"Good work, partner. You might have just solved the crime, although I think you trashed our jurisdiction."

"How's that?"

"What we got here is a good old-fashioned crime of passion, don't you think? Benson barked up the wrong tree. He did Slice's girl. Simple as that. None of this retaliation-for-prosecution shit."

"Huh. Maybe." Was Dan right? It was a simple and elegant solution, yet it didn't feel like the whole answer. "But what about that phone call four years ago? The one from the Blades wiretap that got stolen last night, where Slice and Jasmine are talking about Mighty Whitey?"

"Maybe it wasn't Benson they were talking about."

"Then Jasmine Cruz just shows up on Benson's cell-phone records four years later as a complete coincidence? I don't buy that."

"Hmm. Maybe you're right." They were both silent, thinking. "Hey, what about this? Maybe in the wiretap call, Slice was trying to blackmail Benson or something, you know? Maybe they had photos of him with Jasmine, and if he didn't pay up, they'd tell his wife?"

"Could be. But still, that call was four years ago. How does that get us to killing Benson now?"

"Good question. I don't know. But I bet I know who does."

"Jasmine Cruz?"

"Yup."

"Where is she?"

"Get this. Working as a spokesmodel at the Auto Show."

Melanie laughed. "She's come up in the world. Great, though, I love the Auto Show."

"Yeah? I love the Auto Show, too."

"Let's go, then."

"Only thing is, I'm in Brooklyn, and the bridges are shut now for some kind of enforcement activity."

"Okay, well . . ."

"I'll meet you there, but get started without me."

"I'll have the case wrapped up in a nice, neat package by the time you show up."

"It's a deal."

2 5

His celli ring, it wake him up.

"What?" he said.

"What are you, sleeping?"

Wake him up like that. No courtesy. Motherfucker don't realize he living on the edge already with the way he fuck up the job the other night.

"You know I work last night. The fuck you calling me!"

"Yeah, I know you did. Quite something."

"You next, fool. Waking me up."

"Okay, okay."

"And you calling me here."

"Think I'd do that if I didn't know for a fact it was safe? Besides, this is important. We gotta move on some of these others right away."

"You better get out of my shit. I decide, understand? I'ma do the architect next, that Chinese bitch. That's it."

"Will you just forget her for now? She's not important."

"What you saying? Makes me wonder about you, son. She what the job *about*, far as I'm concerned. We don't get that information, we don't get paid."

"We gotta think about basic survival. We got two problems. First off, Barbie Doll needs to go. Fast, before she talks."

"That ain't my problem. It's yours. You kill her."

"I'll pretend you never said that. Second, Jasmine."

"What about Jasmine?"

"She knows too much. And if they decide to squeeze her, she'll give it up in about ten seconds. She's a weak link."

He paused. "You know Jasmine got my little daughter."

"Well, what do you know? I never saw you shy away from taking care of business before. Very refreshing." He chuckled.

"This a fucking joke to you?"

"Hey, whatever. I'm not telling you how to handle it. I'm just saying it needs to be handled. So forget about the architect and deal with these other two."

"You seem to think you giving me an order."

"Not an order. Just some sound advice."

"You better hope I don't find you, fool, the way you pissing me off!"

He shut the phone and smash it hard against the wall. Fucking worm, telling him how to do his thing, saying he ain't take care of business. He take care of business, all right. But *he* decide who, when, and where. *He* decide, not nobody else. And one day real soon, he gonna decide that motherfucker gotta go. Real soon.

He get out the bed now, drink some Gatorade from the refrigerator. Shit never go bad—leave it in there for a year and it still taste the same. At least something you can trust. He got the humming in his blood again, from that fucking worm getting all up in his face, fucking up his concentration. His head pounding. He gotta try to calm down. Maybe he go down the basement and see No Joke in his special room. He gotta clean up whatever left from No Joke's party anyway. He do the work last night, and the fucking dog get all the reward. That ain't right. Things is fucked up. He need to get his shit straightened out.

2 6

___

ot sunlight shone through the soaring glass ceiling of the Javits
Center, illuminating the tumultuous scene many stories below.
Melanie stepped off the enormous escalator, blinding light and
bright colors hitting the retina of her eye, making her feel like laughing
aloud. She waded through wave after wave of revelers—Japanese busi-
nessmen in monochromatic outfits, bridge-and-tunnel types, gangs of
hip-hop kids with heavy gold-and-diamond pendants dangling down to
their waists—all climbing in and out of gleaming cars that spun on carpeted platforms. Car commercials looped endlessly on colossal video
screens attached to sky-high partitions. She looked up, taking in the
scene. A space-age cobalt blue concept car circled the room on a steel
track mounted thirty feet above her head.

In this chaos she'd never find Jasmine Cruz without asking directions.
Spokesmodels were everywhere she looked. Of every race and color,
they were nonetheless completely interchangeable, with their gazellelike
bodies, heavy eye makeup and identical powder blue leather pantsuits.
Jasmine must be something to look at to get *this* job. Melanie walked up
to the nearest one, a redhead, who stood holding brochures in front of an
acid yellow race car, its doors opening upward like gull's wings.

"Excuse me," she said, "I'm looking for my cousin who's working as a
spokesmodel here. Her name's Jasmine Cruz."

"Jasmine? Hmm. If it's the girl I'm thinking of, try the brochure bar right past Range Rover. Walk all the way to the back, make a left at the Hummer display, and keep going for a while. You can't miss it."

"Thanks."

But following the directions proved difficult in the wildly disorienting space. Screens flashing logos and 3-D diagrams were purposely set at odd angles to create eddies in the traffic flow, making it impossible to walk a straight path. She couldn't get a clear line of sight more than twenty feet ahead. Weaving her way through thick crowds, she made slow progress across the vast floor of the convention center, arriving at her destination drained and a bit dazed.

Two spokesmodels, a blonde and a brunette, stood looking bored behind a tall wood-and-marble bar that displayed an assortment of glossy car brochures. The brunette looked like a cartoon image of a Native American princess, with cheekbones sharp enough to cut yourself on, straight black hair, and coffee-colored skin. Her eyebrows arched dramatically over powder blue glitter eye shadow that matched her leather pantsuit.

Melanie walked up to the bar, deciding to take a chance. "Jasmine Cruz?" she asked the brunette.

The woman looked confused. "Uh-huh. Were you here yesterday?"

Melanie took her credentials from her bag and flipped them open in her hand.

"I need to speak with you. I think you know why, but if you want me to say it, I will. It's just . . . it might be embarrassing." She glanced meaningfully at the blonde.

Jasmine's eyes flashed. "I know the system. I don't need to talk to nobody if I don't want to."

The blonde watched with open curiosity.

"Fi   if that's the way you want to play it, Miss Cruz, then I need to vise   that you're suspected of being involved in the murder of Jed Penso . You're not currently charged with any crime, but I need to ask you some questions. I think it would be in your best interests to answer them."

"I don't even know no Jed Benson. You just hassling me because I'm of color." She tossed her shiny hair dismissively.

"¿Eres boricua?" Melanie asked, in a dead-on imitation of her father's staccato, rapid-fire Puerto Rican Spanish, studying Jasmine coolly.

Jasmine's eyes widened. "Sí."

Melanie tapped herself on the chest with just the right measure of arrogance. "También." Me, too, so don't fuck with me, chica.

"Oh," Jasmine replied, in a more subdued tone.

"And, for your information, you're all over Jed Benson's phone records. Plus, we know all about you and Slice."

Jasmine drew her breath in sharply. "I don't know him neither. I really don't know no Slice. I'm gonna have to ask you to leave, or else I'm gonna call security."

"Perhaps you didn't look at my identification carefully enough, Miss Cruz. I can assure you, security won't side with you in this situation."

They stared at each other. Jasmine looked nervous, but she wasn't giving any ground. The blonde broke the stalemate.

"Go ahead, hon. I'll cover for you for a while," she said, examining her long fingernails, painted the same shade of blue as her outfit, her face expressionless.

Jasmine looked at Melanie for another moment. Then she shrugged, as if the situation were of little concern to her. "Whatever. I need a Starbucks anyway."

She emerged from behind the bar and began walking with studied casualness toward an escalator, looking straight ahead. Melanie fell into step beside her. The escalator led to a mezzanine that held food stands and tables. Their feet hit the first step in unison, and they began to glide up over the crowd wordlessly, as if they shared the escalator by chance.

Melanie leaned toward Jasmine to make eye contact. "Sorry about what I said in front of your friend," she began.

Jasmine turned away, pivoting until she rode nearly backward. She stared at the convention-center floor receding beneath them, jaw jutting stubbornly, ignoring Melanie.

"Jasmine," Melanie continued evenly, "I tried not to embarrass you, but you need to talk to me. You know more about Slice and Jed Benson than anybody left alive. That's a very dangerous position to be in. I'm concerned for your safety."

"Look, you wasting your time," Jasmine said. Her tone was less resentful, but she still wouldn't look at Melanie. "So Jed and me hook up or whatever. He give me money and shit, pay for my implants. That all it is as far as I'm concerned."

"I believe you weren't doing anything illegal, Jasmine, but you need to explain it to me. Help me understand."

"They a lot of shit going on with Jed y'all don't know about. Some nasty shit, too."

"Did it have anything to do with Slice?"

"I told you, I don't know nobody by that name."

"Jasmine, there's no point denying it. Your phone was tapped. I have a tape of you talking to Slice. And he sure doesn't sound like a nice guy."

As they reached the mezzanine and stepped off the escalator, Jasmine turned to Melanie. She tried to look defiant, but the fear in her eyes undermined her cool facade.

"He treat me better than he treat other girls," she said.

"If he treats you so good, Jasmine, why do you look so scared?"

"I ain't scared," she insisted, but her voice shook.

"Come on, let me buy you a coffee. We'll find a table. I'll explain what my office can do to protect you."

A long metal concession counter lined one wall of the low-ceilinged mezzanine. Melanie spied a Starbucks logo halfway down the counter and headed toward it. She was glad when Jasmine followed compliantly. They got their drinks and waited for a table to open up in the jam-packed seating area, not speaking. Only once they were seated did Melanie raise the difficult subject of Slice again.

"Jasmine, I'm here to help you," Melanie began as the girl sipped her iced Frappuccino through a straw, eyes fixed on the table. "We both know that Slice is a cold-blooded killer. That puts you in serious danger.

The closer we get to arresting him, the more nervous he gets. The more nervous he gets, the more likely he'll try to eliminate people who could testify against him. With what you know, you're at the top of that list."

"I know he do some bad things to other people, but he always good to me," Jasmine insisted, looking up at Melanie imploringly. "I'm his baby's mama."

"You have a baby with Slice?"

"Yeah, a little girl. Destiny. She two. He give me money for her, come by, bring her stuff. That's why I always stick by him. I want my baby to have a father."

"Oh," Melanie said, stunned into momentary silence. Jasmine's words hit home. How far could you excuse a man because he was—by whatever your standards—a good father? Should you stay in a bad relationship for your child's sake? In Jasmine's case the answer was obviously no. Staying with Slice could mean the difference between life and death. In Melanie's own life, the choice was less stark, the answer not as clear. Although, deep down, she knew that it wouldn't be good for Maya to grow up with parents who were unhappy together.

"Jasmine, can I tell you something?" Melanie said urgently. "I'm a mother myself. I totally hear you about sticking with your baby's father. But I'm from Bushwick, too. I know what it's like on the block. Some guys are ticking time bombs. You know that, I know that, we both know that just from where we grew up. They can be all right one minute and turn on you the next. Slice is like that. He's killed upwards of twenty people."

Jasmine gasped, shaking her head in mute horror.

"You didn't know?" Melanie asked.

"I know he done murders, but not how many."

"Well, that's how many, and it's a lot. He kills for a living. Not only for a living, for *pleasure*. Maybe he treats you okay sometimes, but I heard him on tape threatening you. Just from what I heard, I could tell he abuses you."

Tears welled in Jasmine's eyes. "Okay, maybe. But I got it under control.

I learn how to not piss him off. He don't beat on me so much these days."

"You're willing to stake your life on that? How long before Slice has a bad day? How long before you say the wrong thing or don't cook his food just how he likes or the baby cries too loud? What happens then? Who's gonna raise your daughter if you're dead, Jasmine?"

Jasmine sprang to her feet, knocking over her metal chair and taking several steps back, her eyes focused on a point beyond Melanie's shoulder.

"Jasmine, please, wait!"

Melanie leaped up and tried to grab for Jasmine's hand, but a vague sense of someone approaching from behind distracted her. She took her eyes off Jasmine for a split second, turning to see who was there. Just then the girl bolted, and Melanie watched in astonishment as Jasmine plunged frantically into the crowd of customers swarming the concession area, running as if she feared for her life. Melanie hesitated for a second, wondering if she should go after Jasmine or let her calm down before they talked more. But the next instant a man brushed by her from behind, following Jasmine's receding figure in its blue pantsuit. Jasmine hurried toward the escalators on the other side of the mezzanine—the man, clad in baggy black jeans and a tan T-shirt hanging to his knees, hot on her trail. He matched Slice's general description. Medium height, slim build, close-cropped brown hair. But didn't a lot of people? Melanie couldn't be sure it was Slice unless she saw his face.

She took off after them, yelling Jasmine's name. Jasmine whirled, panic-stricken when she saw the man gaining on her. As Melanie fought her way through the crowd toward them, Jasmine turned and ran, colliding hard with an overweight woman wearing a loose-fitting black dress.

"Aaagh, you crazy bitch, I think you broke my arm!" the woman cursed, grabbing hold of the lapel of Jasmine's jacket.

Caught in the woman's grasp, Jasmine hauled back and punched her in the head with all her strength. The woman hit the floor with a thud, the crowd surging in confusion around her prone figure, further obstructing Melanie's path. Jasmine ran. The man sidestepped onlookers, doggedly pursuing her. Melanie tried desperately to follow, but it was like swimming against the tide, with more and more people rushing over to gawk at the fallen woman.

"She's out cold! Is there a doctor here?" a man shouted.

"Call 911," somebody else suggested.

Her own progress toward the escalators virtually stopped, Melanie watched with her heart in her throat as the man caught up to Jasmine and grabbed her by the arm. The phony, terrified smile plastered on Jasmine's face as he yanked her around told Melanie everything she needed to know. She'd never gotten a clear look at him, but she didn't need to. It had to be Slice. Who else would Jasmine try to mollify with that pitiful smile? Just then the crowd closed ranks, and Melanie lost sight of them.

By the time Melanie fought her way to the escalators, crucial minutes had elapsed. She hadn't seen which way Jasmine and Slice went, and now they were nowhere in sight. Think, think. Jasmine was trying to escape. She would have headed down, toward the exits. Melanie hopped onto the down escalator, scanning the floor below for them as she moved. Everywhere she looked in the crowd, tall girls in powder blue leather pantsuits tricked her eye. None of them was Jasmine. Desperately, she pulled her cell phone from her bag, dialing Dan's pager as she rode downward, beeping him to her phone. Where was Dan now? Could he already be inside the Javits Center looking for her? Please, let him be. She needed backup, fast.

She stepped off the escalator onto the convention-center floor. Which way would Jasmine have run? Which way would Slice have taken her if he caught her? Straight for the nearest exit probably, but which way was that? She sprinted off in what seemed like the right direction, but again the crowds made for slow going. Running on the uneven floor was difficult—one moment plush carpeting dragged at her high-heeled shoes; the next, without noticing it, she'd stepped onto a rotating platform.

Disoriented and out of breath, she almost didn't stop to investigate when several people ahead of her, who'd been milling around an enormous red Hummer, began pointing upward, toward the skylit ceiling. But then she heard their gasps.

"What the hell is that girl doing?" one of them asked.

"She's out on the catwalk!"

Melanie looked up. Fifty feet above her head, a delicate metal catwalk hung suspended, connecting the mezzanine to the outside of a sky booth that overlooked the main floor. Jasmine Cruz stood completely motionless halfway across its expanse, gripping the flimsy handrail, paralyzed with fear. Up. Running, crazy with fear, Jasmine had gone up.

Melanie pulled out her credentials, displaying them as she waded into the crowd.

"U.S. Attorney, coming through, coming through," she said, elbowing her way to a spot directly under the catwalk.

"Jasmine!" Melanie shouted as loud as she could. "What are you doing? Go back! Go back, and I'll meet you at the top of the escalator."

Jasmine didn't appear to have heard her. The girl didn't move a muscle. Melanie turned and ran back toward the escalators. Her phone began to howl from inside her bag. She dug it out as she ran, nearly dropping it.

"Hello?"

"You beep me?" Dan asked cheerfully.

"Where the hell are you?"

"Just pulled into the parking garage. Why, what's wrong?"

"Slice is here! He chased Jasmine out onto a catwalk that goes to the sky booth! I'm trying to get up there to help her off!"

"Go! I'm coming as fast as I can."

She hung up, throwing her phone into her bag. She was just about to step onto the up escalator when a piercing shriek split the air behind her. She whirled around to see Jasmine's blue-suited figure hurtling to the ground, black hair streaming up toward the soaring ceiling.

MELANIE CLIMBED ONTO the slowly revolving platform and approached the silver concept car, lit so brilliantly by overhead spotlights that it seemed to exude a supernatural force. Jasmine lay on her back on the car's broad hood, staring numbly at the ceiling turning many stories above her. The stretchy blue leather of her pantsuit still hugged every curve of her perfect body, but her slender limbs were oddly twisted—splayed out, rigid, her feet in their stiletto-heeled boots pointing inward. Beads of sweat glistened on the heavy foundation makeup that coated her forehead.

"Just hang on, sweetie, help is on the way," Melanie said softly. Jasmine's hand hung off the side of the car. Melanie reached for it, squeezing the long, slender fingers, already cold and clammy to the touch. Feeling the slightest return of pressure from Jasmine's fingers, Melanie stood on tiptoe and leaned forward.

"Do you want to say something?" she asked.

Jasmine's lips worked, but no sound emerged at first. Melanie leaned closer, placing her ear against Jasmine's mouth.

"What is it? Tell me."

"Des-tiny," Jasmine whispered hoarsely. Her daughter. She was thinking about her daughter, just as Melanie would if she were about to die.

Two paramedics carrying a folded stretcher made their way through the gawking crowd.

"EMS! Over here, over here!" Melanie screamed.

"Somebody move her?" the taller paramedic, a commanding black woman with a powerful voice, asked, climbing up onto the platform. Her name tag read B. JONES. "The call said assault victim on the mezzanine level."

"That's somebody else," Melanie said. "Take care of this woman first. She fell from that catwalk up there."

"Two of 'em? Jesus! Miguel, call for backup while I get the collar on her," Jones instructed her companion as she removed a large neck brace from her satchel. "Decerebrate posturing, indicates brain damage. We need to get her in right now!"

Melanie jumped out of Jones's way, praying something could still be done. But Jasmine expelled a long, sighing breath—and then stopped breathing.

"Shit, went apneic on me!" Jones shouted to her colleague. Clambering onto the hood of the car, she began administering CPR as Jasmine's eyes stared unseeing at the light streaming in from above.

"YOU SURE IT was him?" Dan asked Melanie as they watched the medical examiner's van holding Jasmine Cruz's body pull away from the Javits Center.

The afternoon was hot and airless. The scorching sun beat down on her as she struggled to breathe through the exhaust fumes. Dan and the police had searched the Javits Center thoroughly, but Slice had apparently made a clean getaway.

"How many times do I have to tell you?" Melanie exclaimed furiously, overwrought that they hadn't been able to stop Slice, to save Jasmine, or even to apprehend him after the fact. "I never saw his face, but I *know* it was him!"

"I had the exits sealed as soon as I got off the phone with you. A guy at every door, couldn'ta been more than five minutes after we talked."

"That obviously wasn't fast enough to catch him."

"I'm keeping an open mind, but you should, too, okay? Just hear me out on this scenario. You're putting the screws to Jasmine. She freaks out, gets up and runs off like a bat out of hell, bumping into people left and right. She punched that broad so hard she fractured her jaw, you know. A guy grabs her. Not Slice, okay, just some moke she pissed off by bumping into him. He grabs her, but he doesn't *do* anything to her. End of the day, she's so freaked out, she runs out onto a catwalk, and she falls. By accident. A hundred people saw it. Every one of 'em says she lost her footing accidentally."

Incensed, Melanie shook her head. "No, no way!"

"Okay, why not?"

"*Because!* The guy came from behind me. Jasmine only ran in the first place because she saw him coming, over my shoulder. And he followed her—I watched him. He followed her all the way to the escalator, at least fifty feet through a crowded room, before he grabbed her. That's why!

I'm telling you, it was Slice! I'm not saying he pushed her. But he chased her out there. He *caused* her to fall."

Dan looked down at her steadily, an indulgent smile slowly spreading over his face.

"Okay. Melanie Vargas is so damn sure that's what happened, then that's what happened."

"Don't humor me. It's condescending."

He sighed. "What do you want me to say? Based on all the facts, honestly, maybe it was Slice, maybe it wasn't. You never saw his face, so you can't say for sure. Even if we caught him, you couldn't ID him. Plus, maybe it's too upsetting for you to think Jasmine freaked out after talking to you, ran away, and fell off a ledge, right?"

She grabbed Dan's arm fiercely, her fingers digging into his forearm. "You're kidding me! You're not seriously suggesting I'm imagining things so I won't have to feel guilty? I'm not like that."

"Uh." He looked down at her hand. "No, I take that back."

She let go. "Sorry."

"Man, wouldn't want to face *you* down in a dark alley!"

"I may be upset, but I know what I saw."

"Okay, I hear you."

"Don't you even care that this girl is dead?"

"Of course I care. Jasmine was a civilian, even if she went with that animal Slice. She wasn't a bad kid, and she was actually a decent mother."

"Mother? You knew about her baby?" She looked at him sharply.

"Oh," he said, startled, "yeah."

"You knew she had a baby with Slice?"

"Yeah." He shrugged. "Guess I heard that at some point."

"You heard it *when*? Why didn't you say so when I told you about that tape last night? You acted like you didn't even believe she was Slice's girlfriend!" She took a step backward, hands clenching. "What the *hell* is going on?"

"Whoa, calm down, okay? Let's get my car, and then I'll explain."

"How are you gonna explain *that*? I feel like you lied to me, Dan. You better not've, because you're the only person in my life I trust right now."

As she said that, she realized how true it was. The thought scared her as much as anything else that had happened recently.

He took a step closer, looking down at her with earnest blue eyes. He had such an honest face. Such a handsome, all-American, innocent face. Could he be lying with a face like that?

"Melanie, please. Don't be upset. I promise, I want to catch this guy every bit as bad as you do, okay?"

"Then why cover up the fact that Jasmine and Slice had a baby together?"

"I was protecting a source."

"You were *protecting a source,* so you lied to me?"

"Hey, I didn't lie, all right? Maybe I didn't give up every last detail, but that's a big difference."

She said nothing, shaking her head incredulously.

"You gotta understand," he said, "I have my own priorities and obligations. Every agent does. But we're still on the same team."

"Oh, gee, glad to hear it."

"That's right! Never doubt it either. You're upsetting me, you know."

"*I'm* upsetting *you*!"

"That's right!"

He looked away, seemingly stung. She had a powerful urge to reach out and touch him. But she kept her hands at her sides. Dan obviously had his own agenda, and she had no idea what it was. Maybe this whole thing was a con, start to finish—his admiration, the way he looked at her. She was surprised how much that idea hurt. But it would serve her right, for being weak. She'd known the instant they met that she found him attractive. She knew how vulnerable she was, how devastated by Steve's affair, and yet she'd let her guard down. It wasn't smart. She had to stop. She'd fight it harder. Keep her eyes open. Remind herself not to trust him, not to like him too much.

Dan looked back at her. "I'm only this upset because I care what you think."

Can it, she wanted to say. With everything I've been through, I'm sharp enough to see through *your* bullshit.

"Dan, please," she said instead. "Can we focus on Jasmine right now?"

"Sure. Of course." His eyes were wary, as if he expected her to say something else to hurt him.

"Do you have an address for her?" she asked. "We need to notify the next of kin."

"Us? That's not our job. Somebody from the ME's office—"

"We're doing it," she said flatly.

He looked at her and saw how much it mattered.

"Okay, yeah. I know where she lived. Come on, my car's down in the garage."

OF COURSE JASMINE lived in Bushwick. Dan seemed to know his way around, so Melanie restrained herself from giving him directions. She knew if he went the most direct route, he'd take her old street, drive by the house she grew up in. She planned to keep quiet about it.

She was looking out the window, and, bam, there it was. It'd been years since she'd seen it. The attached brick house looked exactly the same. Maybe a little smaller, but the passage of time played tricks like that. The unisex hair salon that had replaced her father's furniture store on the ground floor was still there. Through the plate glass, she caught a glimpse of Inez, the owner, sitting in a chair smoking. She looked the same. Heavy, with a big mole on her lip. There were no customers. Amazing how these small businesses could survive year after year on practically no income. Her father's store had been like that, hanging on, a fixture in the neighborhood, just surviving. Until, one day, it didn't. *The banners were in English and Spanish. CASH AND CARRY. NAME YOUR PRICE. At the end of the day, as the Salvation Army truck drove off with what was left, Uncle Freddy handed her mother a pile of cash. "But where will Papi work when he comes back?" Melanie asked desperately. Her mother just looked at her, then walked into the house.*

"You okay?" Dan asked, glancing at her with concern.

"Sure."

"I'm really sorry about Jasmine. First Rosario, then her. That's a lot in two days."

"Yeah."

She had no interest in explaining herself. She watched the familiar blocks roll by until they got to Jasmine's street.

The apartment was what she expected—a third-floor walk-up with peeling paint and the smell of urine in the hallway, but otherwise all right. Could've been a lot worse. Standing on the landing, she heard a small child crying inside. She looked at Dan grimly, then pushed the buzzer.

A woman opened the door a crack and peeked out, keeping the chain on. She was short and plump, with dark hair permed into kinky curls, but she had Jasmine's eyes.

"Yeah, who you?" A dark-eyed toddler clambered about the woman's legs, sniffling. She reminded Melanie of Maya. The woman shoved the child back from the door.

"My name is Melanie Vargas. I'm looking for Jasmine Cruz's family."

"The DCYS been here last week already. Why again?"

"No, I'm not from Children's Services, ma'am."

"Oh. You look like the social."

"No. Are you related to Miss Cruz? I'm afraid I have some bad news." Melanie asked.

"I'm her mother."

"May we come in? I'm here with my colleague, Special Agent O'Reilly."

The woman unchained the door and stepped back. Melanie entered the small foyer. It was bare of furniture, decorated with an enormous framed print of the Virgin Mary. The living room beyond was dominated by a large television playing a Spanish-language soap, which faced a battered old sofa. The little girl toddled over and plopped down on her diapered behind in front of the TV. She picked up a plastic bottle filled with apple juice from the floor, put it into her mouth, and proceeded to ignore them.

Jasmine's mother stared at Melanie with wide eyes. The expression on her face was awful to see. She knew what was coming.

"Mrs. Cruz—"

"Yolanda. Call me Yolanda."

"Yolanda, I'm so sorry, but your daughter was killed—"

"*¡Ay, Dios mío!*" Jasmine's mother cried, rocking back and forth and keening. "*¡Dios mío, Dios mío! ¡Mi hija preciosa!*"

As Jasmine's mother sobbed, Melanie patted her ineffectually. She felt so helpless. There was nothing she could do for this woman, so why had she insisted on coming? To see for herself, to bear witness to her grief? As if she needed any more motivation to find the killer, with her background. As if she didn't fully understand the consequences of leaving someone like Slice on the street. She understood better than anybody, so well that she had no words now. Dan took control of the situation.

"Let me help you, ma'am," he said gently, and led the grief-stricken woman to the sofa. Melanie fetched a glass of water and a roll of paper towels from the tiny kitchen.

"There somebody who can come stay with you?" Dan asked.

Mrs. Cruz sobbed into the paper towel Melanie handed her.

"Downstairs," she choked out, "my neighbor, Carmen."

"What's her number?" Dan asked, pulling out his cell phone.

"No, she don't got no telephone. Just go downstairs."

Dan nodded to Melanie, then walked out the door. Melanie sat beside Mrs. Cruz on the sofa and put her arm around her shaking shoulders. The woman looked up, her face streaked black with tears and mascara.

"Where is she? I want to see her! I want to go to her!"

Melanie explained the procedure for identifying and claiming Jasmine's body. Mrs. Cruz resumed crying loudly.

"It was him, wasn't it?" she asked, between sobs. "Junior? I tell Jasmine, that one is gonna kill you someday. But she don't listen. *¡Ay, de mí!*"

"You mean Slice? Yes." Melanie took a business card from her wallet and held it out. "Look, if he comes by, or if you see him, act like you don't know, okay? But then call me. Here's my number. Will you do that?"

"Yeah, sure. I call you," she said, taking the card and examining it through her tears. "Prosecutor?"

"I'm investigating Slice for a murder. I think your daughter knew something about it, and that's why he went after her today. So you'll call me if you see him?"

"Yes, believe me, I wanna get that bastard."

"Good. Thank you."

Dan returned with a thin middle-aged woman, who wore a denim skirt, white athletic socks, and plastic sandals.

"*¡Ay, Yolanda, qué terrible!*" she shouted, and ran into Mrs. Cruz's arms. The two sat sobbing together on the sofa. Dan and Melanie left quietly, pulling the door shut behind them.

In the car neither of them wanted to talk about what they'd just witnessed.

"What's our next move?" Melanie asked, pushing the images from the apartment out of her mind.

"I have Slice's description out to the PD and all the federal agencies. Plus, I'm shaking down every snitch in Brooklyn."

"All good, solid police tactics, but just not fast enough. What's to stop him from striking again while you're doing all that? The city is so big. There are so many places for him to hide. And we don't have enough resources to follow up every lead."

"Those are the constraints we have to work with. None of that's gonna get better anytime soon."

"We've been saying all along he'll probably hit Amanda Benson next. So I vote we set up on her room and don't move till we get him. I'm not leaving that animal out on the street to kill again."

2 7

___

When it came to anticipating where Slice would strike next, Amanda Benson was the obvious choice. The only choice, in fact. Anybody else they could think of who he might go after was already dead. Except Melanie, of course, but she tried not to think about that.

Dan dropped Melanie at the hospital entrance and went to park the car. Riding up in the elevator, she realized she'd been here just about this time yesterday. Seemed like light-years ago.

Amanda's hospital room was situated approximately halfway down a long hallway. As Melanie turned the corner, it popped into view, its door unattended, gaping open. No crew-cut cop, no private guard, no Randall. Wasn't he supposed to be here checking on Amanda? Astonished, Melanie broke into a run, terrified she'd find yet another dead body. But when she reached the door, she saw Amanda lying in bed, alone and unharmed, sleeping peacefully as a soap opera played with no volume on the television set affixed to the wall.

The open door, the missing guard, the vulnerable, sleeping girl. Melanie's scalp prickled with fear, and she turned uneasily to look over her shoulder. Was somebody else using Amanda as bait to lure Slice? Or was she—Melanie—the target? Because this sure felt like a trap, and here she was, standing inside it, right in the bull's-eye. She pulled out her cell phone and dialed Dan's pager with trembling fingers, putting in all sevens. Let him come as fast as he possibly could. She had a bad feeling about this. She found a buzzer attached by a cord to Amanda's hospital bed and pressed it repeatedly, hoping she'd attract somebody's attention. She needed reinforcements. A nurse, an orderly—anybody who would improve the odds and make an attack less likely.

The buzzing noise roused Amanda. Her eyelids fluttered open, revealing eyes bleary and bloodshot, but a startling green against her pale waif's face. When she saw Melanie, she floundered against her pillow, struggling to sit up.

"Are you the nurse?" she asked, sounding disoriented, even frightened.

"No, I'm a prosecutor. Melanie Vargas. I'm working with the police to catch the people who hurt you. How are you, Amanda? I've been worried about you." She kept her voice calm so she wouldn't alarm the girl further.

Amanda's eyes darted around the room anxiously. "Where's my mom?" she asked.

"Nobody was here when I came in a minute ago. Let me help you with the bed," Melanie said. She played with the electronic controls on the side panel and raised Amanda to a sitting position.

"Thanks," Amanda said thickly. "Painkillers. You know, I'm so . . . uncoordinated." She gestured vaguely with her unbandaged left hand.

"What happened to your bodyguard?" Melanie asked.

"That guy? I don't know. He was skeevy, though. I'm glad he's gone."

"It worries me that you're left unattended like this, Amanda."

Amanda looked confused. "Do you have a cigarette?" she asked.

"A cigarette? No, sorry."

"It might help me, like, wake up. Clear my head."

"I honestly don't have one. I don't smoke."

"Oh."

"So your mother was supposed to be here, but she left?" Melanie asked.

"I guess so." Amanda shrugged feebly, but she was obviously upset.

"I'm sure she never would have left unless something really important came up. She was so protective of you when I was here yesterday."

Melanie looked toward the door again. She was beginning to wonder why Dan was taking so long, and why the hospital staff hadn't responded to her buzzing.

"My mom tried to protect me?" Amanda asked, eyes wide and vulnerable. She was still just a kid, a kid going through a terrible ordeal.

"Oh, yes. She wouldn't even let me near you to talk about . . . about what happened." Melanie glanced involuntarily at Amanda's right hand, swathed in bandages.

"Oh, you mean when she wouldn't let you interview me and stuff?"

"Yes."

"Yeah, I heard that. I was kind of, like, half asleep."

"I apologize for being so aggressive with your mother."

Amanda flushed, shaking her head bitterly. "Don't apologize to me about *her*," she said with sudden vehemence. "My mom's a total witch. I hate her guts."

"Oh, don't say that, Amanda. I know you're upset, but I'm sure she had a very good reason for leaving."

"It's not about that. You have no idea. She doesn't care about me at all. First she ships me off to the loony bin to get rid of me, then she abandons me here when I'm, like, in majorly bad shape." Amanda's voice cracked. Tears welled up in her eyes and brimmed over. Melanie handed her a tissue from the box on the nightstand. Amanda mopped at her tears, but they kept coming and coming, rolling swiftly down her cheeks. This poor girl was a mess. Who could blame her?

"I'm sure your mother loves you very much, sweetie," Melanie said gently.

"No, she *doesn't*!" Amanda insisted, breaking into sobs. "You're not *listening*. Only my dad loved me, and now he's dead. I'll never see him again. Do you have a fucking clue what that's like?"

"Yes," Melanie said, hearing echoes of another time. "Yes, I do." *"The bullet is lodged in the right frontal lobe,"* she heard the doctor tell her mother. *"If we try to operate, we risk destroying sensitive speech centers." "Will he ever walk again?" "The paralysis on the left side may resolve with time. But I have to be frank, Mrs. Vargas. It could take years."*

Melanie moved closer and began to stroke Amanda's shoulder. "I hate my mom," Amanda choked out. "She had my dad killed, I know it!"

"Amanda, you're distraught, and you're on painkillers. You don't know what you're saying. Gang members killed your father. It had nothing to do with your mother."

"You're wrong. Why do you think she won't let you talk to me? It has nothing to do with protecting me. She's afraid I'll blab."

"What the *fuck* do you think you're doing? Get away from her!"

Melanie spun around. A large man in a rumpled suit loomed in the doorway. She hadn't heard him come in, so intent was she on Amanda's words. He advanced toward her, his features contorted with fury, tiny red veins popping out on his nose and cheeks. The smell of alcohol rolled off him in waves, filling the room.

"I'm from the U.S. Attorney's Office. This is official business. Who are *you*?"

"I'm her bodyguard, and I don't give a shit if you're the queen of England, lady. Nobody talks to her without my permission. Now, get outta here!" He closed the gap between them and grabbed Melanie's arm. Amanda cowered in her bed.

"Get your hands off me, or I'll have you arrested for interfering with a federal officer!" Melanie shouted, trying to twist out of his grasp. His fingers closed tight as a vise, pulling her toward the door.

"Yeah, just try it and see how far you get. I got friends in high places."

"Get your hands off her, Flanagan!" Dan yelled, charging into the room.

"Fuck off, O'Reilly. This is my gig."

"I *said* let her go!" Dan lunged for him and shoved him hard, pinning him against the wall next to Amanda's bed. Melanie leaped out of the way, rubbing her throbbing arm. The two men were about the same size, but Dan was much stronger. As Flanagan struggled, Dan slammed him back against the wall.

"Touch her again and I'll fucking kill you," Dan said, his voice shaking, holding Flanagan immobile until he stopped thrashing and went limp in Dan's grasp.

"All right! Jesus Christ, I wasn't gonna hurt her or nothing. I asked her to leave, and she wouldn't listen. Let me go already—I won't touch her." After a second, Dan released him and backed away, saying nothing, breathing hard.

Flanagan brushed off his jacket angrily. "You're lucky I didn't go for my gun," he said.

"*You* carry? That just shows how fucked up our system is," Dan said.

Flanagan jerked his head toward Melanie. "What is she, your girl-friend? Nice tits, but a she's a snotty little bitch."

Dan made a move toward Flanagan, but Melanie grabbed his arm. "It's okay," she told him. "It doesn't matter."

"You're right. Who cares what this scumbag says? He was a disgrace to the badge until they booted him, and now he's hanging around like some disease," Dan said.

"A self-righteous prick just like your old man, Danny Boy," Flanagan spat.

"Please, enough already!" Melanie said. "Let's start over, okay? Let's just pretend this never happened so we can get something accomplished here. Mr. Flanagan, is it? Melanie Vargas, U.S. Attorney's Office. So now that you know who I am, I'm sure you won't object if I speak with Miss Benson."

"Fucking right, I object! I work for Nell Benson, and she told me no-body talks to her daughter without going through her first. That's why I was hired."

"Really? I thought you were hired to protect Amanda from her father's killers, not to obstruct a federal investigation," Melanie said.

"Show me a subpoena, lady. Then we can do business."

That stopped Melanie cold. She hadn't planned to come here, so she hadn't brought a subpoena with her. There was no way she could force Flanagan to let her speak to Amanda without one. As an ex-cop, he knew that.

"I hoped we could resolve this without resorting to a subpoena," she said coolly.

"Talk to my boss. If she says it's okay, it's fine by me."

"Where is she?"

"Your guess is as good as mine."

"She left her daughter all alone here, without giving you so much as a phone number?" Melanie didn't believe him for a minute. He could get in touch with Nell if he wanted to.

"What am I, Child Welfare? She hired me to sit here, I sit here. I don't question how she treats her kid."

"Amanda, how can I reach your mother?" Melanie asked, turning to the girl.

"Don't answer that!" Flanagan shouted, flushing an even deeper shade of crimson. He turned to Melanie. "You don't listen too good. I said nobody talks to her. Now get out, the botha youse. You got no subpoena, you got no right to be here, and I'm instructing you to leave. You don't listen, I'm going straight to Mrs. Benson. Then, I can promise you, you won't get within a hundred miles of this girl ever again."

"Mr. Flanagan, please," Melanie said, "can't we work this out? I understand you're trying to do your job and follow Mrs. Benson's wishes. If we could just get in touch with Mrs. Benson and—"

"*Mrs. Benson* doesn't want to get in touch. *Mrs. Benson* just wants you to stop harassing her daughter and get your snotty little ass out of here."

"I'll get a subpoena and be back here in an hour. Let's see how happy Nell Benson is with you then."

"Fine!" Flanagan said.

"Fine!" Melanie shot back. Then, having painted herself into a corner, she had no choice but to march defiantly out of the room, leaving Dan to follow.

"YOU'RE SOME HELLCAT!" Dan said, smiling, as he caught up with her. "I'm very impressed."

"Oh, come on, I completely screwed that up. I lost my temper when I should've just swallowed my pride and backed down, so we could get what we needed."

"And let that drunken bum Bill Flanagan walk all over you? I wouldn't stand for it."

"You know him?"

"My dad was the lieutenant who took away his gun."

"No kidding, your father's a cop?"

"He was. He's retired now. I'm from cops on both sides. My father and grandfather were on the job, a bunch of uncles on my mother's side, some cousins. Everyone else is a rubberman."

"Rubberman?"

"Fireman. Fire*fighter* I guess is what you say now."

"Wow. You must have felt so solid growing up with all that behind you," Melanie said wistfully. How cozy, to come from a nice middle-class background, and just *stay* there. Unlike Melanie, who'd come up so far in the world that she didn't fit in her own life.

"I guess. I liked that I could walk into any precinct in the city as a kid and find somebody to buy me a Coke anyway."

"Speaking of, I could sure use one right about now. Do you have a dollar? Because I only have a twenty," Melanie said as they walked past the soda machine.

Dan dug into the pocket of his khaki pants, pulling out two crumpled dollar bills. He smoothed them between his fingers and handed them to her.

"Here. Get me one, too, wouldja?" he said.

"Is this all the money you have?"

He grinned sheepishly. "At the moment, but I get paid Friday."

"It's only Wednesday."

"Yeah, but you're thirsty now."

She shook her head and gave the bills back to him. He walked right over and fed them into the soda machine. "Regular or diet?" he asked, looking over his shoulder.

"Diet."

Two sodas plunked out. Dan came back and pressed an ice-cold can into her hand.

"You shouldn't walk around this town with no money in your pocket, you know," she said.

"What do I need money for? I got a gun."

She smiled, popping the top and taking a sip, aware that he was watching her.

"I'll never be a rich man, but whatever I have is yours, sweetheart," he said.

"What is that, a marriage proposal?"

"Is it too soon?" he asked with an easy smile, looking down into her eyes.

"No, it's too late." She waved her left hand at him. She'd forgotten she wasn't wearing her rings. The empty space on her finger was conspicuous because of the tan line.

"Huh," she said involuntarily.

Dan stared at her hand and then back at her face. He looked like he'd just been shot through with a jolt of electricity.

"Did you . . . ?" he began.

"Guess I was in a rush this morning," she said quickly.

"Oh." He nodded slowly, not even trying to hide his disappointment. He was standing close enough that she felt the heat of his skin, but he didn't move away. She noticed that her knees were trembling. She sighed and went to sit in one of the orange plastic chairs next to the soda machine. He followed and sat down beside her.

"I'm sorry. Am I out of line?" he asked.

"No, whatever, we're just joking around. But let's talk about work, okay?"

"Okay."

They both sipped their sodas for a moment.

"Where do you think Randall went?" she asked after a pause.

"Good question. He was supposed to be here, wasn't he? I'll beep him." He pulled out his cell phone and dialed but got no immediate response. "Sometimes it takes him a while to answer a page."

"I can't believe I got us kicked out of there," she said, shaking her head.

"It wasn't your fault. I know that guy from way back, and he's a total prick. Plus, it sounds like Nell Benson told him to keep us away."

"Oh, yeah, that reminds me. You know what Amanda told me before Flanagan showed up?"

"What?"

"She thinks her mother had her father killed."

"What, for cheating on her?"

"It wouldn't be the first time," Melanie said. Not like she hadn't thought about it herself with Steve.

"Yeah, but it doesn't add up with gangbangers whacking Benson. How many socialites you know could contract a hit with the Blades?"

"True. Good point."

"Hey, speaking of Benson cheating, you ever watch the video you pinched from that girl's house?" he asked.

"I wouldn't dream of doing that without you."

"You got the wrong guy, sweetheart. It's Randall who likes dirty movies. The brothers trained me good. They used to smack the shit out of us with a ruler if they caught us looking out the windows at girls."

"Oh, so Catholic school turned you off sex?"

"No, not at all. Sex is the greatest thing in life. But only when there's true love."

He looked at her intently, and this time she looked back, trying to figure out if he was for real. She was half falling for him and half convinced he was manipulating her.

"You're full of shit," she said finally.

"Am not. I'm serious."

"You expect me to believe you never slept with a woman you weren't in love with?"

"No, I'm not saying that. I mean, I'm human. But if I did, I felt really bad about it."

"Can we get back to talking about work, please? I can't even remember where we were, the way you're distracting me."

"You were saying Amanda says Mrs. Benson had her husband whacked."

"Right. I'm thinking we should take a closer look at our victim," she said.

"Yeah, in all our spare time. Look, so the guy wasn't a saint. It's an angle, but your other idea was better. Setting up on her room, I mean."

"We're still doing that. Flanagan can kick us out of a private room, but he can't keep us out of the public hallways."

"Okay, so I'll go scout a nice observation post. Someplace I can see Amanda's door without being seen."

"And I'll go back to my office and get a subpoena so Flanagan has to let us talk to her."

"Sounds like a plan. Who knows, maybe our man Slice makes an appearance while you're gone, and I wrap the whole thing up before you even make it back here."

"That would be nice. Although I'd hate to miss the fireworks."

2 8

——

Randall Walker crossed the street, heading for the run-down bar in the middle of the next block. Its grimy windows, covered with iron bars, gave it a blank, vacant look in the blinding afternoon light.

As he stepped up onto the curb, he hesitated. He'd been walking fast, almost as though, if he moved quick enough, he wouldn't have time to think about what he was doing. But he *should* think. It wasn't too late yet. He could still jump off the runaway train. Not go into the bar. Just walk on by, like he was heading somewhere else, circle around back to his car and go on with his day. Just pretend things were okay, that this mess didn't apply to him.

His feet slowed to a stop before he even realized he was standing still. He got lost for a minute, remembering what it was like before he felt so twisted up in his gut. One mistake years ago, and it fucked up his whole life. But no way to go back and change things now. Nope, that was the problem with time—only moved in one direction.

He recollected himself and glanced around nervously, not wanting to be seen yet by the person he was here to meet. He was still thinking he might not go in. The alley between the bar and the next building was strewn with broken glass. He ducked into it for a minute. It reeked from bags of garbage piled high, fermenting in the hot sun. At the sound of his footsteps, a plump gray rat leaped out of the pile, bounded across the narrow alley, and disappeared. What the bejesus was he doing here? Randall asked himself.

He pulled out his cell phone and dialed, to remind himself.

"Hello?" his wife answered.

"Calling to check on you, baby."

"I'm doing fine. Don't you be worrying about me." There was a leaden, groggy quality to her voice that told him she'd taken more than her prescribed dose of antidepressants today.

"It's nice out," he said. "You ought to get out the house."

"Naw, they got an ozone alert on. I'm staying in the bedroom with the air-conditioning going."

"Go downstairs and visit with Della, then."

"It's too hot in her apartment. Besides, I'm tired of listening to her talk."

"No good sitting alone in the house, Betty."

"I'm doing just fine here, Randall. You go about your business now."

"At least get up out of bed. Cook me something good for dinner."

"Aw, come on. You don't even know whether you coming home for dinner tonight."

He laughed hollowly. "You too smart for me, girl."

"You got that right," she said, laughing. Her laugh sounded natural, raised his spirits a little. Only a little, though. She seemed worse to him as time went on, rather than better.

"Okay, I'ma check on you later, and you better be up out that bed, you hear?" he said.

"Mmm-hmm," she said lethargically, and hung up.

RANDALL HUNCHED HIS shoulders as he yanked open the door of the bar, so dark inside after the blazing sidewalk. The air-conditioning in the place was on the fritz, the stench of urine and beer nearly overpowering in the sultry interior. He kept his head down, not wanting to look around, not wanting to see where he was going and what he was about to do. Looking neither to the right nor to the left, he made a beeline for the booth in the back where his associate waited.

"You're late," the associate said, dragging on the last remnant of a cigarette and stubbing it out.

"Yeah, well, this isn't exactly a convenient time for me."

"Where's your partner?"

"Skip the small talk, all right? Let's get it over with."

The associate reached under the table to get something. Randall stiffened, his hand flying to the gun at his waistband. But the associate simply pulled out a thick white envelope and tossed it on the table. It landed in front of Randall with a resounding thwack.

"What the fuck is that?" Randall asked, his voice dangerous.

"What the fuck does it look like?"

"You're very much mistaken. I'm doing this because you're forcing me, not for money. I'm not like you. Don't think I am."

The associate took back the envelope, frowning.

"This 'honorable man' routine is getting stale, Randall. It's about money for you, just like it is for everybody else."

"My pension is something I'm entitled to! Twenty-five years on this fucking job. I earned every penny."

"Yeah, well, I know a few people who wouldn't see it that way if they knew what I know about you."

Randall stood up, livid. "You been holding that one mistake over my head for years. But, you know, I been thinking. You give me up, you give yourself up, too. Why should I even believe you would do it?"

The associate looked Randall in the eye, his expression cold and dead.

"Believe it, friend. That old shit ain't nothing to me now. I got a lot more serious business to worry about."

It was clear he meant it. Randall stood looking at him for a moment more, then sat down.

"Don't call me your friend," Randall said, but they both knew he'd given in.

"Whatever makes you happy."

"Like I said, I don't have all day."

"Well, then," the associate said, lighting another cigarette, "you better start talking."

2 9

In those moments when you have an impossible amount to do and too much on your mind, you have to put blinders on. Choose the most pressing task and perform it as if it is the only one. Block out emotion. Otherwise confusion and anxiety will overwhelm you and you will accomplish nothing. Melanie understood this as she sat down in her swivel chair and logged on to her computer. She was here to type a subpoena for Amanda Benson, period. She wouldn't go through the envelopes piling up in her in-box, wouldn't check her voice mail or e-mail or check in with her boss, wouldn't review the videocassette that was burning a hole in her handbag. She wouldn't think about Rosario or Jasmine or her disintegrating marriage. It wouldn't do much good if she fell apart, would it? Accomplish the task at hand, and get the hell out of here.

She pulled up the grand-jury subpoena macro and began typing information into the blank fields. She tried to keep her mind focused. But her message light was in her field of vision, blinking insistently. Finally she reached for the receiver. She'd multitask—play the messages on speakerphone while continuing to type.

The first message advised her that evidence she'd ordered had been sent out to her office. The second one was about a sentencing in another case she needed to postpone. But the third one—the third one was intriguing.

"You have a collect call from a correctional facility. Caller, state your name, please," said the automated operator's voice. Inmates weren't allowed to dial out directly from prison. Even though she'd heard that same message a thousand times—every time one of her cooperators called her from jail—the name of this caller was totally unexpected.

"Del-vis Di-az," he'd enunciated painstakingly.

Why was Delvis Diaz calling her? She hadn't been at her desk to accept the charges, so he got disconnected before he could explain. Did he want to confess? Unlikely. Cooperate and provide information against Slice? Possibly. Too bad she didn't have time to take a ride up there and find out. She finished typing the subpoena and sent it to print.

There were more messages, but before they could play, the other line rang. Could it be Delvis calling back? She dropped her voice mail and picked up right away.

"Melanie Vargas."

"It's me," Steve said.

"Oh. Hi."

"I left you four messages. Couldn't you tell how upset I am? I can't believe you haven't called me." He sounded distraught.

"I've been running around all day," she said hesitantly. "Really. I didn't even listen to my messages yet."

"You just leave your wedding ring for me to find, like a piece of trash, and then you don't call? That's so cold. Can you imagine what I've been going through?"

"Steve," she said, but then stopped, helpless. Even with all her agonizing about taking her rings off, somehow she hadn't grasped how huge a step it would be in *his* eyes. She felt terrible for the pain she'd caused. And yet maybe it would wake him up. Maybe he'd finally see he had to do better in this relationship, that she wouldn't stay with him otherwise.

"You just keep slipping further and further away," he cried, his voice breaking. "I don't know how to reach you. Tell me what to do, please. Because I don't want this, not for us, not for Maya."

"I don't want it either!" she said with sudden vehemence, the thought of Maya's chubby little face cutting her to the heart. She had to think of her daughter's future. As disgusted and outraged as she was with Steve, maybe she could get over it. But only if she believed he was sincere.

"Tell me what to do," he said. "Anything. You want to see a marriage counselor? I could arrange that. I already got the name of somebody good."

Her other line started ringing. If it was Delvis Diaz, she couldn't afford to miss him. He might give up and stop calling.

"Steve, can you hold on a second?" If she didn't pick up now, she'd lose the call.

"What? No—"

She put him on hold and picked up the other line. "Melanie Vargas."

"You have a collect call from a correctional facility. Caller, state your name, please," said the automated voice.

"Del-vis Di-az."

"Accept the charges," Melanie said eagerly. He was serious about this, whatever it was. "Hello, Delvis. Hold on for one minute, okay?"

"Yes, ma'am."

She switched back to Steve. "Listen, Steve, I have to take this, but your idea about the counselor is a good one. We should definitely do that."

"Uh, okay."

"So arrange it, okay? I have to take this other call."

"Melanie—"

"Bye!" She disconnected him. Amazing what leaving a couple of rings on the bedside table could do for the balance of power in a marriage. It felt good to be the boss for a change. And she felt a real glimmer of hope about Steve's attitude.

"Delvis?" she said. "What can I do for you?"

"Look, I gotta talk to you, ma'am."

"I'm all ears."

"I kinda don't wanna get into it over the phone, you know? It ain't too private over here. Can you come see me?"

She sighed. Was this a game? She'd been through this before with other inmates. Visits from a prosecutor—especially a female one—relieved the boredom of long days on the inside. She could spend weeks trying to drag information out of Delvis, only to find he'd never had any to give. She leaned over, plucked the subpoena out of the printer, and began proofreading it. It looked good.

"No, I can't visit you," she said, tapping her foot impatiently. "Not without more of an explanation. If you have something to tell me, let's hear it now."

"I got some information about the hit. Word I do, ma'am. Like, who be involved and why it went down. You need to come back to see me again real fast."

"Slice did the hit, am I right?"

"Not just him. Some other mu'fuckers, too."

"Okay, I'm listening."

"I can't give you names over the phone, but they gonna surprise you."

"It's not news to me that Slice killed Jed Benson. If that's all you have, I'll add you to my to-do list and get up to see you when I can. But it's a very long list."

She pulled an empty Redweld folder out of her bottom desk drawer, put the subpoena in it, and placed it on her lap. She picked up her handbag and placed it on top of the Redweld, ready to head for the door.

"Please, ma'am," he whispered. "I'd be jeopardizing myself here to say anything more."

She sighed in exasperation. *"Hablamos en español, entonces."*

"Nah, no good. I'm on the Spanish phone. All the mu'fuckers in line be, like, Colombian and Dominican and shit."

That made sense, given what she knew about the extreme self-segregation of prison life. Between the Aryans, the Latin Kings, and the Five Percenters, inmates kept to their own kind just to steer clear of trouble.

"Look, Delvis, you know the game. Risks you take get factored in at the end of the day when the judge gives you credit for cooperation. That's the best I can do."

"It ain't the credit I'm worried about. More peoples is gonna die if this shit don't stop."

Terrible images flooded her mind—Rosario's severed head, Jasmine's bent body.

"More people already have, Delvis," she said, furious. "So if you know something that can help me stop it, you better damn well spill it."

"Benson was dirty."

Melanie laid the Redweld and her handbag aside. "Dirty how?"

"That's what I can't be saying over the phone."

"You mentioned something during the interview about Slice setting you up. Did Benson know about that?"

"Yeah, you real warm, but it even bigger than that. Look, I say this shit over the phone, I'ma end up dead. Maybe you, too."

"Come on, Delvis, don't get all dramatic on me."

"Naw, I'm serious. That's why I'm risking it to call and warn you. You treat me like a human being, so I'm returning the favor. Peoples around you is dirty, Miss Vargas."

"Yeah, like who?"

"Like the ones you brang to see me."

Dan and Randall?

"Delvis, I—"

"Shit. Gotta go."

"What?"

"I'll call you back."

"No! Wait!"

He hung up.

HOW LONG COULD she sit around waiting for a phone call? Twenty minutes had passed, and Delvis hadn't called back. She couldn't work, couldn't think. Was it possible that Dan and Randall were mixed up in something dirty? Every fiber of her being screamed no. They were rock solid, people you could trust with your life. Then again, she trusted her husband, and look what *he* did. People could fool you. She needed to hear the rest of Delvis's information to evaluate it properly. But you couldn't call an inmate on the telephone. Either he called back or she'd have to drive all the way to Otisville to interview him.

Maurice Dawson, the custodian, knocked on her door, interrupting her chaotic thoughts.

"Hey, Melanie, you ask for a VCR? Guys in Audiovisual sent this up."

He wheeled a videocassette player on a metal cart through her door.

"Yeah, thanks," she replied. "Just put it there by the bookshelf."

She made a deal with herself. She'd review the videotape. If Delvis hadn't called back by the time she finished, she'd go to the hospital and find Dan. Maybe if she looked him in the eye, she'd know the truth. Feeling calmer, she took the tape from her bag and slid it into the VCR.

A black-and-white picture of Sarah's bed appeared, neatly made this time and piled with cushions. A date-and-time stamp flashed on, then disappeared. The video had been shot in the middle of the afternoon on the day of Jed Benson's murder. Interesting timing anyway. No people on screen yet, but Melanie heard voices in the background. She knelt down and adjusted the volume.

"*. . . so much stress,*" Sarah was saying.

"*It'll all work out, but that's why I need a little fun. Did you get the ecstasy?*"

The man's voice sounded unfamiliar. Not Jed Benson. But they were still off-screen, so Melanie couldn't be sure.

"*Not so fast, dodo. You wanna fuck, I need some reassurance first, or I can't relax.*"

"*I told you, I have a friend at the SEC. I slipped him some stuff I dug up on Jed. He's looking into it.*"

"*What kind of stuff?*"

"*You don't need to know. Shit, didn't I say white panties under the skirt?*"

Sarah walked into camera range and sat down on the bed. She had on a complete schoolgirl getup—short plaid kilt, white cotton blouse, buckle shoes over white ankle socks, hair up in pigtails. She leaned back against the pillows, letting her legs fall open provocatively.

"*Give it a whirl with these slutty ones. Pretend I'm, like, the corrupt little vixen,*" Sarah said.

A man came into view and walked over to the bed, his back to the camera. He was wearing a dress shirt and suit pants. He sat down and thrust his hand up Sara's skirt, his face visible in profile. It was not Jed Benson. He appeared to be in his mid-sixties, large, hulking, nearly bald, with heavy-rimmed eyeglasses. Sarah writhed under his touch, then pulled away, closing her legs.

"*Come on, I can tell you want it,*" the man said, lifting his fingers to his nose. "*You're all wet.*"

"*Would you just explain to me how your friend is gonna keep the spotlight off what we did on Securilex?*"

"*He already opened a file on Jed, okay? So if and when the shit hits the fan, which hopefully it won't, Jed looks good for it. Satisfied?*"

"*I guess.*"

"*Jesus, now you got me all upset. Where the fuck are the pills? I need one, or I won't be able to get it up.*"

Sarah sighed, stood up, and walked out of camera range. The man turned, looking directly into the camera. Melanie punched the "pause" button, freezing his face on the screen. She studied it. Hmm, vaguely familiar, but she couldn't say from where. Had she seen him at the Reed firm? He must work there, right? She pushed "play."

Sarah returned with a glass of water in one hand. She extended the other hand, palm up. The man plucked a pill from it and tossed it into his mouth, washing it down with a swig of water.

"*You, too,*" he ordered.

Sarah swallowed the other pill. They sat there for a few minutes. He began to fondle her breasts through her shirt.

"*Suck me first,*" he said, and Sarah got down on her knees and unzipped his fly. He moaned.

Not likely to be much meaningful dialogue for a while, Melanie thought. She hit "fast forward" and watched them have speeded-up sex, wrinkling her nose. Jesus, whoever this guy was, he was kinky. And *ugly*! Certainly gave one a different perspective on Miss Sarah van der Vere. Any woman who spent her spare time gratifying this ape must be deeply twisted. Melanie fast-forwarded, looking for some postcoital conversation.

She hit "stop" and then "play" again at what looked to be the end of the festivities. The man lay on his back, spent as a beached whale, saying nothing. Sarah got up, naked, and disappeared in the direction of the bathroom. Time passed. Out of camera range, a cell phone rang, and the man hauled himself out of bed to answer it. Melanie shielded her eyes as his large, hairy body filled the screen.

"*Yeah?*" she heard him answer, off-camera now. "*Oh, hey, Mary . . . right, right . . . Is the general counsel gonna be on the call? Because if not, you can handle it yourself . . . Okay, then set it up for four o'clock, and we'll do it in my office. And make sure you have Word Processing redline the last draft so we can work from it . . . Appreciate it. Bye.*"

Mary. *Hale?* Had to be. So who would speak to the eminent Mary that way, like he was her boss? Only Dolan Reed, the managing partner himself, right? Sarah had called the man "dodo" at one point. Dodo? Short for Dolan? Could be—these WASPs had the queerest nicknames. And if the man looked slightly familiar, come to think of it, he resembled the portrait in the reception area, except fatter and balder.

Something occurred to her. She pulled her notebook from her bag and found where she'd jotted down that cell-phone number she'd gotten from Sarah's caller ID. She dialed it.

"Yeah, hello?" The voice was the same as that of the man on the videotape.

"Dolan Reed?"

"Speaking. Who's this?"

"I'm calling from Verizon with regard to your cell plan, sir."

"Oh, for Chrissakes. I'm in the middle of a meeting. Never call this number again!" He hung up.

Well, well. So that was Dolan Reed petting the kitty with Sarah on the tape. And it sounded as if something suspicious was going on at the Reed firm, having to do with a company called Securilex. Melanie remembered that name's being mentioned in the elevator yesterday. Another lawyer had gotten on and asked Sarah if she was still buried in the Securilex transaction. So Securilex must be a client of the Reed firm.

Something was crooked on the Securilex deal, and Sarah van der Vere was nervous about getting caught. Dolan Reed was involved, too, and was trying to frame Jed Benson as the fall guy. Dolan Reed and Sarah were having an affair, which Sarah was secretly taping. Sarah and Jed Benson were also having an affair. Wow, the girl got around. And all in all, sinister enough circumstances to have gotten Jed Benson killed.

Jed Benson killed over a dirty business deal involving the Reed firm. Yes. She liked it. She definitely liked it. The thing she liked most about it was, it had nothing to do with anybody she was close to. If Jed had been killed over a business deal gone bad, then Delvis Diaz was full of hot air when he'd accused Dan and Randall of being dirty. After all, what possible connection could there be between Dan and Randall on the one hand and the tony firm of Reed, Reed and Watson on the other? The very thought was ludicrous.

MELANIE UNPLUGGED THE VCR and locked the videocassette in her desk drawer. Time to get back to the hospital and meet up with Dan. She might have new evidence on motive and a new lead on who might've hired Slice, but that vermin was still out on the street.

As Melanie picked up her bag to leave, Bernadette barged into her office.

"Melanie Vargas! I must have been on drugs when I assigned you to this case!" Bernadette cried, striding up to Melanie's desk. "I told you to go easy on the Bensons. Romulado called and said Amanda Benson's bodyguard had to physically eject you from her room. Did you think I wouldn't find out?"

"Bern—"

"You're making me look bad, Melanie, and I don't stand for that. If there's one thing I expect, it's obedience to a direct order. If you can't listen—"

"Bernadette, wait, calm down. Bill Flanagan isn't telling the whole story."

Bernadette stopped, mouth half open. "Bill Flanagan? What's he got to do with this?"

"He's Amanda's bodyguard. And he's misinforming Lieutenant Ramirez about what happened."

"Oh, Romulado never said it was Bill Flanagan."

"Yes."

"Huh." Bernadette sat down in a guest chair. "Well. That's a different story, then. I can't believe Romulado didn't tell me that. God, I hate it when people give me incomplete facts!"

"You know Flanagan?"

"Wild Bill? Sure, everyone from my generation in the office knows him. He's famous. Infamous, I should say. I had an indictment dismissed once in the middle of a drug trial because he stole the cocaine from the vault. We couldn't convict without the drugs, so the dealer walked. The only time I ever lost a case."

"Is that when he got kicked off the force?" Melanie asked.

"No, that was something else entirely. In my case they couldn't prove it, but everybody knew it was him anyway."

"I think he's an alcoholic."

"Oh, definitely! The man has an IV drip of booze going into his body day and night. I'm surprised he could get through a job interview without drinking. How do you think Nell Benson hooked up with a degenerate like that?"

"I have no idea."

"I hope Romulado didn't recommend him. He always feels sorry for those boozer types when they're down and out. I mean, buy the guy a hot meal or something—don't give him a security job. Hey, you don't think Flanagan's carrying a gun, do you?"

"Yes, I know for a fact he is. He almost pulled it on Dan."

"Jesus! Can you imagine? Flanagan shoots a federal agent, and it comes out that Romulado got him the job? Oh, God, that better not be how it happened." She dropped her head into her hands momentarily and kneaded her eyes with her fingers.

It had to be tough for someone like Bernadette to be with a guy who was sort of a fuckup, Melanie thought. Not Bernadette's style, but Rommie's dark good looks had obviously won out over her better judgment. *Amor* messed you up like that.

Bernadette looked up at Melanie.

"You don't think Romulado arranged it, do you?" she asked again.

"Gee, I don't know, Bern. But it's not too late to do something about it. Speak to Nell Benson. Maybe she'd listen to you. Amanda's safety can't be left to that guy."

"You're right."

"You know, I only went to the hospital because of this incident with Slice. To warn Amanda, make sure she was safe. When I got there, her door was wide open. Flanagan was nowhere in sight. I waited at least ten minutes before he returned. She was completely vulnerable to attack during that time."

"Yes, I heard about what happened at the Auto Show. Let me ask you, did O'Reilly agree it was Slice chasing this Jasmine Cruz?" Bernadette asked skeptically.

"Dan wasn't even there when it happened. I saw the whole thing, and *I'm* convinced it was him. That's why I'm determined to protect Amanda, don't you see? First Rosario Sangrador, then Jasmine Cruz. This guy is on a witness-killing spree."

Bernadette harrumphed. "That's an exaggeration. One dead witness does not a spree make. Rosario, I accept. She was an eyewitness, about to testify. But Jasmine was Slice's baby's mother. It was probably a domestic dispute. Besides, even if it *was* Slice at the Auto Show, he didn't push her. She jumped."

"She *fell*. He chased her out there, and she fell. She had a little girl. She never would've jumped." Melanie flushed with indignation on Jasmine's behalf.

"You can't know that. Anyway, you shouldn't even have been *at* the Auto Show. Not only did it waste time, but it got you all tangled up in this girl's death. Can't you focus on basic leads to track Slice down? You need to keep your eye on the ball."

Melanie choked back her anger. She needed Bernadette on her side.

"Okay, whatever. But it's still reasonable to think Amanda is in jeopardy, isn't it? She is an eyewitness. Won't you speak to Nell Benson?"

"I don't know, Melanie. Romulado has really begged me to leave the Bensons alone right now."

"Bern, not for nothing, but what is he doing in the middle of all this? First he hires Flanagan, then he criticizes me for interviewing Amanda. Now that Amanda is able to talk, she should be interviewed. Period. I know you agree. You're too good an investigator not to."

Watching the play of emotions across Bernadette's face, Melanie actually felt sorry for her. She wished she could ask Bernadette openly whether Rommie was meddling in the case in other ways and, if so, why Bernadette was allowing it. But she didn't have that kind of relationship with her boss.

Bernadette stood up abruptly. "Here's the deal: I'll speak to Romulado about the Amanda Benson situation. He can talk to Nell. Maybe we can make some progress that way. But in the meantime you need to do your legwork. Amanda is hardly your only avenue of inquiry. Look at this desk! Didn't I tell you to clear it off?"

"Yes, but—"

"No buts! I say clear it off, you clear it off. God knows, you could have Slice's address sitting here in a subpoena response, and you wouldn't even know it." Bernadette looked at her watch. "It's almost five now. You have half an hour. Then you're coming with me to a retirement dinner I have to attend. What do you think of this suit, by the way? Too matronly?"

Bernadette wore a cherry red suit with a short-sleeved jacket, bright gold buttons, and a skintight skirt.

"Not at all. But—"

"Normally I like to show a bit of cleavage for evening. If you've got it, flaunt it, I always say. But I needed something I could wear to that meeting in D.C. this morning."

"It's very sexy," Melanie said. Inappropriate, but sexy, she thought.

"You think so? Good." Bernadette looked down at herself, smoothing her skirt.

"But how can I go to a retirement dinner when I have so much work—"

"Look, Romulado will be there. Maybe we can work something out on the Amanda Benson front. Half an hour, be there or be square," she said, walking out the door, giving Melanie no chance to protest further.

3 0

—

He dialed and listened to the phone ring at the other end, tapping his fingers.

"FCI-Otisville. How may I direct your call?"

"Extension 6239."

"One moment, please."

He lit a cigarette while he waited.

"Inmate Records, Grasso speaking."

"Sal. Hey, brother, how's the Harley?"

"Oh, it's you. What's up?"

"You got that stuff we talked about?"

"You still at that same number?"

"Yup."

"Call you back in ten minutes from another phone."

HIS PHONE RANG about an hour later.

"Hello?"

"It's me," Grasso said.

"That wasn't no ten minutes, pal."

"Hey, I'm doing you a fucking favor here!"

"Not like you're not getting paid."

"With what you're paying me, I'm not risking my job, understand? Now, you want it or not?"

"Depends. Is it anything good? I'm not interested in hearing Diaz jack off for an hour while he talks to some bimbo."

"Hey, don't knock it till you try it. You wouldn't believe some of the shit I hear. Girls moaning and shit, talking dirty. Real graphic. It's like calling a 900 number, except free."

"Ah, you're all fucking perverts up there."

"Okay, so how'm I gonna get the disk to you? I ain't e-mailing it 'cause that leaves a trail."

"Like I said, what is it first?"

"Nah, it's real good. Diaz called a female prosecutor, I forget her name—"

"Melanie Vargas?"

"Yeah, that's it. Says he got some hot information about a murder, and she better come visit right away. But get this: 'The people around you are dirty,' he says, 'so watch out.'"

"Huh. He said that?"

"Yup."

He paused, thinking.

"Hello?" Grasso said.

"Yeah, I'm still here. Do we know if she visited him yet?"

"Didn't get a chance to check the log."

"Well, do that. Right away. I need to know. It makes a difference."

"Okay, but there's gonna be an extra charge for that."

"Don't worry. You'll get compensated. Hey, listen, I got another proposition for you. It requires a little more risk on your part, but the payoff is that much bigger."

"Like, how much you talking?"

"Substantial. Could go into the five figures, depending on the service performed."

"Huh, sounds very interesting. You got my full attention."

"Okay, here it is. What are my options if I want to make this cocksucker Diaz disappear?"

3 1

———

With the afternoon sun behind him, Dolan Reed stood in front of the picture window, towering over his desk like some enormous statue of a dictator. His face stood out bright red against the glare. Only years of practice prevented Mary Hale from cowering as she approached him.

"What the *fuck* is this?" he shouted, throwing a piece of paper across the desk at her. She reached out and took it, forcing herself to move slowly and calmly. She sat down in a chair in front of his desk and settled her reading glasses unhurriedly on her nose. She found it worked best with him never to show fear.

"This is, or would appear to be, a subpoena from the U.S. Attorney's Office for all documents held by us pertaining to the Securilex transaction," she stated matter-of-factly.

"I can fucking see that, you moron. Didn't I tell you to handle this Melanie Vargas person?"

"Served by fax, I would note. Not proper service unless we agree to accept it that way."

"What are you suggesting? Call her up and say we don't accept it? That's idiotic."

"It would buy us a couple of days to respond while they effect proper service," Mary pointed out.

"A couple of days to shred, you mean!"

Her placid face betrayed no emotion. She'd have to consider what she'd do if he instructed her to destroy documents called for by a subpoena. Things between them in recent times had not been to her satisfaction. Cleaning up his messes was no longer as rewarding as it had once been, so why subject herself to criminal liability? Her mind flew forward, rapidly making calculations. She had it in her power to incite a coup. But she'd see. She'd see how she felt when the time came.

Dolan Reed knew Mary well enough to perceive the resistance in her neutral gaze.

"Oh, for Chrissakes, don't go getting all moral on me now."

"Whatever your ultimate decision, Dodo, we'd be wise to at least appear compliant."

The intercom buzzed simultaneously with the door flying open.

"Miss van der Vere," his secretary's flustered voice announced over the intercom as Sarah bolted in.

"Look at this!" Sarah cried, holding out a piece of paper.

"Our Miss Vargas has been busy," Mary noted wryly, taking it from Sarah's hand and perusing it. "Hmm. This one's a bit different. It calls for testimony before the grand jury pertaining to certain criminal acts. I'm a bit rusty on my criminal-code citations. Securities fraud I recognize, but this other one . . . hmm."

Mary got up and strolled over to the bookshelf, pulling out a crimson-bound volume, enjoying the way they followed her with their eyes. She turned the pages slowly, drawing out the suspense.

"Oh, of course! Title 18, United States Code, Section 1951. Interference with commerce by threats or violence. It's the extortion statute. How *could* I have forgotten?"

She snapped the book shut and replaced it on the shelf, then made her way sedately to her seat. Leaning back, she held the subpoena at arm's length to see it better.

"So Sarah's being asked to testify about acts of extortion. And below, in the section relating to documents sought, it asks that she bring any and all videotapes and audiotapes used or intended to be used to extort any benefit, monetary or otherwise, from Dolan Reed, members of the Reed firm, its employees, agents, or clients." Mary stopped reading, raising her eyebrows. "Any idea what that's about, Sarah?"

Dolan was staring at Sarah, thunderstruck. He sat down heavily in his colossal leather chair.

"Mary," he said, in the quiet tone she recognized as his most dangerous, "would you be so kind as to leave us alone?"

32

——

Melanie called home from the taxi on the way to the retirement dinner and told Elsie she'd be late again. She hated doing it. She missed Maya terribly, and what's more, Elsie was starting to make noises about quitting. But Melanie had no choice in the matter. It was imperative that she accompany Bernadette to the dinner. She'd discovered a bombshell, and she needed some time alone with her boss to break the news.

Sharing a cab with Bernadette, Melanie sank back on the ripped leather seat and let Bernadette talk at her. She dreaded opening her mouth. Bernadette wasn't going to like what she had to say one bit. In the mess on her desk, she'd found some devastating information about Rommie Ramirez. Ironic that Bernadette was the one who'd told her to sort through it in the first place, or it might not have seen the light of day for a while.

According to the fingerprint reports she'd gotten from the lab, Rommie had mishandled a critical piece of evidence, possibly contaminated the whole crime scene. Somehow he'd touched the can of kerosene used to set the blaze in Jed Benson's office, leaving his fingerprints on it. It was a major, career-threatening screwup, one he'd be hard-pressed to survive even with Bernadette's support, and it put the whole prosecution at risk of being thrown out. She cringed at the thought of telling her boss, but how could she hold back something so big? There was other new information, too—evidence of Jed Benson's corruption. Maybe she'd begin with that to ease the shock.

When the cab dropped them on First Avenue near the Fifty-ninth Street Bridge, she still hadn't brought herself to say anything. She was getting cold feet. Maybe she should double-check with the lab. Maybe she should call Butch Brennan and go back over the crime scene step by step to figure out how the screwup had happened. Making such a damaging accusation against Bernadette's boyfriend demanded rock-solid information. Melanie could only imagine the consequences if she opened her mouth and then it turned out she was wrong.

Looking up at the bridge's squat outline against the flaming afternoon sun, she marveled at her ability to screw up her own life. To choose this, of all cases, to run after. She could blame it on bad luck, but it was starting to smell like bad judgment. To go after a high-profile, highly political case at a moment of personal crisis? How stupid was that? *Muy estúpido,* but no turning back now. She had important reasons to stick with it. Three important reasons, and their names were Rosario, Jasmine, and Amanda.

She and Bernadette walked into the dark restaurant, Melanie's eyes seeing red echoes from the sun. She trailed Bernadette through the thick crowd, stopping every few feet so Bernadette could talk to the VIPs. Bernadette introduced her to everybody she spoke to, shouting over the din of voices and blaring Irish music. They headed to the bar. Melanie leaned against its dull, sticky surface, looking out over the crowd in the dim light as Bernadette held court. Cops were the worst violators of the antismoking laws: a haze of smoke hung over the low-ceilinged room. Except for a couple of other prosecutors she recognized, they were the only women there. Middle-aged men with aggressive ties and slicked-back hair, mostly bosses in the PD and the federal agencies, kept coming over, offering to buy them rounds of drinks. There would be no chance right now to speak with Bernadette privately. Melanie tried not to feel too relieved.

Bernadette threw herself into networking with frenzied abandon. Pretty soon she was on her third scotch, wheeling and dealing, scrounging for business and making promises, flirting and wangling. She was good at it. Melanie nursed a glass of cheap chardonnay and watched the spectacle, all the while picturing Bernadette's face when she broke the news. By the time they sat down to dinner in the adjoining banquet room, Bernadette was totally smashed. They had lingered so long at the bar that they ended up seated far from the dais, at the back of the long, narrow banquet room. Their table was empty except for two stragglers who sat down across from them. One tall and gaunt, the other with jowls and a beer belly, they greeted Bernadette by name, then fell into animated conversation about the Mets.

"Fucking Siberia. Should've saved a seat," Bernadette complained, her words slurring delicately, her head lolling to one side like a sodden blossom after a rainstorm.

Did it make any sense to tell Bernadette when she was in this condition? She'd be less likely to evaluate things objectively, more likely to lash out at Melanie for being the bearer of bad news. Maybe Melanie should just make an excuse and leave, so she could do her homework properly before dropping the bombshell. She had plenty of good reasons: Dan was still waiting for her at the hospital. Elsie was fuming at home. Steve had left her a message saying he'd gotten them an appointment with that marriage counselor for later this evening. She was pleased by his fast work, but she hadn't even had time to return his call.

"Hey, Bernadette," she began tentatively.

Bernadette didn't hear her; she was too busy signaling the waiter for another drink. Up on the dais, far away, someone tapped on a glass. A powerfully built man with steel gray hair walked up and adjusted a microphone, moving with a boss's arrogance. He winced at the eardrum-piercing feedback, then began to talk. Melanie raised her voice so she could be heard over the drone of his speech and the bursts of laughter from the crowd.

"Bernadette, listen, I was thinking—"

Bernadette turned to her with a warm smile. She looked so relaxed, so normal, that it made Melanie realize she almost never saw her happy. Suddenly she understood it all. How vulnerable Bernadette was at this moment in her life. How dependent she was on Rommie and how blind to his flaws. In Bernadette's mind, Rommie was the only thing standing between her and a lonely, empty middle age. Ugh, Melanie couldn't, she just couldn't shatter that illusion. And she couldn't get up and walk out, leaving her boss sitting alone, drunk, at this table. She'd stay, at least until Rommie showed up.

"I was thinking we should talk about the Benson case," Melanie said.

"Good idea. What new developments do you have to report?" Bernadette dug in her bag and pulled out a cigarette. "Hmm, when are they gonna serve the rubber chicken? I'm starting to get woozy."

"I found out some surprising stuff about Jed Benson," Melanie said. She'd start with the easy part, then see where it went. If Bernadette seemed receptive, maybe she would bring up the fingerprint report after all.

"Nothing you could tell me about Jed would surprise me, Melanie."

"Really?"

"I knew Jed. He *definitely* had a dark side. Mmm-hmm."

Melanie had been thinking about the Bensons' bank records, buried in the pile on her desk and just opened. They were not the bank records of an honest man. But there was something lascivious in Bernadette's tone that made Melanie think she was talking about something else.

"You mean he was a womanizer?" Melanie guessed.

Bernadette's drink came, and she tossed it back like a sailor. "Yeah! In a big way! He seduced me, you know."

"Wow. No. I had no idea," Melanie said. Boy, get Bernadette drunk and no telling what you might learn.

"We're talking a lot of years ago now. It was a pretty tough experience for me. I'm not saying I wasn't willing. But I was naive, and he took advantage. Nowadays I'd have a slam-dunk sexual-harassment claim."

"Why, what did he do?"

"I'd only been on the job a few months, and Jed was the big boss. He was famous and so gorgeous. I had the worst—I mean, *the worst*—crush on him. I used to look up his court appearances in the calendar and then go hang around outside the courtrooms, waiting for him to come out. I was hot back then, honey, lemme tell you. Jed noticed."

The waiter interrupted her, setting down plates of greasy chicken parmigiana slathered in runny pink sauce.

"Yuck, look at this shit. I can't eat this." Bernadette stubbed out one cigarette and fished in her bag for another, fumbling with her lighter, dropping it on the floor. Melanie leaned over and picked it up.

"I had no idea you were such a smoker, Bernadette."

"Mmm, when I drink. Keep saying I'll quit, but it's hard because Romulado smokes, and we spend a lot of time together." She slumped back, smoking thoughtfully, staring off into space. "So one day—one evening, actually—I was working late, and Jed just called me up and told me to report to his office. That's it. He didn't even give me a reason, right? I thought I was getting chosen for some big case or something. When I got there, the place was deserted, so I just walked right in. He was sitting at his desk, talking to a reporter on the telephone. I sat, and he stared at me while he finished his conversation. The way he looked me up and down, I understood right away why he'd called. You know what they call that?"

"What?" Melanie asked.

Bernadette laughed harshly. "A booty call. A goddamn booty call, right there in the middle of the office. But I fell for it—hook, line, and sinker. His eyes were the most unbelievable shade of green you ever saw, like grass in the springtime. So he gets up, locks the door. Doesn't say a word, not even hello. What stays with me is the feeling of my skin sticking to that damn leather couch." She dropped her chin onto her hand and sighed, her hazel eyes cloudy with drink.

"What happened after that?"

"Oh, he'd call now and then. We'd have sex. I kept thinking it would amount to something, you know? I had fantasies he'd leave his wife and marry me. Huh, was I foolish when I was young!" Her cynical laugh didn't disguise the hurt in her eyes.

"Do you think Nell Benson knew about Jed's other women?" Melanie asked.

"Unless she was dumb as a stone. But either she wanted to be with him that bad or else she liked the money. So tell me what you found out. You think Nell had him whacked for the insurance proceeds?" Bernadette asked.

"I can't believe you just said that. All along you've been acting like the only possible answer is the retaliation theory."

"Don't get me wrong—I still think that's the most likely. Romulado's always believed that this was a retaliatory hit, and it makes sense. Jed prosecuted the founder of the Blades, Blades were involved in Jed's murder. Ipso facto. If it quacks like a duck, it is a duck. On the other hand, Nell Benson is an evil fucking bitch, and I wouldn't put anything past her."

The sudden venom in Bernadette's voice startled Melanie, and reminded her of the suspicion she'd had about Rommie and Nell. Did Bernadette suspect something as well? Tit for tat, though. After all, Bernadette had slept with Nell's husband first. Life was too damn complicated sometimes.

"So," Bernadette prompted, "give it up. What did you find on Jed? Some sex scandal? Blackmail photos?"

"A couple of things. Jed was sleeping with Jasmine Cruz, which creates an interesting link to Slice. Dan O'Reilly thinks maybe it's as simple as Benson did Slice's girlfriend, and Slice found out and did Benson."

Bernadette laughed. "Huh, I like that. Has a nice symmetry to it."

"I'm actually more intrigued by another affair Jed was having." She explained about Sarah van der Vere and the wrongdoing at the Reed firm. "So I'm investigating that angle thoroughly. A shady business deal could explain some irregularities I discovered in the Bensons' bank accounts, too."

"What sort of irregularities?" Bernadette asked.

"Let me ask you something. Did you ever wonder where the Bensons' millions came from? I went through their real-estate records just before we left. Do you have any idea what their holdings were?"

"Well, let's see, the town house in the East Eighties that burned—"

"Purchased for almost six million, with two million more in renovation costs," Melanie interrupted. "A large house in East Hampton and a horse farm in Millbrook, worth about three mill each, and a condo in Gstaad that I don't know the value of. Oh, and a place on Mustique. Now, where did all that money come from?"

"Private practice?" Bernadette ventured skeptically.

"No way. What kind of lawyer makes that much money?"

Bernadette sat up straighter, making a visible effort to focus her bleary eyes. Melanie had her full attention now.

"I don't know, girlfriend. You tell me."

"I went through Jed Benson's bank records. There was significant evidence of structuring in his account."

"Structuring?" Bernadette echoed, her brow furrowed.

"Yes, you know, it's a type of money laundering? Numerous cash deposits, all just under the ten-thousand-dollar reporting requirement so the authorities aren't notified."

"Thank you, Melanie, I know what structuring is," Bernadette replied acidly. "How much are we talking about?"

"We're talking about millions of dollars a year. Nearly eight million last year, for example."

"Oh. My." Bernadette looked suddenly green.

"What's the matter? Are you feeling okay?"

"I'd like to believe it's a dirty business deal, Melanie. But in my experience, money that big only comes from one place."

Melanie thought for a moment, then realized Bernadette was right.

"Drugs," she said. "You mean drugs."

"Oh!" Bernadette exclaimed, but she was looking past Melanie, just over her shoulder. "Romulado! I was wondering when you would show up."

33

For the second time in two days, Melanie turned around to find Rommie Ramirez standing behind her. If he'd been listening in on their conversation, he gave no sign of it. He just smiled vaguely, as if his thoughts were elsewhere.

"Had a few without me, Bern? I better catch up." He pulled out an empty chair and sat down beside Bernadette, signaling the waiter for a drink.

"Why didn't you answer your phone or your pager?" Bernadette demanded. "Where have you been?"

"Working. Following up on that cocaine seizure we made last night."

"Oh," she said, nodding, but then looked at him again. "Hey! What's that mark on your neck?"

There was a large red abrasion on Rommie's neck; it looked like a classic high-school hickey. He continued to smile placidly, but a glimmer of nervousness crept into his eyes. Melanie looked down at her plate, feeling embarrassed for her boss. Bernadette would never stoop to showing jealousy publicly if she were sober.

"Oh, shaving burn," Rommie replied after a moment, fingering the red mark.

"You were shaving the side of your neck? Do I look like an idiot to you?" There was an edge of hysteria in Bernadette's voice. Mutt and Jeff from across the table turned to look.

Rommie laughed uneasily. "Come on, Bern. Chill out. Why so suspicious?"

"Why? I can never reach you. You never call when you say you will. And whenever I bother to check, you're never where you're supposed to be."

"Maybe I should go," Melanie interjected, half rising from the table. But Rommie leaned across the back of Bernadette's chair and clutched at her arm.

"No, no, stay, Melanie. What's this you were just telling Bernadette about evidence of structuring in Jed Benson's bank records? I want to hear about that."

So he *had* overheard their conversation. She sat back down, frowning.

"I'm afraid I can't go into it, Rommie. The bank records are privileged grand-jury materials. I can't share them with you if you're not officially assigned to the case."

The waiter set down a double Jack Daniel's before Rommie. He picked it up with a harassed air and took a gulp.

"You always such a stickler for the rules?" he asked irritably.

"Grand jury secrecy, yes, I am," Melanie said with an astonished laugh. "I don't want to get cited for contempt."

"Look, we're all on the same side here, kid, but maybe I feel a little extra responsibility to look out for Jed's reputation. He was my friend. His wife is my friend. And I see how it is. You're out to make a name for yourself. Nothing wrong with that. But let's say you get a little overeager and, in all the excitement, you misinterpret the evidence. I'm not blaming you, but Jed's not around to defend himself. You could do real damage. That's why I want to take a look at the records on his behalf. Where are they, in your office?"

"I'm not misinterpreting *anything*," Melanie replied, flushing with resentment. She didn't need Rommie questioning her judgment in front of her boss. She had enough problems already, with Bernadette thinking she concocted conspiracy theories out of whole cloth. Besides, she was right about Benson's bank records. Those hundreds of cash deposits didn't lie. They all fell between $9,000 and $9,999, just slightly under federal reporting requirements, and they added up to millions being funneled through the accounts. She couldn't imagine clearer evidence of money laundering. Rommie was way off base. But after reading that fingerprint report, she probably shouldn't be surprised. The sharpest knife in the drawer this guy was *not*. Just look how he'd bungled the Benson crime scene.

Melanie needn't have worried. Bernadette was so absorbed in her own problems that she barely registered Rommie's comment. She kept looking at his neck, her face crumpled and sad.

"You were with someone, weren't you?" she said.

"Quit it already. You're drunk, and you're making a scene. People are starting to look."

"You're not even denying it. Who was it, Romulado? Tell me. I deserve that much."

Across the table the thin detective elbowed his jowly companion and made a comment under his breath, eliciting a loud guffaw. That did it! Melanie couldn't stand to watch her boss humiliated for another second. She knew it all: That sick feeling the moment you found out. Constantly picturing what he'd done with the other woman. Asking yourself why he strayed, why you weren't enough. Seeing Bernadette go through what she'd just lived through herself was too painful.

"I should really be going," she said, standing up.

"You're right. We all should," Rommie said. "Melanie, you help me get Bernadette home, and then we'll go take a look at those bank records you're so hot for. Somebody's gotta look out for Jed's memory. Come on, my car's outside." He scraped back his chair and stood up.

"Rommie, didn't you hear what I said? I *can't* show you the bank records. It would violate the grand jury secrecy law. Besides, I don't have time to go back to my office right now. I have some other leads to pursue, and then I need to get home and relieve my baby-sitter."

"What kind of friend are you, Melanie? Can't you see Bernadette's in bad shape? Help me get her home, at least. Then we'll figure out about the records."

"This is between you guys. I honestly don't think I should be meddling in Bernadette's personal life," Melanie said.

But just then Bernadette, who'd been sitting morosely with her chin in her hand, piped up plaintively. "Please come, Melanie," she said, in a smaller voice than Melanie had ever heard her use before. "I don't want to be alone with him."

Bernadette's face was slack and tired-looking. Melanie knew exactly how she felt, and as much as she might have liked to make her escape, she couldn't refuse.

"Okay," she said reluctantly. "If it would make you feel better."

"Thanks, girlfriend. You're a pal."

Having committed herself, Melanie had no choice but to follow when Bernadette and Rommie headed for the exit. She stepped out into the muggy night, kicking herself for agreeing to this.

"I'm parked over there in the tunnel," Rommie said, gesturing toward a stone underpass lined with parking spaces on either side, running directly under the Fifty-ninth Street Bridge. Darkness had fallen while they were inside. Traffic roared overhead, but the underpass was deserted, unlit but for the dim ambient light from a lamppost across the street. Their footsteps echoed against its dank, tomblike walls as they marched, tightly packed on the narrow sidewalk, toward Rommie's car.

Melanie glanced at Rommie, thinking about the fingerprint report sitting on her desk. When she read it, she'd worked out in her mind exactly how he might've left his prints on that kerosene can, and she'd come to the conclusion it was an innocent mistake. Arriving at the scene, devastated by his longtime friend's murder, Rommie forgot all protocol. He walked around in shock and touched things with his bare hands, things he shouldn't. He contaminated evidence. She recalled him vomiting in the corner of Jed's basement office, and it made sense. An awful screwup, likely to lead to disciplinary action, possibly even to the loss of his job, but surely unintentional. Surely caused by emotional shock. Right?

Maybe it was the damp creepiness of the deserted underpass, or the feeling that Rommie was pushing too hard to see those bank records, but for the first time she asked herself whether it was plausible that someone of his experience would make such a stupid mistake. That thought, once she admitted it, unleashed a whole flood of other questions. Why did a narcotics lieutenant respond to the scene of a murder in the first place? Did Rommie know about Jed's money laundering? Did he go there purposely to cover something up? Tampering with evidence was a crime, but he was so close to the family, maybe he'd do something like that to spare them embarrassment. Or worse, maybe he was complicit in the money laundering and had destroyed records at the scene?

Really, she should just calm down. She was letting her imagination run away with her. Rommie Ramirez was a good guy. A dope, maybe, but not a criminal.

They got to the car, and Rommie took Melanie's arm with one hand and drew her toward the driver's-side door, extracting his keys from his pocket with the other.

"Bern, go around. Melanie can sit in the back," Rommie said. Bernadette walked unsteadily around to the passenger side of the car.

Reassure herself as she might, when Rommie flipped the seat forward and gestured for her to get in, she felt unbearably trapped. This was ridiculous, she told herself. She wasn't a prisoner. She could leave if she wanted to. Yet with each passing moment, it got more difficult to find the words to justify her departure. She felt as if she couldn't breathe.

"Look," she said, "maybe I could put Bernadette in a cab or something. I don't have time for this right now. Slice is on the loose, my little girl is home with a baby-sitter. There's just too much going on." Her words rang out louder than she intended and bounced off the tunnel walls, fear audible in her voice.

"Come on, now, Melanie, you said you'd help."

Rommie's tone, though scolding, was pleasant and paternal, so why did she feel threatened? She looked around desperately. Through the window she saw Bernadette slumped against the passenger door, looking ready to pass out. The entrance to the overpass was twenty feet away. Blood pounding in her ears, she took a step toward it but then looked back at Rommie again.

He smiled reassuringly. "Come on, honey. Be a good kid and help me out here. Get in. Okay?"

It was only Rommie, she told herself, getting ready to climb into the backseat. She was overreacting. He was her boss's boyfriend, a decent enough guy, kind of a Keystone Kop. Not a threat. She truly believed that. She must be working too hard. Her fight-or-flight response was set on hyperdrive, and it was messing with her head, because somehow all her instincts screamed that she was walking into a trap.

34

———

S arah wondered what he'd do if she just got up and ran. There were people in the office, after all. He couldn't stop her. She wasn't a prisoner here. She could go call that prosecutor right now and offer to testify. They'd lock Dodo up. That was probably the smartest move at this point, she realized. He was entirely capable of killing her. She knew that. Not that the thought didn't turn her on.

"I'm waiting," he said in that quiet, evil tone. It sent a tiny thrill right through her.

"Hey," she said, "remember that time we did it on your desk while those people from Hudson and Fisher were standing right outside?"

She hadn't been trying to distract him; it was just what popped into her mind. She knew there was no way to get out of this one in any event.

He came around the desk, looming over her chair. She turned her head away, and he leaned down and grabbed her viciously by the chin, forcing her to look at him.

He spoke in a whisper through clenched teeth. *"Where are the fucking tapes you made?"*

"What tapes?"

He raised his hand to strike her across the face, then hesitated, thinking better of it. She smiled, seeing that she would win this round. He wouldn't do anything to her. Not here in the office, with people nearby. She could get away with taunting him.

"What, don't like the idea of your disgusting fetishes broadcast on the six o'clock news, Dodo? You should see the ones where I paddle your droopy old ass while you beg for mercy. You look completely pathetic. Those were Jed's favorites, you know."

The murderous look on his face made her think she'd miscalculated. She stood up and backed toward the door, breathing rapidly. She'd scream if he tried to stop her. But he didn't. He kept his eyes fixed on her but made no move. She got to the door and stopped, hand on the knob.

"You had him killed, didn't you?" she asked, more curious than desperate. "Jed threatened you with the tapes, and you had him killed?"

He slumped, grabbing onto the chair she'd just vacated for support.

"Why, Sarah?" he asked, his face old and haggard. "Why'd you do it?"

"Oh, please, as if you're all pure and I'm the bad one! You knew what I was like, Dodo. It's why you picked me to work on Securilex in the first place. You knew you could trust me not to blab. Hell, you knew I'd even find clever new ways to dummy up the documents. You *love* how bad I am, Dodo."

"You betrayed me!" Sweat stood out on his shiny forehead.

"You're taking this way too personally," she said nonchalantly. "Chill the fuck out, why don't you. It was just a game. I thought you *liked* games."

He sat down clumsily, his face an odd shade of purple. She wondered if he was having a heart attack. Wouldn't be the worst thing that could happen. But she didn't want to witness it and get mixed up in calling 911.

"Look, Dodo, I need some space," she said, turning the knob. "Okay? So don't call me. I'll call you."

35

———

"**M**elanie! Wait up!"

It was Dan, calling to her from the entrance to the under-pass. *¡Gracias a Dios!* She was so relieved! He strode over to them.

"I thought you were coming back to the hospital, and you're out party-ing?" Dan said, smiling. "I should've guessed. You're a wild one, all right."

"Bernadette roped me into it. I told her we had work to do."

"Absolutely. That's why I'm here. I have some information we need to follow up on right away."

"Oh, okay. Sorry, Rommie," Melanie said. "I wish I could help get Bernadette home, but the investigation is at a critical point. I know you understand."

"Sure, no problem. Thanks for helping out," Rommie said noncha-lantly. She must have been imagining things, because if he was annoyed or angry that she wasn't getting into the car, he sure did a good job of hiding it. She walked around to where Bernadette stood slumped against the front door, eyes closed, complexion ghost-white.

"Bern, honey," Melanie said gently, touching her shoulder, "I need to go. Do you want me to put you in a cab?"

She opened her eyes. "No, it's okay. I just drank too much. I'll feel bet-ter in a minute. Rommie can take me home."

"You sure?"

"Yes."

Rommie came around and opened Bernadette's door. He wouldn't meet Melanie's eyes, but she put that down to the embarrassing scene she'd just witnessed. Bernadette got in, staring straight ahead, looking like she might break down and sob at any moment. Melanie's heart ached for her boss, but she understood there was nothing she could do. Some things people just had to work through on their own.

"Call me if you need anything, Bern. Doesn't matter how late," she said.

Without speaking, Dan and Melanie headed for the street, hearing the sounds of car doors opening and closing behind them. The engine of Rommie's car sputtered to life. Headlights threw their shadows into relief on the pavement as Rommie and Bernadette drove slowly past and disappeared from sight.

AS THEY EMERGED from the tunnel, Dan said, "Jeez, that looked ugly. You seemed like you wanted out of there pretty bad."

"Yes, I did. Thanks for rescuing me. You're very good at it." She smiled at him, and he flushed with pleasure.

"Just doing my job, ma'am," he joked. "So what was going on? Looked like Ramirez was practically kidnapping you."

"Yeah, that's how it felt. Listen to this and tell me if you think it's strange: Apparently Rommie's cheating on Bernadette. She was drunk, and they were in the middle of a fight, but then he insisted I leave with them."

"Why?"

"I think what he really wanted was to get me to show him some bank records I subpoenaed from Jed Benson's accounts."

"What's in the records? Anything worth getting excited about?"

"Yeah, like millions of dollars of structuring."

"You're shittin' me!"

"Nope!"

He whistled. "Wow. Millions, you said? It's gotta be drug money, right?"

"That's what Bernadette said, and I agree. But there's more."

He was listening so attentively. She opened her mouth to tell him about the fingerprint report but then stopped herself. Something in the careful way he watched her suddenly struck her as odd. God, she was paranoid tonight! But, unlike with Rommie, where Dan was concerned, she had actual reason to be. She was losing sight of what Delvis Diaz had said to her earlier that evening—that the people she'd brought to the interview were dirty. He didn't mention Dan by name, but still, shouldn't she try harder to keep her guard up, at least until she could get the full story from Delvis? Not that she'd necessarily believe him even if he did implicate Dan directly. Delvis might have reason to lie, and Dan struck her as honest as the day was long.

"What is it?" Dan asked. "You said there's more?"

"Um, lost my train of thought." Not that she seriously doubted him. But still. "So do you think that's weird?"

"That he wanted to see the records? No, not really. Sounds like they're pretty devastating. Besides, Ramirez makes a career out of sticking his nose in where it doesn't belong. You know I think the guy's an idiot. Just look at the fact that he's stepping out on your boss. He's biting the hand that feeds him."

"Why do you say that?" she asked.

"His influence with her is half of why they keep him around. The guy is such a royal fuck-up he's come close to getting booted more times than I can count."

"Yeah, I've heard that before."

"He's been beating this minority thing to death for years, or he would've been out on his ass long ago."

"Hey, watch what you say there, pal!" she said. "*Soy puertorriqueña también*, remember?"

"No offense meant to you, sweetheart. You're, like, the smartest person

I ever met. Which is why people like him piss me off, because they give people like you a bad name." He looked at her and laughed. "You should see your face right now. You're going, 'Who the fuck is this knuckle-dragger I'm hanging out with?' Look, I'll never be politically correct, and you can't take me into polite society. But I promise you, my heart is in the right place."

She laughed, too. It was hard to be mad at him. "You do have kind of a redneck quality, Agent, but I admit, on you it's charming."

"It's the Irish beat cop in me."

"So, hey, speaking of cops, if you're here, who's at the hospital with Amanda?"

"Randall finally showed up. I left him there and came looking for you, see what was taking you so long."

"Where the hell was he all afternoon?" Melanie asked.

"I didn't ask, and he didn't say. Dealing with personal shit, I guess."

"Oh. Right. So should we go back there?" She looked at her watch, missing Maya, thinking of Elsie at home counting the minutes. "It's getting pretty late."

"No need. Randall said he'd beep me if anything interesting happened. So, listen," he said, turning toward her and stopping momentarily, "you wanna maybe go get a drink or something?"

"A drink? We don't have time for that."

"You need to fill me in on those bank records, right? Besides, I need to grab a bite to eat."

"You're crazy."

"Come on, just for a little while. You got a better offer?" he cajoled.

Despite her warning to herself only a moment earlier, she felt powerfully drawn to him. His blue eyes were glued to her face with such intensity that they blazed. And his voice—rough and sweet at the same time—seemed to caress her. But she'd say no, she'd make herself, she had to. She couldn't spend time with him like that, alone in a bar. Bad, bad idea. On a lot of levels.

"I can't. If we're not going back to the hospital, then I need to get home."

"So pick a place on the way, and then I'll drop you. Thirty minutes, tops, I promise. Then I'll take you right home. My treat. Please. Say yes."

He was hanging on her answer. How long had it been since somebody wanted so badly to spend time with her? Had anybody ever? Had her husband? She reminded herself of all the reasons to say no. There were a lot of them.

"Okay," she said breathlessly. *Ay, de Dios,* she was making a big mistake. "Just a quick one."

His face lit up. "Whatever you say. I'm parked right over here."

DAN HEADED FOR a pub he knew on Second Avenue. The whole way there in the car, Melanie felt nervous and guilty that she was even doing this. But now that she'd agreed to it, she couldn't very well make him take her right home. Besides, it would disappoint him so. Just one quick drink, she told herself. That wasn't a crime.

As they looked for parking, she marveled that she'd never been on this block before, a mere five minutes from her apartment. New York was funny that way. A few blocks in either direction and you might as well be on a different continent. On either side of the street, low-rise tenements with lacy ironwork fire escapes, standing since the turn of the last century, alternated with dowdy white-brick high-rises built thirty or forty years ago, after the demolition of the elevated train. The avenue was lined with bars on both sides. Bankers and analysts in their twenties, the men dapper and suited, the women perfectly made up, in heels and skirts, spilled out of the tonier places. In the midst of the frenetic singles scene, a number of Irish pubs hung on stubbornly, one indistinguishable from the next. They stood ramshackle and deserted next to their flourishing neighbors, shamrocks on their tattered awnings, neon Guinness signs in their grimy plate-glass windows. Dan parked in front of one of these.

The place was empty except for a couple of weather-beaten longshoreman types shooting darts in the back. They glanced up as Dan and Melanie entered, then turned indifferently back to their game. A smell of disinfectant from the bathrooms mingled with the yeasty smell of stale beer. Melanie sat down on a stool at a high wooden table. Dan headed for the bar without asking her what she wanted. She watched him walk away. He moved like an athlete, that combination of power and grace. An old jukebox stood tucked in an alcove, and he stopped there on his way, depositing a quarter he took from his pocket. Sinatra came on—"I've Got You Under My Skin." She listened to the lyrics as Dan walked back toward her with two pints of foamy, dark brown Guinness and two meat pies.

"Hey, let me give you some money," she said, reaching into her bag.

"No way. I said it was my treat. Besides, the man always pays."

"But I know you're short till Friday."

"Not necessary," he said, blushing. "I know the bartender. That's why I picked this place."

She saw he was embarrassed and kicked herself for bringing it up. As if she'd forgotten what it felt like to be strapped for cash.

"Okay then, thanks," she said, lifting the beer mug. "Hey, what is this? There's a shamrock imprinted in the foam."

"It's Guinness, missy, real authentic. That's how they serve up a pint in the old country."

She tasted it. "It's so thick. I won't need any dinner if I drink this."

"I can't believe I'm out with a girl who never had a Guinness before. I shouldn't be surprised, though. You're the champagne-and-caviar type if I've ever seen one."

"Right. Every day. Breakfast, lunch, and dinner." She laughed at the thought. The beer was going to her head, coming as it did on an empty stomach and after the wine she'd drunk at the dinner. She'd better watch herself. She was supposed to be keeping her guard up with him, remember? She forced herself to focus on the case.

"So," she said, "after looking at these bank records, I think Jed Benson was killed because he was dirty."

"You're like a bullet headed straight for the target, you know that?" he said, smiling.

"What's that supposed to mean?"

"We just sat down. Can't we talk about something other than the case for five minutes?"

"Like what?"

"I don't know. What you do in your free time, or what your best subjects were in school, or when you had your first kiss?"

"This is not a date, you know."

"Aw, come on. Humor me a little. What's it gonna cost ya?"

Maybe more than either of us knows, she thought, looking into his eyes. The feeling of being with him, of how much he wanted to be with her, was so heady. She was too vulnerable right now, and he was too attractive. She had no idea where this was going, but something told her she should stop it.

"Why do you care when I had my first kiss?" she asked. She'd intended to shut him down, but all this talk about kissing was getting to her. She couldn't help glancing at his mouth. Which was beautiful, of course, strong and sensual.

"I just want to know you better, that's all," he said. He reached for her left hand, taking it in his, and tracing a fingertip lightly across her empty ring finger. "Like, what's up with this?"

She pulled her hand away and picked up her drink again, trying hard to ignore her racing pulse.

"I forgot to wear my rings this morning. So?" she said, looking down into her beer.

"Yeah? Look me in the eye and tell me that."

She looked up. Caught in the tractor beam of his gaze, she couldn't bring herself to lie. "Maybe it's none of your business," she said tentatively, setting the mug back down without drinking.

"Melanie, I'm your friend. At least I want to be. I get this feeling like you need one."

She sighed, saying nothing.

"Believe me, I know where you're coming from," he continued. "I'm a pretty private person myself. I been through some shit of my own and not talked about it. It gets lonely. I don't mean to push. It's just . . ."

He trailed off. There was genuine concern in his eyes, and something else, too. Something like pain. She felt a powerful urge to confide in him, to tell him everything. Not just about her marriage either, but everything about her, from when she was a child. But she couldn't let herself. She and Steve were going to work on things. Today he'd finally seemed ready to. She had Maya to think of. She'd decided all that already, hadn't she?

Dan watched the struggle play out on her face. "It's just . . . I don't want you to be lonely when you don't need to be. Something's going on. Tell me, you'll feel better."

She felt like she was swimming upstream, and all she wanted was to give in and let the current sweep her away. She couldn't help herself. She needed whatever it was Dan was offering her.

"My husband and I, we separated. But it's only temporary. I mean, it may not be permanent."

"Why? What happened?" he asked.

"Oh, the usual story. It used to be the secretary, right? But now it's the—what do they call 'em—the executive assistant?"

"He cheated on you?" he asked incredulously.

She shrugged like it was obvious, but his surprise pleased her.

"What a fucking retard! He never deserved you in the first place. I'll tell him so to his face. Hell, I'll beat the shit out of him if you want me to."

"No, that's okay. Thanks, though. I think." She laughed, shaking her head.

He leaned toward her across the tall table and reached for her hand again. Their fingers intertwined. Her heart began beating wildly. Her brain told her to pull away, but this time her hand didn't obey.

"Hey," he began, leaning even closer. "Can I tell you something?"

"What?" she asked breathlessly, afraid of what he might say. This was moving way too fast. She waited for his next words, but in the second of silence, her cell phone began shrieking inside her bag.

"Don't answer it," he said, but she took her hand from his and reached for her bag. By the time she found her phone, the ringing had stopped. She looked at the number—Steve's cell phone.

"I totally forgot! I was supposed to meet my husband. Hold on," she said, and checked her voice mail. Steve had called from a taxi on his way to the therapist's office to give her the address. "I have to go," she told Dan.

"Why?" He looked crestfallen. "Don't. Not yet."

"Like I said, the separation might not be permanent. We're working on things. We have a counseling appointment."

"All right," he said, nodding stoically. "I understand. Let me drive you."

"That's not such a good idea," she said firmly.

"Why? Where is it?"

"On the West Side, but that's not the point. I can't show up to my counseling session with some other guy driving me."

"With Slice still out there, no way I'm letting you go by yourself."

"No, really."

"Really. I insist. I'll drop you around the corner if it makes you feel better."

"Dan, please."

"Come on, we're wasting time standing here arguing about it."

SHE WASN'T SURE why she ended up in his car—whether it was because he wouldn't let her say no or because she didn't want to.

"Where to?" he asked.

"West End and Eighty-fifth. She works out of her apartment, this woman."

"Jesus, I can only imagine. Some ex-hippie in a caftan with long gray hair?"

She giggled. "Maybe, I don't know. This is the first session."

"I never believed in that counseling shit anyway. Either you make it on your own steam or you don't."

"Yeah? What do you know about marriage?"

"Oh, I know a thing or two, missy, and it ain't pretty. But then, maybe I wasn't married to the right person. Maybe you weren't either. Aren't, I mean." In the light from an oncoming car, he wore an expression of grim determination.

"I had no idea you were married before," she said.

"It's not the first thing you mention when you meet someone."

"So what happened?"

He stared at the road, not answering. The silence grew.

"I'm sorry," she said. "Now *I'm* prying."

"No, no. I want to tell you. It's hard for me, is all. Like I said, I never talked to anyone about it before."

"You never talked to anyone about the breakup of your marriage? Not one single person?" she asked.

"No."

"How long ago did you get divorced?"

"Lemme see. It's four—no, almost five years now."

"That's a long time to keep it inside."

He took his eyes off the road and looked at her. "I told you, I'm very private. I don't just go around telling people stuff. But I want to tell you this, so you know me."

"I understand," she said, looking back at him, feeling something opening inside her heart. He seemed so alone. Like she felt sometimes.

"Simple story, really. I knew my wife—my ex-wife, that is—my whole life, from when we were kids. Everybody expected we would wind up together. She was the best-looking girl in the neighborhood, and I was . . . well"—he blushed in the darkness of the car—"I guess you could say I was a good ballplayer. So, long story short, we got married, young. Too young."

"Yeah, so? A lot of people get married young and it works out okay."

"Jeez, now I see why you get so much information out of witnesses. Gestapo tactics here."

"Sorry. Take your time."

"This is hard for me," he repeated.

"I'm sorry." She reached for his hand, resting on the steering wheel. She'd only intended to pat it reassuringly, but he gripped her hand hard, as if he needed her help to go on.

"Well, it was like this. Diane was from a cop family, like me, so she knew the score. But she was a princess, too. Everybody was always sucking up to her, because she was beautiful. As beautiful as you, but she wasn't smart like you, didn't have your substance."

"You sound angry. Did she leave you?" she asked, paying close attention but also secretly thrilled. He thought she was beautiful!

"Yeah. She got sick of being married to a cop, thought she could do better. Those early years with the Bureau, I'd go on duty, get thrown a case, and call home three days later from the other side of the world. Nothin' I could do about it either, except quit, which I wasn't about to, since I was born for the job. It might have worked out okay if she had more of her own shit going on. But she never wanted to work. And it didn't happen for us with having kids. That was a big disappointment." He fell silent again

"So she left?"

"Yup." He stared out the window at the traffic. "I came home one afternoon from a tour, forty-eight hours straight in the same clothes. Took a shower and crashed. It wasn't until the next morning I realized her stuff was gone. She didn't even leave a note. The divorce papers came in the mail."

"Where is she now?"

"Remarried to a guy I used to play ball with. I think she was cheatin' with him when we were still together, but I can't be sure. He's got a construction business out on the Island. She helps out in the office, drives a nice car. She found what she wanted, I guess."

They reached their destination. He pulled up to the curb a car length away from the marriage counselor's building.

"Hey, can I ask you something?" he said, as she started to open her door. She turned back.

"What?"

"This, you and me. Is it just revenge, for what your husband did?"

His heart was so exposed as he spoke that she could practically see it right there in the car. She wanted to protect him, comfort him.

"I don't think so," she said. But there was a touch of uncertainty in her voice that he didn't miss.

"Anyone ever tell you you're too honest?" he asked, smiling sadly.

He reached out and tucked a stray wisp of hair behind her ear, letting his fingers linger on her cheek. Eyes full of longing, he traced the outline of her lips. She felt his hand tremble. She was mesmerized by his touch, unwilling to stop him. It seemed to take an eternity for him to lean toward her across the small distance between their seats, so that by the time their lips met, the kiss seemed inevitable, preordained. Yet it was the merest taste, sweet and gentle and over much too soon.

He sat up straight in the driver's seat. "You'd better go in. I'll call you in the morning, okay?"

"Okay," she said.

Melanie opened the door and got out, feeling unsteady on her feet. She looked back at him for a long moment before slamming the door shut.

Dan honked the horn as he drove past, but she didn't wave back. Her eyes were focused instead on the brightly lit path under the green awning that stretched from the door of the building to the curb. Steve was standing there, framed by the light, staring at her, shock and hurt in his eyes. He'd seen everything.

3 6

Her first thought was, Hah! Now you know what it feels like! But she wasn't vindictive enough to say that aloud. In Steve's eyes she saw the same sick surprise she'd felt herself, in that awful moment when the bottom had dropped out. That moment when *she* caught *him* red-handed. Infidelity sucked, no matter which side you were on.

"Steve, I'm so sorry," she said. Part of her truly meant it, but another part of her was still in the car, tasting Dan O'Reilly's kiss. And wanting more. Man, she was confused.

Without saying anything, Steve turned his back on her and marched into the lobby.

"Wait!" She rushed to catch up with him. He pretended not to see that she was coming, so she had to stick her hand in the elevator door to stop it from closing. Once they were alone in the elevator, he stared at her as if he barely recognized her. In spite of his anger, he looked amazing. Tall, lean, and tanned, wearing his suit with that careless grace that she loved. This guy could be a model, he showed off clothes so well. Sometimes she thought her whole relationship with her husband was based more on physical attraction than substance. No wonder it wasn't holding up so well under pressure. Hmm, maybe she should marry Dan and have an affair with Steve?

Steve opened his mouth several times but couldn't seem to bring himself to speak.

"I know how that must've looked," she said. But then she stopped, at a loss for what to say next. Because it *was* what it looked like.

They stepped off the elevator into a long hallway wallpapered a dingy beige. The therapist's apartment was directly across from the elevator. Steve pressed the buzzer.

He turned to her as they waited, still looking stunned. "I guess you're trying to get back at me? That's what's I just saw, right? Melanie's revenge?"

The door swung inward onto a narrow foyer warmed by a deep red Oriental rug and smelling of potpourri and scented candles. A petite woman with frizzy red hair and fashionably small eyeglasses greeted them. She was about their age.

"Hello, I'm Deborah Mintz. You must be Steve and Melanie." Neither of them responded. She looked at them and smiled quizzically. "Why don't you come in?" she said. She had a mellifluous voice, unusually deep for such a small woman. To her surprise, Melanie immediately liked her.

She showed them into an office off the foyer, furnished with a brown corduroy sofa and two beige leather chairs. Against the far wall stood a desk piled high with books and papers. Deborah shut the door firmly and went to sit in one of the chairs.

"Please, sit down," she said.

Melanie sat on the sofa. Steve chose the empty leather chair, dropping his head into his hands. When he looked up, his eyes were red and teary. If Melanie had ever thought revenge would be sweet, she was sadly mistaken. Hurting him felt much worse than getting hurt herself.

"It was lucky you called when you did, Steve," Deborah said. "I only have evening office hours once a week, and I just happened to have a cancellation. Now, would one of you like to begin and share with me what brings you here?"

"I cheated on Melanie, and I'm here to take responsibility for that," Steve said firmly, looking at Melanie as he spoke. "Melanie's been acting out, trying to show me how upset she is, and I want her to know that I hear her and that I'm going to do better. For us and for our daughter."

"Okay, well, that sounds like a good place to start. Melanie, would you like to respond?" Deborah asked.

Now they were both looking at her. Steve's words were what she'd been waiting to hear all along, right? So why didn't she feel overjoyed and relieved, like she'd expected to? Why didn't she jump up and throw her arms around him? Could it be that, in her heart, she was already out of this marriage?

"It's not that simple," was what popped out of her mouth.

"Why not? What do you mean?" Steve asked. He looked at Deborah for an explanation, but she just gestured for Melanie to continue.

"When Steve says I've been acting out, I get the feeling he thinks I didn't mean any of it. That I just want attention or to get back at him."

"You did mean it?" he asked, shocked.

"Mean what? Fill me in here," said Deborah.

"She was downstairs kissing some other guy, for starters," Steve said. "Did you mean *that*?"

"Just now?" Deborah asked, raising her eyebrows.

"I think I did mean it." Melanie felt short of breath. Her heart was beating erratically. She'd never had this experience before, of being the one in the wrong. She didn't like it. But she needed to get the truth out on the table here, and the truth was, she felt something for Dan, and she was no longer certain *what* she felt for Steve.

"Who is he?" Steve demanded.

"An FBI agent I work with. We're doing a case together. We only just met a couple of days ago."

"And you're already kissing him? Fast work, Melanie! Are you fucking him, too?"

"*No!* Don't use that word. You must be confusing me with that *puta* Samantha."

"Whoa, time out," Deborah said, making a T with her hands. "Let's try to stay civil and productive. Melanie, please continue. I think Steve needs to hear what you have to say."

"If Steve is serious about wanting to work things out, I guess I'm still willing to try. But we can't sweep our problems under the rug. I want him to know that nothing I've done was for show. Not asking him to move out, not taking off my wedding ring or kissing somebody else. I did all those things because I'm not sure whether I want to continue with our marriage."

There, she'd said it. All of it.

Dead silence.

"Which doesn't mean I'm convinced our marriage is over," she continued, her voice ringing out, loud and urgent, in the quiet room. "Maybe there's—"

Steve stood up. "I need out."

"What? Out of where?" asked Melanie, heart in her throat. Whatever she thought she was up to here, she never intended to end things this minute. She needed more time to decide.

"I can't hash this out in front of a stranger right now. I'm too confused. I'm sorry, Deborah, I know this was my idea. It just— I'm not ready. I need some air." He began to move toward the door.

"Wait!" Melanie said. "Maybe she can help us. We should give it a chance. We should—"

"I can't right now, okay? You really took me by surprise, with this other guy. I need some time to think." He strode out of the room.

"I have to go after him," Melanie said to Deborah, leaping to her feet. "Can you mail us the bill?"

"Of course. And, Melanie, I'm here if you want to come back, either together or alone. Okay?"

"Thank you."

She ran after Steve, catching up with him as he waited for the elevator, leaning against the wall with his face buried in his arms. She placed her hand lightly on his back, making contact for an instant with the well-defined muscles under his suit. The touch reminded her of that morning, doing it standing up in the hallway. What was wrong with her, thinking about that at a moment like this? There was more to marriage than just sex.

Steve angrily shrugged off her touch and barreled into the elevator when it arrived. She followed him. On the street he hailed a cab.

"Is it okay if I come with you?" she asked in a small voice. She hated this. It was actually much better to be the wronged party, the victim. Being the offender felt too terrible.

He opened his mouth to reply but merely clenched his teeth, whistling with a mixture of defeat and scorn, holding the taxi door open for her.

ELSIE OPENED THE door for them, displeasure written all over her face.

"You people realize what time it is?" she said.

Steve took money from his wallet. "Thanks for staying, Elsie. We really appreciate it. Here's your overtime and cab fare."

"That don't make it okay. Night after night being asked to stay late. You-all must think I have no home life."

Steve patted her arm. "We're sorry, really, we apologize. Listen, we're kind of in the middle of something here. If you wouldn't mind, can we talk about this in the morning?" He shepherded her to the door and gently guided her through it. "Thanks again, Elsie. Have a good night."

He closed the door behind her and walked into the living room, sinking down heavily onto the sofa. Melanie came and sat at the opposite end, leaving several feet of space between them. They hadn't spoken the entire way home in the taxi. She looked down at the sofa's once pristine taupe chenille surface, now marred with spit-up stains. She thought of when it was new, of their happy ignorance as they settled into their marital apartment. They'd been so confident of a smooth future, so blind to what could go wrong. Down the hall, as if on cue, Maya started to cry.

"Do you want to check on her, or should I?" Steve asked, sounding tired. He didn't move.

Melanie stood up, but then the crying stopped.

"Stay here. She stopped," Steve said, but Melanie continued heading for Maya's room. She always checked on the baby when she came home. Besides, she'd feel better and think more clearly if she saw her daughter's face.

The nursery glowed with golden light from the night-light. Melanie approached the crib reverently, holding her breath so she wouldn't make a sound. Maya lay on her back, lost in the wild abandon of infant sleep, her arms thrown back over her head and her eyelids fluttering. Looking at her baby daughter, Melanie flashed back to how she felt at her high-school graduation when her father didn't show up, seeing all those other big, happy families. By then it was official that he was never coming home. The doctors had given him a clean bill of health, but every time a date was set for him to fly back to New York, he made some new excuse to delay. Finally she demanded an explanation from her mother. *"Your father wants to stay in San Juan,"* her mother had said wearily. *"But he's better! He can come home now! The doctors said so,"* Melanie had protested. *"You wanted to know, so listen to what I'm telling you. He's not coming back here. We're getting a divorce."*

"What's gonna happen to you, *nena,* if I don't fix this?" Melanie whispered now.

She heard a noise behind her and turned. Steve stood in the doorway, the light from the hall picking up the gold in his hair. He was so gorgeous, she thought, he made great money, and he loved his daughter like only her own father could. What if Melanie's mother was right? Plenty of other women in her shoes would patch things up and consider themselves fortunate. What was her problem? Maybe she should try harder to work things out. If there was one vow she'd ever made, it was that Maya's childhood would be better than her own.

Steve walked over and stood beside her. "She's so beautiful," he said, looking down into the crib. "Like you."

He took her hand and pulled her toward the door.

"Steve—"

"Shhh!" He put his finger to her lips until they were in the hallway, then led her into their bedroom, where he turned her to face him. He kissed her lightly on the lips and began unbuttoning her blouse.

"I thought about it on the way home, Melanie, and I'm willing to forget about this incident with the FBI guy. I get the point. You wanted me to see that other men find you attractive. You think I don't know that, baby? You're so damn hot," he said, nuzzling her ear.

"You're crazy. We need to *talk*, not have sex."

She frowned, but she didn't stop him. This was how he always dealt with their problems, and it wasn't working anymore. Or was it? His touch still made her knees go weak. She wanted to protest, to tell him that Dan was more to her than a point she was trying to make. But Steve was distracting her, sliding her blouse off her shoulders and kissing her neck, then her mouth. She started kissing back. She couldn't help it—he was a great kisser. She'd say that much for him. The way he used his tongue to part her lips, *ay, mami,* so good! And he picked exactly the right moment to slide his hands slowly around her behind and pull her tight against him. She could feel her insides melting.

"Yeah, you have a little wild streak, don't you?" he whispered in her ear.

"You're the wild one, not me," she said, between wet kisses and heavy breathing. "Remember when we first met, at that ski share? You couldn't decide who you were gonna bed first, me or that bitch Kelly what's-her-name. I knew from the start you were a playboy, but you were so handsome I didn't listen to myself."

He pulled back and looked at her, his hazel eyes sleepy with lust. "Kelly? No way. She was boring and uptight. You were always the one I wanted. Like I said, the hottest thing on the planet. Why do you think I married you?"

"Steve, there's more to marriage than just sex."

"Yeah? Who says?" He pushed her down onto the bed and climbed on top of her, nudging her legs apart with his knee. "When the sex is this good, who needs anything else? Not me."

Well, I do, she thought, but she couldn't speak with his tongue in her mouth. Okay, so maybe she'd wait and tell him that afterwards.

"Oh!" she moaned.

"See, baby? Told ya."

SHE HAD TO stop having sex with her husband. Not only was it confusing but it made her feel cheap. Though how could that be? she asked herself, looking at Steve after he rolled off her. This was the man she'd married, in the eyes of God and the law. The father of her child. She was doing exactly what she was supposed to do, trying to work things out with him, wasn't she?

Steve started to snore.

"Hey!" She poked him. "Wake up!"

"Wha'?"

"Wake up. We need to talk. Then you need to go. G-O, go."

"No way. I'm too tired. You wore me out, Mel."

"I'm not kidding about the separation, Steve."

He sat up and looked at her.

"Why? Because of that musclehead creep in the trashy car? I got a look at him. He has 'fling' written all over him, Mel. You're rebounding. I understand, and I'm prepared to forgive. Provided you never see him again, of course."

"You're assuming all I'm after is sex because that's all *you're* after. Dan happens to be a very substantive human being. He's caring and a great listener—"

"Oh, and since when does shit like that even matter to you?" he asked angrily.

"What?"

"Look, I'm not criticizing you or anything. But intimacy is not your strong suit. After the childhood you had, who can blame you?"

"What are you *talking* about?"

"If you don't get it, you ought to take a long, hard look in the mirror, Mel. Think about it. You work all the time. You have no close friends. And you and me—we have fun, and we're really compatible. But this isn't one of those relationships where we sit around blabbing about our innermost feelings. Like you'd ever get that from Mr. Musclehead anyway. Gimme a break!"

She got up and pulled on a bathrobe, then walked over to the window, not speaking, more troubled than she cared to admit by what he'd said.

"You know they never caught the man who shot my father," she began tentatively. "Sixteen years ago, and he's still out there somewhere. That's why I work so hard. To stop other people from suffering what I suffered."

"Hey, like I said, you have your reasons. I'm not blaming you, and I'm not complaining. I'm crazy about you, just the way you are. You're gorgeous and smart and fun in bed. You're an amazing mother. But it doesn't ring true for you to go all psychobabble on me, Mel."

"If it's really like you say, doesn't that mean we need to work on our relationship? And work on *ourselves*?" she asked, turning away from the window and looking at him.

"No! We've got a good thing going here, baby. Let's not overthink it, okay? The best solution is just to forget this ever happened. I cheated with Samantha, then you fooled around with Mr. Universe. Fair's fair. Let's just call it even and put it behind us. I mean, what more do you want?"

More than that, she thought. I want more than that.

Steve sighed and rubbed his eyes. His stomach rumbled. "I never had dinner tonight," he said. "Want to order some Chinese?"

She walked over and picked up his pants from where they lay on the floor, handing them to him. "The diner on Madison is open until eleven. You can still get something if you hurry."

"You're kidding, right?"

"Steve, you may be content to live your life in the kind of relationship you just described, with the kind of partner you seem to think I am. I'm not willing to settle for that."

He sighed, looking down at the pants in his hand. "Fine, if you insist, we'll go back to that marriage counselor. If that's what you need to feel better."

"Don't say that just because you want to sleep over tonight. You need to be sincere. Look, I really think we need some time apart, to figure out how serious we are about fixing this marriage."

He studied her for a moment, then stood up and pulled on his pants.

"Okay," he said. "I'll indulge you for a little while longer, Mel. I guess you're more upset about Samantha than I realized. But I'm warning you, there's a limit. I'm getting tired of sleeping at my parents'. And if you see that guy again, I am *not* going to be happy."

She followed him to the foyer to lock up behind him. As he left, she automatically kissed him good night. The kiss made her sad, but it wouldn't have felt right to let him leave without one either. Old habits die hard.

AFTER STEVE LEFT, she got the munchies something awful. It must be stress. Or all the sex. Lucky Steve was gone, because if he were still here, they'd probably wind up doing it again. Food was a safer option. She'd rather have her stomach full and her mind clear of her husband, so she could think.

She went hunting through the cabinets to find it. The small, square box with the blue-and-gold label that hadn't changed since her childhood. Flan from a mix, her favorite dessert as a kid. And yes, she was an assimilated, mainland Puerto Rican whose *mami* didn't know how to make the real thing from scratch. So what? That's who she was, and she should stop being so down on herself.

That was what she ultimately decided, as she stirred the creamy yellow mixture, savoring the delicious caramel scent that rose from the pot. She needed to think better of herself. In her heart she'd never made it out of Bushwick. She was still the girl from the block, child of violence and divorce, whose father never came back home after that one awful night. Up until now she was grateful to take what Steve offered and not ask anything more.

She poured the sweet molten liquid out into small bowls and stuck them in the freezer to speed the cooling process. She ate two and a half of the bowls before she felt sick to her stomach and dumped the rest in the trash. *¡Qué estúpido!* What was she thinking? She could feel those calories going straight to her hips. Now she'd have to fast tomorrow to make up for it.

She went to her bedroom and turned off the lights, lying on top of the covers and watching the blue shadows move across the room, thinking about what Steve had said. She didn't want to be the person he described. She wanted to jettison all that old baggage from her childhood, so she could be better and braver and take her rightful place in the world.

Now all she had to do was figure out how.

37

———

Bill Flanagan snapped his cell phone shut, a satisfied smile spreading across his broad red face. He hadn't expected this gig to amount to much. But whaddaya know, a phone call out of the blue, and here he was looking at twenty-five grand. Fifteen, that scumbag offered him first, but he negotiated it up. Think Wild Bill Flanagan didn't know the street price for a hit? Think they were dealing with a fucking amateur? Think again, my friend. The timing was good, though. Frankie Bricks was coming after him for that wad he dropped in Atlantic City. He needed a payday if he didn't want to wind up kneecapped.

He'd have to think it through real careful, though. It was such an easy setup, what with him in the room anyway, it was tempting to jump the gun. She'd been sleeping when he left. He could walk back in and take care of it right now with the old pillow-over-the-face routine, then string her up with some rope or, better yet, a torn bedsheet. Make it look like a suicide, the man said. Twenty-five grand for a couple minutes work—not bad. He'd enjoy it, too, big-time. That snotty little bitch waking up terrified when she couldn't breathe, trying to fight him off, writhing under him while he pressed the pillow down harder, then going limp. Wow. Just thinking about it, he got a hard-on for the first time in as long as he could remember. But if he decided to go that route, he'd have to set up his alibi real careful, or he'd get caught.

That was the problem. The easiest thing about this hit was also the hardest. He had total access. That meant they would come looking to him for answers. If they didn't buy the suicide angle, they'd know it was murder; nothing in her condition far as he knew would suggest natural causes. So they'd assume he had something to do with it. Somebody else bodyguarding her might be able to say he'd stepped out to take a piss and get away with it, but not him. They had it in for him, the lousy motherfuckers. He needed something good, something that could be corroborated. He needed to be seen somewhere. The cafeteria, maybe? He could kill her, string her up, then go down there and pick a fight with somebody. That would get him noticed, and it would also have the added benefit of explaining any marks on him if the little bitch resisted. Then he'd come upstairs and pretend to discover the body. It was a possibility.

He went back into the room and sat in the chair in the corner, watching her sleep, thinking about how to do it. It was around ten o'clock. Bright light spilled into the darkened room from the hallway. Still a lot of activity on the ward. Middle of the night would be better, so nobody would hear the struggle. It had to be done tonight—that was a condition of the deal. So he didn't have time to get no heart-attack drug or any fancy shit like that. A knife, a gun, he already had, but they wouldn't fly if he was gonna fake the suicide. Suffocation, then, or maybe strangulation. Strangulation, now there was an idea. The white flesh of her skinny neck under his thumbs as he crushed her windpipe. Jesus, he was turning himself on again.

She stirred in her sleep, sighing and flopping her bandaged arm around on the blanket. He walked over and stood there looking at her. When he was sure she was sound asleep, he carefully tugged the blanket down to her waist, looking at the outline of her body under the thin hospital gown. She was too goddamn skinny. Pointy little tits, she had, needed a boob job. He liked 'em bigger, like that prosecutor today—now, she was a ripe one. The idea of fucking a girl after she was dead had always appealed to him, but this one here was a bag of bones.

There was the DNA evidence, too. Hairs he could explain from body-guarding her, but semen would be a problem. He better watch what he drank, or he'd find himself doing it anyway. Controlling himself was never his thing.

He went back to the chair, sat down, and stretched his legs out. He pulled out his pint, tipped it back and drank till it was empty and he felt that glow. It would be hours before he could do anything. He oughta save his energy. Time for a little snooze.

FLANAGAN WOKE WITH a start from a dead sleep. He'd heard a weird popping noise. Or was it just a dream? It was getting light outside. He pushed the button to light up the display on his digital watch, his head pounding. He'd slept most of the night away. Jesus, better get moving if he was gonna get this job done. He couldn't afford to miss his chance; he needed the paycheck too bad.

The door to the hallway was closed. Funny, he didn't remember doing that. Must've been a nurse. He stood up stiffly and straightened out his clothes, hawking to clear the phlegm from his throat. Sleeping in a fuck-ing chair. Everything hurt. Something smelled funny, almost like blood. He hated hospitals, so depressing. Man, he was groggy. He needed a drink to clear his head. His hands shook as he reached for his pint. Fuck-ing empty! Shit! He didn't remember finishing it off. How the fuck was he gonna do this job without another drink? He might have to go out for some, he was getting the DTs so bad.

He walked over to the bed, remembering that he hadn't decided whether to strangle or suffocate her. Looking down at her, though, it took him a minute to process what he saw. Amanda's eyes were wide open, staring at the ceiling. A neat black hole sat square in the middle of her forehead, as a dark stain spread slowly across her pillow.

He was shaking all over now, trying to work out what had happened—could he have done it and blacked it out?—when he heard a noise behind him and turned. A Spanish guy with a pointy face and little bitty eyes stood there looking at him. Kid was fierce-looking, but small. Fucking prick, stealing his twenty-five Gs. Bill saw in his mind's eye how he'd beat the kid to death with his bare fists.

"Hey, asshole," he said, his voice hoarse, moving toward the kid, "what the fuck you doing? This is my gig."

The kid smiled and raised his arm from where it hung at his side. He held a sleek nine-millimeter with a silencer a mile long coming off the muzzle, pointed straight at Bill's face. Nice piece, Bill thought, listening to the loud pop it made when it went off.

HE WALK TO the elevator and get on, simple as that. It pretty quiet in the hospital this early in the morning. He like the early morning. When he get outside, the street feel real fresh. Garbage don't stink the way it do later in the day, when the sun so hot. Nobody seen him. Even if they did, so what? He left the door closed. By the time they find the bodies, he be long gone and nobody gonna give him a second thought.

He been mad productive lately. It like he unstoppable. Kill people right in front of witnesses, and still ain't nobody catch him. He on a mad winning streak. No reason to stop when you hot. He take care of that Chinese bitch today, that architect. Then maybe he finally get a payday off this fucked-up job.

38

From the depths of her sleep, Melanie heard a telephone ringing. She struggled to the surface through waves of fatigue. By the time she sat up and reached for the receiver on her bedside table, the answering machine had clicked on in the other room.

"Hello? Hello?" she repeated, eyes burning, wincing at the screech on the line as the machine cut off.

"Hello, Melanie, it's Elsie."

She looked at the clock sitting next to the telephone. It was nearly seven. The alarm was just about to go off, and the bed felt empty without Steve in it. She'd barely slept last night, with everything that was on her mind. Given the length of Elsie's commute and the fact that she obviously hadn't left home yet, Elsie was going to be late to work. Which meant Melanie was going to be late to work.

"Hey, Elsie, what's up?" she asked, her stomach sinking. She had so much to do today.

"Did I mention today was my birthday?" Elsie asked.

"No. No, I didn't know it was your birthday. But I'm glad you told me. I'll pick up a cake on my way home from the office today, and we'll celebrate."

"Well, my children want to take me out. After how much I've been working, I need the day off. So I'm afraid I won't be able to make it today," Elsie said.

"I beg your pardon?" Melanie asked, hoping she'd misunderstood.

"I said I can't come in today."

"Elsie, if you want to take a personal day for your birthday, we can talk about that, but I need some notice. I'm in the middle of a major murder investigation." She was panicking, breathing hard.

"I'm sorry, Melanie. I really can't make it today. I'll see you tomorrow." Elsie hung up.

SHE CHECKED ON Maya, still sound asleep in her crib. *Por favor,* stay that way a little longer, *nena*! Melanie needed to concentrate on solving this problem. She made some coffee and sat down at the kitchen table, rubbing her eyes. Tired as she was, coping with this unexpected complication seemed beyond her abilities. Think, think. Who could she call? Well, Steve, of course. He was Maya's father, wasn't he?

She reached him at his parents' and explained the situation.

"Can you believe that?" she said. "I feel so let down. No notice or anything."

"Elsie's probably trying to make a point about how you've been treating her," Steve replied.

"I know. I get it. I'm not stupid. I do need to have a heart-to-heart with her about overtime. But this is her *job*. When I have to stay late, no matter how tired I am the next day, I still show up for work."

"Give her a break. She's been working pretty hard lately, and she's no spring chicken."

"Okay, I hear you. But will you cover for me? At least until this afternoon when my mom gets off work?"

"No, I won't, Melanie. You know why? You need a lesson in what this separation stuff means in real life. Being a single mother is no picnic."

"Steve, this is no time to be vindictive."

"It's not about that. You're rushing into this separation without considering the consequences. Maybe this'll make you think twice, appreciate me a little more. Because I want to be in your life. Yours and Maya's."

"Steve—"

"Think about it," he said, and hung up.

Yeah, she'd think about what a jerk *he* was, that's what she'd think about. As if his refusal to pitch in would make her more likely to reconcile with him. Fat chance. She put the phone down and banged her head several times on the table. Not that that helped anything, but it summed up how she felt.

The phone rang loudly, right in her ear, making her jump. She snatched it up and answered it.

"Hello?" she said hopefully. Elsie, perhaps, calling to say she'd changed her mind?

"Hey," Dan said. "You get some sleep?"

"Oh, hi." She was momentarily disappointed it wasn't Elsie. Things were so screwed up in her life that Dan felt like one more complication. Maybe she should have a talk with him, straighten things out, although that seemed awkward, even presumptuous. After all, nothing had really happened last night. Just one tiny kiss. Mmm, it was pretty great, though. She couldn't help smiling. *He* was pretty great.

"How are you this morning?" she asked, brightening.

"Not so good," he said. "Listen, I got some real bad news."

"Oh." She reviewed all the possibilities in her mind. Could it have something to do with Bernadette? "What? Tell me."

"Slice got to Amanda. She was murdered last night. Shot in the head. Flanagan, too."

A wave of nausea swept through her. She rushed to the sink just in time to throw up. Her eyes were tearing, and she couldn't see. She ran the water, splashed some on her face.

"Melanie? Melanie?"

She heard the phone squawking and looked down in surprise to see that it was still in her hand. In her head she heard Delvis Diaz's voice, telling her the people she'd brought to the interview were dirty. Not just

Randall. Dan, too. Dan, who insisted on taking her out for a drink last night when they should have been at the hospital guarding Amanda. Dan, the man she told her husband she had feelings for, the man she was letting further undermine her already devastated marriage. God, what a fool she was!

"Where the fuck was Randall? Why wasn't he watching her door?" Tears were streaming down her cheeks, but she managed to sound tough, collected.

He paused a moment before responding. "I don't know. I can't find him, and he's not answering his pager."

"Where are you?" she asked.

"At the hospital, but I'm about to leave. It happened overnight. Crime Scene went through the room already and took the bodies to the morgue. I can come pick you up if you want. With Slice out there—"

She hung up, cutting him off in the middle of a sentence.

"Jesus Christ, Melanie Vargas," she said aloud, "you are a fucking *idiot.*"

HER MOTHER COULDN'T get there until after lunch. Melanie said yes to that, then sprang up and paced, racking her brain for other solutions. She grabbed the Yellow Pages and thumbed through frantically until she found baby-sitting services. But no. She couldn't do it. She couldn't leave Maya with a complete stranger. Her sister was out of town. Sophie. Sophie Cho. She realized Sophie had never returned her message from the other night.

She dialed rapidly and tapped her foot, listening to the rings. But all she got was a prerecorded mechanical message: "We're sorry. The number you called has been disconnected. No further information is available."

What? She dialed again carefully and got the same thing. Damn! That was strange. With everything going on, she suddenly felt nervous about Sophie. Why would her telephone be disconnected? Melanie rummaged in the drawer for her address book and found Sophie's cell-phone number. She dialed. *Please answer, please answer.*

"Hello?"

"Oh, Soph, it's Melanie. I'm so glad I got you."

"Melanie?"

"Yes."

"Look, I called you—"

"Yes, I know. I returned your call, and then I never heard back. Is everything okay? Did you disconnect your telephone for some reason?"

"Yes. Yes, I did."

"Why? Are you moving?"

"I'm taking a vacation."

"Vacation?"

"Yes. I'm going up to Vancouver to stay with my cousin."

"Oh, for how long?"

"I'm not sure, but a while. I'm thinking about moving there, actually."

"Oh, my." Melanie's heart sank. It wasn't just because she needed a baby-sitter either. She hadn't realized until just that moment how important Sophie's friendship was to her. Sophie was really her only close friend, other than her sister. "Soph, I'm shocked. I mean, when did this happen? You never mentioned it before. Wow, I'm gonna miss you so much."

"I'll miss you, too. In fact, I was hoping I could come over this morning and say good-bye to you and the baby. If it wouldn't be too much trouble."

"No, no, of course not. I'm stuck home until my mom shows up anyway, because my baby-sitter is taking a personal day. It's awful timing, I'm just frantic at work with the Benson case and everything."

There was a pause on the other end of the line. "Yes. How's that going?" Sophie asked stiffly.

"It's been pretty rough, but I won't burden you with the gruesome details. I brought it on myself, after all. So when should I expect you?"

"Is it okay if I come over now? I put all my furniture in storage yesterday. I'm just sitting in a Starbucks with nowhere to go."

"Of course. Gosh, why didn't you call me? You could've slept on my couch last night."

"It's okay. When is your mom coming?"

"After lunch."

"Listen, if you want me to baby-sit Maya until then so you can go to work, it's no problem. My flight doesn't leave until this evening."

The attendant's booth in the G-car parking lot was locked up tight. Melanie cupped her hands around her eyes, peering in the window, as if someone might be hiding in its cramped, dark interior. The sign posted on the door said the lot opened at nine, and it was only eight-fifteen. She stood there sweating in a tailored shirtdress, trying to think of an alternative to waiting for forty-five minutes. Waiting was not an option at this point in the game.

A faded gray four-door sedan turned into the lot and pulled up beside the booth. With the glare on the windows, she couldn't see who was driving. Then the door opened, and Joe Williams, her colleague from the office, stepped out.

"Joe." She was genuinely glad to see him.

"Why here so early? You have a court date on Long Island or something?" he asked, squinting through his thick glasses against the beating sun.

"Not exactly."

He looked at her closely. "Everything okay? You don't look so good."

"No, actually. All hell is breaking loose. Another witness killed last night. Benson's daughter. We can't seem to catch Slice, and I don't know which way to turn. I need to get to Otisville right away to interview a prisoner. But I can't get a car for another forty-five minutes. Unless you're returning that one," she said hopefully.

"I am, but old Stella here is not in great shape. She's been making a funny grinding noise."

"Hey, I don't care. Beggars can't be choosers. Just give me the key." She held out her hand.

"Are you sure? I don't know much about cars, but she doesn't sound good."

"Joe, it's an emergency."

"Okay." He handed her the key. "If you like, I'll fill out the paperwork for you once the attendant gets in."

"That would be great. You're a pal."

"Hey, anything I can do. Watching you suffer through this case, I actually feel guilty you caught it instead of me."

"Oh, come on, we both know I deserve whatever I get. Teach me to try to further my career," she said. She opened the car door and slid behind the wheel, throwing her bag onto the passenger seat.

"Oh, speaking of careers, I have some news," Joe said, then waved his hand. "But never mind. You're in a rush."

"No. What is it?"

"I'm considering an offer from Fogel, Bingham and McGuire. I may be leaving the office."

Her face fell. Her friends were deserting her. Not like she had many to spare either. Steve had been right about that.

"Oh, Joe! No, you can't. How will I get along without you?"

"It's nice of you to say that. I'll miss you, too. But it's not like we ever see each other, you know."

"But we will, once things slow down."

"As if that'll ever happen. The thing is, Melanie, I need work that challenges me intellectually. No matter what I say, Witchie-Poo keeps assigning me buy-busts."

"When I get a minute, Joe, I'm talking you out of this."

He smiled. "Aw, well, thanks for caring." He stepped back as she pulled the door shut. "Good luck!" he shouted, but she'd turned on the air-conditioning and didn't hear him.

HER LEG WAS cramping from the tension of pressing the pedal to the floor.

"Godamnit, Stella!" she shouted, pounding the steering wheel. Damn thing kept losing power. She had to get to Delvis before the engine died. She had to hear the answer. It wasn't just about catching Slice anymore. If people around her were dirty, she needed to hear the rest. Because the pattern had become too obvious to ignore. The missing evidence. The doors left unguarded. Rosario. Jasmine. Now Amanda. Someone on the inside was working with that animal, tipping him off. She needed to find out who. She had to stop the killings. And, for her own reasons, she needed to learn the truth about Dan O'Reilly.

As she passed through the barbed-wire gates of the prison, she breathed normally again. She made it this far. It wouldn't be long now until she knew. Melanie turned off the engine, wincing at the terrible grinding sound. Then she grabbed her bag and ran for the entrance, clip-clopping in her high heels.

Leona Burkett, the bleached blonde with the wide behind whom Melanie remembered from the other day, met her by the X-ray machine. Melanie flashed her credentials, shivering in the frigid air-conditioning, thinking about what she would ask Delvis. It was amazing how work calmed her, focused her mind. She felt the ground back under her feet.

"You just show up, without an appointment?" Leona snapped.

"I apologize," Melanie said. "This investigation is moving so fast. The need to speak to Diaz again came up unexpectedly."

"Have a seat while I check the computer. I have no idea whether it can be arranged for today."

"Please, whatever you can do. It's urgent."

Leona jerked her head toward a small waiting area to the left of the entrance, then walked away.

Melanie was beginning to get agitated, looking at her watch, when Leona returned about fifteen minutes later.

"Looks like you wasted a trip," Leona said. "This is why I tell you people to call first."

"Why? What do you mean?"

"Prisoner was just transferred to Leavenworth. Went out on the five A.M. airlift."

"Leavenworth? *Kansas?*"

"Yes, ma'am. That scumbag's attitude finally caught up with him. He pissed *some*body off to get sent there. Leavenworth knows how to deal with the hardened cases. I doubt we'll ever see Diaz again, but if we do, let's just say he'll be more cooperative." She snickered.

"No! That can't be right. I just spoke to him yesterday. He never said anything about getting transferred."

"He didn't know. They wake him up, tell him to grab his box of belongings, and get his ass on the plane."

Something occurred to her. "Exactly when was the transfer arranged?"

Leona flipped through several sheets of paper attached to the clipboard she carried.

"Let's see," she said, removing one. "Here's the redesignation paperwork. 'Diaz, Delvis, number A6452-053, designation transfer, airlift, LV.' LV is Leavenworth. This was entered into the computer last night at 1807 hours, so just after six o'clock."

Delvis had called Melanie in the late afternoon, some time between four and five. If she had any doubt about whether the transfer was a coincidence, the timing resolved it. Delvis was transferred for one reason and one reason only—to interfere with her speaking to him again.

"Who ordered him transferred?" Melanie asked.

Leona pointed to a column on the sheet of paper. "See here? It just says *D* for discretionary. That means it was at the discretion of the Bureau of Prisons rather than by a writ. So it was somebody in the BOP ordered it."

"Can I find out who? Ask them why they did it?"

"I told you why. That scumbag was a pain in everybody's backside. I could prob'ly name you ten guys wanted his ass out of here. But who keyed in the actual order, the computer doesn't record that."

"How can I get him back?"

Leona scowled and took back the sheet of paper. "Get him back? He just left."

"But I need to speak with him."

"You want him back, file a sentenced-prisoner writ. But I can tell you, people around here ain't gonna be too happy to see his ugly mug again."

"Okay, how do I do that?"

"Get a writ, get it signed by a federal judge. File it with the Marshals Service thirty days prior to the time you need the prisoner."

"But I need the prisoner now."

Leona shrugged. "Well, then. Guess you're out of luck. Listen, if you don't mind, I got a lot of work to do this morning."

"Oh, of course. Thank you, Leona. You've been very helpful."

"Don't mention it, hon."

MELANIE CROSSED THE blistering-hot blacktop back to where she'd parked. The way her day was going, she had a sinking feeling that the car would decide not to start. And that was *before* she saw the oily reddish brown puddle seeping out from under it.

She opened the driver's-side door and felt waves of hot, acrid-smelling air rush out at her. Of course she hadn't thought to park in the shade. She got in anyway, wincing as her skirt rode up and exposed the backs of her thighs to the scalding Naugahyde seat. Leaving the door open for air, she found the key in her bag, stuck it in the ignition, and turned it.

A strange whirring noise emanated from the engine, but when she put the car in gear and stepped on the gas, nothing happened. Stella refused to move. She pressed her foot to the floor. Still nothing.

"Come on, Stella. Come on, baby."

The whir became a grind and then a screech, but no matter how hard she pressed, the car wouldn't budge. She put her head down on the steering wheel, eyes completely dry. What good would crying do? Besides, she was too tired.

"Car trouble?" said a voice beside her.

She raised her head. Dan O'Reilly stood there looking down at her, the sun glinting off his thick, dark hair, a smile lighting up his handsome face.

4 0

———

"Lucky I showed up," Dan said. "Your transmission is shot. You'd better come with me."

Standing there in the sunlight, he looked so trustworthy he practically sparkled, but appearances could be deceiving. If she really wanted to get the truth, she'd go with him now. She'd play along, keep her eyes open. If she said no, he'd realize she suspected something, and she'd lose her advantage. She wasn't scared. She refused to believe Dan would hurt her. She would never believe that.

So she pretended to smile back at him and got out of her car.

"I'm parked right over here," he said. "I'll get the A/C going for you, see if I can find a garage out here in the middle of East Buttfuck."

He opened the door of his car for her, then walked around to the driver's side. She got into the passenger seat. He must've had the air-conditioning going just minutes earlier, because the interior was cool. It smelled of coffee and, beneath that aroma, something clean that she realized with a start must just be him. She breathed deeply, then caught herself. What was she doing? She couldn't let herself feel anything for him—not trust, not physical attraction, nothing. She'd decided that already.

She reached out and touched the coffee sitting in the drink holder. It was still hot.

"That's for you," he said. "Bought it at a diner down the road. Thought you might need some caffeine."

"You were expecting to see me? So I guess it's no coincidence you're here?"

"No, of course not. You hung up on me this morning. I got worried about you, so I tracked you down."

"How on earth did you find me?"

"Trained investigator, sweetheart."

Yeah, right, she thought.

He flipped on the air-conditioning, turning the vent to point directly at her. A blast of air whipped her hair up into her face, where it stuck to her lipstick. She brushed it back with her fingers.

"Cool enough for you?" Dan asked.

"Definitely."

"See? Who's your daddy? Do I take care of you or what?"

"Why didn't you just call me, rather than driving an hour and a half to Otisville?" she asked edgily.

"With how upset you were, I figured you wouldn't answer your phone."

"You thought I wouldn't answer, so you hopped in your car and drove for two hours instead? That makes no sense."

His cell phone rang.

"Oh," he said, pulling it from his pocket, "I'm working a lead. This might be it.

"Yeah?" he answered. When he heard the voice on the other end, he looked at Melanie like it was important. Holding the phone with his shoulder, he set the timer on his digital watch. "Fucking right I was out there last night. . . . Look, you don't want me shaking the trees for you, you fucking return my beeps. . . . When? You been telling me that for three days. How long am I supposed to wait? . . . You know the game. You want any protection, you gotta give me something. . . . I told you, you deliver Slice and I'll take care of that. . . . I'll handle it when the time comes. . . . This afternoon or nothing. This is the end of the line. . . . Where? . . . Okay, yeah, four o'clock, but if you don't show, that's it. You're fair game on the street. And you know how people get hurt in an arrest situation, regrettable as that is. . . . Right, bye."

"Who was that?" Melanie asked when he hung up.

"Snitch of mine. He could deliver Slice on a silver platter if he wanted to, but the guy's fucking playing me. He won't come in, won't meet. So I'm trying to track him through the phone company." He dialed his phone hurriedly. "Yeah, gimme the Compliance Department. . . . Vinnie Maresca, please. . . . Yeah, Vin, Dan O'Reilly. Did you get it? Great! Hold on a second."

He leaned across her and rummaged through the glove compartment, his body inches from hers. She closed her eyes and held her breath, willing herself not to feel anything. Sexual attraction, *claro*. A chemical thing. Her brain could override it, she told herself. He pulled out a pen and a small notebook and sat up again. She breathed out. She opened her eyes and saw him scribbling something down.

"Millbrook, New York. Never heard of it. . . . Dutchess County? Huh. Strange. Listen, thanks though, I owe you a beer. Later, buddy." He hung up and turned to Melanie. "Where the fuck is Millbrook, New York?"

"Millbrook? It's a fancy little town just south of here. Horses, antiques, that sort of thing. Jed Benson had a country estate there. Why?"

"Huh, that's gotta be it. Why else would a scumbag Bushwick drug dealer be in Millbrook? My snitch must be at Benson's place. Looking for something. You don't happen to know the address?"

"Of Benson's house? Yes, actually I do. I reviewed those records just last night, and I remember it. Why?"

"We need to get there right away. If I can get my hands on this guy, he can take us right to Slice."

DAN FOLLOWED THE signs back to the highway, then pulled a road atlas from the space between the two front seats and flipped it open in his lap, consulting it as he drove.

"So who's this snitch? Would I recognize his name?" she asked, studying his profile.

He smiled. "You're very nosy, you know that? So many questions to-day. How about I ask a few for a change?"

"What do you want to know?" she asked warily.

"I want to know why the first thing you do after Amanda gets hit is rush up here to talk to Delvis again? What did he have to say that was so important?"

"I don't know. I never spoke to him."

"Oh? Why not?"

"He was transferred to Leavenworth this morning."

He took his eyes off the road and looked at her with genuine astonish-ment. She made a mental note. Whatever Dan was involved in, he hadn't known about Delvis's transfer.

"You look surprised," Melanie said.

"I am. Diaz has been at Otisville since day one. It's weird he'd get moved all of a sudden. Why do you think they transferred him?"

"Leona said there was no reason given in the order," she said, evading his question.

He looked over at her quizzically. "Any relationship between you com-ing up here and Delvis getting moved?"

"Why do you ask?"   ·

"Hey, can we stop playing games here? What's the matter, you don't trust me or something?" He looked upset, kept his gaze on her. The car swerved slightly in its lane.

"Will you watch where you're going, please? I don't want to end up dead," she said.

"Answer my question."

"Of course I trust you."

"Well, you're sure not acting like it."

Dan's mouth set in an angry line. They drove on in silence for some time. Eventually, he signaled and pulled off the highway onto the exit ramp for Millbrook. Within minutes they were on a winding road flanked by views of red barns and pastures dotted with creamy white sheep and picture-book horses. Dan consulted the atlas sitting open in his lap and adjusted the route slightly. They drove for a while longer, the scenery getting better by the minute. On either side were gentleman's farms, graced by painstakingly restored nineteenth-century farmhouses with freshly painted shutters and elegant landscaping. Their late-summer gardens competed in lavish display with the first blazes of color appearing in ancient, towering trees.

Dan focused on the road, staying quiet.

Finally he asked, "Is it that you're upset with Randall? I vouched for him, and he didn't come through? If that's it, you should tell me."

"Naturally I'm upset," she said, seizing on the explanation he offered. "I know he's your friend, but his performance has been a problem, and it's past the point where it can be overlooked. Blowing that interview with Delvis was one thing. But he was supposed to be guarding Amanda. And now she's dead."

"I know, I know. You're right," he said, shaking his head.

The pain in his voice sounded real. She studied his face in profile, wishing she could see through into his brain. Every instinct told her he was just as true-blue honest as he looked, but the facts suggested other-wise. And after all, how well did she really know this guy?

"Were you able to get in touch with him this morning?" she asked.

"No, and that has me worried. I can't get him at home or on his pager. Oh, hey, I think this is it."

Dan pulled into a gravel driveway that sloped gently up and away from the road, got out and opened a latched iron gate that stretched between two large brick-and-limestone portals on either side of the drive.

"Wow. Not bad," Melanie said when he got back into the car.

Farther up the drive, though, the Bensons' spread started to look less scrupulously tended than the neighboring estates. A small outbuilding on the way to the main house had two broken windows. Its door sat slightly askew, blown open by the wind. The fenced paddocks sloping away from the drive on either side were emptied of horses and badly overgrown.

"Looks abandoned," Dan remarked.

"Yeah." Melanie shivered slightly in the air-conditioning.

At the top of the rise, a semicircular drive led to a gracious Georgian brick mansion, its three stories perfectly symmetrical, with evenly spaced mullioned windows and white shutters. The house veritably gleamed in the hot sun, yet the windows seemed blank and dark. A separate four-bay clapboard garage stretched off to the right, one of its bays, oddly, thrown open.

"Do you think your informant's still here?" Melanie asked, a high-pitched note of anxiety in her voice.

"He better be. If not, I'll prob'ly never get my hands on him. Place sure looks empty, though. Let's check it out."

"We don't have a warrant."

"So what? The garage door's open. If you're nervous, stay in the car."

"I'm not nervous," she said. But she was, terribly. Palms sweaty, heart rate elevated. She couldn't decide whether to follow Dan into the garage, on the theory that she was safer with him than alone, or stay in the car, on the theory that he might be leading her into a trap.

Dan sprang out of the low seat and strode deliberately toward the open garage bay, hand at his waistband near his gun. She opened the passenger door and got out tentatively, lingering in the drive. From the top of the rise, the blue shadows of the Catskills were visible to the west. A delicious summer breeze washed over her, carrying the scent of wild anise and a whiff of animal dung. The deep lowing of a herd of cows made its way up from the valley, providing a counterpoint to the high chirp of sparrows and jays from the surrounding trees.

She looked longingly at the cool grass under the trees. It was so beautiful here. Suddenly she felt exhausted by all the sad things that had happened. For just a minute, she wished for a completely different life. She and Dan, no murders, no Benson investigation. Up here for the weekend, as lovers, maybe even married to each other, with a picnic lunch. As if they'd met when she was single, before Steve. But then she shook herself. If she'd never married Steve, she wouldn't have Maya. Not to mention that Dan might somehow be complicit in a string of brutal murders. Oh, yeah, that.

"Hey, nature girl," Dan called from the gloom of the bay door. "There's a brand-new Hummer in here. Thing is fucking huge. You like cars. Come check it out."

Inside, it took a moment for her eyes to adjust. She flipped a switch near the door, turning on overhead fluorescent lights to reveal a well-maintained garage, its floor freshly painted a glossy gray. Five heavy-duty black rubber trash cans stood along the far wall, their lids off, empty but still emitting a sour smell. A large refrigerator stood beside them.

"Did you check the fridge for bodies?" she joked.

"Yeah, actually, that's the first thing I did. There's some skanky-looking meat in there, but I'm pretty sure it's venison. Get a load of this car, though. I found it sitting open like this."

He stood in front of the only car in the garage, an enormous black Hummer with aggressive metal piping, a row of spotlights across the roof, and military-style flat windshields. Solid and massive as a bank vault on wheels, the vehicle sat with its four doors wide open.

"Wow," she said.

"Yeah. Thing's insane, but you gotta love it."

"You think it was Benson's?"

"Who else?" he said. "Look at it, it's like a fricking death star. I'll tell you, it sure looks like it belonged to a drug dealer."

"Or else some crazed rapper."

"Same difference," he said.

Dan climbed up into the high front passenger seat, rummaged through the glove compartment, and brought out a handful of papers. "Yup, it's registered to Benson," he announced. "Bought two months ago."

From where she was standing, Melanie noticed an odd glint of red shining in the lower-left-hand corner of the small rear windshield. She came around to inspect it, running her finger over a metallic red sticker. It was affixed on the inside and bore the image of the Looney Tunes Road Runner cartoon character.

"Hey," she called to Dan. "You were right, drug-dealer car. There's a Road Runner sticker back here. This car has a trap."

Dan jumped down from the front seat and raced around to where she stood. Like Melanie, he instinctively brushed his finger over the sticker. They'd both done enough drug cases to know what it meant.

"Jesus, whaddaya know. Jed Benson with a trapped-out car."

The Road Runner was the most famous trap installer in the five boroughs of New York City and had been for a decade. He'd never been caught. Traps—also called hides, stashes, or secret compartments—were the kingpins' preferred way of moving contraband. If you wanted to transport drugs, you needed one, a good one, one nobody could find. The Road Runner's were the best. Legend had it he'd been a structural engineer back in Colombia, and it showed in his work. His traps were customized to fit into the least expected places in bad guys' cars, with the carpeting and leather matched exactly to camouflage their location. Their triggering mechanisms were the most sophisticated ever seen, opening hydraulically on complex, coded electronic sequences sent by normal vehicle functions. You could rip a car apart down to the floorboards and still not find his traps, unless you knew the precise code for opening them. The traps were so good that bad guys could afford to indulge themselves by flaunting them with the Road Runner's signature sticker in the rear window. It was a status thing—show off for your homies, taunt law enforcement. Yeah, I have a trap, asshole, the sticker said, but you'll never find it.

"I can't believe it," Melanie said.

"I'll say. Last time I checked, the Road Runner was charging ten grand for his simplest trap. To trap out a car like this, you gotta figure fifteen, twenty K easy."

"Laundering money is one thing. But why would Benson have a Road Runner trap unless he was—"

"Unless he was moving drugs?"

They looked at each other. "Yeah," she said, "moving drugs. Our victim got his hands dirty."

"I'm really starting to believe you about this guy," Dan said. He walked to the front and climbed up into the driver's seat. Melanie followed, coming to stand beneath where he sat.

"Do you know how to open it?" she asked.

"Every trap is different. The Road Runner's sequences are so complicated it's almost impossible to figure them out without a snitch or an expert." The keys were sitting in the ignition. Dan turned the car on, and the engine sprang to life with a rich, satisfying roar. "I can fiddle around with things and see if we get lucky, but I don't think we have time."

"You mean if we want to find your snitch?"

"I mean if we don't want him to find us first. I'm betting he was sitting right here before we showed up, trying to open this trap just like we are."

Dan wasn't prescient. He just had good instincts, refined by many years on the streets. At that very moment, as their eyes met and the significance of his remark hit her, she heard a low growl. An enormous black dog, clad in a biker's regalia of harnesses and chains, stood at alert in the open garage bay ten feet from them, salivating and poised for attack. She froze, rooted to the ground, fascinated by the intricate pattern of scars on the dog's battle-worn hide. He's not real, she thought as he leaped directly at her in slow motion.

"Slice's dog! Get in!" Dan shouted, grabbing her around the waist and hauling her into the car as he stepped on the gas. She sprawled across his lap, then righted herself and clambered on all fours into the passenger seat as the car charged forward. Dan slammed his door. Off balance, she reached for the handle of her door, leaning out over open space for a harrowing second before managing to yank it closed, sitting up just in time to see the dog disappear with a thunk under the front wheels of the vehicle. They lurched out into the sunlight and hit the crunchy gravel of the circular drive. Instinctively they both turned to look back through the rear window. The dog jumped up, uninjured, and bounded after them.

"Shit! Get the back doors!" Dan shouted.

She threw herself over the gearshift and toppled into the backseat, her fall broken by soft, fragrant leather, pulling the driver's-side rear door closed just in time. The dog bounced off it with a loud thumping sound, barking wildly, the second after it slammed shut. Melanie reached out for the passenger door and slammed that, too. The dog continued to pound insanely against the other door as they both gaped at him in astonishment, his powerful back legs propelling him all the way up to the high window, which threatened to shatter under the impact.

"Duck!" Dan yelled, drawing his gun, "I'm gonna shoot the fucking thing!"

"No, don't!"

"Get down!"

Dan reached over the seat with one hand and pushed the top of her head. She hunkered down on the back floor as he leaned over, aimed, and shot through the closed window. The dog yelped; small chunks of shattered window glass rained down on her.

"Shit, only grazed him!" Dan fired three more shots in rapid succession. Melanie raised her head and climbed shakily up to the backseat, brushing away pebbles of sea green glass. Dan opened his door and stepped down, leaning over to examine the dog.

"Is he dead?" she asked, looking out through the empty space where the window had been.

"Yeah."

Melanie descended gingerly from the Hummer, picking her way over to where Dan stood. She looked down at the viscous puddle seeping into the white gravel under the dog's carcass, and then back at Dan.

"Look," he said gently, reading her face, "I hate to hurt an animal, sweetheart. But this one, Slice ruined him. It's like he was rabid."

She nodded. Nervously, she looked over her shoulder toward the house. "Wait a minute, now. How do you know this was Slice's dog? Why would your snitch be here with Slice's dog?"

"I ever tell you you ask very good questions?"

Standing over the dog's carcass, scanning the seemingly deserted house, he snapped the cartridge from the base of his gun, examined it quickly, and snapped it right back in. Before she could ask him another one, the glass of the Hummer's side window exploded, followed a split second later by a loud pop that reverberated from somewhere above them. Suddenly she was on the ground, breath knocked out of her, hands and knees scraped, with Dan's bulk on top of her.

"Shit! We're under fire!" He held her head down with one hand as he shot off several rounds toward the house. A window shattered on the second floor, followed by silence, the only sound the rustling of leaves in a sudden breeze.

"Is he still there?" she whispered after a moment. "Did you get him?"

"No way." He spoke into her hair, his warm breath tickling her ear. "He's inside. The only way to get him is gonna be to go in after him."

"So let's go," she whispered harshly.

"I can't take you into a gunfight. This ain't no exercise—these are live rounds we're talking."

"Okay, so you go. I'll make a run for the garage."

"He'll pick you right off. He's got a bird's-eye view from up there."

As if to emphasize Dan's point, several more rounds exploded in the gravel around them, ricocheting wildly, kicking up clouds of dust.

"Oh, my God!" Melanie cried, hunkering down in the scratchy gravel, finally comprehending the danger they were in.

"See? Jesus, what an idiot I was to bring you here!"

"What should we do?"

"The car is between us and the house," he murmured. "In a minute I'll start shooting. That'll provide some cover for us to get to it. Stay low to the ground. I'll make a run for the driver's seat. You jump in the back and stay down on the floor, okay?"

"But then we won't get him."

"I'll drive you to a safe spot, you jump out, and I'll come right on back and find the guy."

"Okay." She wasn't about to argue. She wanted to live to put her daughter to bed that night.

"Here we go. Ready? One, two, three—"

She could feel the kick of the gun in the way his body jerked into hers as he fired. Ears ringing from the deafening reports, she ran, crouching as low as her legs would allow, and dove headlong onto the floor of the backseat. None of the rough chunks of glass she landed on had edges sharp enough to cut her. She knew that Dan had made it into the driver's seat only because the car lurched forward. That was when she realized that the shots whizzing past the remaining windows were not from his gun. A bullet buried itself with a clang in the side of the car. The acceleration kicked in, and they shot down the driveway. She lifted her head enough to see out the side window. They careened off the gravel and bounced over grass and flower beds, sideswiping a picket fence before righting themselves. They made it to the main road, and Melanie grabbed the front seat, vaulting over the gearshift to settle in beside Dan. One side of his yellow polo shirt was streaked with blood.

"My God, are you hit?" she cried.

He looked down in surprise, nearly swerving off the road before righting the steering wheel.

"I didn't feel anything."

"Keep driving!"

She turned sideways in her seat and tugged on his shirt with both hands, pulling it up to expose his abdomen, slightly sticky with blood, but smooth and unmarred. She ran her hand around his belly, and he drew his breath in sharply.

"I think the blood must be from the dog. You're fine."

After a few minutes, he pulled off the road into the parking lot of an old metal-sided diner.

"Here we are." He nodded toward the diner. "I hear the blue plate special is good. Get me one to go."

As he leaned across her and pushed open her door, the inch of space between their bodies seemed to vibrate like a magnetic field. She wondered if she would ever see him again. Her suspicions about him temporarily forgotten, she stepped down, her legs shaky as her feet touched solid ground, and looked back up at him for a long second.

"Please. Be careful," she said.

"It's nice to know somebody cares." He flashed a gorgeous smile and winked at her, then slammed the door and backed up. She watched until the now battered Hummer disappeared from sight.

4 1

—

olan Reed was no stranger to the concept of suicide. He was one of those oversize personalities who couldn't tolerate defeat. And while his lack of scruples meant he rarely lost in business, in his personal life he hadn't been so lucky. Rejection sent him spiraling into paroxysms of self-pity, which in turn provoked thoughts of sucking on a tailpipe or rigging up a noose. When life slapped him, rather than accepting the insult, he preferred the thought of telling life itself to fuck off. Especially if he could go out in a way that would hurt the one who spurned him. Hurting Sarah. That was the main thing on his mind right now, as he sat at his desk contemplating death. His *and* hers.

Sarah deserved to die. There was something wrong with her, some black hole in her heart that shocked the conscience. Even he could see that. What she'd done to him was but one small success in a long and distinguished career of shattering lives. He wasn't the first, but he could make himself the last. Wouldn't be difficult to arrange. He had a shotgun in the country that would do the job nicely. If you planned to kill yourself, the logistics of taking someone else with you were tremendously simplified. No need for tiresome details like escape routes and alibis.

So that was the plan. Two loud blasts in the middle of the office in the middle of the afternoon. Lots of ugly publicity. He only wished he had copies of the videos Sarah had made of them. He'd leave them playing silently on a large monitor facing the door, the first thing people would see as they entered. Oh, his wife would love that. Hah, the bitch! She'd be so humiliated in front of her society friends. The tapes would bother her much more than his death. The more he thought about it, the more the videotapes seemed essential to the plan, a sort of fabulous, graphic suicide note. The absence of that one special touch would spoil the whole effect. And not only because of his wife either, but because he wanted Sarah exposed for the two-faced, low-life whore she was.

When he couldn't think of a way to get his hands on the tapes, though, he considered whether there might not be another path to revenge. He would regret giving up the sensual pleasure of blasting a hole in Sarah's chest wide enough to rip her heart out through. Yet wasn't that approach a bit garish, a bit lacking in finesse? Surely he, with his first-rate mind, could come up with something cleverer, more devious. Something designed to make her suffer more exquisitely, and for longer.

Then he remembered. Of course. Yes. How perfect. He chuckled to himself. He had tapes of his own he could use. Sarah wasn't the only one skilled in the discreet art of electronic surveillance. Dolan's office was rigged with a recording system Richard Nixon would have envied.

Extracting a small gold key from the pocket of his suit jacket, he knelt in the well under his desk and pulled up a piece of the custom-dyed Stark carpeting, exposing a small trapdoor. He unlocked it and reached his arm in, pulling out a manila envelope, then covered everything back up. A moment later he was seated at his desk, having selected and cued up a particular tape on the elaborate sound system concealed within his credenza.

He had to fast-forward a bit to get to the spot he wanted.

"... *never do anything of the sort!*" he heard his own voice saying. Why did he always sound so fucking nasal?

His blood pressure shot up at the memory of this argument. God, he'd hated Jed. Hated him, and found his murder gratifying in the extreme. Dolan had been sitting in his big leather chair, just as he was now. Jed sat across from him, smug in a perfectly tailored, five-thousand-dollar

Brioni suit. Dolan remembered just *itching* to take a crowbar and bash Jed's handsome face to a bloody pulp.

"Unfortunately, Dolan, you'll find it's necessary to protect your interests," Jed's recorded voice had said.

"Twenty percent for nothing? That's outrageous. Go fuck yourself! Get out of my office!"

"My silence is not nothing. It's highly valuable, a bargain at twice the price," Jed had said smoothly. That phony-baloney baritone of his. So fucking full of himself. *"With what I know about the transaction and my contacts in the U.S. Attorney's Office, you'd be risking a nice long jail term, Dolan."*

"You're bluffing. I don't think you have a fucking clue what went on with Securilex."

"Oh, really? I understand how the stock was manipulated better than you do. Would you like a summary?"

Dolan punched "stop," his chest heaving with fury. To his chagrin, Jed had proceeded to outline the transaction in minute detail. Looking back, of course, he realized Sarah had double-crossed him, had divulged everything to Jed. At the time he'd been positively flummoxed about that. Had no idea how Jed had found out. Never suspected her for an instant. He had to hand it to her—the girl was a truly gifted double agent. She put Mata Hari to shame. And, if he had anything to say about it, she'd meet the same fate as the famous spy. Death, ultimately, but only after a long and harrowing prison sentence. He'd get her convicted for Jed's murder. This tape was the means to accomplish that. He fast-forwarded and hit "play."

"Of course," Dolan had protested to Jed, *"what you're suggesting puts Sarah van der Vere at terrible risk. You realize that? She'll be the innocent victim in all this."*

"Hardly innocent. Sarah's getting caught would be regrettable. She's a charming young woman. But I always say, don't do the crime if you can't do the time."

Dolan hadn't known then that Jed was fucking Sarah. The conversation was all the more remarkable now, in light of that knowledge. Jed hadn't cared about her in the least. All the damage he'd done, and he never even cared.

"Oh? I guess you don't practice what you preach, then," Dolan had said sarcastically.

"What are you talking about? I had no role in Securilex."

Dolan felt a vein in his temple pulsing as he checked himself from shouting at Jed. Throwing all the dirt he knew about him in his smug fucking face. Because Dolan knew a lot. Jed had been a thorn in his side for long enough that he'd taken steps. Had him followed, investigated. He knew about the money laundering for sure. The rest, he guessed at. But he didn't say anything just then. Wouldn't be good poker.

"So you'd let Sarah be ruined? Arrested, even?"

"Cost of doing business," Jed said with a nonchalant shrug.

"Well," Dolan said, *"I'll let her know you feel that way."*

He never had, but he could say he did. Yes, it would do nicely. An excerpt of that tape, a few doctored e-mails, and a long, confessional suicide note from him. Presto, Sarah had motive. Jed had threatened to expose her, ruin her career. Sarah had come to Dolan seeking advice. Against his better judgment, he'd helped her arrange the murder. That last part would be more difficult to fake. He knew very little about murder contracts. But he kept a highly proficient private investigator on retainer. The man, to be effective, naturally had underworld contacts. He could surely provide sufficient insight to manage that aspect of it.

Dolan nodded grimly to himself, finally satisfied with the plan. He would spend the day preparing his package for that prosecutor. Put it in the overnight mail. Then drive out to the country later this afternoon and eat his shotgun for dinner. All the while crowing over the thought of Sarah's getting arrested. His only regret would be not witnessing it himself. But he could imagine the scene vividly enough. After all, he knew what Sarah looked like in handcuffs.

4 2

——

Sophie Cho pushed the baby stroller down a pathway darkened by an overhang of lush late-summer trees. With the sun high overhead at eleven o'clock, it was ninety degrees in the shade in Central Park. The air smelled of ozone and baking pavement; the pathway was completely deserted except for a professional dog walker escorting a lethargic group of terriers and poodles. She wondered where the experienced mommies went on a stifling morning like this. They had a secret gathering spot, she was sure—an air-conditioned museum perhaps, or a coffee shop.

She was heading for a sculpture she'd noticed and admired many times in the past, a whimsical brass rendering of Alice in Wonderland characters that she'd often seen covered in small, climbing bodies. She'd imagined herself there, shouting at a child who had her hair, her eyes—be careful, don't fall. But as she wilted more with each step and Maya began to fuss, she knew she'd made a bad choice. That sculpture was best on a clear, cool day. Going there in the heat, like so much else in her life these days, was a mistake.

Dead calm, without the slightest stir of breeze in the trees. Sophie leaned down into the stroller and blew lightly on Maya's face, earning a delicious giggle for her troubles. How could she possibly run away to Vancouver and leave this baby behind? Melanie's job was so demanding, and her marriage was on shaky ground. As time went on, Aunt Sophie's role in the little girl's life would grow and grow. She imagined buying her clothes, taking her to tea at the Plaza, listening to her childish confidences. Giving up those dreams would feel like ripping her fingernails from her flesh. Yet she'd reached the point where she saw no other way out.

Maybe if she'd told Melanie that first night, when Jed was murdered and the fire broke out. Then it wouldn't seem so much like she had something to hide. But would that have made any difference? Either what she did was a crime or it wasn't. She didn't know the exact legal answer to that question. The only person she could think of to ask was Melanie. But asking, of course, would reveal her secret, and then Melanie would never let her care for Maya again. Yet if she ran to Vancouver, she wouldn't see Maya anyway. She just went around and around in terrible circles.

She reached the sculpture and took a seat on a bench, lifting Maya out of the stroller to sit on her lap. As she'd feared, they were the only ones here today. The sun beat down on her head as she pulled out a bottle filled with a mixture of one part apple juice to two parts water, exactly as Melanie instructed. She'd measured it out with great care. She held it for Maya, who began to suck happily, oblivious to the heat now that she was enjoying her favorite treat.

"Good girl. See, look over here, Maya. See all those funny critters? Aunt Sophie's going to tell you a nice story about them. Once upon a time, there was a little girl named Alice."

They were no longer alone. A young man came and sat down on the bench opposite. She smiled at him, proud to be observed mothering this child, wondering if he had children, too. Because, despite his intimidating appearance—he had small, cold features and multiple tattoos—he seemed to listen to the story with great interest.

4 3

—

They eat lunch early in cow town, Melanie thought grimly, taking a seat on a red leatherette stool at the counter of the metal-sided diner. It wasn't even eleven-thirty, and all the tables were occupied, the patrons an odd mix of farmhands and flamboyant city types in fashionable outfits. The smell of frying bacon hung in the air, overpowering and unpleasant on a scorching day. A tired-looking waitress with bluish hair slapped a menu down in front of Melanie. Having just been shot at, Melanie was hardly in the mood to eat, but she didn't think the waitress would take kindly to her sitting there without ordering. Her handbag was where she'd left it, on the floor of Dan's car. If he didn't come back for her, she'd be stranded with no money and no identification.

She ordered egg salad on whole wheat toast and an iced tea, then sat waiting for it to come, spinning back and forth on her stool like an anxious child. She could barely keep her body still. The possibility that the informant might shoot Dan flooded her thoughts, making her crazy with worry. She'd seen so much tragedy in the space of a few days—Jed Benson, then Rosario, then Jasmine, now Amanda. She'd kept going by focusing on getting Slice, on locking him up for the rest of his life. But now, thinking of Dan O'Reilly lying broken and bleeding on the ground, she came undone. Even if he was—maybe, possibly—involved in a string of brutal murders. Even if he'd lied to her. Even if nothing more ever happened between them.

She checked her watch again. How long should she wait before she asked to use the diner's phone to call 911? He'd been gone only ten minutes. Dan was an FBI agent, after all. Presumably, if he needed reinforcements, he'd have the sense to call them in. Then again, maybe not. She knew him well enough to imagine he'd be touchy and secretive about soliciting help. The Bureau bred that in its agents, playing things close to the vest. Plus, she thought grimly, there was always the chance he wouldn't call the police because he was really one of the bad guys.

The sandwich, when it finally came, looked decent enough, so she forced herself to eat it. Food might seem repellent, but she needed to maintain her strength. She chewed mechanically, barely tasting it, still hearing the sound of bullets whizzing past her ears, still seeing that vicious dog lunging for her. Dan said it was Slice's dog. How could he know that? Had the snitch told him? Was the story about the snitch even true? Dan had protected her, put his body between her and the bullets. Surely that meant he was on her side. Or was it a show? Designed to convince her he was still on Team America when he wasn't?

This diner brought out the child in her, or maybe anxiety was making her regress. She used her straw to slurp the remaining iced tea from the bottom of the glass, her mouth puckering at the tart bite of juice from the lemon slice. She swung her stool around backward, dangling her feet, looking through the plate-glass window. To her astonishment, as she watched, Dan's G-car pulled into the parking lot. He was alone, and he'd been gone only twenty minutes.

HE WALKED INTO the diner holding her handbag, and she'd never felt so happy to see anybody in her whole life. But the next second, all the doubts rushed back in.

"Your phone just rang, but I felt funny answering it," he said, handing her the bag.

"What happened? Where's the informant?"

He slid onto the stool next to her. "I missed him. But I got some other leads instead."

"What do you mean, you missed him?" she asked sharply.

He avoided her eyes. "He was gone by the time I got back. Win some, lose some, I guess."

She searched his face apprehensively. His nonchalance at the informant's escape seemed like an act. She felt certain he was hiding something.

"What'll it be?" asked the blue-haired waitress, shoving a menu at Dan.

"Nothing, thanks." He waved the waitress away and turned to Melanie. "Listen, your car's safe enough sitting in the lot at Otisville. You can deal with it later. We need to get back to the city and find Slice."

"I agree completely. Let's go."

Once they were on the highway, Melanie pulled out her telephone and checked her voice mail. The missed call had been from Sophie Cho.

"Uh, Melanie, it's Sophie. I'm in the park with Maya and we're having a slight problem. Can you call me on my cell phone please? Oh, it's just after eleven on Thursday."

Sophie's voice sounded quiet and anxious, giving Melanie a moment's worry. Darn, Sophie didn't leave her cell-phone number, and Melanie didn't have it with her. She wished she were one of those people who programmed every number she ever came across into her phone. What could the problem be? Was Maya not feeling well? She'd been in perfect form a few hours earlier. Had Sophie gotten locked out of the apartment? Melanie's mother had keys, and she should be arriving within an hour. But even though Melanie was sure it was nothing serious, Sophie's message weighed on her mind. Without a way to reach Sophie, though, there was nothing Melanie could do except hope she would call back.

She closed her phone and leaned over to put her bag in the back. A large green trash bag sat on the backseat. It had not been there earlier when they drove from Otisville to Millbrook.

"What's in that bag?"

"Oh, yeah," Dan said offhandedly, like it had slipped his mind, "I opened the trap."

"*What?*"

"The Road Runner trap? You know, in Benson's car? I managed to get it open."

"Let me get this straight. You're gone for maybe twenty minutes total. In that time you manage to search the entire Benson estate, figure
out the snitch is gone, *and* open the Road Runner trap? How is that
possible?"

"Hold your horses, princess. I'll tell you the whole story."

To hear Dan tell it, his return to the Benson property had been largely
uneventful. He drove back up the driveway to find the dog's carcass gone
and an eerie silence pervading the whole property. He drew his gun and
kept his eyes open, moving stealthily around to the rear of the large
house, until he found a sliding glass door on the terrace, already jimmied
open by somebody else. Then he did a quick room-to-room search for
the informant. He didn't find him, but he found plenty of evidence that
he'd been there. The place was ripped apart. Every drawer, every cabinet,
every closet had been emptied, its contents scattered wildly across the
floor. Furniture was upended and pictures torn off walls, presumably in
search of hiding places. Sofa cushions and mattresses bled stuffing where
they had been savagely slashed open.

"He was looking for something. Probably what I got out of the trap,"
Dan said.

"I don't get it. How the hell did you figure out how to open it?"

"Dumb luck. My specialty."

The search of the house had taken no more than ten minutes, start to
finish. Once he was confident the informant was no longer around, Dan,
unwilling to give up on the Road Runner trap, sat down at the wheel of
the SUV and fiddled with the controls, searching for the magical sequence that would pop it open.

"In the trap-recognition course I went to, they told you which vehicle
functions can be used as triggers. You know, wipers, signal light, whatever. They said the Road Runner likes sequences of six, so I sat there and
tried every sequence of six I could think of."

"That's practically an infinite number. I can't believe you hit it—and
so fast."

"Fortune was smiling on me. I knew I got it right when I heard the hydraulic lock release. The sound came from under the backseat, so I got down on all fours and felt around in there. I found this little opening, maybe eight or ten inches across. You woulda never noticed it, it was carpeted so good. But I was able to get my fingers along the top and yank it open. The trap went back at least two feet under the rear compartment. And I found a lot of nice goodies inside. Three handguns—two Tec-9s and a Glock, all with defaced serial numbers. A pair of metal handcuffs, a bag with about fifteen grand cash in it. Oh, and some blueprints. You know, like architectural drawings? Those, I don't really know what they're doing in there."

"Are you being straight with me?" she asked, eyes wide, mouth open with pure astonishment.

"Why wouldn't I be?"

"How did you possibly manage to accomplish all that in the twenty minutes you were gone?"

"Fast hands, sweetheart."

Coming from Dan, she almost believed an answer like that. Almost, but not quite.

Curious about what he'd found in the trap, she reached behind her and felt around inside the trash bag, extracting a long, shiny red cardboard tube. She pried off the inset plastic lid with her fingernails and held the tube up to her eye. A ream of grayish white onionskin paper lay coiled inside. Working it out with her fingertips, she unfurled it. There were at least twenty sheets of thick, spongy paper, smelling of ink and toner, bearing delicate blue elevations of the interior and exterior of a town house. In the lower left-hand corner was written Jed Benson's address and the legend "Sophie Cho, architect."

"Hmmm. These look to me like the blueprints for the renovation of the Bensons' town house. A good friend of mine was their architect. I can ask her take a look and verify that's what they are. But isn't that strange? Why would Benson hide blueprints in a trap?"

"Beats me. That one I can't answer."

She put them in her handbag, where they protruded from the top.

The thought of Sophie made her anxious. She pulled out her phone again and called home. If her mom had arrived, she could find Sophie's cell-phone number in the address book and read it to Melanie. But nobody picked up.

"Okay," she said, turning back to Dan, "next question: Why was your snitch up here trying to open the trap in Benson's car?"

"I wondered that myself. Why drive all the way to Buttfuck just for a couple of guns and some cash? They got plenty of that stuff in Bushwick. He musta been looking for something else."

"Who the hell is this guy anyway?"

Her cell phone rang.

"Saved by the bell," Dan said.

She answered it, hoping it would be Sophie calling back to tell her all was well.

"Hello?" she said.

"Melanie? Butch Brennan."

"Butch! Are you still at the hospital? I'm just sick over what happened to Amanda."

"No, we wrapped up a while ago. The bodies were discovered first thing this morning, couldn't've been more than an hour or two after it happened. Real clean MO this time. One shot each, smack in the middle of the forehead."

"Did you recover the bullets?"

"Yeah, in fact we got preliminary ballistics already. Gives us a ninety-nine percent probability the bullets were fired by the gun that killed Jed Benson. I'll have final confirmation in a couple days. But it looks like the same killer."

"No surprise there," she said, then held the phone away and placed her hand over the mouthpiece. "Butch Brennan," she told Dan. "He says the bullets that killed Amanda and Bill Flanagan came from the same gun that killed Benson. Presumably Slice's."

"But, hey, Melanie," Butch called.

She put the phone back to her ear. "Yeah?"

"Why I'm calling is about your message last night. You know, about those latents on the accelerant can? The ones come back to Rommie Ramirez?"

"Oh, yes, right. What can you tell me about that?"

"Are you alone?"

"No." She forced herself to keep her face blank, not to look over at Dan. She cupped the phone closer to her ear so Dan couldn't hear Butch's end.

"Who you with, O'Reilly?" Butch asked.

"Yes."

"Look, nothing against O'Reilly. But I'd keep this to myself for now if I were you. Till you follow up and check it out more."

"Of course," she said.

"I never been one to drop a dime on another cop. O'Reilly's an organization man, and he don't like guys ratting each other out either. This is real sensitive information."

"I understand," she said. Dan was listening intently to her end of the call, but she didn't think he could hear Butch.

"Here's the deal, okay? No way Ramirez's prints got on that can legitimately," Butch said. "It couldn't have happened when Ramirez was working the crime scene. You see, my boys got to the scene first, before any other cops. The initial call came from the fire department. Ramirez only showed up afterwards. Frankly, I have no idea who the hell called him, but it wasn't us."

"So what does all that mean, Butch?"

"We had total control of that crime scene before Ramirez ever set foot in it. We already collected the can before he got there. If those are really his prints, maybe he thinks he can explain them away, but I gotta think they were there from before."

"Before when?"

"Before. Like during the crime. Unless the fingerprint report is wrong, Ramirez was there when Benson was killed."

"WHAT WAS THAT all about?" Dan asked when she hung up.

She'd never been so aware of the muscles in her face. How could she arrange her expression so she didn't look like she was in complete shock?

She met Dan's gaze. "Oh, just ballistics stuff," she said, trying to sound casual.

Dan's eyes bored into hers. She marveled once again at their exquisite clarity. The eyes of an innocent man. They demanded the truth, made her feel treacherous for deceiving him. She told herself it was merely a physical thing, that she shouldn't be swayed by it.

"You're lying, I can tell," he said. "Are you holding something back from me on our investigation?"

"Of course not," she said, but her voice came out small and uncertain.

He smashed the heel of his hand on the steering wheel, making her jump.

"What was that for?" she said, annoyed. If he was going to act threatening, she would feel no compunction about misleading him. But he looked over at her with terrible hurt in his face.

"I can't believe you just looked me in the eye and lied to me," he said. "I thought we trusted each other. I thought we had something, that we were a team."

"Hey, pal, let me tell you something," she said, anger coursing through her veins. "Team is a two-way street. Who's the one who won't give up the name of his informant? Who's the one with his own agenda to protect? On the day you come clean with me, you'll be justified in acting self-righteous. But today you're out of line."

He looked back at the road, shaking his head, whistling through his teeth.

"Well?" she said.

"You're tougher than you look, you know that?"

"Never doubt it."

44

___

Dan dropped her at her office after a hellishly tense ride, claiming he was going to look for Randall and would call once he found him. She got out without a word and slammed the car door. He sped away, not looking back.

As she rode up in the elevator, exhaustion and depression overwhelmed her. She was in the middle of a murder investigation, and everybody assigned to help her was now on her list of suspects. *Dan* was now on her list of suspects. She had every intention of getting Slice. But she'd never counted on having to do it by herself.

She stepped off the elevator.

"Hey, Melanie!" the guard called from inside his glassed-in booth. "Lady here to see you."

He pointed to the adjoining small reception area, where Mary Hale sat ensconced in a chair surrounded by at least twenty cardboard file boxes.

Mary stood up. "I'm responding to your subpoena."

"So I see," Melanie replied, startled. "But the subpoena said Mr. Reed should bring the documents to the grand jury himself, tomorrow morning. I don't have time to review all this now."

"Mr. Reed isn't going to show up. He saw your fax and instructed me to start shredding."

"Do you realize what you're saying?" Melanie asked. "Destroying documents sought by a subpoena is a crime. Why would he do that, un-less he had something to hide?"

"Ms. Vargas, I *always* realize what I'm saying," Mary replied.

"So you're telling me the Securilex deal was rigged?"

"Oh, my, yes."

"And Mr. Reed knew that?"

"He didn't just know it, he set it up," she said, almost gleefully. "When Securilex went public, Mr. Reed structured the IPO. He demanded kick-backs from any investor who wanted to buy large blocks of stock at the insider price. All *carefully* disguised as legitimate payments, of course."

"Does he know you're here?"

"No, and when he finds out, he'll do everything in his power to stop me from talking to you. I suggest we get down to business. There are years' worth of documents in these boxes. It'll take time to go through them."

Melanie looked at her watch and then back at the boxes. Even if Securilex had played a role in Jed Benson's murder, poring through boxes wouldn't help her track down Slice and get him off the street any faster. On the other hand, if she uncovered enough evidence to arrest Dolan Reed, that *could* help find Slice. Reed would flip in a heartbeat and start talking. White-collar types like him couldn't stomach the inside. And since there was at least some chance Reed had ordered the hit, he might have a way to get to Slice. A thought flashed into her mind. A way to get the work done and do a favor for a friend at the same time.

"Ms. Hale, could you wait here for just a moment, please? I'll be right back," she said eagerly.

"Certainly."

Melanie swiped her card key through the magnetic lock and raced to Joe Williams's office halfway down the hall, stopping, out of breath, in the open doorway. Joe looked up in surprise, chopsticks poised above a white paper carton.

"Joe! Sorry to interrupt your lunch, but I need a few minutes of your time. More than a few, actually."

"Sure. Everything okay?"

"Yes! Guess what? I have the perfect case for you."

AFTER SHE SETTLED Mary and Joe in a conference room, Melanie dashed back to her office to figure out her next step. It wasn't until then that she noticed her office door was shut tight. Strange, she'd left it wide open, as usual, last night when she went to the retirement dinner. She reached for the doorknob, sensing that something was wrong. Inside, the furniture seemed disturbed, as if someone had moved it and put it back in slightly different places. The cleaning service? Was she getting paranoid?

She walked over to her desk. The second she looked down at it, she knew for sure—the carefully arranged piles covering its surface had been tampered with. Somebody had been here, looked through them. She rifled through the piles frantically. The Bensons' bank records. Gone! She immediately thought of Rommie Ramirez's behavior last night. Despite her rebuffs, he'd repeatedly insisted on seeing them. Would he have gone so far as to sneak into her office and steal them? Who else had known about the bank records besides Rommie? At the very least, Bernadette and Dan. Neither of them was above suspicion the way things were going, although certainly Ramirez had expressed the greatest degree of interest. A highly unusual degree of interest, as she recalled.

Wait a minute! She looked through the piles a second time. The fingerprint report identifying Ramirez's prints on the kerosene can was gone, too. Now she was convinced it was Ramirez. There were a few too many coincidences. Like the fact that he'd sneaked up on her in her office the other night, right before she got chased in the basement. Normally cops couldn't just come and go as they pleased in the prosecutors' offices. But Rommie had special access. Bernadette let him in.

Blind with rage, she backed out into the hallway. Before she thought twice, she was in the anteroom to Bernadette's office.

Shekeya's two daughters, maybe four and six, played jacks on the linoleum floor while Shekeya typed. Intent on their play, they granted

Melanie only the same brief, resentful glance she received from their mother. Shekeya kept typing, not bothering to explain their presence, a foul silence hanging over her.

"Bernadette in?"

"What you think? It's the middle of the afternoon," she said coldly, eyes on the keys, not looking up a second time.

"It just seems quiet."

"Quiet like a snake before it bite you."

Not troubling to decipher that comment, Melanie walked in unannounced. Bernadette looked up from a paper she was reading. The afternoon sunlight glared through the window behind her desk, hurting Melanie's eyes, making it difficult to see Bernadette's face. Melanie knew that her boss had placed the desk there for precisely that reason, to gain advantage, to unnerve visitors.

When Melanie's eyes adjusted, what she saw surprised her. There wasn't a trace of last night's excessive drinking or its stormy aftermath. Bernadette looked fresh, better than she had in recent memory. Her eyes were clearer, her color better, her carriage more vigorous and erect. She looked like a woman who had come through a terrible ordeal relatively unscathed and finally figured out who she was and where she stood.

"Sit down," Bernadette commanded. "You've saved me the trouble of summoning you. We need to talk about your handling—or should I say mishandling?—of the Benson investigation."

"What?" Melanie exclaimed, shocked, stumbling as she backed into a guest chair. Her heart began to pound.

"I assume you've heard about Slice's latest victims? Amanda Benson and her bodyguard?"

"Yes," Melanie said warily.

"I was just proofreading this memo. Here, take a look."

Bernadette slid a piece of paper across the desk with her fingertips. Her fingers were gruesome. Like Dorian Gray's picture, they revealed the strain that didn't show in her face—red polish horribly chipped, cuticles bitten to bloody shreds. Melanie picked up the memo, saw it was from

Bernadette to the U.S. Attorney, dated that day. It announced Melanie's reassignment to administrative duties. The Benson case would be handled by Bernadette herself.

"Did Rommie Ramirez put you up to this, Bernadette? You know it's completely wrong."

"Wrong? I'll tell you what's wrong. Assigning this case to *you* was wrong. Rommie's been telling me that all along, and now I finally see."

"You know why he wants me off the case? Because I'm getting too close."

"Close? You're not even in the ballpark, girlfriend. I gave you a chance. But enough is enough. You're parading around like a hotshot, screaming about conspiracy theories while the killer picks off your witnesses one by one. Do you have any idea what it means that Amanda Benson was killed? Any minute we can expect her mother to march into the front office and demand our resignations. I can't believe it hasn't happened yet."

"Do *you* have any idea what it means that Amanda was killed, Bernadette? She was a scared, confused little girl. Fifteen years old, and now she's dead. She'll never get a chance to grow up. And you're sitting here worrying about how it looks to the front office."

"Yes, I'm worried," Bernadette snarled. "You should be, too. With the way the bodies are piling up, we look downright incompetent."

"Oh, it's a lot worse than that!" Melanie cried.

"What is that supposed to mean?"

"It's not incompetence, it's corruption, and your boyfriend is in the middle of it. Rommie told Slice where to find all my witnesses. He was involved, Bernadette. Open your eyes! His fingerprints are all over a can of accelerant found at the scene of Jed Benson's murder. I'd show you the report proving that, but it was stolen from my office last night, along with the bank records Rommie was so interested in at the retirement dinner. Funny coincidence, isn't it? Was Rommie here last night, after the dinner?"

Bernadette's mouth fell open, all color draining from her face.

"He was, wasn't he? He has free run of our office after hours, isn't that right, Bernadette? That's how he found out where Rosario Sangrador was sequestered, I bet. Who let him in here, any idea? Would it happen to be you? Don't you think the front office would be interested to know *that*?"

"I don't know what the hell you're talking about," Bernadette said, her voice fierce and quiet.

"Let me explain it more clearly, then. The fingerprint analyst compared the print on the kerosene can to all law enforcement present at the crime scene. Rommie's prints matched."

"Well . . . so?" Bernadette stuttered. "He messed up. Didn't handle evidence properly. That's bad, but it doesn't mean—"

"I already spoke to Butch Brennan," Melanie interjected. "The can was recovered from the scene before Rommie ever arrived there. So it couldn't have been a mistake."

"No. No, there has to be some other explanation," Bernadette declared emphatically, shaking her head. "You're just confirming everything I said about crazy theories. To accept that a fifteen-year veteran could be involved in murder, rather than doing the extra work to find the right answer. It's . . . it's . . . why, it's just ludicrous!"

"I believe the evidence I see before my eyes, Bernadette. Maybe I don't have personal motives for disregarding it."

They stared at each other. Melanie imagined she saw a second's hesitation, a moment's doubt, flicker on Bernadette's face. But then Bernadette squelched it out. Doubt was not an emotion she tolerated.

Holding Melanie's gaze, Bernadette pressed the intercom. Shekeya came into the room.

"This memo is fine. Distribute it!" Bernadette snapped.

Shekeya took the memo without so much as a glance in Melanie's direction. She must have typed it right before Melanie walked in. No wonder she'd acted so hostile; she was covering up her embarrassment. She knew that Bernadette was about to deliver a humiliating blow, yet she'd presumably been instructed not to tell Melanie.

"It's done," Bernadette said dismissively. "You're off the case. I'll handle this matter from here on out. If you want something done right, do it yourself, I always say. Oh, and by the way, I made you a list of new assignments, starting with a week of bail duty. Idle hands do the devil's work, after all."

She thrust a piece of paper at Melanie, who took it without looking at it.

"You're going to find out I'm right, sooner or later," Melanie said, standing up, looming over her boss's desk. "Let's just hope nobody else dies in the process."

Melanie turned on her heel and marched from the room. When she got out to the hall, she took Bernadette's list of bullshit administrative chores, ripped it to shreds, and threw it in the nearest trash can. She wasn't about to get sidelined. Damned if she'd leave that animal and his cohorts on the street one second longer.

4 5

—

Only once she hit the street did Melanie ask herself where she was going. New York was a big town. Slice could be anywhere.

The basic principles of investigation counseled starting with his last known location. That would be Mount Sinai Hospital, last night, wielding a nine-millimeter. The way things had fallen to shit on this case, she doubted anybody had even canvassed the hospital staff to pick up leads. She hailed a taxi. She'd do it herself. And if somehow she managed to find him, then she'd figure out how to take him down. No point worrying about that now.

Settling back into the seat, finally catching her breath, she noticed a red cardboard tube protruding from her handbag. The blueprints. They reminded her of Sophie. She'd never heard back from her friend about the problem in the park. Checking her watch, she saw it was nearly three o'clock. Sophie should have delivered Maya to Melanie's mother some time ago. Quickly, Melanie dialed home.

"Hello?" her mother answered.

"Hi, Mom. It's me. Everything okay?"

"No, as a matter of fact. I've been waiting for over an hour, but your friend hasn't showed up yet. I don't know why I had to leave work early to sit around your apartment all alone, Melanie. I have a real job, too, you know."

Melanie went cold with fear. Sophie had been gone for hours longer than she should have been. Had something happened?

A persistent clicking could be heard on the line.

"Oh, hold on," her mother said. "It's this damn Call Waiting."

"No, Mom, wait—"

Her mother put her on hold. Outside the taxi window, the blocks flashed by. Inside, Melanie sat utterly still, frozen in time, each second lasting a lifetime. She wouldn't breathe again until she knew that her daughter was safe.

Her mother came back on the line.

"Melanie?"

"Yes! What is it?"

"Don't snap. That's your friend. What's her name again? Lucy?"

"Sophie!"

"Right. Sophie says she needs to talk to you."

"Well, why didn't you tell her to hang up and call my cell phone?"

"Watch your tone of voice, please. She can't very well call you while I'm talking to you."

"Mom, whatever, just tell me. Did Sophie say anything was wrong?"

"It's not like we had a whole conversation, for Pete's sake."

"Okay, okay." Melanie took a deep breath, telling herself that shouting at her mother at this juncture would not be productive. "Please. Just have her call me on this phone right now. You have the number, right?"

"Give it to me again?"

She gave her mother her cell-phone number, then hung up and waited another eternity for her phone to ring.

Finally it did.

"Sophie?" she practically shouted.

"Melanie?"

"I didn't have your cell number with me, so I couldn't call you back before. Is everything okay?"

"Never mind that. Thank God I got you this time!"

"Why, what's the matter?"

"There's a guy following me."

"You mean, like a mugger? Where are you? Is there a cop around? Is Maya okay?"

"No, I don't think he's a mugger. We were sitting in the park before, and he was watching us. After a while it creeped me out. Thank goodness more people came, so I was able to walk out to the street. But we've been walking around for a while now, and wherever I go, I see him."

"So Maya's okay?"

"Yes, she's fine, although her diaper needs to be changed. You know I hate to let her sit with a dirty diaper. But I didn't want to go back to your apartment and lead him there. I think he has bad intentions."

"What do you mean, bad intentions? Can you see him? What does he look like?"

"No, I can't see him right this second, but I know he's here. I'm in a supermarket. He's probably waiting outside. He's thin, not super tall. Fade haircut, sharp features. And a big tattoo on his arm. Like a knife dripping blood."

"Oh, Jesus! That's the C-Trout Blades' gang tattoo! Sounds like Slice!"

"Who?"

"The man who murdered Jed Benson."

There was complete silence on the other end of the line.

"Sophie? Are you there? Sophie?"

"I was afraid of that," Sophie said quietly.

"Of what? Sophie? Why on earth would Jed Benson's killer be following you? Following *me* I can understand, but *you*? Do you know something about the murder you haven't told me?"

"I can't talk over the phone, but yes. It has to do with the Bensons' house."

"The Bensons' house? What about it?"

"Listen, Melanie, this is serious. I did something wrong. It's why I was running away to Vancouver. I need to meet you somewhere to explain."

"What did you do?"

"Well, for one thing, the blueprints I filed with the Buildings Department, they were fakes. I mean, that was part of it. Part of what I did."

"Fakes? I don't understand."

"I knew I shouldn't have, but that job was so important to my career, and Jed convinced me it would be all right. I should never have listened to Jed. He was bad, Melanie."

"Yes, I know. What do *you* know about that?"

"Oh," Sophie exclaimed, "I think I see that man! He's in here, inside the supermarket! What should I do?"

"Okay, okay. Where are you exactly?"

"In a Food King a few blocks from your apartment."

"Take Maya home. Those are crowded blocks between there and my house. You'll be safe. You might even see a cop along the way if you're lucky."

"But this man will see where you live."

"I don't care about that. He probably knows anyway. I just want her safe. Give her to my mom and wait in the lobby. I'll come as fast as I can, with the police, and we'll arrest him, okay?"

"Are you sure?"

"Yes! You can't keep walking around forever, and he's not gonna just go away."

"Okay, that's what I'll do then."

"Try to act natural, so he doesn't realize you know you're being followed. And call me right away if there's a problem. Or better yet call 911!"

MELANIE TOLD THE cabdriver to drop her at the corner across from her building. She thought about calling the local precinct for backup. She thought about calling Dan. But she couldn't decide. Going through normal channels with the PD could bring Ramirez down on her head. Calling Dan . . . well, that would bring Dan down on her head. Much as she hated to admit it, either option sounded more dangerous than going it alone.

She jumped out of the cab, deliberately refusing to look back over her shoulder. She assumed that Slice was somewhere in the vicinity. Because of the mug shot, she would recognize him if she saw him, but she had no reason to think he knew what she looked like, not yet anyway. She wanted to keep it that way. Years of writing arrest warrants had taught her that glancing around furtively like you thought you were being followed attracted people's attention. She didn't need Slice to notice her.

Sophie was not in the lobby as they'd discussed. Had they made it safely home? Melanie tried to shut off her mind until she got upstairs, so she wouldn't go crazy with fear. She acted normal the whole way up in the elevator, making conversation with an elderly lady who lived on the floor above her. But when she got to her apartment, her hand trembled violently as she turned the key in the lock. She raced down the hall to Maya's room, where her mother was just lifting her baby, freshly diapered, off the changing table. Melanie swept Maya from her mother's arms and held her close, putting her lips to Maya's silky dark hair.

"*¡Nena preciosa!* Mommy missed you so much!"

"Mama!" Maya said for the first time.

"Did you hear that? She said 'mama'!" Melanie cried, tears standing out in her eyes.

"Oh, Melanie, she's just babbling. Babies that young can't talk," her mother said impatiently, crossing tanned arms over her pink polo shirt, pursing her coral lips. "What I want to know is, if you were planning to be home so early, why did I have to upset all my plans and come into the city? I try to help out, but you abuse the privilege."

"Sorry we're such a burden on you," Melanie said, squeezing Maya even tighter.

"That's not what I meant, and you know it. I'm just saying, I'm the one who's always here for you, unlike your father, who's never even bothered to make the trip to *meet* Maya. And you don't give me credit."

"Do we have to get into all this now, Mom? Where's Sophie?"

"Oh, yes, your friend. A very sweet girl, that one. Very polite, unlike some people I know," she said, casting Melanie a reproachful glance.

"Where'd she go? Is she in the bathroom?"

"Oh, no. She left."

"Left? When? Did she say anything?"

"Yes, as a matter of fact. She said tell you not to worry, that she would lead him away from here, and to come find her at the model-boat pond. I thought that was odd. Who was she talking about, do you know?"

Before her mother had even finished the question, Melanie sprinted into the kitchen to get Sophie's cell-phone number, then ran straight out the door.

4 6

—

Dan O'Reilly walked up the steep front steps of the Brooklyn row house. He hadn't been here in years, not since the service for Randall's son. The block was beautiful like he remembered, but shabbier now. Paint peeled off Randall's house in strips. Garbage and graffiti were all around, and a bunch of teenage mokes stood outside the bodega on the corner, looking like they were pitching drugs. They checked him out warily, and he nodded back. Not here for you today, fellas. Used to be, a few years back, this city was shiny as a new penny. Even out here in Fort Greene. But not anymore. Fucking economy these days, bringing everybody down.

Randall lived in the third-floor apartment. Dan found the button on the intercom panel and pressed, glancing up at the sky. Looked like rain, any minute. Smelled like it, too.

"Who's that?" asked a woman's voice after a moment. She sounded hoarse, tired.

"Betty?" he asked, leaning down to speak into the intercom.

"Yes?"

"Dan O'Reilly. I gotta talk to Randall. He around?"

In answer the buzzer sounded, and he pushed in the heavy wooden door.

Dan always noticed architecture, and he took a second to admire the once spectacular foyer. It smelled like cabbage or some other type of greens boiling. The parquet floor was black with grime and rotting in places, the carved mahogany staircase missing rails, covered with dingy carpeting. Damn shame it wasn't being kept up. He should offer to come out here some weekend, strip the wood and refinish it. He'd done enough construction in his day to be pretty good at it. Not like he had anything better to do with his time. But who knew? Who knew if him and Randall would even be talking after this.

He heard a door open somewhere above his head and sprinted up the three flights. When he got to the third-floor landing, Betty Walker stood waiting with the door open, her face haggard. It shocked him to see how she'd aged in the past few years. She used to be a good-looking woman. Sharp dresser, hair always done. Now she looked like she never made it out of the old bathrobe she wore.

"How you doing, Betty?"

"Thank the Lord you're here." She spoke urgently, in a low voice. "Whatever's wrong, it's beyond me to help. Maybe you can talk sense to him."

"Tell me what happened."

"I have no idea. But he been up drinking all night, and he's talking all crazy now. Like he might hurt himself."

"Where is he?"

"In the second bedroom. Used to be Darnell's room. Straight to the back."

She held the door open and stepped aside for him to pass. The apartment was laid out front to back like a railroad flat. He entered directly into the kitchen, which boasted gray metal 1950s cabinets and a Formica table that was new back when cars had fins. You could get good money for this shit these days—he should tell Randall that. He continued on through the small living room, which consisted of two plastic-covered recliners facing a large-screen TV, and made his way back to the bedrooms. Behind the door of the farthest one, he heard a ruckus. Sounded like things getting torn apart.

The door was slightly ajar, so he pushed it in. Randall had just ripped a drawer from the dresser and turned it upside down, spilling its contents across the narrow twin bed that occupied one wall, beneath an enormous poster of Tupac Shakur burying his face in be-ringed hands. Randall rummaged frantically through clothing and other objects, oblivious to Dan's entrance.

Dan stood dumb. He'd come all this way, and he couldn't think of a word to say.

Randall seemed to have found what he was looking for—a packet of papers in a manila envelope. He sat down on the bed to review them and spotted Dan.

"What the fuck—"

Randall jumped up, and only then did Dan realize he was drunk. Dan had seen Randall drunk only once before—in this house, in fact, at the service for his son. Randall was no drinker. Dan always ragged him about that, about how his own partner was the only cop in the whole PD who wouldn't lift a pint with him on a Friday night. Now, as he saw Randall's clothes disheveled and his eyes wild, Dan's heart sank. Things were as bad as they could be.

"Hey, hey, calm down," Dan said, raising his hands, taking a step toward Randall.

"What the fuck you doing here?"

"Your wife let me in. She's worried about you."

"Oh, really? The shoe's on the other foot for a change," Randall said bitterly.

"Is this about you and Betty?" Dan asked, confused.

"None of your goddamn business."

"What's going on? What's in the envelope?" Dan asked.

Dan advanced another step, and Randall jerked the envelope around behind his back, as if Dan would try to rip it from his hands.

"I said none of your goddamn business!" he said.

"Hey, come on. We've been partners for years. I came here because I know something's up. I want to help. Whatever it is, whatever you need, I want to help."

"You wanna help? Go away and leave me alone, then!" Randall shouted, the alcohol from his breath reaching Dan's nose.

"Randall, you're gonna have to tell somebody sooner or later. At least me, you can trust to put your interests first."

"Oh, is that so? The hell I can. I know you better than that," Randall said, words slurring slightly.

"What's that supposed to mean?"

Randall backed away a step, muttering something inaudible.

"What's that you're saying? Speak up," Dan demanded.

"You and your goddamn code!" Randall said.

"What code?"

"I used to have a code, too," Randall said, his eyes glazed as if he were talking to himself. "Fucking lot of good it did me. You don't know shit about my life nowadays."

"Try me. Explain to me. Maybe I'm more understanding than you think."

Randall thrust the manila envelope at Dan. "You wanna know what's in here? My life insurance. I'm reading it to see if it got an exemption for suicide. Because if it don't, I'm thinking I'm gonna eat my gun so Betty can get the money."

"They all do. Exempt suicide, I mean," Dan said.

"Even the cop ones?"

"Yeah, sure. Especially the cop ones. Those insurance companies are smart. They'd be paying out left and right."

Randall looked at Dan for a minute, then started to chortle. He sat down heavily on the bed, laughing uncontrollably until tears streamed down his face.

"Cop ones exempt suicide! Oh, boy, that's a good one!" Randall screamed, holding his sides. After a moment, though, he stopped, straightened his shoulders, and looked up at Dan, wiping the tears off his face with the back of his hand.

"I know there's an explanation why you left the hospital," Dan said soberly. "Tell me, and we'll take it to the right people. We'll work it out so it doesn't affect your pension. I know you're worried about that."

"Oh, I'm worried about more than that right about now."

Dan studied Randall's face gravely.

"What happened?" he asked again.

"I was sent on an errand."

"On purpose?" Dan asked.

"Did I realize it was to get me out of the way? No. But maybe I didn't let myself think about that."

"Who sent you?"

"Ramirez."

"Jesus. What's he got on you?" Dan asked incredulously.

Randall's face was sunken like an old man's.

"Long story, my friend. Long story, from a long time ago."

Dan pulled over a plastic chair from the desk in the corner and sat down straddling it, looking at Randall.

"Might as well get started," he said. "Once I know the extent of the problem, I'll figure out how to handle it."

SARAH VAN DER Vere paced around the main entrance to the U.S. Attorney's Office, sucking a final drag off her cigarette. It was about to pour, and she just *had* to be wearing her favorite outfit. She shared the space grudgingly with a tacky-looking secretary on afternoon break, who apparently hadn't heard that teased hair went out thirty years ago. The woman smiled at her, so Sarah flashed a condescending smile and turned her back. Damn antismoking laws—they really threw you in with the riffraff. If she needed a hit of nicotine before she did this, wasn't she entitled to some privacy? Even when they planned to execute you, they let you have your final cigarette in peace.

She threw the butt down and stamped on it but still didn't feel ready to go inside. She stalled for a bit, contemplating the passing traffic. Taxis and trucks sped by, spewing black exhaust into the humid air. All those people, going about their pathetic lives. At this low moment in her personal history, Sarah still thought highly enough of herself that she didn't envy them. Even if she was possibly about to get arrested, it was still better being her. Arrested. Now, *that* would be upsetting. But there was no way to turn Dodo in without incriminating herself, and she'd come to the conclusion that she needed to turn him in for her own protection.

But she'd take an extra moment, think it through one more time. Had she missed anything? Any out, any escape valve? She wasn't in a rush. It wasn't like she had an appointment. Melanie Vargas might not even be in her office.

If only she didn't have to worry about Dodo killing her. She'd been worried about that ever since Jed's murder. It was why she'd approached that prosecutor in the elevator in the first place. But when Melanie Vargas came to her apartment, she'd chickened out. It suddenly occurred to her that giving evidence against Dodo would reveal her own involvement in Securilex. So she made a major scene to get the woman out of her apartment. Sob, sob, like she'd ever let herself cry like that over a man. Hah, fat chance. But it worked. The prosecutor had left her alone. Only now Sarah had changed her mind, after seeing how angry Dodo was yesterday.

The situation was truly maddening. If she hadn't felt the need to defend herself by launching a preemptive strike against him, she'd be enjoying a normal afternoon. At her desk sipping an iced cappuccino and doing some research, or sneaking out to do a little lingerie shopping. Something pleasant and unremarkable like that. Instead she was about to go confess to a major fraud. Which was rather interesting, admittedly, but damn upsetting. Although maybe it would get her on television. She *would* like that. She should give a little thought to what she'd wear on her perp walk, maybe get her hair blown and makeup done beforehand. She'd find herself a lawyer with good press contacts, somebody well known—cute, hopefully. Maybe there was even a book deal in this somewhere.

But she should at least consider the possibility that she was overreacting. After all, her fear that Dodo might harm her wasn't based on much. Only on the belief that he'd ordered Jed killed. Otherwise she had no reason to think he was capable of murder. In his treatment of her personally, he'd never been violent. Okay, maybe when they played S&M games, but that was consensual. And even then he was pathetic. She'd known a lot worse. In fact, she liked worse, she liked rougher. That's why she'd ended up making him be the bottom, because she couldn't stand the squirrelly way he whipped her. Earlier, in his office, he'd actually seemed like he might hit her. She wasn't surprised when he didn't. Disappointed, but not surprised. Even when he was so upset, he couldn't. Poor thing, she really did treat him mean. She couldn't help it, though. He was so tiresome sometimes.

So okay, what made her think Dodo had Jed killed? What was the basis for that belief? She had to admit she didn't have one shred of proof for it. It boiled down to *someone* had Jed killed, and who else could it be? Dodo had motive, he had money, and he hated Jed enough to do it. But did that prove anything? Knowing Jed, she was sure that plenty of other people probably wanted him dead, too. Jed was deliciously corrupt, the only person Sarah had ever met whose aura was darker than her own. She was quite broken up by his death. But just because she didn't happen to know who those others were didn't mean they didn't exist. Maybe Dodo was innocent.

If only there were a way to find out, before taking the drastic step of incriminating herself. Maybe she should just *ask* Dodo whether he'd killed Jed. He'd probably tell her. It was the sort of thing she could imagine him bragging about, if he'd actually done it. Of course, she could imagine him bragging about it even if he hadn't done it. But no, Dodo was a lawyer at heart. He didn't like needless exposure to liability, any more than she did. She didn't really think he'd confess falsely.

She opened her bag. It was that Louis Vuitton one with the pink flowers and the little gold lock that Dodo got for her. She loved pink. Come to think of it, he did buy her some nice things. It was worth giving him another chance. She pulled out her cell phone.

"Dodo. Cell," she said, enunciating clearly so the voice recognition would register. It rang three times. She was just about to hang up when he answered.

"Sarah," he said. The way he said her name, he sounded terribly upset. But she wasn't interested in his mental state right now.

"So, Dodo."

"Yes?"

"I have a question for you."

"What?" he choked, almost as if he were crying.

"Did you or did you not order Jed Benson killed?"

The snorting and grunting emanating from the other end of the line was Dodo sobbing, she decided. Really. Couldn't he just answer the damn question? Crying could mean guilt, or it could just mean he was a pathetic fool. Now she was going to have to coax it out of him, and she was tired of standing out here already.

"Now, Dodo, please. Don't be so upset. Dodo?"

"I'm going to kill myself," he sputtered. "I'm driving to the country. I'm in the car right now. And when I get there, I'm going to shoot myself with my hunting rifle."

"Why on earth would you do a stupid thing like that?" she asked with true bewilderment. Sarah couldn't imagine suicide. Her survival instinct was much too robust.

"Because," he choked out, "I hate you. I hate you, and I want to hurt you."

She laughed, a light, trilling giggle.

He stopped crying instantly. "Why is that funny?" he asked.

"Because, silly. There's a logical fallacy there. What makes you think it would hurt me if you killed yourself? It would actually solve a lot of my problems."

"Oh, it'll hurt you, all right, you ungrateful whore. I've made damn sure of that."

He spoke with such utter conviction that she got nervous.

"Oh. How's that?" she asked.

"Maybe I did order Jed killed. But maybe it was at your insistence."

"What *are* you talking about?"

"Melanie Vargas is about to receive an interesting package in the mail. It's going to lay out for her how you persuaded me to put out a contract on Jed, so he wouldn't expose what we did on Securilex. What we *both* did, Sarah. And I have proof. Very persuasive proof."

"That's ridiculous, Dodo. I had nothing to do with Jed's murder."

"Neither did I. But once the prosecutor reads what I sent her, she'll think otherwise. Happy landing, Sarah! I'll be waiting for you in hell."

Melanie was in terrible shape. Those ten extra pounds—she felt every one of them. Rushing toward the model-boat pond in her high-heeled shoes, gasping for breath, she had an agonizing stitch in her side. The paved pathway was nearly deserted in the stifling heat, the air wet and pungent, smelling like rain. Her body ached to stop, but she had to keep going, had to find Sophie Cho before the skies opened.

Slice didn't fuck around. He would murder Sophie with less thought than he'd give to crushing a cockroach under his shoe. Melanie refused to let that happen. Whatever Sophie's entanglement with Jed Benson, she was fundamentally a good person, whereas Slice was an animal. Thinking about Slice hurting her friend, pure rage shot through her. She felt capable of terrible violence, imagined hurting Slice, clawing him with her fingernails, ripping into him with her teeth. She felt the animal within herself.

She got to the open plaza housing the model-boat pond and slowed to a walk. The sweat dripping down her back made her dress stick to her skin. Black thunderclouds loomed overhead. In the gathering gloom, she focused her mind, scanning the shiny green benches around the pond's perimeter. They were largely deserted because of the heat and the threatening rain. A few people sat fanning themselves, waiting hopelessly for a cool breeze, but Sophie wasn't among them. Had Slice overtaken her on the empty pathway? Was she lying dead or injured in the bushes Melanie had just passed? Central Park was a big place. She could use some help, but there was no one to call, no one to trust.

Not seeing Sophie, she picked up her pace again. The sky darkened to a lurid gray-green. The first fat drops of rain hit her arm and forehead. Within seconds it became a downpour. Everybody scattered. Melanie flew up shallow bluestone steps to a small brick building housing a concession stand, huddling along with several others under its green copper awning. Rain beat down on the metal like sticks on a tin can. Drops fell sideways in sheets, pricking her skin and stinging her eyes.

If Sophie wasn't at the model-boat pond, where was she? Hands racing, Melanie dialed Sophie's cell phone. It picked up on the first ring.

"Yo, Big, what up?" a man's voice answered, low and dangerous. She recognized it instantly, from the tape.

"Slice," she said.

"Who this?" Slice asked.

"Where's Sophie? What have you done with her?"

The phone went dead in her hand.

If she hadn't been certain before, she was now. Slice had Sophie's cell phone; ipso facto Slice had Sophie. Melanie trained every neuron on figuring out where he would take her. She felt the answer beckoning just at the edge of her grasp. What was the connection between Sophie, an architect, and Jed Benson's murder? It had something to do with the town house, with the blueprints Sophie had filed with the Buildings Department. They were fakes, she'd told Melanie over the phone. Fakes? Fakes! Duh! Melanie didn't realize she'd spoken aloud until the woman standing next to her looked at her with a start. No, she wanted to say, I'm not mentally ill, but I *am* a complete moron.

Melanie reached for the red cardboard tube she'd been carrying, protruding from her handbag, since this morning. Why would Jed Benson bother hiding blueprints of his town house in his trapped-out car? Why would Dan's snitch travel all the way to Millbrook to find them? Because the blueprints were valuable, that was why. She'd been carrying around the originals, the real ones, the whole time. They revealed something, hid something, contained some secret, that the phonies on file with the Buildings Department didn't. Based on what she knew, the secret must be about one of two things: either the Securilex deal or drugs. The evidence pointed to one of those two motives being behind Jed Benson's murder. Melanie was betting on the latter. Something that had to do with drugs. Drugs, drugs, drugs. Yes! She thought about the Road Runner sticker on Benson's Hummer, about the secret trap in his car. It all made sense. She held the real blueprints in her hand, and with them the key to the whole case.

SHE SPRINTED TO Jed Benson's town house in the pouring rain, skidding and slipping, wrenching her ankle, swearing. People on the street got out of her way as if she were a crazy woman. Her dress was soaked, her hair plastered to the side of her face, but she wouldn't stop. Slice was taking Sophie there to find what was hidden in the blueprints. Once he got what he wanted, he would surely kill her. Every second that passed brought Sophie's murder one second closer.

Adrenaline pumping, Melanie didn't spare a thought for her own safety, until suddenly she pictured Maya's precious, funny face. Maya made her want to take care of herself, to take precautions. If ever there was a moment to call in reinforcements, this was it, but who to call? Damn that Dan O'Reilly, making her feel she couldn't trust him. Because there was simply nobody else. Randall, Bernadette, Rommie Ramirez. All of them would hurt her before they would help her. Wouldn't they?

Before she knew it, Melanie stood panting, gazing up at the Bensons' town house. Boarded-up windows lent its facade an eerie, derelict appearance. The rain was letting up, but the sky overhead was still black with storm clouds. Once she caught her breath, she crept around to the basement entrance. It was hidden from the street, tucked behind the grand, curving limestone steps to the main floor. Tattered remnants of yellow crime-scene tape fluttered from its carved wooden door. She rattled the heavy brass doorknob. It wouldn't budge. Just as well. She needed time. Time to gather her nerve. Time to formulate an escape plan.

She did the only thing she could think of to alert anyone to her whereabouts—dialed Steve at work. No matter how things stood between them, he cared about her safety. The thought gave her a sharp pang of nostalgia for him. But his secretary came on the line and said he was out of the office at a meeting. Melanie left a quick voice mail saying where she was and hung up wondering if she'd achieved anything beyond telling him where to find her dead body.

She stashed the blueprints in a nearby planter and knelt down to examine the lock. Maybe she could jimmy it with a credit card like she'd seen in the movies. She'd give it a try, maybe do a little reconnaissance, but not go inside just yet. She was digging in her handbag for her wallet when she heard a noise behind the door.

It swung open, and before Melanie could get to her feet, two men sprang out, one lean and slight, the other huge and hulking, both wearing black ski masks over their faces. The big one tackled her. She went over backward, slamming her head against the rough sidewalk, letting out a startled grunt.

"Yo, what you up to, bitch?" the small one asked in a low, intimate tone, leaning down so she felt his fetid breath, warm on her face. He thrust a large silver semiautomatic against her cheek. She felt it there, enormous and cold, blocking her view of the sky.

"Well, lookit this, Bigga. It the prosecutor. Melanie Vargas. She come for a visit. Ain't that nice? You got something you wanna tell me, Melanie?"

It frightened her that he knew her name. Obviously she recognized him, even through the ski mask. Not just from his old mug shot either, but from everything she'd heard. The height and build, the attitude. Killer's freaky energy radiating through the ski mask, body twitching with adrenaline. This guy had to be Slice. But the fact that *he* recognized *her*—what could that mean, other than that he'd followed her?

"I know you come for a reason, bitch, so don't play cute," Slice repeated softly, prodding her cheek even harder with the gun. The answer he was looking for was in the blueprints sitting a foot away in the planter, obscured by dark leaves, but she wasn't about to give it up so easily. The information was too valuable. She would use it to trade—for Sophie's life, for her own.

Slice nodded at Bigga, who yanked her up and twisted her arms roughly behind her back. Dragged to her feet so suddenly she saw stars.

"Where's my friend?" she demanded when her vision cleared.

"You hear that, Big? This bitch think she in charge. She gonna learn her lesson when she dead 'fore the night's through." Slice's tone was casual. Killing was just what he did.

"If you let my friend go, I have some information for you."

Melanie heard the deadly calm in her own voice. She wasn't afraid. This felt like a dream. Or a nightmare, really. A nightmare she'd lived through before. *The man behind the door, the blast, her father lying in a pool of blood, eyes staring, breathing ragged.*

"What information?" Slice asked.

"No. First you show me she's okay," Melanie insisted.

"Who you talking about? That Chinese bitch? The architect?"

"Yes."

"She your friend? Small world, ain't it? She inside, resting. Come on in, we'll have a nice talk." He laughed deep in his throat, like a growl.

Slice went inside, and Bigga shoved her through the door after him. The lights were on, the foyer looking just as it had when she'd been there the night of the murder. It smelled different, though—the burned-flesh odor replaced by a powerful, acrid combination of basement damp, water damage, and the smoky aftermath of the fire. Thick enough to taste, but better than a charred corpse. Slice headed down the hallway toward Jed Benson's office, and Bigga pushed her from behind, making her follow.

As she walked through the office door, she saw two feet sticking out from behind the blackened remains of Jed Benson's desk, and she gasped. The feet were clad in Sophie Cho's favorite black Nikes. Melanie lurched forward, trying to reach her friend, but Bigga grabbed her arm savagely and stopped her.

"Where the fuck you think you going?" Bigga yelled.

"That's Sophie! What did you do to her?" Melanie exclaimed, craning her neck but unable to see any more of Sophie than her feet.

"She fine. We just give her a little taste of something, keep her quiet on the way here," Slice replied, a sadistic glint in his tiny eyes.

If Sophie had been unconscious since they brought her here, Melanie realized, they couldn't have gotten any information from her yet. That was a positive sign. Because the second they had what they wanted, Melanie knew, they would have no reason for keeping Sophie alive. Or Melanie either.

Slice shoved Melanie down into a damaged leather swivel chair. Popped springs from the scorched seat poked into her back and thighs. She wondered if it was the same chair Jed Benson had been tortured and died in. The thought made her angry rather than afraid. Slice leaned close, his sweaty ski mask emitting a sour wool smell.

"Listen up, Melanie," he said, "we can do this real easy or we can do it the hard way. The easy way, you tell me what I want to know. The hard way, you end up dead like Jed."

"Dead like Jed," Bigga said. "My man shootin' the rhymes."

"You a pretty girl. Be a shame if you got cut so you wasn't pretty no more," Slice said, rubbing his gun along her cheek, pushing back her hair with the barrel. The sexual menace in the gesture enraged and nauseated her. She honed the anger, realizing that it was helping her stay in control.

"If you want to talk to me, Slice, back the fuck off," she commanded icily, as if she were in her office. She'd talked to scumbag criminals like him a hundred times before. Pretend this is no different, she told herself. She was the boss. She wasn't surprised when it worked. Confidence was everything in life. Slice laughed and took several steps backward, dropping the gun down to his side.

"The bitch got cojones, I say that much," he said to Bigga. "And she know our names. No point in being uncomfortable, then. We can go plain-face."

Slice stripped off his ski mask. Bigga did the same. Melanie was overwhelmed with rage, this time at herself. By using his name, showing him she knew who he was, she'd signed her own death warrant for sure. No way he would ever let her live, now that he knew she could identify him. Her only remaining chance was to drag out giving him the information he wanted as long as possible, and try to figure a way to escape. She had no hope that anybody would come save her. She'd have to rely on her wits.

"What is it exactly that you want to know?" she asked, making an effort to keep her voice steady.

"Don't play games, bitch. Where the product?" Slice demanded. "We know it's here. You show us where."

"We know it's here, you show us where," Bigga chanted, laughing. Slice shot him a look, and he fell silent.

So her theory was right. There was an elaborate trap built into the walls of Jed Benson's town house, concealing a king's ransom of drugs, revealed in the blueprints she'd left outside. Sophie, Sophie, what did you do? But Sophie, lying on the floor in deep sleep, couldn't answer her silent question. It had been a classic home invasion from the start. The bad guys were looking for drugs, like they always were. When Jed Benson wouldn't give up the goods, Slice killed him, as often happened. The same brutal story had played out a thousand times before on the streets of Bushwick. She just hadn't recognized it in this fancy neighborhood.

Just then the cell phone in her pocket began to howl. Somehow she knew it was Steve; she could feel his worry in each piercing shriek. Slice leaned over and dug his hand into her pocket, his fingers creeping grotesquely against her thigh. He withdrew the phone, turned it off, and threw it to the floor. It skidded to rest against the desk. Melanie looked at it longingly, saying a silent prayer that he would call the police.

"Guess they'll have to leave you a voice mail," Slice said, smiling sarcastically. "Now, about the merchandise . . ."

Drag it out longer. Maybe somebody will come, she told herself. "What merchandise?"

"Don't be acting like you don't know. That would upset me. You don't wanna see some shit I do when I'm upset, you feel me?" he said in a low, intense tone. He had the eyes of some night creature—tiny, gleaming, dead eyes much too small even for his narrow face.

"I'm gonna tell you everything, okay? I don't want to get hurt. I need to make sure we understand each other, that's all."

"What the fuck merchandise you think I'm talking about? Ladies' underwear?" Slice yelled. Bigga laughed uproariously.

"You're saying there are drugs hidden here? Why would there be drugs hidden in Jed Benson's house?"

She didn't even see it coming, he was that fast. In the blink of an eye, Slice smashed the butt of his gun against the side of her head. Pain exploded in her skull. She shot back in time. *"Daddy! No! Noooo!"* *"Shut the fuck up, bitch!" A blinding blow to her head, then darkness.* But a second later, she was back in Jed Benson's office, conscious, hearing and seeing better than she wanted to. She raised her fingers to the spot the pain radiated from. They came away bloody.

The blow might have thrown somebody else into a panic. But for Melanie it served as a wake-up call. It reminded her. You had to fight back, or the animals would win. They'd won last time. Things had never been the same after the robbery. Her father had never spent another night under their roof. Years of rehab in San Juan, and then he ended up leaving them, marrying his nurse. She'd seen him twice in the last ten years. She wouldn't let the animals win this time, goddamn it. She found her rage and, at the heart of it, her calm.

"You think I won't hurt you? Next time it's a bullet, bitch!"

"Okay," she said, "I hear you. I'll play ball." *Until I can figure out how to kill you, you scum.*

"Where the fuck the drugs? And don't you be acting like you don't know, because I know that's why you came here."

"I'm getting to it. You know we were up at Benson's place in Millbrook this morning, right?" She was breathing heavily, her ears still ringing, but she was more determined than ever before.

"That true, Bigga?" Slice asked.

"Toldja they's somebody with that police who killed No Joke," Bigga said.

"It was her? Why the fuck you didn't body 'em when you had a clear shot, then? They killed my dog." He grabbed Melanie by the throat. She struggled for air. "Fucking bitch, you killed my dog! That dog was a warrior. You know what his name was? No Joke, because he wasn't no fucking joke. Me and him been through mad shit together. You gonna have to pay for that."

He let go of her throat, took a step back, and raised his gun. She couldn't let him shoot her, because then he would win. She didn't care if *she* lived or died, but she cared if he did.

"Stop!" she yelled. "We found the trap. The trap in the car, okay? I have the blueprints to this house."

"Yeah, Slice, get the product first, then body her," Bigga said.

"Okay, right, Big." Slice dropped his arm. Melanie breathed again. "I get carried away. Then I don't get the information I need. I got to focus. One thing at a time. Yo, thank you, son."

"That's what I'm here for," Bigga said.

"So you found the blueprints. Where they at? 'Cause this bitch useless," Slice said, pointing at Sophie, lying so still she might have been dead. "Think you mighta OD'd her on that shit, Big."

Melanie's brain felt intensely focused. She saw an opening.

"Dan O'Reilly, the FBI agent, he took them to my office and put them in the evidence vault," she lied coolly. "We were planning to show them to a trap expert to help us figure it out."

"If that's true, why you here now?" Slice asked.

"I wanted to get a head start. You know, take credit for finding it first."

Slice nodded. He believed her.

"So she got to call O'Reilly and tell him to bring the blueprints here, then," Bigga interjected.

Yes! That was exactly the result she was aiming for. Better Dan than nobody. At least she thought he'd try to prevent her death. But Slice was too smart.

"What the fuck, Big? This why I tell you to keep your stupid-ass mouth shut. That would get us locked up. We use our own people. Here, take my heat and watch her while I make some calls."

Slice handed Bigga the gun and retreated to the hallway, pulling his cell phone from his pocket as he went. She heard beeping as he hung up and dialed repeatedly. He was paging somebody. Melanie tried to focus, but she couldn't help replaying what he'd said a moment earlier. Calling Dan would get them locked up. So Dan wasn't on their payroll? He wasn't working with them? God, she prayed that was what it meant!

Out in the hallway, Slice's cell phone rang, and he answered. His voice filtered, low and intense but clearly audible, through the open doorway.

"Yo, son, you ain't jumpin' on my beeps like you should be," Slice said. "Don't gimme that shit. Now you gotta prove your loyalty. I need you to do something for me. . . . Yes, now! . . . I don't give a fuck if you busy. This more important. . . . Don't you be making me think nothing. . . . I ain't your bitch, so why you trying to fuck me? . . . You better be jumping on this, or you gonna wake up dead. . . . Okay, that's more like it. . . . Good. . . . This is what you do. The blueprints be in the vault in the prosecutor's office. I need you to go in there and get 'em."

Slice had spoken of using his own people, but he was obviously talking to an insider, to one of Melanie's people, somebody who could get into the vault in her office. Rommie Ramirez. It had to be.

While Slice talked, Bigga stood leaning against the massive wooden desk. He had the sort of fat, doughy face that looked benevolent on some people. On him it was merely vacant and self-indulgent. His arms crossed, he held the gun casually against his chest, watching Melanie quietly.

"Who's that on the phone with Slice, Rommie Ramirez?" she asked.

"Shut the fuck up. We ask the questions 'round here," Bigga said.

"Whoever it is, maybe if I talked to them, I could give them a better sense of where to look for the blueprints."

"Open your mouth again and I tape it shut."

As she watched him warily, something clicked inside her throbbing head. She put two and two together. Bigga was the one who'd shot at her at the Benson estate this morning. Bigga was Dan's snitch. But no sooner had she taken heart from that thought than warning bells went off. Which way did it shake out for her prospects of survival that Dan and Bigga were working together?

A FEW MINUTES later, Slice walked back into the room. "Now we in play. If the blueprints be where she say, they're on the way. If not, she don't live another day."

"Awright!" Bigga said admiringly. "Now what?"

"We wait. Keep the gun on her."

Slice kicked aside debris to clear a space on the floor and, extracting a small GameBoy from the pocket of his baggy pants, slid down to a sitting position against the wall near the doorway. The beeps emitted by the video game lent an incongruously festive air to the dismal basement. Bigga stood watching Slice.

"I said watch *her.* What the fuck you watching me for?" Slice barked.

"Nuthin'. Whatever."

"So don't fucking look. You disturbing my concentration."

"I'm hungry," Bigga whined.

"You always hungry. That's how come you so fat."

"I'm starving, bro. I need me something delicious. Lemme go get some Chinese or something before the action start. I saw a place when we was driving."

Slice looked up from his game, annoyed. "You remember that last job we pulled in Bushwick? You couldn't climb in the window because you was so fucking fat, and that motherfucker Arturo broke out. We didn't get nothing off'n him?"

"Yeah?"

"So I'm putting you on a diet. No food for you."

Melanie had followed this conversation intently, flooded with relief that Slice wouldn't let Bigga leave. She cherished the hope that Bigga was on Team America, working for Dan, and that when push came to shove, he would help her out. Despite her bravado, she had no interest in being left alone with Slice. She might be reckless, but she wasn't stupid. Slice would kill her just for kicks, even if it made no sense for his game plan, so how could she predict his next move?

Bigga sighed and sat back down on the desk. Slice returned to his GameBoy. As they sat there, the silence broken only by beeps from the GameBoy and the noise of Bigga's stomach growling, the air putrid with a wet, burned smell, Melanie's confidence withered and disappeared. She realized she was right near her apartment, that her beautiful baby was mere blocks away. She thought about going out with the stroller on Monday night, smelling the smoke, following it here. Her foolish pride had made her run after the Benson case, and now it would cost her her life. And ruin Maya's. Maya would be motherless, Steve left to raise her alone, and Melanie had only her own ego to blame. She knew what it was like, growing up with one parent, always feeling the absence of the other, and now she'd inflicted it on her daughter, something she'd vowed never to let happen. In spite of herself, Melanie started to heave and shake with suppressed sobs. Goddamn it, she was thinking, she wouldn't give that bastard the satisfaction of seeing her cry! But thinking also about the gaping hole she'd be leaving in her daughter's life, she couldn't help it.

"Aw, fuck, shut the fuck up!" Slice yelled. Just then Bigga's stomach let out a loud rumble. "You, too, shut up with that foul shit! Between her whining and your disgusting noises, you both making me sick."

"I need something to eat," Bigga said calmly.

"So go get it, then. I can't fucking concentrate with shit like this going on."

"You want me to bring you back Chinese?" Bigga asked.

"You crazy? I ain't eating on no fucking job."

Bigga shrugged. "Okay, I'll be back real fast," he said, handing Slice the gun.

A moment later the door to the street slammed behind him, leaving Melanie alone with Slice.

4 8

———

Slice played with his GameBoy for what seemed like a very long time. Eventually it let loose a particularly loud series of beeps, then fell silent. The game was over.

"Hmm," Slice said aloud. "My game all through. What I'm gonna do for some fun now?"

Melanie had stopped crying a while ago. Her eyes clear and dry, she watched Slice with heightened senses. Slowly he pulled himself up from where he sat against the wall and replaced the game in his pocket. He tucked his gun into the waistband of his baggy pants. Deliberately he walked the few steps to where Melanie sat in the swivel chair, pulling a roll of duct tape from his pocket. She knew what it was for. She hadn't been afraid before, but she was afraid now. She began to tremble visibly, and a savage smile curled the corners of Slice's lips.

He leaned over and whispered in her ear, "This my favorite part, bitch."

He jerked her arms forward and taped her hands together at the wrists.

"The way I see it," Slice said, "now we know where the blueprints is at and I sent somebody to get 'em, I don't really need you no more. I'm free to do as I please. Don't you agree?"

Melanie opened her mouth to speak, but only a wet, choking sound emerged.

"Cat got your tongue?" He tugged up his baggy pant leg and pulled a large knife, its curved, ten-inch blade glinting hypnotically, from a tan leather sheath strapped to his shin. He hefted the knife in his hand, testing its weight.

"You took No Joke. But I still got my knife. You know, my knife my favorite way to kill. I much prefer it to my gun. Just, like, a personal-taste issue, you feel me?"

He reached behind her and grabbed her hair, snapping her head back viciously to expose her throat. She exhaled all the air sharply from her lungs. The cold blade slithered along the skin under her chin. She felt the slightest sting.

"Yup, still real sharp," he said, holding it before her eyes. The edge of the blade bore a tiny bit of blood. Melanie began to shake with pure terror. Slice laughed.

"WHAT THE FUCK you doing, you fucking idiot?" cried Rommie from the doorway, his face contorted with rage. As Slice turned toward the sound of Rommie's voice, brandishing the knife, Rommie swiftly closed the distance between them. Slice jabbed the knife straight at Rommie's face.

"You psycho piece of shit!" Rommie screamed, jumping back, chest heaving. "You gonna kill her? You always have to hurt somebody for kicks, and all it does is fuck my shit up! Those blueprints weren't where she said. You kill her, we'll miss the stash again."

"She saw my face. She can ID me. How I'm gonna let her live?"

"Get the fucking product first. Moron!" Rommie's mouth was wet with spittle, his face rabid, transformed, nothing like the hail-fellow-well-met guy Melanie knew. He reached his hand inside his elegant, dark suit jacket. Anticipating shots, Melanie threw herself off the chair, rolling away from them to a sheltered spot behind Jed's desk. Focused on each other, neither man stopped her. She nearly cried out at the sight of Sophie's inert body on the floor; she'd almost forgotten she was back here.

Melanie watched until she saw Sophie's chest moving up and down. Thank God, alive! Then, needing to know what was happening, she inched forward on her stomach and peeked around the side of the desk.

Rommie and Slice loomed between her and the door, circling each other like boxers in a ring. By menacing Rommie with his knife, Slice managed to prevent him from drawing his gun. Rommie should have overpowered Slice easily, given his larger size. But Slice was lightning fast and armed. He danced around on the balls of his feet, his knife blade floating before him. As she watched, Rommie lunged for Slice's wrist. Slice angled the blade just right so it slashed deeply into Rommie's extended right hand.

"Aaaaagh!" Rommie screamed, clutching his bleeding hand against his chest and backing away.

"See what you get, fool?" Slice taunted.

Slice advanced toward Rommie, ready to stab, and Rommie went for his jacket again, with his left hand this time. Just as he managed to pull out his gun, Slice pounced, slashing. Rommie ducked aside, but not fast enough to stop the blade from making contact with his left arm. Slice couldn't halt his forward momentum. The tip of his knife pierced the wall near the door and stuck in the decayed plaster. As he yanked it out, Rommie swung around wildly, howling with pain from his slashed arm. His gun went flying from his left hand, sliding across the floor and coming to rest near the swivel chair Melanie had just vacated, a few feet from her face. She stared right into its gleaming barrel. It was a sleek Glock nine-millimeter, and she'd fired one just like it recently on a courtesy visit to the DEA range.

Melanie thanked her lucky stars that Slice had taped her hands in *front* of her. The darkest parts of her past had prepared her for this moment: You acted. She'd learned that the hard way. You acted, or you became the victim. She lunged forward with all her strength, clasping the gun and rolling back into a sitting position, raising it in her bound hands to point straight at them.

"Drop the knife!" she shouted.

Slice whirled around and saw her holding the gun. Then he did something she hadn't anticipated. He smiled, a condescending smile, as if the sight of her sitting there pointing a gun at him amused him considerably. His smile unnerved her for a second. But then it pissed her off.

"Drop it, or I'll blow your fucking head off!" she shouted again.

Adrenaline pumping, breath coming in gasps, she lurched forward onto her knees, then sprang up toward Slice. She skidded to a halt less than five feet from him, pointing the gun straight at his head. Point-blank range, and she had decent aim. Assuming she was capable of pulling the trigger, she wouldn't miss. But did she really have it in her to shoot another human being? Even this one?

Rommie, who'd been staring at his own blood dripping from his hands, looked back and forth between Slice and Melanie, dumbfounded, and did nothing.

Slowly and matter-of-factly, holding Melanie's gaze, Slice pulled up his pant leg as if he meant to sheathe his knife. Did he think that would satisfy her?

"No, I said drop it! Drop it on the floor!"

She watched in mute horror as he slid the knife into its sheath and calmly reached for the gun stuck in his waistband. The trajectory the gun followed from his waist to pointing at her head seemed to happen in slow motion. She closed her eyes and squeezed the Glock's trigger. A long time later, she felt the kick. Seconds seemed to last hours as she saw her daughter's face. An enormous wave of sorrow washed over her. Far away, an earsplitting report sounded, and a fine spray of blood covered her skin and clothes.

4 9

—

How funny, Melanie thought, dying *does* feel like you're still alive, but there's no white light. The next second she opened her eyes. Slice slumped to the ground, a flap opened in the top of his skull.

"Nice work," Rommie said. "It was him or us. Motherfucker woulda bodied us for sure."

Wearing an expression of pure disgust, Rommie flipped over Slice's lifeless body with his shoe so it lay facedown. Melanie was shaking all over. She couldn't believe it. She looked down at the gun clutched in her tightly bound hands, and then back at Slice. She'd just killed a man.

Seeing the state she was in, Rommie pressed his advantage. He leaned over, picked up Slice's gun in his left hand, and leveled it at her.

"Okay, Melanie, you had your fun. Enough cops and robbers. Drop the weapon."

Rommie looked dangerous as a stray dog in pain. Sweat poured down his forehead into his eyes. He wiped his face with his cut right hand, leaving a trail of blood. This was a side of him she'd never seen before. Unbeknownst to her, he'd already walked a mile down the path of corruption. No telling how much farther he'd go. He'd probably be willing to kill her. Dropping the gun was not a risk she could afford to take.

"No," she said, raising it instead, to point at his chest. "You drop yours."

The surprise in his eyes was gratifying. But then his expression changed.

"Wait a minute," he said. "That's my gun, isn't it? You picked it up off the floor?"

"Yes."

He laughed. "It's empty!"

She studied his face, holding the gun as steady as her shaking hands would allow. Rommie didn't look like he was lying.

"I don't believe you. You're bluffing," she said, trying to sound strong despite the trembling in her legs.

"I went to the range this morning because I was due to qualify," Rommie said. "Emptied the clip, except for one bullet, which you did me the favor of pumping into my friend's head there."

Holy shit, was he telling the truth?

"You would never leave your gun empty like that," she said, definitively, as if she could will it to be so. "You would reload." Then again, remember the fuck-up she was talking to.

"Sometimes it pays to be sloppy, kid."

Rommie advanced on her with an evil grin, his gun pointed right at her head.

"What are you doing?" she shouted. "Get back!"

"You worried I'll kill you, Melanie? L'il ole me? I'm flattered."

Panting in terror, but determined, she pointed the gun at Rommie's legs and squeezed the trigger. Right away, she knew it felt different. There was no tension. The trigger snapped back uselessly, making a hollow, clicking noise. Rommie closed the gap between them and ripped the gun from her hands. He shoved it into his waistband, then grabbed her by the throat with his blood-slicked hand, backing her straight up against Benson's desk.

"Everything I did for you, and you try to blow me away? What kind of friendship is that? I'll remember when the time comes to figure out what to do with you. Which is right after you tell me where those blueprints are."

"Let go!" she choked out. "Let go, and I'll tell you!"

He dropped his hand and backed off, and she sucked in a ragged breath. Adrenaline born of pure fear was the only thing keeping her functioning. She needed a plan. She needed more time, and a way to call the cops. But how? The blueprints were right outside. And after the wild-goose chase she'd sent him on once today, Rommie wasn't likely to fall for another.

As if to confirm her thoughts, he raised Slice's gun and placed it to her temple.

"*Now*—or you're fucking dead in five seconds."

"Outside, in the planter next to the door," she blurted. *Shit!* She'd given up her last bargaining chip. But she had to. Rommie, like his buddy Slice, was stupid enough to kill her without getting the blueprints first. Now she'd have to come up with another way to stay alive.

His eyes narrowed. "Why there? Why should I even believe you had 'em in the first place? You fed Slice a line so he'd let you live. Who's to say you're not playing *me* now?"

"I had them, I swear. I got them out of the trap in Jed Benson's Hummer."

That registered. Rommie obviously knew about that trap.

"How?" he snarled. "When nobody else could figure out how to open that fricking thing?"

"Dan did it."

"O'Reilly." He nodded. "But you stashed them in a *planter*? Ohh, I get it. You want to go outside. This is all a goddamn scam, isn't it, Melanie? I take you outside to get the plans. You make a scene on the street. Start screaming or something. And somebody calls the cops. You must think I'm pretty fucking stupid."

He jammed the barrel of the gun hard against the side of her head, making her wince. But still, she'd heard it. She'd heard her opportunity, clear as a bell, and it gave her hope. He had the gun, but she could outwit him. She had to. There was no other choice.

With the gun pressed to her head, she managed to feign a shrug of indifference. "If you don't believe me, make me stay here, and you go check it out."

Rommie cast her a savage look, but her playacting had worked. He relaxed and backed off a step, keeping the gun leveled at her, albeit with visible effort. She could tell he was in pain.

"This better fucking be straight."

"It is."

"The upper floors are sealed off, you know. The only way out is past me," he said.

"I'm not going anywhere, Rommie."

"I come back and a fucking hair on your head moved, you're dead."

"I understand."

He backed away, keeping his gun trained on her until he reached the hallway, then turned and made rapidly for the basement door.

As his footsteps receded down the hallway, Melanie hurried over to the desk and dropped to her knees. Heart pounding, she retrieved her cell phone from under the desk where Slice had thrown it, what seemed like a lifetime ago. It *was* a lifetime ago—Slice's lifetime. She glanced at his stiffening corpse, lying inert on the floor like some grisly piece of debris, surrounded now by a shiny, dark pool of blood. She wouldn't let herself think about what had happened, what was still happening. Not now, or she'd fall apart. She had to get herself out of here, so she could live, so she could see her daughter again. Tiny baby girl, *nena preciosa.* Get home to Maya, then think about everything else. She'd have plenty of time later to come to terms with it all. She'd have the rest of her life.

Clutching the phone in her bound hands, she turned it on. She dialed Dan O'Reilly's pager number as fast as her thumb would move, the whole time thinking she might just be calling another calamity down upon herself. But even if Dan was bad, wouldn't he save her life? She just couldn't believe that their whole relationship—everything she'd read in his eyes, the things he'd said, that kiss— was all an elaborate act. Anyway, she was running low on options. At the prompt she punched in the numbers for the town house's address, followed by the code she and Dan had come up with. Lucky seven, he'd said. It damn well better be. Then she turned off the phone, threw it back under the desk, and hurried to the exact spot where she'd been standing when Rommie left the room.

ROMMIE CAME BACK carrying the red tube. He hurried over to Jed's desk, pried off the lid, and spread the blueprints on the marred surface.

She took a step closer, and he spun around with lightning reflexes, raising his gun.

"Stay away, Melanie. Now that I have these, I'll blow your fucking brains out if you mess with me!" His eyes were deadly. He wasn't bluffing. She backed off a step.

"I was just curious about the trap."

"Yeah, well, curiosity killed the prosecutor," he said, breathing hard, still sweating profusely. He gestured with the gun to a spot right beside the desk. "Get over here where I can keep an eye on you."

She moved as commanded, watching him warily.

"This is no game, understand? There's two hundred kilos of Colombian heroin stashed somewhere in this room. I'm not talking about stepped-on shit either. I'm talking pure. You know what that's worth? Twenty million wholesale!"

Her eyes went wide. This was even bigger than she thought.

"Yeah, that's right. Don't look so surprised. You think I'd risk myself for small-time shit?" She didn't answer. "Huh, Melanie?"

"No. Of course not." She needed to calm him down. Drag things out. Keep him talking until help arrived.

"Everything you know, and you hadn't figured it out?" He eyed her skeptically.

"I knew Jed Benson's murder had something to do with corruption, with drugs. I figured it was related to Delvis Diaz and the old Flatlands murder case. I knew that much. But that you were involved? No. I never guessed," she said. Until I learned your fingerprints put you at the scene, you scumbag, she thought.

"Yeah, I was pretty careful, wasn't I?" A boastful smile crept across his face. This wouldn't be so hard after all.

"You covered your tracks pretty well, Rommie. How did you manage it?"

"I guess I can afford to tell you now, huh?" he asked, gesturing meaningfully with his gun. "How's that saying go? 'If I tell you, I gotta kill you?' So anyway, it was like this: Jed and Slice teamed up years ago. They locked Diaz up for those kids Slice bodied, and then they took over the candy store. Threw me a piece of the action now and then, enough to support me and all my alimony payments in fine style anyway, though not near as much as I deserved. Slice was the front man, Jed laundered the money, and I kept the cops off. Pretty good scam, huh? It woulda kept going, too, but Jed started holding back. There's a major shipment stashed in this room somewhere he didn't want to share. He figured Slice wouldn't find out, but he didn't count on me. See, Jed took my loyalty for granted. A lot of people did."

So that was it. All those years, when Rommie was the butt of jokes, he'd had a chip on his shoulder.

"Jed didn't respect you?" she prompted.

"That's right. And he found out how wrong he was, the hard way." He smiled savagely.

"There were four or five guys in the room when the murder went down. I take it you were one of them?"

He shook his head. "Nuh-uh. Don't go there, Melanie. Don't be stupid."

Knock yourself out, you scumbag, she thought. I know you were in on it. I have your prints on the kerosene can. You're dead in the water. If I get out of this room alive, that is.

"Whatever you say," she said aloud. "So who did kill Jed, then?"

"Just some mopes from Slice's crew. Blades."

"Any insiders? Law enforcement?" she asked.

"You mean like Randall Walker?"

"Randall was involved in Jed's murder?" she asked. So it was true. But at least he hadn't mentioned Dan. *Yet.* Had her call for help been in vain?

Rommie chuckled mirthlessly. "In the murder? No way. Guy's fucking useless. I had to practically hold a gun to his head to get anything out of him."

"Then why did you bring him up just now?"

"I thought that's who you meant when you said law enforcement. Randall did only, like, low-level shit for me. Mostly tell me what *you* were up to, so I could keep tabs on the investigation."

Jesus, who could you trust? People really sucked. She had liked Randall, liked him a lot.

"*Why?* Why would he do that?" she asked.

"He didn't have much choice. I had something on him—we're talking ancient history now, but it was major. We were doing an undercover deal, years ago. The buy money disappeared. Twenty large, to be exact, not chickenshit. I pinched it, but Randall didn't know that. He signed it out from the vault, so his ass was on the line. I convinced him his only option was falsifying the reports. So we both said the perp pulled a gun and stuck us up. Swore out statements and everything. Once Randall lied under oath, I had his pecker in my pocket. Simple as that."

"Did he set up my witnesses? Did he give you Rosario Sangrador? Or Amanda Benson? Is that how you got to them?" She felt sick to her stomach at the very thought.

"No, he wasn't in that deep, and I didn't need him for that anyway. I had an in over at your office, remember? With your boss? Show up a few minutes early for a date. Wander around. Take a peek. No telling what you could learn. I had the run of the place."

"*You* killed them?"

"You think I'm stupid enough to get my hands dirty like that? No way. I gave Slice the locations and took care of the doors. Like, I sent Randall Walker off on an errand. But Slice did the rest. That's why I'm gonna get away clean."

Rommie giving up those innocents to be slaughtered by an animal like Slice. Who ever knew a cop could be so twisted?

"But it *was* you who stole the bank records and fingerprint reports from my desk," she said.

"Can you blame me? I asked nicely first, but you wouldn't share."

"And down in the file room the other night, when the tape was stolen from my bag? That was you, too, wasn't it?"

"Uh-huh."

"Bernadette didn't know anything, did she?" Melanie asked.

"Nah. Nothing. She never would've gone along with it."

"So you used her."

Rommie shrugged. "You could put it that way. She's all right, your boss. But not really my type, if you know what I mean."

And Bernadette was so far gone on this guy! *¡Hombres desgraciados!* Men were such dogs! Speaking of, it was time to ask the question she'd been dreading. Even if the answer wasn't the one she was hoping for, she had to hear the truth, if only to better estimate her own chances for survival.

"What about Dan O'Reilly?" she whispered. She held her breath, waiting for his answer.

Rommie stared back at her in surprise. "O'Reilly? You're fucking kidding me! He's a goddamn choirboy."

The relief she felt at that answer was greater than when she'd opened her eyes to find herself still alive and Slice dead on the ground. Dan was clean! And that made her happy for a lot of reasons.

But her exultation was short-lived. A cloud passed across Rommie's face. She'd come to the end of his patience.

"You got me fucking wasting time here!" he shouted suddenly, his face reddening. "Just stand there and shut up, or I'm gonna decide I don't need a hostage, if you see what I mean, Melanie."

He looked down at the blueprints. After a few minutes, he walked over, nearly tripping on Sophie's legs, and pressed a small switch set into the wooden bookshelves behind Jed Benson's desk. With a fluid glide that spoke of Sophie's talent, a section of the shelves slid inward, opening a narrow doorway to the hidden room beyond.

"Shangri-fucking-la! And so easy! Only that moron Slice coulda missed it the first time. I'm going in, but don't you move, you hear me?" Rommie waved his gun at her, then disappeared into the opening.

After only a few seconds, he stumbled back through the opening to the trap, looking almost drunk.

"The drugs!" he shouted, coming over to her, searching her face desperately. "The drugs are fucking gone! First the money in the bank account, now the drugs!"

He pulled out a cell phone and dialed frantically, his hands, covered with now-drying blood, shaking violently.

"Disconnected!" he shouted, pitching the phone across the room with all his strength. "Fucking bitch disconnected her phone! She took the drugs, the money, everything! She double-crossed me!"

"Who, Bernadette?" Melanie asked, confused. Hadn't he said Bernadette knew nothing about this?

"No! No! Nell!" He slumped against the desk, burying his face in his hands, pulling at his hair. "Fucking bitch! I did all this for her! The way Jed treated her. A fine woman like that, and he's doing every stripper in town. She said she loved me, wanted him dead so we could be together. Just pinch one shipment, she said, and we'd be set for life, get a big villa in the Caymans right on the beach. All I needed to do was bring Slice down on Jed. All this for her, and she stabs me in the back!"

"So you lied before when you said Jed held out on Slice. You were covering for Nell. Jed never held out. You set him up."

"He deserved it, the bastard. Treating me like a fucking lackey. Jesus, I can't believe it. Nell, that double-crossing bitch!" He kicked the desk furiously, several times in rapid succession.

"Any woman who would condone the killing of her own daughter . . ."

"Of course she didn't condone killing Amanda. She didn't know. I even tried to avoid it because I knew it would upset Nell." He drew a sharp breath. "Oh, my God, that's it, that's it! That's got to be it. She must've heard about Amanda. She's upset with me. That's why she ran. I have to find her."

"I'm not so sure about that," Melanie said.

"What do you mean?"

"Nobody could locate Nell to break the news of Amanda's death. So when I was driving back to town before, I called her hotel. They told me she'd checked out. The concierge had booked her a ticket to Switzerland. He booked it *yesterday*. Before Amanda was killed."

Rommie's face crumpled.

"Switzerland. Beyond the reach of any extradition treaty," Melanie said.

Rommie shook his head in disbelief, looking to Melanie as if she could explain this terrible betrayal. He had a wild glint in his eyes that made her think she'd better get out of the room fast. She started to move toward the door.

"Where the fuck do you think you're going?" he yelled, raising his gun once again.

5 0

——

The next moment Dan and three other agents burst into the room, weapons drawn. Dan body-slammed Rommie, who crashed to the floor, a flash of light and a deafening report issuing from the barrel of his gun. Seconds later chunks of plaster rained down from the ceiling.

Dan landed on him and managed to yank the gun from Rommie's injured hand, throwing it clear. They somersaulted over Slice's corpse, punching at each other furiously, until Dan ended up on top and smashed Rommie hard with the butt of his own gun. Rommie reeled back, stunned. Dan grabbed Rommie's arms, wrenching them savagely, flipping him over, and handcuffing him. Rommie exhaled in defeat, his entire body deflating, seeming smaller, as if his very flesh understood it was all over. Two of the agents pulled him to his feet. He staggered between them, his eyes hollow with shock, as they dragged him toward the door. Melanie almost felt sorry for him. The third agent, gun still drawn, went to examine the contents of the secret room.

Dan knelt and checked Slice's pulse, then stood up and looked at Melanie. Her face and dress were spattered with blood.

"I shot Slice," she confessed, and started to shake again from head to toe.

"*You* killed him?" He looked at her with a mix of concern and admiration.

"Yes." Tears welled and brimmed over, rolling down her cheeks. Dan came over and wiped them away with his fingers.

"First off," he said, turning over her hands to inspect the duct tape, "you need to understand you did the world a huge favor. That little prick was a stone-cold killer. He wasn't ever gonna stop. You gotta look at it like what you did saved lives."

"Okay," she said, still shaking violently.

"I mean, think about how many murders he had left in him. And if you hadn'ta stopped him tonight, the next one would've been *you*. Hear what I'm saying?"

"Yes."

He picked at the tape with his fingernail, then tugged. It made a loud ripping sound as he unwound it from her wrists. She shook her hands out, feeling the warm blood rush back into her tingling fingers.

"That brings me to my second point," Dan said. "You oughta be proud as shit you made it through this alive. I know *I'm* proud of you. Between this piece of garbage on the floor and that psycho Ramirez, most of the cops and agents I know would've folded. But not you. You beat 'em. You know what that makes you?"

"What?" she asked, voice tremulous, looking up at him with huge eyes.

He brushed her hair back off her face. "You're a survivor. You're a fucking survivor. That's what you should carry around with you for the rest of your life. If you ever find yourself in a tight spot again, you think back on today and you say, 'I took out Slice. A killer with fucking twenty bodies on him, and I took him out. I'm a survivor.' That's what you say, you hear me?"

"Yes. I know you're right, but—"

"No buts. I understand you didn't sign up for gunplay. That's supposed to be my end of the operation. But it was life or death in there. You had no choice. Do you hear me?" He grasped her chin, looking intently into her eyes.

"Yes. Thank you. That helps," she said, taking a deep breath.

He let her go and walked over to where Sophie lay, behind the desk, still unconscious.

"Is she okay?" Melanie asked, rushing to kneel beside him. "She's my friend. The architect I told you about."

"Out cold, but her pulse is strong. What happened to her?"

"Apparently they drugged her to get her over here. I don't know what they gave her, but I'm concerned about an overdose."

"Don't worry. When people OD, it happens right away. They foam at the mouth and stop breathing. She's fine, she's just knocked out. She'll wake up with a headache, that's all."

The other agent emerged from inside the secret room. "Empty," he said, "but that's some fucking trap."

"Empty?" Dan asked, springing to his feet. "My snitch told me Benson had two hundred keys stashed in there!"

"Apparently Nell Benson stole it," Melanie explained.

"What?"

"Long story."

Dan laughed. "You had quite an afternoon. I can't wait to hear the details." He turned to the other agent. "Call an ambulance for the woman on the floor, and notify the ME to come get this piece of garbage."

"Yup, I'm on it," the agent said.

Melanie stood up. "Where's Randall?" she asked Dan guardedly, not sure how much he knew.

"I took him over to Internal Affairs and left him there."

"Oh." She nodded with understanding.

"You knew?" Dan asked sharply.

"I suspected. Well, yes, after this afternoon, I knew for sure. Rommie confirmed it. I'm really sorry. It must be hard for you," she said, reading the pain in Dan's eyes.

"People fucking suck."

"That's exactly what I said when I heard about it. But Randall's a good man at heart. I want him to come out of this okay. What'll happen next, do you know?"

He shrugged. "I put in a word for him. I owed him that much, all we been through together, but I don't give a shit after that. With everything he was into, he's dead to me," he said bitterly.

"Come on now, I know you feel let down. But it sounds like Randall was up against a lot. Ramirez had him over a barrel."

"Don't make excuses for him," Dan said, shaking his head with disgust. "So he was worried about his job and his pension. So what? It all comes down to money. Same shit that brought down every dirty cop from the beginning of time. My old man told me from when I was a kid, on this job you face temptation a hundred times a day. If you ever once let it be a question in your mind, you're fucked."

"Well, I hope after things calm down, you'll think it over and maybe give Randall another chance. I have to admit, though, I'm relieved at your attitude. I was having some doubts about *you,* you know."

"Me?"

"Yes, you. Things you knew that you shouldn't have. The way you opened the Road Runner trap in, like, sixty seconds. That struck me as pretty far-fetched."

"Yeah, you're right. A guy with my IQ cracking the code that fast? No way."

"I'm serious."

"So am I."

"What are you saying? You didn't open the trap?"

"Bigga opened it. He found out the code."

"So you lied to me."

"You could say that—a white lie, though. Look, Bigga was my snitch. The one you've been asking about? That was him. I mean, he was a good snitch back in the day, but then he went south. Participated in a murder. Wouldn't return my beeps. It didn't look too good. If you knew I caught him, you would've told me to lock him up on the spot, right?"

"Yes," she admitted.

"Of course. You would've been justified, too. Especially after he shot at us, right? But I knew he could take me right to Slice. When I got back to Benson's estate, I parked down the road and got the jump on him. Wasn't too hard. He was right inside Benson's house, talking on his cell phone and eating some Doritos. I had him in cuffs in about ten seconds. I got him to open the trap for me as a showing of good faith, and I sent him back out there. I knew you wouldn't approve, so I kept it to myself. But, look, he came through with flying colors. He called in the marines when it counted. He saved your life."

"Him? What did *he* do? I'm the one who beeped you!" she exclaimed.

"Yeah, I got your beep. It confirmed Bigga's information for me, but I already knew. Good thing, too, because that extra time was critical. Bigga called me, and I was at fucking IAD with Randall. I had to get here, call for backup, set up on the place. I'm telling you, you owe him big-time."

"No kidding. All in the guise of going out for Chinese food."

Dan laughed sheepishly. "Actually, Bigga did grab some Chinese before he made the call. He had it with him when we picked him up. Hope it was enough to last him for a while. He's sitting outside in a blue-and-white, cuffed up all nice for you, looking for a little time off his sentence for cooperation."

"Wow. Maybe I should go shake his hand."

"I wouldn't go *that* far," he said with a laugh as the paramedics arrived to take care of Sophie.

MELANIE EMERGED INTO the twilight and breathed deeply. The air after the rainstorm tasted as sharp and clean as ice water. Patrol cars and ambulances were parked in front of the town house, their flashing lights reflected in the slick black pavement. Home was only a few blocks away, but she had unfinished business here first.

Knowing she needed to give a detailed statement, Melanie headed for the cluster of conferring officers standing by the patrol cars. She glimpsed Rommie handcuffed in the back of one, Bigga in another. As she approached, though, the sea of uniforms parted and Bernadette emerged, dressed in tight jeans, stiletto-heeled boots and blazer. She hurried toward Melanie, arms outstretched.

"Melanie, thank God!" Bernadette yelped, embracing her. "I was so worried about you! Once I stopped being angry, that is, since of course you're no longer assigned to the Benson case and I don't know *what* you thought you were up to."

"How did *you* get here?" Melanie asked, immediately extricating herself from Bernadette's grasp.

"Your husband called me. He was in a panic. He wanted to come find you himself, but I refused to give him the exact address. We don't need civilians interfering. But he obviously adores you, Melanie. He was practically hysterical," she said.

Melanie stared at her boss with frosty eyes. Bernadette was not blameless in this fiasco. Her carelessness had allowed Rommie to get to Melanie's witnesses. Her continuing skepticism, even after Melanie told her of the fingerprint report, had perpetuated the whole conspiracy. If Bernadette had listened sooner, some innocent people might still be alive and the whole ordeal tonight could've been avoided.

Bernadette saw Melanie's stony expression and wilted. "I don't know what you're thinking, girlfriend, but please. You have to believe I didn't know."

Melanie glared at her. "I believe you didn't know. But you *should* have known. After what I've been through tonight, don't expect me to let you off the hook."

"I know, I heard all about it. I *cannot* believe you personally shot Slice! Very impressive. I mean, that guy was a serious player. And look at it this way: If you'd caught Slice and taken him to trial, you would have asked for the death penalty, right? Same result, but you saved yourself years of appeals."

"Bernadette, this is not a joke."

"Okay, fine. I see you're angry. What do you want me to say? That you were right?" Bernadette asked.

"Yes! It would be a start."

Bernadette tossed her head irritably. "Fine, then. It turns out you were right, and I commend you for astute investigative work. But you have to admit, from where I stood, your theory looked pretty implausible before tonight. I was entitled to trust Romulado, after all. I'm not speaking about our personal relationship, but about his fifteen years' service."

"Oh, come on, I pointed out all the warning signs," Melanie said. "I even told you about the fingerprint report, and you discounted it."

"In the glare of hindsight, I admit, I made a few errors in judgment. Maybe I didn't take you seriously enough. Romulado accused you of blind ambition, and there was sufficient truth to it that I let him convince me. I was wrong. You deserved more credit than that. Okay? Satisfied now?"

The stricken expression lying just beneath Bernadette's bravado took away any pleasure Melanie might have felt in her victory. Ramirez's treachery was a personal tragedy for Bernadette on a magnitude Melanie hated to think about. Besides, who was *she* to lecture anyway? Maybe Rommie's lie was bigger, but Melanie had trusted Steve and been proved wrong. She'd also failed to trust Dan when she should have. Her judgment of men's character was hardly foolproof.

"Thank you for admitting you were wrong, Bern," Melanie said, softening. "And now that you explain it, I understand why you trusted Rommie over me. When someone you're close to lies to your face, it's natural to believe him."

"People can fool you, Melanie. That's one hard lesson I've learned in life. You never really know another person the way you think you do." Bernadette looked wistfully in the direction of the police cruiser where Rommie sat.

"I'm sorry for you, Bern."

Bernadette drew herself up straighter. "No need to feel sorry for *me,* hon. I'll be fine. Anyway, look, I'm gonna call first thing and see if I can get you into that PD posttraumatic-stress counseling. And I want you to take tomorrow off."

"No way. Too many loose ends to tie up. Like, I have to file a habeas petition to vacate Delvis Diaz's conviction, since now we know it was Slice who killed the Flatlands Boys. And I have to check on the Securilex case," Melanie said.

"Oh, yes, that reminds me. Who made you a supervisor, miss? Since when are you empowered to make assignments?" Bernadette asked.

"Ah," Melanie said with a laugh, "you mean Joe Williams?"

"Yes, that's exactly what I mean. I just signed off on an arrest warrant for one Dolan Reed that had Joe's initials on it instead of yours."

"Man, that was quick! That Joe is a whiz!"

"Apparently a second witness surrendered this afternoon, a young woman from the Reed firm—"

"Sarah van der Vere?"

"Yes, and she had some *gruesome* story about blackmail and suicide. The Connecticut State Police picked Reed up at his country place a few hours ago, drunk as a skunk and babbling about blowing his brains out."

"Wow, what a juicy case. Juicy *and* document-intensive. Joe deserves to work on it, Bern."

"Did you hear me say no? He can help you out on this one case, but next time I'm disciplining you for insubordination. Understood?" Bernadette's smile belied her scolding tone.

"Yes, ma'am."

"All right." Her smile turned sad, then disappeared entirely. "Listen, I need to go deal with Romulado. He'll have to plead, of course, but at least I can help him get a decent lawyer. I'll catch up with you later."

Bernadette took a deep breath and walked off in the direction of the police cruisers. Melanie watched her retreating figure with some measure of disappointment, leavened by a grudging, but definite, respect. Bernadette would come out of this smelling like a rose. She always did.

MELANIE STOOD SCANNING the crowded block with a vague sense of urgency and unease. When she spotted Dan O'Reilly talking to one of the cops, the palpable relief she felt told her he was what she'd been searching for, though she hadn't realized it.

He must have sensed her eyes on him. He looked up immediately and met her gaze, then patted the cop on the arm and excused himself. As he walked toward her, their glances holding the whole way, she felt her heart pounding.

"Hey," he said, when he reached her. "C'mere."

He took her hand and pulled her into the shadows near the basement entrance, away from the crowd, where they wouldn't be seen. She didn't protest. Hardly. Her eyes closed and her lips parted of their own accord as he drew her into his arms, up against his chest, which felt solid and unyielding as steel. His mouth on hers was sweet and demanding at the same time. When he set her down after a moment, she was utterly breathless.

"I'm not gonna lie to you," he said grimly. "I'm falling for you so hard, Melanie. I don't know how to handle it."

"You say it like it's a curse."

"It *is* a curse. You're married."

"You're right," she conceded, sighing. He wasn't letting himself forget the complications. She shouldn't either.

"What can we do?" he asked, taking her by the shoulders and looking down into her eyes. *Mira,* what was it about this man? The rough caress of his voice, the clarity of his gaze, his magnificent height? She was actually trembling at his touch. She tried to tell herself it was accumulated stress, but she didn't think so.

"I know what I *should* do," she said. "I should tell you I can't see you right now. That I need to sort things out with my husband."

"But he doesn't treat you right," he protested. "I saw it in your eyes the second we met. I said to myself, Something is screwed up here. This girl needs me. And come to find out, it was true."

"It's not so simple," she said, in a small voice. "It's not just myself I have to think about here—it's my daughter. Divorce is really tough on kids. Believe me, I know that firsthand."

"Oh. You never mentioned that before," he said.

"Yes. My parents split. My father lives in Puerto Rico. He has a new wife, a second family. I never see him."

"Jeez, I'm sorry."

"It's sort of ancient history, and yet it's not. It affects me in a lot of ways. It definitely makes me think long and hard about whether to end my marriage."

"I understand. I respect that. You take commitment seriously. But a bad marriage isn't good for kids either. Besides, what about this? I mean, what about . . . about . . . us? Isn't this— I mean, don't you—"

She reached up and touched her fingertips to his lips to silence him. "*This?* This is a powerful thing, Dan O'Reilly. Like nothing I've ever felt before."

He took her hand from his lips and kissed it, looking into her eyes with barely suppressed exultation. "No problem, then. I'll wait. I can be very patient."

"Even if I'm not sure how long it'll take? Or what the outcome will be? I want to be completely honest with you."

"Don't you know me by now? I don't scare, and I don't give up. You do what you have to do. I'm not going anywhere."

She shook her head in confusion. "I'm not even sure whether we should see each other while I'm trying to work this through."

"We can see each other as much or as little as you want. How about I bring you a good case? Terrorism, maybe? Lotta shit going on down on Atlantic Avenue these days. We can work together, hang out, maybe grab lunch or a drink now and then."

"Maybe." She hesitated. "But I don't want to put you in a difficult position."

"Hey, sweetheart, you're talking to Mr. Self-Discipline here. I'm the king of cold showers. I can keep my hands to myself if we're working a case."

"Maybe you can, but I'm not sure *I* can," she said. After all, in her thoughts, hadn't she already imagined it? Weren't they already *amantes*? She knew herself, and, more than that, she knew how much she wanted him.

"Come on, say we can at least work together," he said. "Think about all the good we could do. The honest citizens out there counting on us to keep the streets safe. And think about how much fun we'd have, the two of us, locking up the bad guys together."

She laughed. "Now, how am I supposed to say no to something like that?"

"You're not."

"Okay, but listen. For the foreseeable future, we're the greatest team in law enforcement and nothing else. You got that? Anything else remains to be seen."

"Yes, ma'am. You got yourself a deal." His eyes were fixed on hers. She could tell he wanted to touch her, but he wouldn't let himself. He took a step backward. "But I like a challenge. So don't think this is over. It's just getting started. And you'll be hearing from me, like, first thing in the morning."

He turned and walked away, smiling, his step confident, not looking back.

ONE OF THE paramedics who came for Sophie looked in Melanie's eyes with a flashlight and told her she didn't need to go to the hospital. So she spent some time giving her statement to a detective and headed for home.

Madison Avenue was bustling, the rain-soaked darkness made glamorous by the lavish displays in the shop windows and the expensively dressed people walking by. Her head still throbbed, yet when she breathed the night air, she felt a sense of clarity and anticipation. In a strange way, this case had cleared her mind. She was ready to move on to the next phase in her life. She would work hard, be a good mother to her daughter, and figure out what the future held for her battered heart. But Dan was right. She was a survivor. And that was a joyous thing to be.